SAYULITA MARIPOSA, SAYULITA BUTTERFLY

Saludos de Sayulita
Eric Rudd

A NOVEL
ERIC RUDD

SAYULITA MARIPOSA, SAYULITA BUTTERFLY - A Novel, is a work of fiction, albeit based loosely on actual events. The use of Elizabeth Taylor, Richard Burton, John Huston, Andy Warhol, Mary Meyers, Walter Hopps and other people and organizations is purely fictional. Names, characters, places, dialog and incidents are the products of the author's imagination and are not construed as real. Any resemblance to actual events, locales, or persons, living or dead is entirely coincidental.

Printed in the United States of America.

SAYULITA MARIPOSA, SAYULITA BUTTERFLY - A Novel
Copyright © 2015 Eric Rudd.

All rights reserved. No part of this book may be used or reproduced in any manner whatsoever without written permission from the author.

Text design by Keith Bona
Jacket design by Keith Bona and Eric Rudd

Published by Cire Corp - Publisher, an imprint of Cire Corporation of MA, North Adams, MA.

Library of Congress Cataloging-in-Publication Data
Rudd, Eric.
Sayulita Mariposa, Sayulita Butterfly/Eric Rudd. –1st ed.
p. cm.
ISBN: 978-0-9709959-8-8
Electronic Version ISBN: 978-0-9709959-9-5
LCCN: 2013946625
1. Art-Fiction. 2. Kennedy Assassination- Fiction. 3. History/Politics - Fiction.
I. Title
PS3606.L935G66 2015
813'.6-dc23

For information address: Eric Rudd, c/o Cire Corp,
189 Beaver Street, North Adams, MA 01247
First Edition: October 2015
Printed in the United States of America.

ALSO BY ERIC RUDD

THE SLUMS OF HEAVEN
(NOVEL)

MAPLE SYRUP AND FISH SAUCE
(NOVEL)

STRATEGIES FOR SERIOUS OLDER ARTISTS

THE ART WORLD DREAM
ALTERNATIVE STRATEGIES FOR WORKING ARTISTS

THE ART STUDIO/LOFT MANUAL
FOR AMBITIOUS ARTISTS AND CREATORS

A PORTRAIT OF THE NORTHERN BERKSHIRES

THE DAY SOMETHING STRANGE HAPPENED IN SAYULITA
(BI-LINGUAL/ILLUSTRATED/CHILDREN)

WET PAINT
(PLAY)

Acknowledgements:

My thanks to all the people in the arts and to the residents of Sayulita whom I've known over the years. I've learned a lot about the events portrayed in the novel, some of them first-hand. The events of the filming *The Night of the Iguana*, property purchases by Elizabeth Taylor and Richard Burton as well as the film's director, John Huston, paintings done by Andy Warhol, and the mysterious killing of Mary Meyers on Washington's C&O Canal, all have a basis in fact. I've spent my life as a visual artist, participated in such events as the Corcoran Ball, and knew the working habits of many, including Walter Hopps. All these events played out while dramatic national changes were occurring. Of course, I tried to link up these events and people into an intriguing novel. At the very least, I hope I've wetted the reader's appetite to visit Puerto Vallarta, Mexico and to venture a bit north to Sayulita.

This novel is dedicated to those people who have enriched my life.

CHAPTER ONE

Bart Singleton's flight, which originated in Miami with a change of planes in Mexico City, arrived on time at the Puerto Vallarta airport. Immigration had all been taken care of in Mexico City prior to his local connection to Puerto Vallarta. His main bag, recently purchased at a chain department store, was small enough to be carried on, even with his shoulder bag, so he decided not to check it. Since he was a tallish middle-aged man in good shape, he had no problem carrying both bags. He never liked the suitcases with wheels and just used the shoulder straps instead. He went with the other passengers directly to the exit area and into the main lobby. Local flights are not met with the herd of hotel and taxi representatives that camp outside the international lobby looking for arriving tourists. He exited the airport and opted for the pedestrian ramp that went over the highway. Once on the other side, he walked into the first taco restaurant and ordered a marlin burrito to go. He watched as the cook put the fish on the flat griddle with the other ingredients, and then once cooked, tossed the pile onto the tortilla, rolled it over, cut it in half and then stood each end up so the cut sections could get seared, then wrapped up in paper and tossed into a plastic bag along with a tiny bag of sauce. Bart chose a coke from the glassed cooler and paid for his food with the pesos he had gotten at the money exchange in the Mexico City airport. He walked down the two blocks to his hotel, a newly built Holiday Inn Express that catered almost exclusively to passengers arriving or departing the airport.

His prepaid reservation was confirmed at the desk. The clerk gave him his access key card and he started to go upstairs. Prior to getting on the elevator, he was approached by two Mexican men with whom he had expected to meet. The three went up to his room silently. Without asking, one of the men used the bathroom in Bart's room even before inquiring if Bart, having just arrived, might have needed it. They sat down, and the two men gave Bart his instructions and items he needed. They shook hands and the two men left. Bart finally got to wash up.

He turned on the television and settled for a soccer match of two national teams he knew nothing about. He sat on the bed, with his shoes off, spread one of the white bath towels across his lap, and ate his sandwich and coke. Later he would shower and retire, wearing just boxer shorts and choosing just to read a travel magazine left in the room by the hotel. When he felt a bit sleepy, he turned off his bedside light and slept soundly.

The next morning, Bart woke late but with a one-hour time difference from the East Coast, it was still relatively early. Not needing to be out before ten o'clock, he decided to just buy a breakfast sandwich at the McDonalds adjacent to the hotel. He stepped outside to a sun so bright he had to squint. Even though it was only a stone's throw away, he got out his dark sunglasses and put them on, instantly relieved by the improved visibility, and strolled next door. The restaurant was identical to the ones in the States except that all prices were in pesos. He sat eating his egg sandwich and a less than satisfactory coffee. To kill time and to stretch his legs, he took a walk down a few blocks, and then crossed the highway and walked back. There was little of interest in the immediate vicinity of the airport. He browsed the windows of the few stores geared for tourists, a couple of taco and chicken joints, and a small shopping plaza. Most of the retail stores had not opened yet or were just getting ready by sweeping the outside and setting out enticing merchandise on display. He returned to the hotel, collected his bags, checked out and returned to the airport by the same walking route that he had made the afternoon before.

The departure lobby was just becoming alive with activity but being quite early for Aeromexico's first flight of the day and having a first-class reservation, he didn't have to wait more than a few minutes to get to the counter, where he checked in for his international flight to New York. As he was busy at the ticket counter, he thought he spotted one of the two men he had met with in his room the day before, but since they had no reason to talk to one another, he made no attempt to connect. Aeromexico's counter agent examined his passport, checked on their computer to confirm the reservation, checked his one bag that didn't even weigh a third of the maximum weight, and gave him his boarding ticket and baggage claim. Thanking the agent, he threw the strap of his carry-on bag over his shoulder and allowed the next passenger to have access to the counter. The entire procedure had only taken three or four minutes.

Before going to the escalator leading to the gates, he walked just outside the lines and paused against a column, watching the main entrance door for some time. Dozens and dozens of families and couples and singles were hauling bags from taxis and vans pulled up outside, or using porters to get their things to various airline counters that lined the far side of the lobby. Most were coming in to get to departing flights since international arrivals, once exiting customs, entered the airport lobby at another part of the airport, where taxis and resort vans were lined up. Bart seemed to be looking at the passengers who came to where he had just left, lining up at the Aeromexico counter. After ten minutes, he seemed satisfied. He went up the escalator, past the food and retail venders and lined up to go through security. He showed his passport and boarding pass, pulled off his loafers and put them and his bag on the conveyor belt and walked through the scanner without incident.

Once on the gate side, sliding on his shoes and picking up his bag, he decided to grab a sandwich at the main café that was situated beyond the security gate and where they had tables along a window so passengers could view some of the planes at their gates. He had a full hour before his scheduled departure. He sat and watched the other passengers passing by. He also was curious if the two men whom he had met the previous evening, one of whom he thought he had spotted downstairs, were also going to a departing gate. Would they perhaps try to contact him again with last minute changes? He watched for twenty minutes while he ate his sandwich, ample time for someone to find him, but finally concluded that they had no further business to discuss. Perhaps, he reasoned, they had already left the airport.

*****

Ramos pulled up the freshly washed white SUV to the Gustavo Diaz Ordaz International Airport in Puerto Vallarta, Mexico, having driven 45 minutes from a private home located a mile outside the town of Sayulita. He got out and walked around to the front passenger side and opened the door. Out stepped Felix Peters, a man of 94 years but agile enough not to need real assistance other than the use of a cane, which was carried just in case but rarely of essential use. Felix would have been happier with the cane if he could brag it was either filled with red wine or tequila. Nevertheless, it was a compromise he had made with his doctor and family, to show that he was being careful in his extended independence. They all thought that any man of his age would need full-time home care. He assured them that it was none of their business to tell him how to live. Most car passengers would have opted to sit in the back seat, but Felix had known Ramos for many years and was on friendly enough terms to just sit with him up front. Felix turned and grabbed his small shoulder bag while Ramos retrieved from the back seat a standard rolling bag and escorted Felix inside the terminal, leaving his vehicle blinking. Felix told him not to worry, smiled, stroked his white hair back so it wouldn't be going down his forehead, popped off his sunglasses that were around his head on a lanyard so they hung on his chest, took the rolling bag handle and continued on the smooth marble floor to the Aeromexico counter. Ramos knew well enough that Felix would not call him on his cell but once in his car, he pulled down so he could wait; he assumed check-in wouldn't take long, based on the quick glance he had of the line for

Aeromexico. It would have been irresponsible to be a greater distance away just in the one-in-a-million chance Felix needed assistance. He had reminded Felix to call him if the flight was unexpectedly delayed or if there was any other problem. Knowing that Felix was a bit stubborn, Ramos would call anyway.

The line moved quickly and Felix showed his Mexican passport rather than his American passport once he got to one of the counter agents, and the female clerk, seeing that Felix looked 'norteamericano,' politely spoke to him in perfect English even though Felix was fluent in Spanish. His bag was weighed and then checked and he was handed a departure form. When asked, he politely said in Spanish that he did not need special assistance, and especially did not need a wheelchair to get him to the gate. He restrained himself from telling the agent in Spanish that he had lived in Mexico since before the agent's grandmother was born.

He walked across the terminal to the immigration desk to get the special form stamped so he could return as a Mexican resident instead of using his American passport. Once he showed his stamped card to the counter agent again, without having to wait in line, he received his boarding pass. Putting away his sunglasses inside his carry bag that he carried on his shoulder and held close to him with his arm, and holding his cane with his other hand, he started for the gate. As he approached the escalator, Felix's cell rang. Fetching the phone out of his jacket pocket and hearing Ramos asking if all was on time. Felix assured him that the flight was on schedule and insisted that Ramos drive back - he was on his way to the gate and Ramos should not waste more time! Ramos politely exaggerated by telling him that he was already halfway back and once again wished him a safe flight.

It was at that moment when Felix hung up his cell phone that he spotted two Mexican men looking in his direction. They did not seem to be passengers, at least they had no bags and were not in any line or doing anything other than standing and watching him, so it appeared. It unnerved him a bit.

He had no choice but to walk as fast as his old legs and cane could get him to the escalator and to the security gate. He looked back as he rode up and then made the right turn, past the last eatery in the main lobby, past the last few tourist stores, to head towards the security check-in. He tried to see if they might be following. He was relieved not to see them, although he wondered if they might catch up or even be on the same flight. Of course, there were many Mexicans taking international flights; there would be dozens on his plane. Maybe he was being silly with his fears. And would he even know if they followed him? The two who were observing him were quite far away, and he didn't really see their faces clearly. How would he know if they were on the same plane or not?

Once on the other side of the security check-in, he felt safer and slowed his walk as he ventured forth to his gate. A security companion might have been prudent, but just as he never would have allowed someone to put him in a wheelchair, he didn't feel it necessary to call out the reserves. He was still agile enough to get about and it would have been difficult to quickly describe to someone why he was anxious.

The plane was boarding shortly. He looked at his boarding pass. He was pleased to have a first class ticket. Normally he flew economy, but this ticket had been purchased by the museum. They did things in style, he thought. They were taking his contribution and the presentation very seriously.

*****

Bart Singleton went into a stall in the men's bathroom to pee before boarding his flight. Nature called for him to relieve himself but he always added an element to peeing. He couldn't help it. Ever since he became fascinated as a teenager with military bombing raid stories and vintage war movies that came on late at night, when he looked into the toilet bowl water, he saw islands and cities in the clusters of bubbles that his pee created. What remained his private secret was that almost every time he peed, he practiced aerial bombing by dropping spit from his mouth, aimed at the half dozen larger bubble-targets. Each burst bubble would be a successful bombing of a major war target, whether an industrial complex or just a large city. The political implications had no bearing. He pretended hundreds if not thousands of lives were living in those bubbles, but it never bothered him that he might be eliminating those lives if his spit were actual bombs, only how accurate his aim was. Often the targets drifted, but his mouth held enough saliva to make three or four drops before flushing the toilet. That's why he preferred the stall rather than the urinal; the entertainment added just enough excitement to make the bathroom routine less boring.

He was a bit nervous this afternoon. The airport was air-conditioned, but he still looked like he had been sweating, not because he was boarding an international flight to New York, but because of the job he had been given. He washed his hands and then looked about. No one was using the group sink anywhere near him. He took a small bottle of pills out of his carryon bag and checked its contents. It looked like any cold medicine purchased from a drug store. He was all set. He put the bottle into his pants pocket where it would be easier to reach.

He glanced into the mirror. No one would take him for anything other than a normal middle-aged American returning from a meeting in Mexico. He even had a bit of a tan from his Miami stay. He ignored any implications and just observed the superficial aspects -making sure his almost blond hair with just a bit of white showing near the ears was combed nicely, making sure that he had not missed any hairs from the close shave that he did with an old fashioned razor shaver that morning, and making sure he liked his blue and white striped shirt, nicely tucked into khaki slacks with an adjustable pull fabric belt. He had purchased all his clothes at a Target in Miami, paying with cash shortly before his trip. He didn't want to think about his life, whether he liked his job or disliked it, or whether it was what he had hoped to do a decade earlier-- he had accepted life and fate and that was it.

He had been married, had had a kid, had been divorced and had been out of touch. For the past many years, he had lived a fairly solitary lifestyle, but he was content enough and if things turned on him, he didn't have enough vested in life to care much one way or another. He was satisfied having no real ambition and more importantly, no better expectations than whatever the next day would bring. He was thinking about this as the voice from the loudspeaker announced his flight to New York. He returned to the gate just across from the restrooms and sat down.

Boarding was beginning. First invited to board were passengers who needed special assistance. There were several in wheelchairs and one or two with young children and carrying a pile of associated equipment. Thinking that he'd be sitting for several hours, he got up in anticipation and leaned against the wall near the agent, watching the other passengers assemble their bags. He rarely flew in first class; still, he had been given the ticket for a reason, so when first class was called next, he quickly got into the front of the line to hand his boarding pass to the agent. These days, people didn't seem dressed any differently in first class than in economy; several were still in their Mexican vacation clothes like they had come directly from the pool terrace. His turn came and he showed his boarding pass for the final time and disappeared into the tunnel gate. The line was shorter than he had been accustomed to when doing economy boarding. He found his row and sat next to the window.

*****

When they called for pre-boarding, Felix had no intention of joining the wheelchairs and parents with young children. He could have, of course, simply due to his age and cane, but he was too proud of his independence. As he was sitting at the gate, he glanced about at his fellow passengers. Most had just vacationed in one of the area's resorts and were tanned and dressed very casually, laughing and chatting and enjoying their last few hours of vacation before returning to their homes and jobs. A few were Mexican nationalities, most likely visiting relatives in the United States or they had just visited family in the area and were returning as permanent residents or citizens of the U.S. There were two men who seemed, to Felix, out of place, not the same men who were downstairs but in similar dress, that is, they had on dark business suits, white shirts with no ties, but they looked a bit like they had slept in them. They also seemed to be looking at him. He got up and went to the water fountain and then switched to a different seat. Again, Felix thought they were observing him. It made him uncomfortable. Normally, he might have assumed they were from the town of Sayulita and simply recognized him, since most residents in the small town knew his face more than he knew their faces, but by the way that they were dressed, more formal than anyone in Sayulita would be dressed even if they were on a trip, they seemed to him not to be someone from the town. They, of course, could simply have been Mexicans traveling from or through Puerto Vallarta for scores of reasons, and he normally wouldn't have given it a thought if they hadn't been eyeballing him and if he hadn't been carrying something in his bag.

Then he heard the announcement calling for first class passengers. He saw the Mexicans still look in his direction. He saw a taller American leaning against the column also looking in his direction, but that man quickly got into line ahead of Felix and so Felix only became concerned about the two Mexicans. He strolled to get in line but a few more passengers had quickly positioned themselves ahead of him. He pulled out his boarding pass and presented it to the same agent who had earlier checked him in. She was very nice and wished him a great flight. Before entering the gate tunnel, he took a final glance; the Mexicans were still looking in his direction but were not getting in line.

*****

"Excuse me, I think that's my seat," said the white haired gentleman, sporting a grey summer jacket over a shirt that hung out.

"I always have window," replied Bart but to be polite, he checked his boarding ticket. "Oh my goodness, they must have made a mistake. I'm sorry," he tried to say sincerely, "my agent must have made a mistake with my ticket. Not your concern. I'll take it up with her tomorrow."

He got up and into the aisle so the old gentleman could get in. Bart watched the man looking around, as if wondering if he could recognize anyone. Someone getting into the plane might have alerted the old man, because he quickly ducked his head. He put his carry bag on the seat, removed his jacket and reached to store it above, but Bart quickly grabbed it and put it neatly on top.

Felix acknowledged the help of the tallish passenger with a quick smile. Turning to see the back of a Mexican passenger walking towards the economy section, Felix squeezed by the man who was still standing. Felix was wearing just his long-sleeve yellow shirt and sat down, simultaneously picking up his bag, which he then held on his lap after connecting his seatbelt.

Bart noticed that just the boarding passes were sticking out of one of the pockets of his fellow passenger's bag. After the old man was settled, Bart sat in the adjoining aisle seat that corresponded with his ticket. He fastened his belt and took from the pocket the airline magazine and held it in his lap.

Felix strained to stretch his neck in order to look behind him but the seat was too high and he was too short to see anyone. Giving up, he took out a sketch notebook and pen from his small carryon bag that he had kept beside him and stared down at it, and then started doodling, but he looked up so many times it was obvious that he was more interested in the passengers walking by than whatever was on the page.

Bart wondered who the old man was looking for. He joined the old man in eyeballing each of the passengers as they walked past going to find their economy seats. With good peripheral vision so he didn't have to turn his head and seem too obvious, Bart then noticed that the old man seem to pinch his lips as two Mexican men walked past. Bart saw that he made a sudden movement to look away as if he didn't want them to recognize him.

He didn't know if there was a reason for the old man's seeming discomfort. Nevertheless, Bart didn't see anything out of normal. There didn't seem to be anything odd about the men from the quick look that he had, nor did he recognize them. He wondered why the old man seemed spooked. Nevertheless, it was a long flight and he was more concerned about his aisle seat. He wondered how filled the plane was, in case he wanted to sit at a window for a while. He was on assignment and the tickets were not given to him for his enjoyment, but still, he always disliked being in motion and not being able to see out, or in this case to see down. He had remembered mentioning to someone about his seat preference, but his ticket was arranged at the last minute and his assignment took priority over his seating comfort.

"We have a full plane today, so please help us leave on time by storing your carry-on bags wherever you find space and getting into your seat, " said the speaker.

That took care of Bart's question. There'll be a movie, and a snack. I can stand the five hours, he thought. Besides, I should be concentrating on my job.

*****

After the checking procedure to see that all passengers had their seat belts securely fastened, enduring the safety instruction video on the screens, taxiing to the runway, a smooth liftoff, then the noise of the wheels being closed inside the plane as it gained altitude and the attendants preparing to serve all the passengers a drink, with first class getting special cups and a better choice of snacks, Bart started to read the airline magazine. First he flipped to the back section to see what movie was being presented. He had seen the movie. Too bad, he thought; now he was hoping reading the articles would make him sleepy enough to doze for an hour.

Felix was looking down but glancing at the man sitting next to him. He normally didn't sit in first class but the museum had insisted on sending him a ticket once he told them which flight he wanted to go on. Perhaps that made a difference - first class felt a bit more secure than economy - really, did bad people sit in first class? They must have been somewhat successful to make that standard. He glanced at the man sitting next to him. He looked fine. He was obviously an American, casually but respectfully dressed in a short sleeve casual shirt, khaki pants, and loafers. His hair was trimmed like he worked for a large company with dress standards. Might he have no choice? After all, the man happened to be sitting next to Felix exactly at a time when the old man had no one else to turn to.

It seemed to Bart that the old man had observed most of the passengers going past after he had seated himself. Although all the passengers seemed normal to Bart, clearly the old man was alarmed about the two Mexicans. He couldn't understand why - there were many Mexicans onboard - that was normal for a flight leaving Puerto Vallarta.

Felix tried again to see if they were still watching him. The seats were just too large to see more than a couple of passengers sitting across the aisle, and he had no idea where they were seated. In addition, the airplane hung a curtain to block off the economy class from seeing into the first class section. Of course, perhaps there were other suspicious people aboard that he might have missed with the fuss he had in claiming his rightful seat. Nevertheless, he had spotted those two, and that gave him enough to worry about. They had been definitely watching him near the gate area, well, looking in his direction - it was hard to tell their actual intentions - and now they were aboard the same flight somewhere behind him. The more he thought about it, the more he was suspicious. Had they boarded this flight for the reason that Felix feared? And if he might be in trouble, did he have anything to lose by conversing with the young man sitting next to him?

"Excuse me, but may I talk to you?" said the old gentleman to the man next to him. "My name is Felix Peters."

"Oh, hello. My name is Bart Singleton."

"I know I may be presuming too much, but you look like an

intelligent man, and I have something of an urgent matter I'd like to discuss, if you would spare me a few minutes."

"I'm all set with insurance and financial planning," Bart said in a friendly tone, making it sound like he was assuming this was a sales pitch of some sort.

"Really, it's nothing like that," Felix said seriously. "I think what I have to tell you might be of importance, and since there's no movie for a while, I wonder if you'll let me explain."

"Go ahead," Bart said, still doubtful but what else did he have to do? "Don't worry about the movie; I've already seen it, so it has no interest to me anyway."

"As I said, my name is Felix Peters. I mostly live in a small town not far from Puerto Vallarta. I'm not Mexican, of course, but I'll get to how I came to live there. I want to tell you a story in order to give something to you.

"Why me?" asked Bart. "You and I have just met."

"Because, Bart… may I call you 'Bart'? Because there is a likelihood that I will be dead by the time the plane lands, and I have no one else that I can reasonably tell this to."

This was a dramatic statement and Bart turned to him fully, to see if this was a complete nutcase.

"Do you need medical help?" was Bart's instinctive reply.

"No, no, nothing like that. I think I saw the men who will… please let me explain. I might not have much time."

"I did notice that you seem to be worried about something. But don't worry. You won't die. Why, you look very healthy and we only have a few hours on this flight."

"You are kind to humor me, but let me tell you my story. There is a reason for my concern. Do you have to do something else?"

"Not a thing. I'm done with this magazine," putting the closed magazine back into the seat pocket. "It's a long flight, so go ahead and tell me your story. I'm your captured audience. My ears are at your disposal."

"Thank you. Then I'll start at the beginning. I won't rush it because the more details you hear, the more you'll understand why I'm in the circumstance that I find myself."

CHAPTER 2

"Where should I begin?" asked Felix to Bart. "An introduction perhaps. You don't know who I am at all. I was an artist. Actually, I am an artist and I even consider my actions on this flight to be part of my life's work. Specifically, I did large abstract paintings, using objects but still considered to be abstract, contemporary. I started at a time when contemporary art was just getting off the ground in the United States. I started with serious figurative work, but abstracted like Picasso and others were doing in Europe, and it wasn't long before I got swept into the non-objective movement that took off with a vengeance in New York. Pollack was one of the leaders, as was Gorky, Still. You get the idea."

"Mr. Peters, I'm afraid I don't know anything about art - old art or new art."

"Please, call me Felix. Everyone in Sayulita does. And not knowing about art - that's okay. Suffice it to say that I was taken seriously by the galleries and even by some museums. Since I was among the early practitioners, I got some degree of success. Had I continued doing that kind of work, I think I would have disappeared into oblivion. But I continued to experiment. I started once again using objects, but attaching them, painting them; a bit advanced but there were others, in New York, also doing that."

"What kind of objects?" asked Bart.

"I started attaching all kinds of things to my canvases. At first objects from my studio, like brushes, cups and old palettes. Then I'd haunt the thrift markets around Puerto Vallarta, then L.A. and I'd collect some funky things, like dolls, knick-knacks, household items. Eventually large things, like sections of boats, beach umbrellas, you know. Anyway, I'm not saying I was the only one to do this or that I didn't get inspired by work I saw by Rauschenberg or Dine or Wesselman and others, but I caught the first wave of what a curator coined as "Pop Art."

"I've heard of Pop Art. It's comic book stuff, but paintings. Right?"

"That's more or less correct. Pop art dealt with popular life - consumer products. Really no different than what the masters painted centuries ago."

"How so?" asked Bart.

"You've must have seen some paintings in museums, painted by old masters - still life paintings of wine bottles, bowls of fruit, hanging rabbits and such?"

"You're right, I went on a high school field trip. I remember seeing a lot of violence and even the paintings without people in them, there were hanging slabs of meat and knives on the table. I wondered why they wanted to paint a butcher's shop."

"Because that was common then. That's what was in every house. You won't see hanging rabbits being prepared in our kitchens. Our meat comes in wrapped packages from the grocer. Today, we have fewer wine bottles and more soda bottles. That's why the Pop artists might paint Coke, Campbell's soup or cigarette packages. Even our landscape is different now; it's littered with advertisements and billboards."

"I see. You artists like the new stuff."

"To a degree. But I was different from the most noted artists - mostly from New York - who were doing that art. I lived for many years in Mexico, so that influence was part of my work. In fact, many curators would group me as a Mexican artist rather than as an American artist. And being removed from New York gave my work a distinctive style. I was probably among the first on the West Coast to be part of this style. When a group of artists have a certain style, they call it a "school." I was part of the Pop art school. I guess I was also part of the West Coast school, and one critic called it L.A. Pop. You see you can be part of more than one school."

"That has at least doubled my knowledge of art. And your story is just beginning!" joked Bart.

"The early years were meager and I didn't make life easier by being out of the country and then on the West Coast, but eventually history caught up and my name was added to the list. In some circles, second tier perhaps, but at least on the list. After the famous artists were collected, if a museum wanted to fully document the period, they eventually might round off their collection by finding one of my works. Because of that, my work is in many museums, more often in storage to be shown once in a blue moon. I didn't make the very big time - to be a household name. I was not a Picasso or Warhol, to name a couple. But for millions of artists, that's the same, although in my case, I think the name Peters stood above most others. I was respected, I was collected and I did achieve limited fame. In fact, my life might be worthy of being studied by those younger artists who are climbing up the ladder."

"I guess that I'm understanding you, but ......" Bart started to say with some hesitation. Felix acknowledged with a nod.

"Anyway, that's enough about the art aspect, until I tell you the specifics. I mentioned that just to put my professional work into a context in order to tell you my story and my predicament. In some ways, it's symbolic that we are flying from Puerto Vallarta to New York. It's a journey I made many, many years ago, but of course, in reverse."

"You see, I was a young man in Mexico, really just hitchhiking around the country. I had a few dollars in my pocket, not much by today's standards, but Mexico was poor in those days and so it was enough. A few cents here and there got me rides, a meal, even a mattress once in a while. I ended up on the west coast, near a fishing village called Puerto Vallarta. Oh, I know, it's a city now, but in those days, just fishing boats and a sleepy little town. Ha, the airport had just gotten paved for small planes."

"But even then, I didn't stay long. I hitched a ride on a boat that went up the coast to a tiny speck of a village, called Sayulita. You could count the number of buildings in two minutes. Like all Mexican towns, it had a small plaza, maybe two little places that served tacos and a beach. Oh, what a beach. The fishermen would bring in their catch each morning and what they didn't need, a boat would take down the coast to Puerto Vallarta, to sell to the markets and restaurants. And they'd take these little coconuts that they harvested from the tall palm trees and sell them. They contained little drops of oil, not huge quantities but very rich oil that was much in demand. Not regular oil; this oil was used for a fancy soap, mostly, very prized at the time. That's how this little village made its living. But that's just the backdrop for my story. Should I continue?"

"Please do," said Bart, "but what does this little village have to do with your situation now?"

"Patience, my new friend, for the connection will become clear soon enough."

*****

"I guess I'm jumping ahead if I'm already talking about Sayulita. Let me give you a brief glimpse of my life, and how it all fits into this puzzle. I'm 94 years old, celebrated just a month ago."

"Congratulations. I assumed you were quite a bit younger."

"Thank you, but I only mention that to put the years in perspective. You see, when I say I was a young man, that means I'm going back more than seventy years. That's ancient history to someone your age, I suspect."

"Well, I'm in my mid-40s, so it's before my lifetime. Please, I don't mean to interrupt." Bart was smiling politely and encouraging his fellow traveler to continue.

"Ask whatever questions you want as I tell my tale. How far back should I go? Well, since we have time and you seem to have the patience, let me start by telling you a bit about my family pedigree. My grandmother was born in Mexico and moved to the United States. My grandfather was a mixture of European and some Scottish ancestry, but basically a good old American boy. He met my grandmother in Los Angeles, they got married and my grandfather finished his degree in engineering. I'm not sure what type except that he was an expert in water systems."

"He got an opportunity early on to go work in Mexico. I think it had something to do with silver mines somewhere in the middle of the country, except they needed water, either for the industrial process or just because they were setting up camps for thousands of workers and needed basic services. Again, I'm not sure and maybe it was for both reasons.

In any case, they decided it was a good opportunity for him, and since she was Mexican, they could take advantage of the fact that my grandmother was fluent in Spanish and could help him if language became an issue. They were young and adventurous. As part of the two-year job offer, they were given a modest house with servants, so they really were living quite well for an engineer just starting out. After a year, my grandmother became pregnant and things got a bit harder. The available medical services were minimal where they were, and so they planned to return to the United States for the birth. But you know how things can go wrong. They did manage to get to Mexico City just in time, and their baby, my mother, was born there."

"Eventually, the city of Los Angeles called for engineers to improve the water services - they were expanding their capabilities as fast as they could- and so my grandfather was in great demand upon his return. They lived in the Hollywood hills, had three more children, and my mother was basically a Hollywood-L.A. brat of sorts, with no real ambition other than to work until she married and had kids. This was during the pre-depression years, when life was fast and fun. She barely looked even half-Mexican, and dressed in trendier clothes, she looked like a Californian with a darkish complexion."

"Then my mother went to community college outside of San Diego, which in those days was really a vocational college, and studied to be a secretary and to do some basic accounting. She liked to party and met my father, who was in the Navy stationed in San Diego, and they hitched up. That was around 1930 and I came along two years later. Dad got assigned to a good job in Washington D.C., and so they pulled stakes and ventured all the way to the east coast, a vastly different environment than the Los Angeles life style. My mother, who spoke Spanish mostly to her Mexican family and friends, would soon find out how few of her kind lived in the east coast, or at least in Washington. New York might have been another matter, but D.C. was like light years away from there. So there was not much need to speak Spanish after we moved, and consequently, I didn't learn that much. I sort of knew the basics but as a toddler."

"The first twenty years of my life is really of no importance. I was only two when we moved to the nation's capital. In those days, Washington was a smallish southern town. Most residents even had southern accents; they were more at home in Virginia than anywhere else. The blacks lived on one half of the city or at least in specific neighborhoods, and the whites lived in the other half. Georgetown, one of the most expensive places to live now, used to be the home of the servants. There were sections where they wouldn't allow Jews to live. Only because there were Embassy families living there, Washington had some semblance of a more cosmopolitan city, but that was a small component. Why, I remember there were even a few cow pastures around, but they didn't last for long. The government kept expanding and builders were putting up houses as fast as they could bulldoze the fields."

"No one would ever think my mother was part of a minority group, which Hispanics were in those days, and I escaped any of the dark hair. Instead, I had sandy light brown hair and we looked like any middle class American family. My folks found a two-story Cape Cod house in a nice residential neighborhood called American University Park. Our home was really a mile away from the college but at least we could walk three blocks to the grocery and drug stores and a few other shops. We lived near one of the main thoroughfares, Massachusetts Avenue, so although my father often drove to work, he could take the bus if my mother needed the car that day. My father was officially stationed at the Pentagon, but his actual work was more often at the Naval Yard, smack in the middle of downtown, near the Capitol. As I grew up, World War II brought the city alive with more and more military personnel."

"I think they were trying to have other kids, but for some reason, my mother didn't get pregnant again. It was during the war, that my mother got very ill, and was in and out of hospitals for about two months. I think they finally decided it was cancer but the testing wasn't clear in the beginning. Then she passed away. We, my Dad and I, were lonely of course, but the war effort kept Dad busy and I was in school. Somehow we managed. During summers, I mowed lawns and worked part time for the local gas station."

"After the war, Dad decided he liked Washington well enough and decided to stay. He had his Navy buddies and connections by then. He retired from the military, and got into construction, working at first for one of the large builders and supervising many of the houses going up. As an only child, I had a very close relationship with my father, but at the same time, I was yearning for some independence. Nevertheless, I became more familiar with the building aspect of the growing city, often accompanying my father to his building sites on Saturday mornings. I never really got to experience the government side, although the fathers of most of my friends worked for the government. In any case, I graduated from Wilson Public High School, and Dad wanted me to go to college, and if not, join him in the construction industry, but I had a hankering to see the country, so with some savings and a gift from my dad, I traveled all the way to California, met up with some of my Mexican relatives there and picked up more Spanish. When my funds finally ran out, rather than get a regular job or retreat back to Washington, I followed my father's foot steps and enlisted in the Navy."

"I was a bit late for most of the Korean War, but got into the last three months from afar being on a ship. Those three months of action were close enough for my taste; I saw some of the wounded men who were transported to our ship; glad I was too late to see more battle action. The Navy was still doing some cleanup efforts in the Pacific from WWII damage, and I saw a fair bit of that part of the world."

"After I returned, I ended up in San Diego when my enlistment expired, and I took advantage of the Federal G.I. Bill programs and went to college there. My Dad was happy I was safe and in school, but not happy with my interests. He wanted me to study business or engineering or law. I was interested in the liberal arts. Although I studied philosophy and history, I happened to take a painting course and got hooked. I had been interested in art growing up, and often went to the museums. In fact, the best Saturdays for me involved taking the bus downtown, going to one of the Smithsonian museums which are always free, but always including the National Gallery of Art, then walking a few blocks to the F Street area of stores and doing some window shopping, buying a Eddie Leonard's foot-long subway and sneaking it into a matinee so I could watch the movie while I ate my sandwich. That was a full day. But it never occurred to me to become an artist, that someone could actually plan that as a career."

"After my second year of college, I went home one summer. My Dad had met a woman, named Beatrice, and she had a son and daughter a bit younger than me - the daughter was just starting college and her son was finishing high school. Beatrice worked as a paralegal in the small law office that did all of Dad's building contracts. She was very attractive, almost as tall as Dad, with dark brown hair that was beginning to show grey streaks. She had been born in Maryland, near Annapolis, and was a die-hard sailor when she was younger. Beatrice's ex-husband, a lawyer working for the Justice Department, had been caught having one too many affairs and that was that. Dad and Beatrice decided that a June wedding at their new house would be in order. They had purchased a contemporary house in the suburb of Bethesda that Dad had actually built for a client who then had to bail. He had sold the District house that I grew up in and during my visit, I was asked to go through boxes of my stuff that had been packed. Since I was coming for the ceremony and didn't have any summer commitments in San Diego, my Dad offered me a summer job at his company, a small building concern that he formed with two partners. They were building suburban houses in the Bethesda area, and had several crews working. Part of the reason for the offer - Dad was hoping that I would be enticed to stay and to get into a more suitable profession.

"I arrived and met my new family, and their cousins and uncles and aunts- a full company of names had to be added to my memory. They were all nice, but Beatrice's kids were heading into medicine and law, and all of her friends and relatives had similar practical careers. Beatrice was well grounded, very nice and clearly organized and scheduled. I think she made a good partner for Dad, plus I saw that Dad was happy again, as he had been with Mom."

"I did stay that summer. I was an assistant supervisor on his construction jobs, and I must say, I learned a lot. Often it was just a matter of making sure materials and tools were on the job when they were needed, but just as frequently, some problem would come up and the crew needed an immediate answer. On weekends, Dad took me golfing. I wasn't very good but he was trying to show me the lifestyle that I could choose to have, if I wanted to - if I worked at something a bit more practical."

"It was the first time that I really spent time in Washington as an adult, so every chance I had, I drove into the city and went to the museums. The Philips Collection, a small oddball museum that occupied a large in-city house and had expanded to the adjacent townhouse, had early modernist art. There I saw my first Rothko paintings, in their Rothko gallery. It felt like a small meditation room - that's how I thought of it - with three incredible Rothko paintings on three walls. Rothko was the painter who basically did rectangular shapes of color. His work, and I suppose Pollack's, stimulated more cartoonists to make fun of abstract art. Anyway, the first time I entered the Rothko room, surrounded by these minimalist paintings of colorful soft boxes, I couldn't leave the room for at least a half hour. Everything that I was learning about paint and concept in school came together for me at that moment."

"There was more to see in the city other than the Phillips Collection. I spent less time at the National Gallery because I was more drawn to the Corcoran, which was showing some contemporary artists from New York. I thought about my future, and contrasted the life my Dad was advocating for me- two cars in a carport next to a contemporary four-bedroom house on a half acre lot, membership at a nearby golf club with swimming privileges, steady employment at a company that was bound to grow and all within a metropolitan area that was experiencing the first fruits of culture - compared to a life of a struggling artist. As comfortable as that lifestyle might be, it was not the one I could force myself to go with. My epiphany that I experienced at the Phillips sealed the deal. By late August, I was heading back to San Diego."

"I won't say I didn't continue to have some doubts from time to time, but by graduation, after having my work hanging in the student show at the university's museum and seeing my friends pursuing a life in the arts, I had made up my mind. I announced to Dad that I was going to make my mark as an artist. That would not help in making a living, said my father to me on many occasions and in many different ways. His upbringing did not include the arts as a respectable way to live. He wanted me to reconsider, but he didn't push it other than making suggestions; he and Beatrice both said that they would support my goals, no matter what I chose. My mother had had a lot of design sense, mostly in fabrics. I used to watch her sew various scraps of colorful cloth together, and she used to say that what she was doing was really a craft and not an art, so I never really appreciated her creative side as much as I should have. After her death, her artistic fabrics became my most treasured memories of her. I wondered if she would have approved of my art, at least more than Dad did. Perhaps I would have been encouraged to go that way after my trips to the National Gallery, if only my Mom had still been alive. One wishes one can turn back the clock or undo events, but of course, that's not possible."

"The decade of the 50s was an exciting time to mature. Jazz was out in front followed by Rock and Roll, French writers were making noise, and in the visual arts, semi-abstract art, especially, was just getting noticed in some circles, a bit late compared to European standards, but American artists were adopting it with a new slant."

"Socially, I had a serious girlfriend whom I met in my art classes, who also wanted to be an artist, but she wanted to settle and work from a studio, and I wanted to venture to faraway places and carry my supplies with me. I wasn't ready to commit, and I suppose Ms. Mary Owens, a pretty brunette with a short Bohemian-style haircut, looking perhaps a bit French, who wanted to create the artwork that would be taken very seriously by the best museums, concluded that she couldn't wait for me to get my wanderings over with. We just weren't ready for each other from a practical point, although I think I can say we both loved one another. I met up with her several years later, but that comes later in my story."

"Although I saw a bit of the world during my time in the Navy, I can't say I experienced those places outside of tight supervision or during short shore leave jaunts. This time, I wanted to meander my way at my own pace, so I sold anything I couldn't take, withdrew my savings-- which was not much, probably less than $2,000 but enough if you travel frugally - kissed Mary goodbye, who by that time seemed sad but genuinely excited for me to be off on my adventure and probably glad that she no longer had a conflict to deal with, and I took the bus to cross the border in Tijuana, then headed down the coast and across to La Paz, near where the Baja ended. From there, I got a seat on the boat to a port near Los Mochis, and continued wandering along the west coast of Mexico, stopping along the Pacific beaches."

"Mexico was pretty laid back in those days; a few bucks went a long ways. Tacos cost a few pennies and I could sleep for a dollar, at most, at decent enough hotels. Of course, a decent bed with a bathroom down the hall was acceptable to me. I was less fussy in my youth than I'd be today. I was young and my stomach was pretty strong, although traveling on the cheap, I had my share of stomach sickness. That's pretty much forgotten now. Travelers to Mexico were pretty brave in those days, but I suppose that's true for those who went to Asia or even post-War Europe. I drank a lot of Coke then. It was the safest drink to have, non-alcoholic, bottled and sealed. We didn't have those plastic water bottles like today. At night, a 'cervesa' or two did the trick."

"Anyway, I kept heading down the coast, one town at a time in some cases, unless I got a ride to a decent next stop to wherever that particular truck or bus was heading. I had my share of adventures and excitement, but I don't mean for this to be a travel memoir. The main point is, I landed in the small coastal town of Puerto Vallarta. Yes, the same Puerto Vallarta that we just took off from!"

"It was a lovely town of about 40,000 inhabitants, just big enough to have a variety of activities, although fishing was the main industry there. In the old section, I liked the way houses were stacked up the hill fronting the plaza, most with nice views of the bay. Others eyed this as well, as eventually foreigners started buying in this area, which then quickly became known as Gringo Gulch. But when I first landed there, tourism was just beginning, which meant you could count the tourists by your fingers for the most part, and there were a couple of decent hotels along what's now the Malecon. I'm sure you walked the Malecon - that walkway along the waterfront with the art-deco statues - during your visit? That's become the main tourist attraction, along with the church there, and the front is solidly lined with restaurants and craft shops."

"Yes, I was there," replied Bart. "I didn't have much time. Not this trip. On a previous visit. Puerto Vallarta seems lovely indeed."

"Back then, however, most of the town was just a plain vanilla nondescript assemblage of one-story buildings and the waterfront was cluttered with hundreds of fishing boats. You couldn't cross the beach without stepping over one net after another. The beach was not for enjoyment as it is today-- it was only for the fishing industry and some transporting of goods. But it had an appeal to me; it's hard to explain why. Laid back, easy and lively enough and easy on my pocketbook, friendly town-folk who accepted a stranger without suspicion, and of course, the weather was perfect - at least for half of the year. Hardly a drop of rain or even a cloud would be seen day after day, week after week. For me, it was paradise except there weren't a lot of cultural offerings. But I wanted to create art, not look at more art. As artists, we just need some space, some materials and some time to work! Before I left San Diego, I was just beginning to develop my own style; I didn't feel like I wanted to see other artists on a daily basis and be accused of copying or being influenced. I wanted my voice to come out in my art in a pure way. Oh, I was so idealistic then. I just needed a cheap studio and some time to explore my ideas-- to make some art. I wondered if I might find a place to plop myself down. But before I got into those practicalities, I wanted to know what else was around the town."

"I explored the area a lot and ended up hitching a ride on a small boat that was picking up daily catches of fish from a village about an hour and a bit up the coast. I got off at this tiny hamlet called Sayulita. The beachfront had just a few small concrete buildings. The plaza area with the town's only cobbled streets was a block inland. The plaza itself was small, with a few trees and not much upkeep. The small dirt roads that emanated out from the plaza had a few more buildings, but there were no more than a few stores catering to local needs. On the corner nearest the beach side was a basic grocery store. On the other side of the river, which was small and which had just a trickle of water running in the sand during the dry months, there were a couple of additional produce stands and a place that made tortillas every morning and sold them by the stack."

"Most of the residents either fished or picked these special coconuts - native to the area and about the size of baseballs - that grew way up in the tall palms. About as laid back as I could imagine, it was the cheapest place I'd found in the entire trip. For a few pesos, pennies in today's rates, I found a place to stay and I could draw on my pads that I had brought with me, and think. Thinking was important then. I was trying to push ideas and it's not always about production. I needed to know what I wanted to produce, but once I got my ideas together, I needed space to work. I also needed more supplies, which were not easy to get, not even in Puerto Vallarta. Basic paint was available, but not artists paint. Canvas was available because there were some fishing sailboats and they used canvas. Wood, of course, was plentiful enough, but mostly a special type that termites couldn't eat. But I only needed a few stretchers to work on since I could roll up the paintings once they were completed. So eventually, I found a supplier in Guadalajara for my paint and with some correspondence and help from, of all things, a plumbing distributor near Puerto Vallarta who went there often, I was able to get the paint I needed."

"Anyway, that came a bit later. I had just landed in Sayulita and it just felt like a place that I would like to hang out in. I'm not sure why I chose Sayulita at first when Puerto Vallarta seemed small enough at the time. Maybe just the feeling I got when I walked about. No one seemed to mind another hippie-type person being there. If I may say so myself, I was a fairly good-looking chap, with a boyish face, nicely suntanned, and fairly tall, but not quite six foot. When I used to be measured in the Navy, I would try to stretch my spine that extra fraction but I never could get past the five foot eleven mark. Just under. My sandy brown hair lightened under the hours in the sun; some reddish streaks would show, I suppose a bit of Scandinavian DNA mixed in."

"When I first started on my trip, I knew enough Spanish to get by, certainly I could ask for things that I needed but I progressed to where I could have conversations about all sorts of matters. The hard part was in understanding the fast-paced Spanish of the locals, but my ear was acclimating to their speed. And Sayulita had its own funny accents. Perhaps a bit like listening to English from a resident of a small town in South Carolina verses the English from a college graduate in Pennsylvania. It was certainly not the Spanish that was taught at home, or used by my Californian relatives, or used in school. For the most part, this was just small town of uneducated Mexicans who worked hard for a basic living. But I liked the flavor - it was authentic and full of connotations. I connected with it. And I suppose that after a couple of months of traveling, it was easier to stay in a tiny village where I didn't have to go very far for anything, not that much was available anyway. Just a few feet up the hill, I found a nice room to rent with a shared kitchen in a house with a private balcony just high enough to see the ocean above the palm trees. Next door was a taco place that served breakfast and meals until dusk. For studio space, I could take my paint and canvas outside and work almost anyway I pleased. A few residents might come over to watch, but after their first few times observing me, their interest would wane. The entire village became my studio."

"One day, as I was having a leisurely light lunch, a young, very attractive girl hanging out on the plaza across the way with a couple of girlfriends gave me the eye, or I gave her the eye. I say a girl, but so mature. What did I notice first about her? You'll never believe it but her ankles. She was sitting on a low wall that served as the plaza bench and she had crossed her legs. I just saw these beautiful ankles attached to her tanned legs sticking out of her pants. She was barefoot. Then I looked up at her body and saw that face, looking at me and smiling - not flirting, not inviting, just smiling in a way that said that she found my presence amusing."

"At that moment, I was at one of the three taco stands that the town had, discounting the many houses that opened when they felt like it to give dinner to neighbors at low prices and indicating that they were open for business by just putting a table or two and some chairs on the street outside their kitchen doors. I was eating a taco with a Pacifico beer, enjoying the midday warmth, when I happened to gaze across the street towards the plaza. There were a couple of other residents also sitting and they noticed that I noticed that she noticed."

"That's Maria. She's a difficult one. Fussy for the locals," they laughed. "Her mama wants her to have more schooling. She's almost twenty and still not married!"

"Now from that little exchange that I had, during my taco, actually told me a lot about her and about her folks. It wasn't like I was making moves; I had assumed that most women and their families would treat me more or less as an alien rather than as a suitor or prospect. Gringos were not that common, and the few that happened to find their way into Sayulita were hippies of sorts, not always clean and almost certainly with rough beards and weird long hair. And of course, I don't think I made the best impression wearing clothes that needed washing and probably a pressing which I couldn't do. I was almost as hippie as any other wanderer and certainly a bit Bohemian for the local population. However, my hair was shorter than some and I never grew a beard; that's why I seemed a bit better, I was eventually told."

"When I had finished eating and walked over to her, she was brave enough to converse with a gringo, not that many outsiders visited the village speaking Spanish well enough to converse. Her friends were shy, but not this one. She also was different in that she was not married or engaged. Most of her friends, even a bit younger, had one or even two or three kids by her age, but she didn't. An inch or two taller than many girls, like most Mexicans, she had black hair, hers was cut shoulder length. A perfect face with high cheekbones and she accented her dark body wearing a white blouse, with the bottom ends tied into a knot just above her navel, and her khaki pants were rolled up above her ankles. To this day, I find it sexy for girls to have white blouses with the bottoms tied up above their waists. But I must sound very old fashioned?"

"There were only three cobblestone streets around the plaza, and all the rest of the roads were dirt. As I said, to the casual visitor, there were few redeeming features in this dusty, dull and forgotten little fishing hamlet. Except the beach was pristine, bordered with palm trees and then hills that went steeply high just yards away. A few small huts were built up there, taking advantage of the breezes and views, although most of the houses had been constructed in the more practical flat areas, just yards from the sand."

"From anywhere else, the town wasn't easy to get to. You could get there by car but not easily, unless you had a jeep and then only in the winter dry months because the one paved road from Puerto Vallarta was not in great shape and would take you a couple of hours on a good day but if it rained, you were out of luck. Plus not that many people had automobiles, mostly small trucks used for work. That's why people moved supplies by boat, and that's how all the fish and coconuts got transported to the Puerto Vallarta port. How many tourists would get into boats to go to a little village up the coast? Not many at that time. All this was about to change, however, as the government was widening the road from Puerto Vallarta to the state capital called Tepic, and that road went right by the entrance to Sayulita."

"Anyway, that girl, unlike almost all girls in the village and in fact, unlike most of the boys who only went to school through the 6th grade because classroom education was not thought of as that necessary in those days, was set to become educated. She had no way to really enter college, which was too expensive, but she did go through Secondaria and then attended high school in the next town. At 19, she was past due for marriage by the town's standards, and the entire boy population wanted her, but she had a sense not to marry a local kid. She wanted something more. I think that's why she was intrigued when I landed that day and stayed around."

"In such a tiny village, it's hard not to bump into everyone all the time. After we struck up that first conversation, we saw each other daily, in the beginning by chance then quickly by plan, and developed a friendship right away. She loved to see my sketches in my drawing pad and to learn more about my cultural pursuits. She'd often sit near me as I painted outside for two or three hours at a stretch. It never bothered me because painting is a slow process and I'd much prefer chatting than listening to static songs on the radio. As we talked, my Spanish got better, and she got used to my "accent" as I got used to how she talked. Being very considerate, she slowed her speech just a bit, perhaps 10% for my sake, but that made a difference. It was just a matter of a day or two until we were both fluent and comfortable with each other."

"She loved to read although finding books was not easy; there weren't many books in the entire village. Occasionally when she went into Puerto Vallarta, she was able to buy second-hand books, and would read them over and over. After that day, every time I went to Puerto Vallarta, I brought her books that I found in the two second-hand shops in town. They had a better effect on her than if I had brought flowers."

"She wanted to know about the world. No one in the village had a television then, there wasn't reception. People went to Puerto Vallarta for various reasons, and if they had time, they'd stay around and have a meal at a restaurant that might have a television going. Usually there'd be sports on, soccer was the big sport of interest, but often a bit of news would also come on. These news stories would be retold back at the plaza in Sayulita."

"Maria had tried to learn a little English prior to our meeting and when I offered to practice with her, I discovered how fast of a learner she was. I found some elementary English books and within a week or two, she had digested them and begged for something more advance. After a few months, I think half the time we used English, just so she could practice."

*****

"Sometimes when things don't make much sense to the outside world, they make perfect sense to you. I don't need to tell you that I stayed in Sayulita, and after six months, we decided to get married. She was not cultured in the formal sense, had never traveled more than a hundred miles except for one trip to Mexico City which had changed her perspective of life forever, and yet, she was more poised, more responsive than any of my college friends or even art friends back up north."

"I won't say we behaved perfectly, and certainly I wasn't as loose as I had been in the past. Maria was not terribly religious but her family was and she was very respectful of their beliefs, so I'll simply say that we were pretty good - okay, good enough - until we got married. Once it was legal and once our union was blessed by the family and by the church, then I can state that in my limited but not total inexperience, Maria was the most passionate, the most fun partner I ever had. We enjoyed sex and although always private, we made love in many places spontaneously."

"Her family gave us a traditional large wedding party. I felt somewhat guilty at not inviting my Dad and Beatrice but they were both busy in Washington. Beatrice had to supervise her son who was finishing school, and Dad had some health issues so that I'm sure they were grateful that I didn't insist they venture all the way to Mexico. At least I mailed them a letter and enclosed a photograph taken at the wedding, and explained how I was settling down at last. I promised we'd travel to see them at some point, but I was vague enough not to be pinned down to a date. In his kindness, Dad wired a substantial amount of cash to us, enough to get our married life off to a good start. On the day of the wedding, when we went to Puerto Vallarta for the start of our honeymoon, which really was a trip to a small resort in Manzanillo, then a day's journey down the coast, we called Dad long distance and he got a chance to actually talk to Maria directly. Maria was very nervous, speaking live with Dad and then briefly to Beatrice, but she did great and I think Dad was especially welcoming."

*****

"It was her insistence that we move permanently to Puerto Vallarta. Her family was fine with that decision since it was easy enough to visit on Sundays, an excuse for them to come to Puerto Vallarta and besides, they believed that were more opportunities for us in the bigger town. Of course, Maria and I would continue to visit them in Sayulita,"

"By that time, I was so fluent in the language, I could talk like a native, so with the tourist industry just getting off the ground, I ended up acquiring a panga which is what the common open fishing boats are called, and giving day tours up and down the coast as well as land tours within the town. Since land and buildings were so cheap, my little money went pretty far and we were able to purchase a small house up the steep hill from the main plaza and beach. The main rooms and the main terrace had a spectacular view of the bay. I was always a sucker for a place with a view, often not minding serious defects if I had a place for a comfortable chair and I could wake up or go to bed looking at the distant horizon. The sea was my magical stage with the open spaces of water and sky."

"Right behind the house was a second building, once a house but then used for commercial purposes and run down inside, but because it was built of stone and concrete with a ceramic tile roof, it was structurally sound. That's all I needed and we purchased that as well for my art studio. I was far removed from the action of Paris or New York or even Los Angeles, so in most likelihood no one would ever see my work, but I had a respectable studio and ample time to make art even while earning a living helping with tours and tourist development."

"And so we started our life as a couple together, secure with home and studio, building up a business helping tourists, and establishing our reputation as the perfect bridge if anyone - company, tourist, new resident - needed assistance. It gave us variety, and I'm happy to say, the income was consistent enough that it wasn't necessary to worry about next week's bills."

*****

"One day, on one of our Sunday visits to Sayulita at one of those big family meals that her mother and father produced for the children - Maria was the second youngest of eight children - and grandchildren and quite a few close relatives, her parents told us that they wanted to take us to a special place."

"'Come with us,' said Papa Rodriquez after a heavy lunch that started with tamales and elote, which is a kind of milk and corn drink, and continued with tacos, pollo and arroz and of course, several cervezas and after many of the guests started to go home or simply wander off."

"Maria and I, with Papa and Mama, walked past the plaza towards the beach, then along the beach road and through the local cemetery, past the smaller Los Muertos beach and along the jungle path. We walked for a good half hour until we turned off the main path and onto a small path that I never would have spotted. After just five minutes through dense jungle, I heard the roar of ocean waves and we came onto the most splendid, the most exotic piece of pristine sand I've ever seen. Bordered by rocks on each end, the quarter mile of sand was a light color with just a few streaks of black sand that the dark rocks created as they got eaten away by waves. A small stream of water emanating from the hill broke into and through the sand, near the rocks where a few pools of fresh water could mix with salt during high tide. A few yards inland, the land gently rose a good hundred feet and I could see how clearing just a few of the high shrubs would create a wonderful vista."

"'We own all this land, many hectors including land closer to the village,' began Papa after we had absorbed the totality of the landscape. 'And we have divided up the land between all our children. The others wanted more practical land. They wanted the ability to harvest coconuts or build on land near to the village. You two have a life in Puerto Vallarta and you are growing your business there. You don't need working land or land to build your permanent house. What we wanted you to have is God's creation for your use someday, or when you come to visit us in Sayulita.'"

"'This beach, from that end where the rocks are, to where we are standing, and going inland for a hundred meters, is our gift to you,' added Mama."

"It's hard to explain how unusual it was for Maria's folks to give us this gift. Most families only valued land by what it could produce - what it could grow, what animals could be raised and fed, or how it could be used for boats. Land was valued by the number of palm trees that produced the prized coconuts that it contained. If a hector had 100 trees, and another much larger parcel had only 50 palms, it was the small land with the most palms that would be worth more. This beach, a good 30-minute walk from of the village, was remote and forgotten about, and of little value. Yet with the insight that Mama and Papa had about their daughter and me, they knew that this would be of greater value to us than any practical piece of land."

"It is far away from the village, but one day, that small path will be widen, maybe enough for cars, and someday, when the village gets crowded, maybe this will be your paradise. If not for you soon, then for your children, and their children. No matter what happens, we want you to keep this in the family, in your family, because we are sure that God will bless you someday," said Papa.

"'With more grandchildren for us!' added Mama with a smile, in case we didn't get the point."

"Maria and I walked the entire length of our beach, holding hands, while her folks sat under a shade tree at the edge of the sand on a small blanket they had brought. We waved to them from each end, and as we looked up, near the middle but not quite, about three stories up from the beach, lay an opening with rocks that protruded from the slope, and a flat area."

"'One day, we'll build a small house, right there,' I said."

"'Let's go look, now,' squealed Maria as she led the way up from the beach."

"We scrambled up and quickly stood a few meters above the sand. The view just opened up, as the entire Pacific seemed to be under our gaze."

"'Yes, we'll build here,' she agreed, with a kiss to my lips to seal the deal. 'We'll sit and watch our children and watch the sun go down.'"

"'Mama, Papa, we so love this gift,' Maria said as she hugged each of them when we rejoined them. 'Did you see where we climbed? That's where we'll build!'"

"They smiled, and I smiled and gave each a hug, too. But I was quiet. They knew that I was too emotional and simply didn't have the language ability to improve upon my hugs. 'Muchas gracias' just didn't say enough."

CHAPTER 3

"The winters were heavenly, but the summers were less than congenial. Everyday it rained, but luckily mostly during the afternoons and evening hours. Unfortunately the rain didn't cool things down; it just got everything muddy. When we went to Sayulita, it was worse. Most of the town roads were dirt, except the few cobblestone streets around the plaza, but with the mud flowing down the dirt roads that climbed the hills, the cobblestone soon became buried in the same brown gook. Walking about was not something that anyone did with good shoes on. Puerto Vallarta was only slightly better. Although most of the Centro had cobblestone streets, there was still enough mud up in the hills and from the adjacent neighborhoods to mix with the water and cover the lower streets with a wet, brown slip."

"Almost all summer until late fall, it was hot and sticky, almost unbearable at times unless there was a decent ocean breeze. People just slowed down, stayed in the shade and moved their muscles a bit less. And always a beer was on hand, or something stronger, like Tequila, at dinnertime. The breeze kept most of the mosquitoes away, but at times when the breezes stopped, even the screen canopies draped over the beds were not enough to prevent sleepless nights. Perhaps in the same way that one gets too much winter snow and cold up north but then spring finally emerges, just when one has had enough of the rain, it stops, the breezes build up a bit, the mosquitoes seem to fade, and life gets back to almost being perfect. That's also when tourists come, to escape the cold of the north."

"I set up shop in my studio as Maria set up the house. It was easy to buy local furniture and supply the house with an ample amount of dishes and hand-made ceramics. Maria would cut some bougainvillea from the outside bushes and always kept the vases filled with color."

"Maria stayed busy helping me. Whenever tourists needed shopping companions - especially the wives so that the husbands could go out on fishing boats- that was more Maria's expertise. Her English was so good that no one needed to concentrate to understand her. She knew the town as well as I did, and so as a team, we excelled."

"My artwork was heavily into pure abstraction. That is, I left all images out; not a trace of people, objects. I was dealing with colors and shapes, but harsh, aggressive shapes, often with hard edges. A few years later, I started to put images back in, but just hints at first, like shadows of things, and eventually, I actually attached objects to my canvas. Very strong work, but at this period, I had to work through all my semi-abstract schoolwork and find myself. That is, I needed to come up with an individual and unique style. My emotions were strong enough where I didn't feel it necessary to use imagery - real objects - to make my work be forceful. Not that I ever desired that they should be pretty. I was not painting for the tourist who wanted to bring home a colorful souvenir from Mexico, with many flowery shapes of bright colors. Later, I reversed course about the use of images, but at that point, I wanted the most distance from anything resembling paintings of fishing boats on a beach or palms trees swaying in the sun, or even the stacked up houses of Puerto Vallarta. I wanted to paint meaningful work, like Pollack, like Kline, like Newman. Oh, you don't know those artists, either, but they broke away from traditional painting. Some by splattering paint, some by using huge brushstrokes just in black and white, and some by using hard edges - controlled, tough, minimal."

"I used a lot of black - I was not a colorist by nature, and I'll admit, black and white paint was easier to get and certainly cheaper than artist's colors. Cadmium yellow and orange and red, oh, they were so very expensive. I used those colors sparingly. But I also discovered that a speck of red in a painting that was mostly black and white, well, it just had a very powerful impact that you just had to see in person."

"I'm talking about the art again, I know. I'm sorry. But you see, for more than seventy years, that's been my life's work. Everyday, I think about what I can create on a blank sheet of paper or a blank canvas that will be interesting, new, exciting, powerful - something that not only won't be forgotten, but something that feels like it was meant to be. An image that if I didn't create it, someone would have to because it's too important for it not to be born. Do you understand what I'm trying to say? I didn't paint because I was producing something to sell, or because I thought it was a fun club to be in. I created because I felt I had to. There was something driving me to do so. Yes, of course, fame supports the process. When you are an artist and you are having an exhibition, you are the star of the show, the centerpiece, if you will. I don't deny enjoying those moments. But the casual viewer forgets that for 99% of the time, the artist spends it alone in the studio, struggling to make a work survive and then thrive. There are many deaths in the studio; not all are meant to live. That's just how I see it."

Bart tried to be sympathetic to Felix's passions. "I do understand that you took your art very seriously. I admire people who are dedicated to their craft."

"Yes, the craft is important, and the dedication. But mixed with all of that is talent. At least for the masters. The ones who really stood out. There are thousands upon thousands of artists. The ones who stand out, I used to wonder why - is it talent or dedication or the ability to make it happen? A combination or is one thing more important than the other?"

"I think you must have talent," responded Bart. "Like a sports player. Without talent, all the training in the world won't get you into the major leagues. I know. That's what I always wanted to be. A baseball player; I just wasn't good enough, they said."

"I'm sorry you couldn't follow your passion. You are right my friend. And how many people can get into the major leagues? Maybe there aren't enough teams? At least, that's the way I felt. I worked hard but felt that there weren't any teams to appreciate my work, or even scouts coming my way. I'm not complaining. I knew it was my choice to be away from the big American cities where the galleries and museums were. Those are the equivalent of teams, in the art world. But I also felt that I had some time. First, I needed to create a body of work that I felt good about, and with the income Maria and I were earning, I was able to purchase the materials necessary to produce a lot of paintings. Maria supported my habit as much as possible. She never complained that I spent so much time in the studio. She found activities to keep herself busy, and often, she came and helped me prime canvases and even to clean the studio so I didn't have to waste time doing that. She wanted me to create as much as I wanted to. I couldn't have asked for more."

*****

"'Felix, am I still pretty?' Maria said to me one afternoon."

"'Are you pretty? Maria, my love, you are the most beautiful girl in all of Mexico. And I only have eyes for you,' I said with a passionate kiss thrown in."

"I won't be soon. My tummy is growing."

"Sometimes I'm a bit slow, I don't know what went through my mind- perhaps if she ate too much for lunch or something. But then I caught on. I took her arms, looked carefully again at her body, then pulled her to me and hugged her. Her sandals left the floor as a twirled her around. Inside, I was a bit terrified at first, but the joy replaced my fear. Of course, we had to wait until the following Sunday's gathering to break the news to the family, and while Mama and Papa were ecstatic, her siblings, who already had many children of their own, took it in stride."

"Maria broke tradition and insisted on having the baby in the hospital in Puerto Vallarta, rather than having Mama or one of the aunts deliver at home or at the Salud in town. Mama insisted on coming but the baby came quickly and was born before Mama arrived to the hospital. Mama stayed with us for a week, as Maria and I got used to caring for our daughter, whom we named Daniela."

"Our Sunday boat visits to Sayulita continued, except during the summer months when we avoided the storms. On most trips, with Daniela in tow, we hiked to our beach, which we nicknamed "Private Beach," and we started to place stones marking out the outside walls of our future house. Each time we added features we wanted, sparing no expense; that was easy since it was just imagination at that point. We were there at all times of morning, afternoon and evening, even sleeping overnight at times on blankets. We were there in each season, noting the winds, the rains, and sunsets and sunrises and how the tide would come in and go out. We wanted to leave nothing to chance in planning where we would sleep, what we would see upon waking, where we might eat breakfast and dinner, and where we might relax. We also wanted to incorporate the best of the natural features, from rock formations to the little stream nearby, calculating which trees we would preserve and the few that we might take out for a better vista. The beach was, of course, public but the access to the beach was difficult by any means other than through two private properties.

Although it was our personal stretch of oceanfront, we knew there'd be another home there someday, but we didn't care. We had ample distance to the property line, giving us abundant privacy for our needs. It would never be like the town's beach, where chicken-filled tamales were already being offered by venders strolling the beach for the few tourists who ventured that far north of Puerto Vallarta. By the time the summer ended, our plans were pretty well set and we were both anxious to get something built so we could use it on our overnight visits."

*****

"'Let's get the foundation poured for the entire house,' I said to a crew of nine workers."

"'You said a 'small' house, remember my sweet?' reminded Maria to me on countless occasions, as we both watched over the work going on."

"'I know, but you see, projects grow, like our family. We must be prepared. Besides, with your Dad's friends, we are getting a deal.' I kissed her each time we disagreed on anything. That was my way of making sure it didn't stay a disagreement. 'We aren't going to build the second story now, anyway, but at least structurally it'll be ready when we are,' I added."

"We had planned our house in phases. I was the one that kept expanding the house, allowing for several bedrooms and bathrooms, for studio space for my work, for patio space, for a sun terrace, for a rain terrace, for a moonlight terrace, and my list went on. We eventually compromised and decided to try to get the basic rooms built - a living room and kitchen, a outdoor dining terrace that was large enough to have couches or hammocks on, and two bedrooms - one for our bedroom and one for our daughter-to-be. Of course, I also planned an additional guest bedroom, additional work and studio spaces, storage spaces, an indoor eating area and play room, and ample hallways, atriums, spaces for plants and trees, a laundry room, and bathrooms. If I had the money, I would have done it all at once, but I was satisfied with the compromise to build the first spaces in order be able to sleep in the house and acclimate to the environment. And besides, Maria kept reminding me, this was a second home and it would be quite some time before we could spend a lot of time in it. We only needed a small place for those occasional overnights to visit her family."

"All in all, we were very satisfied with our plans, which we had done ourselves but then brought in a seasoned concrete supervisor for his advice. Of course, our plans were not much more than a sketch with rough measurements, and then drawn in the dirt once the area had been cleared; not at all like blueprints, but that was enough. We very quickly settled on a schedule, which really meant that we'd begin the very next week."

"There was a dearth of construction in town and so whenever someone had a project, an ample number of competent construction workers showed up. In the village and certainly at this remote site, everything was done by hand, without electricity. The foundation was excavated by hand. Of course, we made sure we started in the dry season; digging ditches during the wet season is a no-win effort, because a heavy evening rain would wash out all the work before any concrete could be poured. Once the ditches were ready, and once the dirt path was widened by manually cutting down growth until it actually could be called a road, a few trucks could get close enough to wheelbarrow the sand and concrete mixture to the site, plus of course, we needed the water truck to keep filling the temporarily constructed holding tanks. Each day more and more foundations were poured. Workers would constantly be shoveling and mixing the sand, concrete and water into piles on small cleared dirt pads, while others carried the ready concrete in buckets the remaining few meters to the site where the pour was happening that day. For the pour days, there were probably twenty guys working like a fire line. I had to scramble a bit to keep up with the cash flow, since everyone had to be paid in cash. But the wages were very low and a crew of twenty probably cost the same as having three workers in the States. Plus they built quickly with this process, so the outflow of pesos would not last long."

"Inside a week's work, the basic foundation was constructed. Then additional rebar was set and framing was placed around it so the main columns could be poured. Each day, only four columns could be poured, but again, within a second week, the basic form of the house had taken shape."

"Bricks were purchased from a nearby town north of Sayulita and used for the walls between the columns while basic electric, which we didn't yet have but anticipated having at some point, and plumbing lines were installed, and then the rough concrete was given a trowel finish by the workers throwing handfuls of concrete hard enough against the rough ceilings and walls so they would stick. A lot dripped immediately onto the floor, but enough stuck so the material could be trowel into a smoother finish. Even at a fistful of concrete at a time, inside a day, one worker could do at least two or three walls or ceilings."

"After that, it was a matter of small details. No matter what was forgotten, it appeared not to matter; they could just chisel away the concrete and put in whatever was needed. When the walkways were poured, the more experienced workers would inlay pebbles collected from the beach into a variety of designs. Others used heavier stone to form cobblestone type driveways and walkways. The most interesting process was adding pigment to the concrete, then smoothing and glazing the material into beautiful counters for the kitchen and bathrooms, as well as for the floors in the main living areas. The locals were highly seasoned craftsmen and with just a few tools, they knew how to craft almost any shape and design in concrete."

"What was fun for me was to incorporate curved walls into the design. In fact, sometimes a curve was easier to construct than a corner or even a straight wall. We had curved terraces and curved concrete railings and a few curved walls here and there. When we added the finishing materials, which also were a variety of concrete, stone, tile and texture, we turned the house into a living sculpture."

"The roof was another art form. A few of the smaller roofs were formed in concrete. They were engineered to allow for a second story at a later point. For the palapa roofs, which overhung the main living area and where we wanted a much higher ceiling, a special crew came with wood that had been shaved down to a smooth round consistency, and then they built a teepee structure using just a few nails and by tying the pieces together with strong rope, usually in batches of three posts, until the main posts were secured. Then, adding horizontal braces spaced a meter apart, they added the covering. This was made of special fronds that came from palm trees growing several miles away in the jungle. Handfuls of the fronds were tied, one bunch at a time starting at the bottom and then overlapped until a multi-layer thatched roof emerged. Believe it or not, a palapa roof is stronger and would last longer than most conventional roofs."

"Inside of two months, we had our basic dwelling. Each time we visited, we got more and more excited. Maria would walk through each room and along each walkway, way before the walls were completed, just to make sure all was right. In fact, she had the workers make small changes as she realized an extra few inches here or there might make a difference, and in one case, she wanted more light and so she had them cut open a wall and add an extra window. These things all could be done while construction continued, since it was just a matter of moving where a form would allow the concrete to be poured, or even punching a hole into a completed wall and smoothing out the change with extra concrete.. We only had to abide by the foundations that had already been poured but within that space, or by adding an extension to a foundation, we could design and amend our home as it was being built."

"And then I added a large room. But room is not the correct word for it. In Mexico, where the weather is almost perfect, all one needs is a floor, four columns and to connect the columns with poured beams, invite the palapa crew and quickly there's a big room. With a second palapa, our beach house was looking pretty grand, larger than most houses in the village. But the second palapa would allow me to do large studio work there, and I knew - just felt - that someday we'd be more in Sayulita than in Puerto Vallarta."

"Oh, I'm rambling again about the construction. But keep in mind I grew up with house construction. My Dad did that. I often went to his projects, where he was supervising the crews. In the States, everyone wanted more and more mechanical help. Carpenters still did the framing and finish work by hand, but as many materials as possible came in to be cut and put into place with the least amount of labor. Concrete came already mixed in huge trucks and was poured directly where needed. Dad never had a construction site so remote and without modern machinery. Within the Washington metropolitan area, there were hundreds of supply houses handling every aspect of construction. In Sayulita, in those days, we had to improvise. I found that very refreshing; one of the things I enjoyed so much being so far away from home was having to come up with creative solutions. Dad would have been genuinely intrigued with my project, so different from how he worked."

"Although the methods were different, I did learn - that summer working for Dad - the basics of building foundations, walls, roofs, windows and doors, walkways and driveways and doing electrical and plumbing, and my Dad always, always would emphasize to me some of the aesthetic qualities. He'd use to say, 'anyone can build a box with a few rooms, doors and windows, but take a good architect, and the resulting house will be something in which you can enjoy living in. Of course, the architects are not always right, and that's where I come in. I interpret their ideas and give them the form and function to make it work. I often have to modify their plans. Sometimes I'll discuss the changes with the designer and we work together fine; other times we butt heads and I just have to do what I have to do to have the quality that I want. I don't care what the architect says, if he's wrong, it's not going to be junk built under my supervision.'"

"We used local knowledge and skills but I added some of my Dad's sensibilities and I think it added to the project. And so it went, my first education about Mexican building and design. Some of those ideas carried over from my art, and I enjoyed the creative input. Once I caught on to how they made local houses, I got excited about what else we could invent. They wanted to buy cheap bars for towel bars and flimsy soap holders. Instead, Maria and I found large flat rocks on the beach; the laborers just chiseled away a hole in the concrete wall, shoved in the rock and filled it around with new concrete and voila, there was the perfect, natural soap holder without spending a peso. I asked the palapa guy to use the same poles he used for the roof to also make curtain rods and towel bars. We had to use some metal for some extra security since the house was remote and would not be watched every night, so I designed some of my abstract shapes on the ground, and the metal guy bent rods to mirror my design and welded them together to form artistic gates and window bars. Once the guys saw some of the highlights I wanted to do, they offered even more suggestions, like intricate stone designs around the edges of the walkways and broken tile with a few decorative tiles from Guadalajara for accents; the broken tile areas had more grout, therefore they were safer when wet.   You see, form and function can come together splendidly. Details all, but they added up to give the house a beautiful finish, and the extra labor really didn't add that much to the cost."

"When we could, we stayed over a few days in a row, trying to be on site enough to give it our creative supervision. Our Puerto Vallarta business suffered a bit; I was getting hectic messages from tourists who had been given my name as "the only one to use." But all in all, we balanced things the best we could. That's why in Mexico, 'mañana' is often meant as "tomorrow" but which "tomorrow" is not always clear. It could be some tomorrow that occurs the following week as much as the next day."

CHAPTER 4

"This building process happened over a six-month dry season period, but not everyday. I'd get everyone motivated and be there and there'd be a scurry of activity, and then when I left, the guys would seem to find other work to do as their priority, so when I would return the following week, I'd have to gather them up again and get them to complete the project. These were either friends of family or distant relatives, so I had to really bite my lips at times. They were being paid, but they acted like they were doing me a favor."

"To finish our construction, Papa was as involved with helping us as much as he could. He owned a few properties and ran the main grocery store that had expanded and now included a general store - at least he was the owner - one of Maria's brothers was running it by that time - so he had adequate income and felt that Mama's and his time were put to better use helping the kids and grandkids by babysitting, cooking, caring, or whatever."

"We balanced it all - with Daniela and Maria and my work, Puerto Vallarta and Sayulita. I wanted to take them to Los Angeles or Washington or both, but then we found out that our second child was on its way. Now, Maria and I had no intention of continuing the Mexican tradition of having a dozen kids-- I'm not kidding - I think the average Mexican family had eleven kids if my memory serves me correctly, anyway, we loved having Silvia, a little sister to Daniela, and Mama and Papa were ecstatic. They had been a bit worried when we married, thinking an American might not want a family for some reason, not really because I was American but also an artist which was about as foreign to someone living in Sayulita as one could get. Since they had plenty of grandkids from the other siblings, the quantity wasn't as important as long as we had more than one."

"Living in Puerto Vallarta proved a bit more difficult since we couldn't access Mama and Papa's help more easily, but down the street was a lovely young woman who needed some income, and so we employed her to help with our girls so we could do our work. Of course, Mama came often enough. The road was improved and they could actually drive in and do some shopping and other errands, so Papa would drop Mama off and go off to his supply houses. We were a modern couple since we both worked and hired childcare, which is average now, but in the early 60s in Mexico, it was still considered a progressive lifestyle."

"When Silvia came in the middle of the summer, it was not the easiest time to get to a hospital, bring home a baby and enjoy her. It was constantly raining, hot and muggy. Of course, I guess the reason no one is as bothered by the summer as much as new people is that the kids get acclimated to it from day one."

"The second child is always easier than the first - after all, we knew the routine and were better prepared all around. Now we were a family of four. Yes, I guess I had a slight feeling of wanting a son, after all, males are all raised to think of handing things over to our sons, but on the other hand, I was a strong feminist before that word ever got popular, and there was no way that our girls weren't going to have the same opportunities and the same experiences as boys. In fact, I went out of my way to show the girls how I worked - my tools, how the house was constructed, whatever I would have naturally wanted a son to know. You know what? When they grew up and married, I think they wore the tool belts around their waists fixing whatever needed attention in the house, rather than their husbands. And they certainly were not timid about traveling alone. Tough but cute, that's what I used to think. They both had Maria's complexion and features, especially their eyes and their smiles. That was important for me, as you will find out."

*****

"We were doing quite well. At least one day a week, and often two, I was in Sayulita; the rest of the time I was in Puerto Vallarta working my tail off. Of course, evenings I spent in the studio, and some afternoons - as much as I could. But during the day during the tourist season, I couldn't turn down good money. I was involved with almost any tourist who stayed more than a few days and who wanted to see something more interesting than the main church and plaza. They had just started flights originating in Los Angeles with a stop in Mazatlan but with Puerto Vallarta as the end destination. More and more what I called regular tourists started to enjoy the town. Prior, there had been some, but many were writers or early Bohemians who wanted an offbeat experience. Once everyone saw that the town was enjoyable, the government took greater note that the city was a gold mine for future development aimed at tourism. Soon enough, they expanded the airport, expanded roads, started to give the city a better infrastructure with better sewage and water service, and every year or so, contractors would show up and re-do some area, like along the water front or in the old town section. Then too, that was done in conjunction with deals made with large developers who started to put up luxury hotels. Up to that time, accommodations were okay but not great. Within a year or more, I could already see the difference by the increase numbers of Americans visiting. It would take a couple of years more of this effort and the actions of a certain movie director to create the explosive expansion, but even on its own, the town was beginning to come alive."

"The word had gotten out that Felix Peters could take them on tours, help them find accommodations, even find them a house to buy if they fell in love with Puerto Vallarta. Maria was always there with me helping, and her English got better than my Spanish within a year. We were gearing up for a better business future, while I was also gearing up to do more and more artwork."

"I was immersed in our life in Mexico, although I was an American and trying to keep up with the main stories from the States. I'd read some international news in the local newspapers and I'd see an occasional International Wall Street Journal or even a Los Angeles Times when a tourist would bring it and ask if I'd like to have it before throwing it away. I was always anxious to hear any art news and occasionally someone would bring an art magazine and I'd get a glimpse of what was happening in my world."

"Maria heard it first at the local grocery and didn't even bother to finish her shopping. Carrying Silva and pulling Daniela in order to run to tell me, she went directly into my studio where I was up to my arms in wet paint. 'They shot your President!' she said in a very urgent voice."

"Who? What?"

"Kennedy. President Kennedy. They shot and killed him! I heard it at the grocer's. It's on the radio."

"I washed up as quickly as I could and lifting Daniela while Maria carried Silvia, the four of us almost ran to the nearest restaurant three blocks down the hill, where I knew they had a television. Already a small crowd had gathered as the national news station broadcasted non-stop the latest information and pictures coming in about the assassination in Dallas. Several men turned to me as if I held some inside information about the significance of the event. We watched for at least an hour, when Maria finally took the girls home. I continued to watch, trying to make sense of it all and trying to understand if I was lucky to be in Mexico and away from the turmoil happening at home, or whether I should feel like a deserter, absent during a time of need."

"I walked home and gave my sleeping girls an extra kiss. When I finally climbed into bed with Maria, I had a hard time closing my eyes. I stared for a long time at the motionless ceiling fan."

*****

"One day, I heard about some film people from Hollywood, based in a small bay about ten miles south of the city, looking about for lodging, vehicles, caterers, and all sorts of set design materials. Tourists were getting common enough but a group this size going to places a bit off the path soon got people talking. I wondered if I should go snooping but soon enough, I got a knock on my door."

"'Mr. Peters? Glad I found you. Are you available to help us?' asked a man who introduced himself as Andrew Heron, an assistant to the assistant director."

"'I might be,' I replied. 'Can you tell me what's going on? I only heard that you are trying to make a film.'"

"And we heard that Felix Peters is the person to see if we want some local help. That he's an American artist living here and knows practically everything."

"I smiled."

"Please, come this afternoon and meet my boss -near the Posada Mismaloya. You know it, I'm sure. We have set up a film set less than a kilometer down the road. You can't miss it."

"'Of course, ' I replied."

"That late afternoon, I drove south of Puerto Vallarta, about twenty minutes taking it slow since the road was in bad condition, to a speck of a inlet call Mismaloya. Just past and above the boats was a complex of palapas, obviously erected recently. I could tell by the freshness of the palm leaves used; they had not yet dried out and turned the dusty brown color. There must have been a dozen or more Americans moving about, and an equal number of local workers that had been hired to do the lifting. I'd seen a few movie shoots during my California days, and this group seemed highly professional. I could just imagine what it took to get all that equipment into Mexico and to this remote location."

"I went up to the first American I saw and asked where I could find the assistant director. "Try that hut over there," he replied without any suspicion about whether I was expected or not. In the distance, I spotted some of the actors who were sitting in an open-air table, under a palapa for shade and, I suspected, rehearsing their parts. I couldn't make out the individuals from my vantage point, since there were equipment and people moving in front."

"I went up to the directed hut and asked, 'Is the assistant director about?'"

"'And who might be inquiring?' came a very husky but not unfriendly voice. In the back portion at a desk, sat a middle-age man with wrinkles and a beaten up cowboy hat, wearing glasses and looking at a huge pile of papers."

"My name is Felix Peters. I've been living here for a few years and I was told that you might be interested in my services."

"'And what services might that be,' replied the voice, as I had my first introduction to a rustic faced gentleman named John Huston. He was friendly while always getting straight to the point. 'Oh, I'm teasing. Not to worry. I know about you. Glad to meet you. I'm the director. John Huston,' he said standing up and putting aside his papers to greet me. 'I certainly could use you,' he continued."

"Oh, I was asked to meet your assistant."

"Max. Later. Talk to me. We're making a movie. Filming starts in a week, that's my task. We are scrambling. We've decided on a location here, but we need help with details. And I'd like to find some more places to rent. And I have a list of equipment and stuff we need. An old bus to begin with. I hear you are an artist, too. True?"

"'Yes, true,' I said. 'And I'll be glad to work with you.'"

"And my man will discuss our pay. I'm sure you'll work it out, although we don't pay well. Tight budget. You see, we are on a tight timetable. I want to complete the film in three months - not one day longer! Everyone has obligations and so I work hard to stick to my schedule. We hire top people."

"I'd be happy to. It's an exciting project. I'm surprised you picked such a place like Puerto Vallarta. It's not very well known and it doesn't have every modern convenience."

"That's what I love about it. It's authentic. I don't like fake sets when I can come and get the real thing. It's as important for my movies as the actors. And I happen to love it here. Do you know I bought a house not too far away?

"I heard someone did. To tell you the truth, I heard that an eccentric gringo put good money down for something away from town."

"Ha. Eccentric, am I? That's fine with me. I get along. They'll get used to me. Meanwhile, I'm paying lots of locals to feed us, move our stuff and allow us to work. They seem okay with that."

"What's the film about?"

"John Huston grabbed a thick booklet from a stack of them. 'Here, take a script if you'd like to read it. Ever hear of Tennessee Williams? He wrote it. He's coming in a few days. You can help with the next arrivals. Can you?'"

"Thanks. I'll read it right away. And of course, I'd be happy to pick up whomever you want. My wife, too. She's Mexican but is fluent in English and is very capable. However, she needs to know in advance so we can have her mother take care of our kids."

"Bless your heart. You have a wife and kids here too. Wonderful. What kind of art do you make?"

"People always ask and it's hard to describe in words. Abstract. Tough. Large canvases when I can get the supplies. I try to push. But I guess some Mexican influence. Rivera is a big hero of mine."

"Hell, mine too. We'll get along fine. I'd like to see your work, but not now. For the next three months, I have one purpose and except for evening meal time, when we all try to relax and restore our energy - well, hell, get over the anger we have for each other and get back in unison for next morning's work - it's pretty intense."

"Just then, a man not much younger than Huston walked in."

"Ah, here's Max. Max is my main assistant. He's the one you were supposed to meet, but I'm glad we talked. He'll show you around and give you the lists of needs. That bus. That's at the top of my list today. I need an old bus. I have one we can use but I don't like it. I want to find one a bit different. Max knows."

"Huston shook my hands again and laid his other hand on top. It was a warm, welcoming handshake and his smile was infectious. I'd say lovable but there was too much seriousness in his work to be taken casually."

"As I started to reply, he corrected himself, "Oh yeah, I'll pay you well. Mr. Greene will give you the numbers. You'll be pleased. I was just joking with you - about the low pay; just wanted to see what kind of guy we're bringing into the family."

As Max and I were leaving the hut, he called after us, "Felix, join us later for our afternoon drinks and early dinner. You'll meet the gang."

"I nodded. Max added, 'It's a great group of actors and filmmakers here. He's taken us to this God forsaken place but just you watch, you'll see a masterpiece come out.'"

"How long have you worked for him?"

"This is my third film with Huston. He's great. Knowledgeable. And he takes chances to make a film better. But he's focused on getting a bus. The one we came up with is not what he wants."

"'What's his budget?' I asked."

"You know, whatever is fair. We aren't here to quibble. But don't get the wrong idea, we don't want a new bus. We want a beat up bus that looks like it's on its last legs taking tourists anyplace."

"I know of a few busses; parked behind the electric company. I'll bet I can get you one tomorrow."

"'Show up with the right bus, and he'll be loyal to you always,' joked Max."

"We did a short walk around the complex. Workers were constructing walls around an existing old building."

"This is our main set. It's supposed to be a hotel, of sorts. Funky."

"Not so funky here. It's pretty typical, actually."

"That's what the director wants. Authenticity. They say you're the man here-- you and your wife. Are you onboard? Don't answer. Just work it out with Mr. Greene."

"Max ushered me into another small building, with a more substantial roof I gathered to protect the papers just in case of inclement weather, which was rare during the winter but not unheard of, and I met Mr. Greene, the moneyman on the set. Max told Mr. Greene that I was to be hired, along with Maria."

"Mr. Greene was strictly business. 'We can pay you $40 a day, in U.S. dollars. Your wife can earn $25. We are paying you more because Mr. Huston expects more from you. Hours are loose; if it goes way overtime, we'll add on. Is that fair?'"

"I agreed to the pay. It was actually more than I'd make on an occasional day, and this seemed like it would be steady for at least a couple of months, and besides, I found the entire project exciting. It was just up my speed, an art project except in motion."

*****

"I stayed until the crew gathered for late afternoon drinks and tacos. There was a Vietnamese man there, cooking Asian food."

"Huston found him. He loves Asian food. Crew does, too. But he makes tacos just as well as the Mexicans."

"'The Mexicans don't use fish sauce in their tacos!' laughed a crew member who had been overhearing."

"For some, it was dinner. For others, it was appetizers. I saw some of the actors. Richard Burton was there, by himself. His new girlfriend, actress Elizabeth Taylor, was joining him soon. Ava Gardner was there, as was Deborah Kerr and the very young Sue Lyon. They all had partners or chaperons or some sort of family around. Then there were the crewmembers - assistants to the director and to the actors and those who had their special skills in camera work, sound, set design, and so forth. About forty men and woman all together. They were staying at various houses and hotels, some in the posada in Mismaloya and others in the south end of Puerto Vallarta, in the old section, so they could commute more easily."

"After everyone had heard about the new guy on the set, Richard Burton blurted out, "Felix. I'm playing you. You're the real life tour guide in Puerto Vallarta and that's my part in the movie. Of course, I drink too much. Do you?"

"'Not in front of my tourist clients,' I joked in reply."

"You are few years younger than I am. By the time you catch up, you'll be as miserable to your tourists as I am in this film."

"Anyway, from that day, I had constant jokes about how my life was parallel to Richard's part, and did I steer clients to seedy hotels for extra commission on the side?"

*****

"Family was the right word, because inside of a week, I became familiar with each and every crew member - their wishes, their demands, their problems, and how it might affect that day's filming. It took another two weeks to get all in order before the main scenes could be filmed. To finish the film, it took John Huston just three months and one week - just a few days longer than Mr. Huston had scheduled. Max told me that Mr. Huston was always a bit optimistic on what others could accomplish. Nevertheless, he was set to do the filming in three months including all of the preliminary work, and you know, he just about succeeded in meeting his deadline."

"What was the name of the film?" asked Bart.

"*The Night of the Iguana.* It's very old now. You can still find it online. A classic. It's in black and white. It's the reason that you and I are flying out of an international airport today. It made the town. Gave it worldwide publicity. Puerto Vallarta grew from 40,000 to a city of 250,000 today; doubled its population within the first decade, mostly from all the attention that movie started. Of course, the government got in on it and helped. But it was Liz and Richard who set it all off."

"Who?"

"Elizabeth Taylor and Richard Burton. Surely you've heard of them?"

"Yes, I've seen some of the old movies. They were Hollywood legends."

"They were already famous when I met them. As was John Huston. I don't think anyone understood what this movie would mean to our lives. Anyway, that very first day, after we had eaten, I told them I needed to go look for a bus for Mr. Huston and would be there later the next morning because I would need some time to try to secure one. I didn't even have to wait 'til morning. That evening, on my way home, I actually saw my guy outside at a taco stand before I got to my street and told him what I wanted. We set up a time for early the next morning. I met him at the depot. He thought I was looking for the best conditioned bus; I told him I needed the cheapest bus, so he steered me to the one that I had spotted a week earlier, and I agreed to purchase it only subject to Mr. Huston's approval. Meanwhile, I gave him a few pesos to let me go drive it to the set and show it. If they consented, the film studio would pay him immediately, in cash, I promised."

"Well, you would have thought I was bringing in a food truck to starving prisoners, because when I drove that bus past the gate and into the set compound around mid-day, I beeped the horn and John Huston himself came out of this hut and started to clap his hands. That stimulated everyone else to stop and look and they too started to clap their hands. In fact, I think they clapped for a full five minutes, because the entire crew knew that the director had desperately wanted a more simpatico looking bus and had told everyone to be on the lookout, and he had become increasingly edgy about not having it, so when I pulled in and it was exactly what they wanted, there was a big sign of relief from everyone, all played out with their thunderous applause."

"I left the bus right in the middle of the lot so everyone could inspect it from all sides, put it into park, pulled the handbrake and turned off the ignition and got out. Huston came over to me with outstretched arms and grabbed me almost violently and hugged me tight. Then he gave me a big theatrical kiss on my cheek in full view of at least twenty cast and crewmembers. Boy, his laugh was contagious and I was grinning ear to ear."

"Felix, your first day and you did it, boy! You're incredible! I was almost ready to offer my daughter in marriage I wanted that bus so badly. How did you know this is exactly the look I wanted?"

"'Because it's a typical run-down, Mexican-maintained old bus, and I knew you wanted authenticity,' I beamed."

"You know, we only need to do the most minor alterations to it. We were ready to beat up a newer bus and paint in all the dents; you showed up with exactly what I had in mind!"

"I had an idea it would work and I was right! I had skimmed the script he gave me before going to bed, and I sensed that the bus was an essential part of the story. If you ever see the movie, you'll see that bus in quite a few scenes."

"Things only got better after that. I seemed to be the guy that everyone turned to when in need. Maria worked as well. Maria had seen only a few movies in her life, mostly during trips to Guadalajara, and here she was fitting right in. She was able to find all sorts of small items that they needed -you'd be surprised at the amount of small items that fill up a set, from glasses to plates to clothing and tools - even to the critters which might be walking or crawling about - and she also was great at taking non-working crew and actors and their companions on tours and shopping trips."

CHAPTER 5

"I was standing around on the set, after I had done my preliminary work and just observing how the company was preparing for yet another day of filming, when a very attractive young lady approached me."

"You must be Felix, are you not?"

"I am. Felix Peters. Miss… Taylor?"

"Yep. Elizabeth. How are you? Richard is on camera today, but I wonder if you have some time to drive me around and show me some properties. We thought that maybe we'd see if we could buy a Mexican escape. What do you think?"

"'I do know some nice properties,' I responded. 'Are you looking for something remote like Mr. Huston bought, or something in town and more convenient?'"

"In town, easy. We don't want to rough it the way John seems to enjoy."

"Up on the hill just two blocks behind the main church gets you a sensational view. But you are a two-minute walk to the bay and to shops and restaurants along the Malecon."

"Show me, please. Now? Can you? And call me Liz."

"I'd be delighted. Since we are heading back to town, can my wife come along? She knows properties better than I do."

"Of course. Where is she?"

"Maria was on the set helping to collect the objects being used in the hotel set. I waved her over. 'Maria, this is Elizabeth Taylor. She's an actress in the States. She's here because of Richard.'"

"Very pleased to meet you, Maria. I actually heard that you've been taking people on shopping trips. You know, I love to shop. You'll have to help me, too."

"It would be my pleasure, Miss Taylor."

"And with that, Liz quickly said, 'And no more of that 'Miss' stuff. I'm Liz.'"

"We took one of the rented crew cars and I drove from Mismaloya back to the center of Puerto Vallarta. Having hunted a year earlier for ourselves, Maria and I both knew several properties and the easiest thing to do was just look from the outside, and if anything hit her fancy, we could knock on the door. There really weren't any real estate agents in those days. "

"Elizabeth Taylor was a knockout even in simple clothes. She was in her early thirties at that time, fun, vibrant and willing to explore and we hit it off. She didn't want nor need to be pampered; she was as regular as our next-door neighbor, or anyone on the film crew for that matter. And I was intrigued that my Maria didn't look that dissimilar to the actress. Both had dark hair, dark features and they had about the same figure. Maria was ten years younger, but they looked like sisters walking together. Liz liked white blouses, too, because it showed off her tan; that was something else they had in common. Of course, Maria didn't have the international stardom, but she was a star in my world! For that reason, I treated Elizabeth just like one of Maria's friends. And Elizabeth treated Maria like the younger sister she appeared to be."

"'We're going just a block up from the church. I'll try to get the car close. Then we'll walk; it's easier,' I said as we parked the car."

"Are you implying that I can't hike up a steep hill? This is easy to walk; I don't mind hills. And we'll not have a car when we come-- probably just take taxis or walk. Well, maybe not Richard as much, the climb that is. But it'll be good exercise for him. Then we can come back and relax. Four blocks to the beach is fine, and the view! That's what we like. Imagine having cocktails with this view!"

"We walked along the streets, climbed another level to almost the top street where there were two lovely houses, each on the corner, facing each other, the smaller one slightly below the larger house."

"'These used to be for sale. I think they still are,' I said."

"'Let's please try to look inside!' exclaimed Liz."

"Maria and I knocked at the door of each house, and explained in Spanish that we were possibly interested in buying the house. We were instantly welcomed in. Gringo prices were probably triple what a Mexican would likely pay, so the owners were anxious to show us. Of course, I knew how to bargain their asking prices down to more realistic levels if there was serious interest."

"'It needs redecorating, but look at the views from the window!' exclaimed Liz."

"'There probably is a roof terrace with even better vistas,' I replied."

"We climbed the stairs to the outdoor terrace. There before us was the entire pueblo of Puerto Vallarta and just beyond, the entire Bay of Banderas."

"'Wow,' was Liz's remark. 'It won't take much to make this really comfortable.'

She was right because each house had ample bedrooms and bathrooms, with a large family kitchen and living area for entertaining."

"This is a very substantial house. The woman's father, who had been living with her, died last year and so she wants downsize and move into their son's house. The other house is for sale because the owner died and the family wants to sell. So both houses are available. We even looked at them a year ago but even this one seemed too large of a project for us."

"I'm glad they're still available. We must show them to Richard. Your studio is nearby? Can you show me?"

"'Sure,' I replied."

*****

"Liz brought Richard one weekend and we met at the house. 'Look who I got on a day off? John works them to death but even the crew needs a day off. You can't go 24 hours for 90 days without a few breaks. If the actors take a break, it helps the crew get a break.'"

"'I'm not here for long; John wants us back on the set this afternoon,' explained Richard. 'I like it here. Liz wants to buy. I'm game. John already bought. We need a retreat. There are too many reporters already here; you can imagine how bad it'll be someplace more convenient. So if Liz is happy here, I'm happy here. We'll have more time after the filming wraps up.'"

"'We like details done right, but tell us what are things we need to consider?' asked Liz sitting next to Richard on the terrace gazing out upon the bay."

"Well, construction in Mexico is different than in the States. I'm building a modest home right now, so I can tell you lots that I've learned.

We use concrete and tile for obvious reasons, wood does not do well in this humidity and with termites. The termite nests in trees can be as large as a refrigerator. For kitchen cabinets, closets, and doors, there is a special wood that locals use. It's very pretty, medium-dark with a nice grain, but the wood is like poison to the termites, so they don't touch it. They also use the branches from the same tree to make decorative woven front panels for doors and cabinets."

"For everything else, think concrete and tile. But they can smooth and glaze the concrete with color for bathroom and kitchen counters. You might like this look rather than tile. And the less metal the better. Everything rusts here. The more metal, the more painting you'll be doing each year. You'll need some for windows and locks but I would try to keep it to a minimum."

"What about railings? I've admired some artistic railings."

"We have some great metal craftsmen here. If you want iron railings, I can arrange for that, but they will need painting each year."

"'What are the alternatives?' asked Richard."

"Some people use wood and bamboo and rope, but I think they require more maintenance than metal. Others are using concrete to make railings that look like bamboo - they just paint them bamboo color. But for you, I think you want something more elegant, so black iron railings with lots of curves would liven up a terrace."

"'And for the floors?' asked Liz."

"Tile is used for almost everything - floors, benches, walls, wherever you want it to be more decorative."

"'What about marble, can we get marble here?' asked Richard."

"Mexico has everything- and it's all reasonable. Maybe not as much is available in Puerto Vallarta. This is still a fishing port. We can go to Guadalajara or even to Mexico City, but that's farther. Guadalajara has just about everything we'll need. And they have all the crafts and decorative items you might want."

"'I'll be glad to take you. I know the shops quite well,' added Maria."

"'"Then we'll schedule a trip there at some point,' smiled Liz. 'When Richard is not along. He has no patience for shopping.'"

"'But always design with views and breezes in mind, and remember, although many houses are very open, during summer storms it's possible to see rain going uphill-- the wind can be that strong,' I joked."

"'We don't anticipate being here during the wet season. Of course, we don't want water coming in, even if we aren't here,' said Liz."

"'Ocean breezes are nice during the day; we can also design your house to enjoy the breeze coming from the jungle hills, because the wind reverses each evening,' I added. 'For a roof, you can go with tile, concrete or palapa-- the thatched roofing that you've seen all over. But I'd stick to tile here, and just replace the older tile that's on it. You can add a palapa to the rear terrace. You might think they will blow away in a hurricane but in reality, they are as strong as any other type of roof.'"

"'Felix, you know your stuff. Please help my 'novia' and I'll make sure you get paid on time,' said Richard. 'Is that a deal?' as he put out his hand and we shook."

"Yes, but I owe my time first to John Huston, for the next two months, until the film wraps up. By the time you own the house, I'll have a full crew working. And Maria can help Liz find the furniture and decorations and we can store them for a couple of months."

"On the way out, Richard talked to me one on one while Liz and Maria were chatting. 'Listen, I love it here, don't get me wrong. And I'm astonished Liz came. We are in love, so I suppose I shouldn't be surprised. But Liz has her own career and she's not used to being around a film set and not being one of the players. This is a new experience for her. So I'm excited that she's gotten into this project. It'll keep her busy and happy to be with me, without feeling left out. I know you are busy helping John but just tell Maria to spare no expense. What Liz wants, she gets. Keep in mind, she always wants something special.'"

"You know, there are not many homes here that come up to your level of style. It'll be fun to see it happen. This is a perfect house, and the one across the street would make an interesting package. They are large enough to remodel into whatever you dream."

"And by the way, I like your art. I saw the one that Liz already purchased from you. She had it hung it in my hotel room. We couldn't stand what was on the wall when I arrived. I'm glad you're one of us-- a creator. "

"That was nice of Richard to say. He didn't have to, but I think he genuinely was impressed."

"In the end, I put in bids for both houses, around $16,000 each as I remember, which was probably double what the owners thought the houses were worth. Over the next year, acting as Liz's local agent and general contractor with communications by letter, phone and wire, I probably put in double that amount in updating and decorating the houses. Then upon their next visit, Richard and Liz proposed connecting the houses by building a small bridge over the street from their second floor terraces, so each would own one house but they could live in them as a couple. The residents were so perplexed when they saw this structure going up. People just didn't splurge like that; no practical purpose could be found for not just crossing the street and using the normal front doors."

*****

"Maria was hired to help purchase furniture and decorations, but the truth was that Liz loved to shop, and they ended up making special trips to Guadalajara to a special area called Tonala, where most of the craft goods in that region of Mexico was sold to retail as well as wholesale customers. It was a long drive in those days, probably more than seven hours, and my Maria was a talker-- I suspect that she told Liz every aspect about her family and me. I can just imagine Maria driving carefully and yakking away while Liz is smiling and just looking out upon the hills and valleys and waving to every farmer in the field and every kid when they cruised through the small towns. Their shopping trips were great successes, I heard. Maria said that she had a very quick and good eye for the best items, paid fairly but never overpaid, and came back with the car stuffed with items. Larger items were trucked for just a few dollars more. Meanwhile, I commuted between the film set and Liz and Richard's new houses to get things planned, and then after the filming had ended, I worked full time to get enough completed before their first return visit so they could visualize the end result. A few rooms needed only minor work, so they were soon ready to fill with many of the purchases Liz had made."

"It would take another four months and two return visits before all was completed. Soon enough, with the final tile finished and everything painted, the houses were amply filled with furniture, vases, crafts and artwork - most from local or regional artisans. But Liz's property appetite didn't end there; she just got more and more excited. We did a brief shopping trip just a half hour north of the airport and she got so excited about that town, that she bought a beachfront house almost on the spot. She never really used it for anything other than storage, but she was impetuous and properties were so cheap, she just couldn't resist."

*****

"While it was a nice carry over to be involved with Liz and Richard's two houses, and then furnishing them, I was very sad when the filming ended. Just about everyone left and locals went back to their regular jobs. It felt like kids leaving at the end of summer camp. There was a lot of work left to do on the film, but it all had to take place in Los Angeles with editing and sound work, adding titles and then of course, distribution deals had to be made, and so forth. John Huston had his house just south of Puerto Vallarta, but he was going to be so busy, I didn't think he'd return until the next winter, no matter what happened politically in the United States. Of course, he reminded me often that his bag was always packed in case all hell broke loose and he had to escape the country's downfall in a hurry. I didn't hold my breath, although he did convince me of many of the dangers the nation faced. The entire crew had been devastated with the loss of Kennedy, and not one cast member had a positive feeling about Johnson."

"Almost all the tasks I had been assigned by John Huston had been successfully completed, so I'd say he was more than happy with me. Two days before they were departing, when for the first time, his responsibilities were somewhat lessened since others were in charge of the packing and transportation aspects, John spotted me as we were both in a Centro hotel saying goodbye to two of the actors, and called me over."

"Felix, I want to see your studio. We're downtown and need lunch anyway, so can we go see it on the way?"

"We hopped in my car, and I took him directly to the studio that was behind our house. He had never been there. He was quite impressed just getting out of the car."

"Looks great. Not as big as what you got for Liz and Richard, but nice."

"Their houses are just six blocks over."

"I was driven by with Richard. I actually peeked inside. They have their work cut out for them but I hear you are doing it all for them. That's good. I wanted more distance from civilization-- that's why I bought down the coast. I like it there. But living in town is also nice, and more convenient for them."

73

"I led him into my studio and he just stood there. Quiet. For once, he didn't say anything for about three long minutes; he just slowly turned his head and took it all in. I was not prepared for a visitor, so par for the course, I had canvases spread all over in a mess, and three big ones against the main work wall that I was working on."

"Felix, did you know that I studied art? I still paint, some. I wanted to be an artist, but then drifted into film. Got that from my old man. But man, I never guessed. I'm sorry, I should have. Knowing you, I mean. This is tough shit you are doing."

"He stepped closer to a couple, and hesitated, 'may I?' He indicated he wanted to see the painting that was partially blocked by a canvas in front."

"'Of course,' as I rushed over and moved the small front painting aside."

"'Man-oh-man,' he exclaimed again. 'This is good stuff. Boy, I'm glad I didn't leave without seeing this. When are you exhibiting this work?'"

"I don't know. I haven't lined anything up yet. I'm here and it's hard to make contact with U.S. galleries. Liz bought two large paintings and is taking one back for her L.A. house; says she will contact a friend who has a gallery."

"Hey, with Liz behind you, you won't go wrong. Listen, when I get back next trip, let's get together and talk art. At my place. I'd like that."

"We ducked into the house where he could see some more of my paintings on the walls, and Maria was there with the girls. She offered food and drinks, but John said he was on a mission with me, and just wanted to make sure he said goodbye to them properly, before the last minute rushing started. He gave Maria such a nice hug and kiss, and then the girls, seeing their Mom getting kissed and perhaps wondering, received the same - in fact, he picked up each girl and swung them around."

"'I'll be missing you two,' he said to them, although he had only seen them a few times and not for long. On the few times we brought them, Maria and I made sure they had stayed in the background so as not to interrupt any of the filming that was going on."

"John and I got a quick taco at a place near the hotel; we started to chat, but then a couple of the crew managers spotted us and joined us and our talk morphed to shop talk. But as we were splitting up, John said, 'you've got a great family and you are doing great art. Keep it up. Don't slack, at all. You have too much talent, and I'm an insider, so I know what I speak. See you next visit, my man.'"

"Then as he took a step to depart, he added, 'Felix, you helped me greatly on this film. I'm very grateful to you. Muchísimas gracias, mi amigo.'"

CHAPTER 6

"The film came out. It was a huge success, but no one in Puerto Vallarta saw it. There was no movie theater to show it and no one had bothered to arrange for a showing. It was at least a half-year before we finally got a reel and were able to arrange a showing at the new hotel that had just opened."

"By that time, the news of Liz and Richard's affair, the movie, the glamour and romance of old Puerto Vallarta had been written about in newspapers around the world. Suddenly, we were living in the new jetsetter destination."

"It was really the fact that Liz and Richard were having the affair that caused all the reporters to come to Puerto Vallarta. Once they were there, they needed to get the most bang for their buck, so they wrote also about the filming, and the other stars, and then about the beaches and the charm of the town. That went to millions of readers who had never even heard of Puerto Vallarta but suddenly, it was as much on their minds as Nice, Acapulco, Rio de Janeiro and Capri were on any jetsetter's list of escapes. It made the population of the city double within the decade, and double each decade after that. Rapid growth brought opportunities for many."

*****

"One day, I got a message to go to the wire office. In those days, there was one place that handled the little mail that came into town, and they had a public telephone where you could pay to make long distance calls or where you could send or receive telegrams. The few people who wanted to be in touch had that address and number. But when something came in, maybe after a day or so, someone in the office might deliver the message or mail. More frequently, someone in the office would mention it to someone who knew the recipient, and by word of mouth, the intended recipient would get word that the postal office had something. That was how I heard that there was a cable for me."

"I walked over one afternoon after hearing such a rumor. Sure enough, there was a telegram. It was from Beatrice. The telegram said that Dad was in the hospital and had wanted me to know that he'd be okay."

"Of course, when my Dad said he's okay but it was serious enough for me to know about it, I knew it was very serious."

"I deliberated on my walk home, how to take a leave of absence. I had dreamt of having the entire family see the United States on some imaginary vacation, by car, and ending up in Washington D.C. But the girls were too young, I had commitments for all the tourists I was helping and Maria always had her hands full. What to do? I decided to go alone. It was going to put a dent in our growing savings account, but what could I do?"

"My love, my Dad is sick and in the hospital. I think I need to fly there and see him. It's not the best time to do a family trip, even if we could afford it."

"Of course you need to go. We'll be fine. I can get Mama to come and help. How long do you think it will be?"

"A week, maybe longer. I don't want to be long. And I have all those clients."

"I can help them. I've helped you enough to know the work. You know that."

"'I'll go to the airport tomorrow and see what I can get for tickets,' I said."

"They were beginning to use jet planes to Puerto Vallarta and travel was improving, although getting to the east coast generally meant going through Los Angeles, with an occasional flight to Dallas. The airport wasn't much to look at, a non-descript block building with fans struggling to keep it bearable inside but they were building a large extension. I went up to the Pan Am window and asked about flights. I managed to book passage through L.A.. Depending on how my visit went, I thought I might have time on my way back to stop off in L.A. for two days and see some friends and try to reconnect with a couple of galleries for my work. I then went to the cable office and sent off a cable to Beatrice telling her that I was coming in a few days."

"I had not left Mexico in several years, so in some ways, I was excited. I wondered if I should suddenly realize, upon stepping on American soil, all the creature comforts that I had been missing. My life was pretty complete and I was working hard on my art on top of everything, still, I knew how primitive our life was compared to living in the States. I worried that I might be looked upon as a country bumpkin. My clothes were all work clothes or shorts and short sleeve tropical shirts. I didn't have any city clothes. Even my suitcase was an old bag that most people might have tossed in the trash. I was not the best example of a well-heeled traveler, although my "artist" profession allowed me some freedom, I rationalized."

"I kissed the girls and Maria extra hard, after they drove me to the airport and stayed to watch my plane take off. The girls were as excited to see the planes up close and so were less thinking about the fact that I would be leaving them for the first time in their memory. The United States was something they knew a lot about, but only from my stories and books."

"In no time, I was in the air, going to a new world."

*****

"Dad was home and doing okay. Beatrice had everything organized and a nurse came once a day to check on him. His biggest hurdle was quitting cigarettes. All over the government had new warnings of the danger of getting cancer, and Dad had it even worse with emphysema. He was stabilized and recovering. He was able to take time off from his business, he had good partners, but he waffled in committing to retiring. He felt he had another good ten years, but that was if his health allowed him too. For now, he could barely walk down the block before he had to sit down. He wasn't used to a slower pace, and the frustration showed."

"I helped him around the house, but only to the extent that he welcomed it. He couldn't drive without Beatrice, not with his medications and lack of strength, so he encouraged me to take his car and to enjoy the city. It had only been a few years, yet I could tell how it had grown by leaps and bounds since my last visit."

"Of course, he was referring to buildings that had mushroomed all over the downtown. Most of the new housing had expanded outside the boundaries, into the Maryland and Virginia suburbs. I actually was more interested in the museums and to see what art activity there was. I had to revisit the Philips Collection and take a peek at the Biennial Exhibition at the Corcoran, and I had to have at least one visit in the National Gallery, revisiting some of my favorite masterpieces. That had stimulated my first interest in art and probably was the reason I even signed up for that first painting class in college. I walked the Dupont Circle area where a dozen small but credible galleries had blossomed. I heard that the best ones were showing paintings where the artists stained the paint onto raw canvas in various basic geometric shapes. I heard the name, the Washington Color School, a term that referred to about a dozen artists working in this style. A couple of the artists had already shown in New York and had started to get mentioned nationally."

"On a side street just off Connecticut Avenue, I walked up to the second floor of a small commercial building and into the Jefferson Place Gallery. It was one of six new galleries within that block. Galleries often find it better to be close together because if a client goes to one gallery, he or she will visit the others if they are close by. At the Jefferson Place Gallery, there were large square paintings and some circle paintings, all done like a pie shape divided into slices, each slice a different color. Very strong, I thought. I walked into the second main room, and then I saw the name on the wall - Mary Owens Meyers. Mary! My Mary? I glanced at the bio that was on the desk. Yes, the same Mary that studied in San Diego. What was she doing showing in a Washington D.C. gallery? I glanced into the third exhibition room and there was a woman staffing the gallery."

"Excuse me, but can you tell me about the artist?"

"'Her name is Mary Meyers,' said a thin, red-haired middle age woman with an English accent."

"Yes, I know. I mean, I know her. I used to. In San Diego. Does she live here, now?"

"Yes, she's been here for a couple of years. Made a name for herself. Do you like the work?"

"I do. But it's so different from the work I knew. Can you tell me how to contact her?"

"You say you know her?"

"We went to art school together. We were very close. I'm an artist, too. My name is Felix Peters."

"Not a problem, then. I'm Nesta Dorrance, the gallery director. Just had to ask." Nesta grabbed a small sheet from her pad and wrote down Mary's information. "Here's her telephone number. You know, she often drops in the gallery, just to see how things are going. I'm surprised she's not here by now."

"May I use your phone, to call her?"

"Of course. I'll try for you, but she's probably not in at this time. As…"

"Just then Nesta looked up and smiled. My back was towards the stairs. I heard a 'Hi Nesta,' just as I turned around."

"Mary stopped dead in her tracks. She was dressed in stretched black slacks and a light jean jacket over a red blouse. She was in absolute shock, I would say. I just stood there, allowing her to take it in."

"'Felix, what in hell? Felix! Oh, Felix!' as she came running into my arms and hugging me. 'Why are you here?'"

"You forgot. I'm from D.C."

"'But you left. To Mexico. I lost track of you. Wow, let me look at you,' as she let go of me and took a big step back. 'Wow! Tanned, and healthy! What are you doing here? Have you moved back?'"

"Mary saw Nesta just standing there, and had to explain."

"Nesta, this is my friend, oh, more than friend, he was my first and true love. We should have been married but I was too much into my schedule. I know, I'm saying too much. He's going to blush. But Nesta knows me. She won't tell. Especially my husband. But this man, he could almost make me do anything. But I was too stubborn in my youth… oh, wasted youth."

"I smiled. 'Mary exaggerates,' I said to Nesta. Turning back to Mary, I said, 'But the bigger question for me is, what on earth are you doing in this town? You were California freedom.'"

"Nesta smiled as well. 'Felix, believe me, Mary is still California freedom. She's twirling the art world until they are dizzy. Washington has not seen the likes of someone like Mary in a long time!'"

"And you Felix. I did hear something about you being married and with kids, for God's sake. How many?"

"Two."

"Two! And you are Mexican. Nesta, he's a Mexican artist. He was good. Very good. But I haven't seen your work in years, Felix. Nesta, this man left me to run off down the coast and now lives in Mexico. In some town you've never heard of. Are you still painting?"

"Very much so."

"Thank the lord at least for that. "

"But why are you here?"

"Let's go grab some coffee, or tea, or whatever you drink these days. Margaritas, I bet. Anyway, let's go have some lunch at least and we can catch up with each other. Nesta, please excuse us. Oh, any more sales?"

"That collector is coming back tomorrow….for another look. Wants to bring a sample of the fabric, to see if the colors will fit."

"You see Felix. I want to make art for museums. Instead, some buyer just wants to see if his decorator will approve."

"'Sales are sales. Besides, eventually, they give their art to museums. It just takes time,' responded Nesta."

"See you later."

"Nice meeting you, Nesta."

"You know, Mary, you should bring me some slides of his work. There are embassy connections here. I wouldn't mind showing a Mexican artist."

"'You see, Felix, already you have offers. Just keep close to me, you'll be famous by the week's end,' laughed Mary."

"We went out and up the block to a café right on Dupont Circle. The circle was where all the liberal young people hung out. By day, it was mellow when the surrounding cafes did business with the office crowd. By evening, it was the hippies and performers who came. It was the closest thing in Washington to what was in every town and city in Mexico, a 'plaza principal.' There were larger places, of course, like the Mall, but Dupont Circle was the nucleus of the 'scene.' Within the surrounding blocks, were the new bookshops, the only theater showing art and independent films, about a dozen galleries, the leather sandal shops, the small clothing boutiques, and about a handful of decent but economical eateries. Mary went right into Herb's. I knew why the minute we stepped into the main dining area. Hanging on the walls were hundreds of 8x10 framed photos of artists and actors and writers and who knows who, they all seemed like celebrities, about three rows high, frame to frame around the entire room."

"See over there? That's me, in front of my painting that was in the Corcoran show last year."

"So you are a celebrity, I see."

"Ha, I only wish. A bigger fish here only because this is a pond. Take your photo to Herb, and he'll put it in a frame and hang you. It's his connection to the artists, and guess what, that's why the artists all come here to eat and drink. Herb likes to think he's competing with the restaurants that do the same thing with political celebrities. It's at least an important acknowledgement. In this town, if you hang a photo of yourself with Johnson or Rusk or O'Neil, it's much more of a social statement than if you have a de Kooning painting on the wall. Most of this town wouldn't know who that was; they'd ask if he was the new ambassador from Holland. If they saw the actual painting, they'd say 'my two-year old can do that!'"

"We sat down and each ordered a sandwich and a glass of wine."

"I'm glad you still drink wine. I thought maybe you'd only be drinking tequila and beer."

"My favorite is still a glass of red wine. We can get Chilean wine. It's good. The Mexican wine has a ways to go to get up to speed. So tell me, how and why and you know, what's going on?"

"After you left, I was pretty devastated. I know, I pushed you to go without me. I thought that's what I wanted. I went into my studio and worked for a few months. That was good. I developed my way through a lot of ideas. But then reality started to sink in. I needed to make money; my funds were running out. I was lonely. Everyone I met didn't come up to my standards, which really meant you, my love. You were that high bar, and I couldn't match you."

"She paused to sip some wine. 'So I decided to widen my circle. I took a few classes in other things and I tried hard to meet folks outside of the art world.'"

"How so?"

"You know, meet normal people. Not just artists. And I met Charles. He wasn't an artist. Not an actor, not someone in any of my former circles. But thank goodness he liked art. He was an international affairs guy. Had been in the army, like you. Well, you were in the Navy, but it's the same. But he didn't have a creative bone in his body. He's a smart guy. Very savvy. Interned for the state department. Went back to California for some advanced studies. At Berkley. That's where we met. I went up there for a summer. I thought he was a liberal like most of the students there. Turned out he was, just not a radical, just liberal. A Kennedy man. Kennedy all the way. But only within the system, never buck the system. You know, that was refreshing,"

"All my friends in one sense or another were struggling and wanted to change the world. They don't have a prayer to do so. I know that now.

They ignore the work that others are doing, like Charles."

Mary took a couple of bites and continued with her summary. "They look down on someone like Charles because he wears a jacket and tie. His way is to work within the system. There are bad things going on in the world and he wants to help fix all that. We can't control everything but there are things we can do, and for that, he's a team player. And he was as strong a Kennedy supporter as I. Anyway, he represented intelligence; you know how I need that in a partner. He's very well read. He makes a living, so he could support my habits. He's been my cheerleader, too. He studied things that he didn't understand. It doesn't come natural to him as it does to us, but he did make it his business to read art history books and when we go on the gallery rounds, he looks carefully and asks me how it connects. He's pretty knowledgeable now. You know, he can hold his own at any art party. And I've cleaned up my act. I can hold my own at one of his parties."

"So he got a job here?' I asked."

"He got drafted by the CIA. It's kind of hush-hush, I suppose, and I'm not supposed to ever say he works for them. I'm supposed to say he works at the State Department. So you never heard that, okay? Anyway, I'm in enough trouble already."

"So we came to this miserable political town. No offense, Felix, but there wasn't much art going on in your hometown. Well, the last couple of years it's improved. Unless my standards have simply come down. There are a few good galleries. Kennedy was making a difference. That's why I wanted to come too. I met enough people to push things. Charles was doing his thing but maybe we jumped the gun a bit. I mean, what was novel and refreshing eventually got a bit less glamorous. But the radical in me, that stayed, and access to a new government, that made a difference. I had the luxury to not only paint, but to lobby. You know, Kennedy was so open- he wanted to establish a commission that would actually give grants to artists. And the government has a fabulous contemporary art collection that was just in storage, so they are starting two new museums, and one will show contemporary art. And all sorts of people from L.A. to New York are coming to town to help make all that happen."

"Charles started taking me to these Washington parties. When Charles went overseas or stayed for twelve hours in his office, I started going to the parties alone. These parties are work parties, Felix. That's how Washington works - over Martini's and shrimp. And they listened to me. Maybe being female helped. Maybe there aren't enough young ladies pushing. But I was invited to special conversations."

"Mary lowered her voice, and looked about. There were only a few diners and no one within range, but she seemed afraid. 'Okay, I think it's safe. I don't always know. I'll tell you but you can't repeat this. Promise. You don't have to promise. I know you won't. But I don't have anyone else I can confide in.'"

"I assured Mary of my ability to keep secrets. From the way she sounded, I suspected that she was going to tell me that her husband was not being faithful."

"Felix, don't think less of me. But my marriage is not what I thought it would be. Charles tries to be supportive, I guess, but he's too much of a team player and not the initiator. I want to help the arts, by being a good artist and by encouraging the government to help. You know, in Europe, governments do a lot for the arts. Here we are the richest country in the world, and we give nothing to the arts. Not to museums, not to artists. It's wrong."

"'That's a pretty open fact, not a secret,' I said."

"I was invited by some White House staff. And I got to meet Kennedy. Actually talk to him. He, we, or, shit, I met with him quite a few times, late, if you know what I mean. He was open. I liked him. God, I liked him. He liked me. And the arts. And my ideas. And he was trying, but then, they, you know, they got him. They killed him. I was depressed. For the entire winter, I didn't leave the studio. Charles thought I was just working hard. I was. But I was crying, too."

"You mean...?"

"Charles knew. He must have. After all, he's a spy. Oh, I shouldn't say that, openly. That's why I'm in trouble. I have a big mouth. And he's not. In that sense. He's an administrator. But he's in charge of them. And he can spy on anyone. He could be spying on me right now. We'd never know it. They are that good. And now he's a Johnson man. But he's in trouble because they know that his wife was a Kennedy lover. And that's tricky. They want the world to go on. They don't want to have the world see their dirty dishes. They have them. Dirty dishes. And I'm one of them. Because they think I know too much. Charles is caught in the middle. He must have known. He's putting up a front, but I'm sure it's difficult for him. And that report that they are doing. On the assassination. Do you really believe it was that simple? I know too much. Others do to, but they have the power and they can control what gets out and how. The media, they try to be smart but they just aren't in the same league. They don't have the same resources. Felix, are you sorry you ever bumped into me again?"

"I had no idea. I'm so far away from all this. The only thing I read might be a newspaper that's two days old, when I can get it. We get the basics. We have a few televisions in the town, at the cafes. That's about it. I follow it, but not too closely."

"It's good to be away. This is not fun stuff to deal with. You still need stimulation, don't you? You must have some friends down there?"

"I got to know John Huston. You know the movie director. He did a film in Puerto Vallarta. It came out, about two months ago. If you haven't seen it, go. I'm not sure where it's playing. Anyway, he's very political and sounded like you. He was very depressed about Kennedy. When he drank, it came out. That's why he bought a house down there. He thinks the country might sink. As does Liz Taylor."

"Elizabeth Taylor? The actress? I met her, at a D.C. party. She was the guest of honor."

"Yes, we're friends. I've been helping her. And she's with Richard Burton you know. I've been making a living and working as I continue my art, helping tourists and people like Liz. My wife helps too. We're doing fine but it's cheaper there. Anyway, you're right, Liz was close to Kennedy. She also was disgusted about what happened. "

"I know. I only talked to her briefly, but she was making enemies quickly at the party. There were lots of White House folks attending, and all she kept talking about was how much the country missed Kennedy and how the Warren Commission had not done a good job and how they were too quick to say that Oswald was the lone gunman - not the thing that Johnson's folks wanted to hear. There was enough criticism on that; they didn't need to hear more from someone they were trying to honor."

"But Liz thinks Johnson is at least carrying out many of Kennedy's programs. And probably with more success had Kennedy lived. Sad isn't it. You have to be a martyr to make real progress."

"Yes, but your friend got off script; she should have only talked about how she was supporting current programs, if that's what she believed. She's right that Johnson is doing some good programs. He's also waging war. And he's spying on people. He's also evil. Evil. But I shouldn't say that within a range of a microphone, should I? Let's get out of here. Can you walk with me? I like to walk along the canal. It's very peaceful. That's where I think. No one bothers me there. Come, can you?"

"'Sure,' and we paid and left the restaurant. Mary hopped into my car and we drove to the outskirts of Georgetown and parked. We walked over one of the small locks that used to lift the barges that the mules would pull along the edge."

"'When I grew up, they were still using the barges from time to time,' I said. 'Now there's just one barge left in Georgetown that's used for tourists.'"

"We walked along the C&O canal path, away from town where the houses and buildings soon disappeared. A few walkers and a couple of people running for exercise passed us, but by and large, we were by ourselves."

"I can talk more freely here."

"I'm surprised that you feel so afraid."

"Me, too. How's your Dad? You mentioned you were visiting."

"He almost died. He was in the hospital and it was serious. That's why I hustled here by myself. The girls are too young and it's tourist season, so Maria had to stay and carry out our commitments, and besides, it's not the time to take the family on a trip. Someday. Anyway, Dad is home now. He remarried a while back; his wife takes good care of him. But he has emphysema - needs to take it easy. He should retire, but he won't. He's only in his late 50s, too young for all that. But it was from smoking. Glad we quit."

"Almost. Actually, I try to smoke no more than seven cigarettes a day. That's my limit that I gave myself. And once in a while, weed. Do you know weed?"

"Only from tourists. Haven't tried it except I did inhale someone's smoke once. I hear it's getting more popular."

"'I brought some to the White House,' Mary said with a devilish grin."

"You what?"

"Not my idea, originally. I mentioned it. It was requested. Let's just put it that way. I've changed now. I'm not the cheery optimist. I'm a beaten, depressed, but interesting artist. My work is good. I know it. What did you think?"

"Your show? I'm very taken with the art. I saw some Louis paintings reproduced. And Frankenthaler. It's not what I'm into, but it's good. I haven't seen enough of the new stuff. I want to go to New York on my return. I need art supplies anyway. It's hard to get in Mexico, even in Mexico City. I'm going to go to Pearl Paint and take back a hundred pounds of Bocour paint. That'll last me a few months. And I want to see the galleries."

"Maybe I'll take the train up and go with you. I try to go regularly."

"That'll be fun. You know, at one time, we thought of going to New York - together."

"I didn't forget. For the east coast, I picked wrong. Instead of being here, I should have gone there. The joke is that collectors find the chicken in New York and only the leftover chicken salad in D.C."

"'California's scene was only marginal, too. Remember?' I reminded her."

"I do. And it's really not as bad here as I sound. Each year it gets better. The best thing is that there is a faster train now and I can hop it from Union Station and be in New York in less than four hours. I go up there once a month. So I keep in touch.

"And you are working; that's important. And showing."

"Listen, I have a thing I'm supposed to go to; some friends are waiting for me. I can't take you. It's strictly a girl's thing. But every day I walk the canal. At ten in the morning. It's my break. I work for two hours, and then go for the exercise. Can you meet me tomorrow? How long are you staying?"

"About a week . That's all I can. Dad's okay so I don't have to stay."

"There's a party at Alice's house. You can go. She's the dame of the arts world here. She knows how to bridge the government and arts circles. We're close even though she's much older than I am. Tomorrow night. On R Street, facing the park, near Wisconsin; on the curved part. Her house is in the middle; you can't miss it. Around 7ish. She always has a catered dinner. I'll tell her you're coming. And you'll meet Charles. He'll be back in time. I want you to meet him. But I'll see you tomorrow. Here. First. Promise? At this spot. If you can't park, go to the next lock and park there. There's always space there. You'll spot me somewhere between the two locks-- I'll be the only one there. At ten. Promise?"

"I promise."

"And Felix… " she started to say as we were back at the car, "Oh, never mind. We'll chat tomorrow. I'll walk from here. I'm meeting my friends in Georgetown, in a new remodel. It's close to here. One of them will drop me off afterwards at the gallery." She hesitated again. "I don't want you to take this the wrong way. I know you love your wife and your daughters and all that. I just have to."

"Have to what….?"

"Before I could finish asking, she pulled me and gave me a passionate kiss on the lips. I melted. I was ashamed in some ways but for Mary, as I thought about it afterwards, it was just a way to experience what she had left behind. It was obvious, to me, that she was crying out for some love, some support, some care. Whatever she had in her busy life - and I could tell how full it was - something was missing. She knew it and perhaps she sensed it even more with that kiss. How did I feel? That's hard. I loved my wife and I was happy in my choices. But yes, Mary was a magnet. I could talk to her and I could have taken her to bed without hesitation, as if we had never said goodbye those years earlier. But we had. We both knew the barriers. Mary just wanted a taste, a reminder perhaps, of what we had. A memento that perhaps could help her decide, I'm not sure what. Something was going through her mind; I could tell. She was planning, something. I wanted to talk to her some more, but she had to go. Anyway, I'd see her the next morning. I was thinking all this as she walked away, but then she seemed to hesitate, turned and walked back to me."

"I'll tell you my secret. I'm going to change. My life. I'm still going to work as an artist. That won't change. But I'm going to change how I act. I'm even going to drop my maiden name altogether and just use my married name! Mary Meyers. That's for the next show. I'm going to tell Charles. He's away in Miami, some business. He comes back tomorrow, in the afternoon. I'll tell him and then we'll go to Alice's party. You'll meet him. He's going to be so happy. You see…I'm pregnant. I'm going to have a baby! Don't get the wrong impression. This is Charles' baby. I mean, he's the father. I'm sure. And I'm going to be a good team player and we're going to have a great life here. Nesta is really making a difference and the Corcoran, it's a good museum and they are showing contemporary art and they are showing some local artists and some of us are even showing in New York. So the future looks good. Really. I believe that. So be happy for me, Felix. Please."

"Felicidades, mi amiga."

"Si, soy amiga, ahora? I used to be more than just a friend. I know. I'm giving you a hard time. And someday, my family will meet your family and we'll all be happy and successful. Okay, mum's the word until tomorrow. I'll tell our friends at the party. But join me in the morning. We'll discuss babies. You must be an expert. "

"Mary ran off. I got into the car and sat for a moment. I needed to absorb what Mary had told me. About her past, and now her future. I was happy for her."

"I decided I had time to see the Corcoran. That was my day and when I met up with Dad and Beatrice late that afternoon, we decided to eat at home. Beatrice had prepared dinner; Dad had to be fairly careful in his diet, but it was still a lean steak, potato and vegetable dinner; I had almost forgotten how American a meal could be."

*****

"I've spent a lot of time talking about Mary. It's funny but you know the old saying, about six degrees of separation. I've found many truths in life, living to be as old as I am. It's that life goes in circles and often people you know from one era of life reappear later on. There are always connections. Mary was someone whom I thought was just part of my early life, and now she reappeared and soon would mean something different. She certainly had a different life than I had could have predicted when I knew her in San Diego. Who knew she would be close to the President of the United States. But on the other hand, I was close to Elizabeth Taylor. And you know what, when you get up close to folks like that you find out that they are just like you and I. They are in the spotlight, they have talent and power, but they are also normal, if you know what I mean, like you. You seem as normal as anyone on the airplane, and yet I'm sure you have some special talents."

"Well, my life is not nearly as interesting as yours, I'm sure," said Bart.

"One never knows, but you are still young. Who knows what the future will bring to you? I'll continue with my story. Your story is for another flight, perhaps."

"So you were going to meet Mary the next morning - that's where you left off," said Bart.

"Yes, I was to meet Mary. I ate a light breakfast with Dad since Beatrice had to go out. Dad needed something from his closet, up high, so he asked me to help. I left a few minutes late. But I knew Mary was not waiting, she'd just walk to the other lock if I were a few minutes late. I drove down to Georgetown. Nine-thirty was after rush hour, so I had no problem in traffic. Besides, the city was coming back to me and as a former native,

I knew the side-routes, New Mexico Avenue that I could then cross over to MacArthur to save a couple of minutes. See, after all these years, I still remember the names of the streets."

"I decided to park at the second lock thinking I'd actually be closer to where Mary was walking. If I parked in the first lock, then I'd have to run after her, so I thought that I'd make it easy for her. I parked and spotted a figure in the distant, coming my way. I started to wave, but wasn't positive it was Mary. I didn't see anyone else so I assumed it was but I couldn't be positive. I saw a car parked off to the side on MacArthur. Not a place to park. It must have broken down, I thought. Then I saw another figure, this one definitely a male. In a suit, it seemed. And he wore a hat, I remember that. Funny to be on the canal with a suit on. The canal's walking path was used for recreational running and walking. Then I saw the man approach the figure and I started to walk faster towards them but I was still a good ways off. Suddenly, I heard a gun go off. It was definitely a gun, not a backfire. The woman dropped. The man in the suit ran off, back towards the lock and around, and into the car parked by the side of the road. As I was running to the figure on the ground, the man got into the passenger side and the car roared off. There must have been a driver, waiting. I ran faster. I didn't want it to be. It was. It was Mary. She was lifeless. She had blood all over her chest. I slide onto my knees, hoping that I could do something. I picked up her head, gently. Mary, my dear Mary. I was crying. I was crying loudly. Tears were flowing down my cheeks. I looked around. 'Help! Help,' I shouted. No one was near. I saw cars whizzing by in the distance. No one was coming. She was not breathing. I could do nothing. I cried."

"I had to leave her. I had to leave to get help. I ran to the first lock. No one was there. I ran to the road, and flagged down a car. Help! She's been shot. Get an ambulance. I never said police. I only wanted to save her, somehow. I knew it was too late, but I didn't want to believe it."

"I ran back. The police came, within a few minutes. I heard sirens in the background."

"Are you the one who called for help?" an officer asked me running up to us.

"I am. She's been shot. Some man. He took off. Help her. Please help her."

"He got down. He took her wrist. He looked closely. 'The ambulance is on its way. I'm afraid it's too late.'"

CHAPTER 7

"That awful day on the C&O canal. I'll never get over it."

"It must have been traumatic. There's way too much violence in the world," remarked Bart. "Please, continue."

"I stayed. They came, the whole battalion of rescue and police vehicles. A few bystanders gathered. I explained I was at the other lock. I could only make out a male figure. The police insisted it was a robbery attempt gone array. I voiced my objections. They didn't want to hear that. I said I only knew her slightly, from many years ago. I emphasized how innocent our meeting was, to just catch up. My Dad was home sick, and I had to go back to Mexico to my wife and kids. I said enough. They took down my address and telephone number. They had enough. They could tell that someone shot her and that it had nothing to do with me. But they weren't too happy to hear of the getaway car. I said it was a dark car. But it, too, was far away from where I first saw it happen. They called my Dad and asked him of my morning. He confirmed that I had to meet some friend with whom I had gone to school with, but that's all he really knew. They did their due diligence. They didn't' dig very deep. Mary told me to never repeat what she had told me. I thought it best not to mention that we had gotten together the day before. I didn't want them to ask me what I knew about Mary. They said that they knew who she was and would contact her husband. I was the only person who knew she was pregnant. Except her doctor, I suppose. Would I tell Charles that, if I should meet him? I didn't know. I was too much in love with Mary. I knew that. It's possible to love more than one person at a time. I knew nothing would have happened between us. Mary was going to have that happy life, but someone got in the way. It was too much of a coincidence for this to be the random robbery attack that the newspapers later reported based on the police statements. They wrote that there were no witnesses, just a bystander who was too far away to see any details of the attack, but had appeared quickly afterwards and had called for help. All that was reported was that it was a male, who had driven away in a dark car and he had used a gun. It was another violent crime only different because of the location - it was unusual for something like that to happen in broad daylight on the C&O Canal, and that the victim was a prominent female artist, married to a State Department official."

"That came out the next day. But that day, the first few hours, were the hours that were so painful, so vivid, so punishing to me. How can anyone plan life when shit like that can happen?"

"I was despondent. I needed to talk to someone. That day. I needed to have some contact. I went back to Dad's house. I cried in my room. I took off my shirt and pants that had Mary's blood all over it. I didn't know what to do. I didn't know if I was abandoning Mary by putting them in the trash. I certainly didn't want to wash them and try to ever wear them again. Dad asked me some questions. He knew I had witnessed it, but I tried to minimize it. I didn't want to upset him and cause him to have health problems."

"It was evening. I needed to do something. I decided to see if the party was still happening at Alice's. The few hours at home gave me some distance from the police, the questions, the blood. I couldn't stay with Beatrice and Dad. I sat while they tried to push some dinner into me, but I didn't really eat more than a forkful or two. I excused myself and I drove back into the city to R Street. I found the house, it was lit up and lots cars were outside. I went in. The party didn't seem to be festive. I assumed it was because they heard the news. I asked a guest who Alice was. I was pointed to an elegantly dressed woman in a dark print dress, a pearl necklace and her grey-turning-white hair swept to one side."

"Alice? Hi, I'm Felix Peters. Mary was…"

"Oh, poor Felix. Poor Mary." Alice gave me a hug like we had known each other, as if we were best friends. "She called me yesterday - told me she was bringing you to the party. Told me that she and Charles might have some news. Oh, poor Mary. Are you the one? I mean, were you there? Are you the one who was reported to having seen it? I heard it on the radio. You were there. From a distance. You've been crying. I can see the red around your eyes?"

"If I had been a few minutes earlier, I might have prevented it."

"You mustn't say that. Fate happens. Don't punish yourself. Whoever did this, I know it wasn't a robbery. It was an assassination. I don't know why, but I can sense that. The whole room can. These were her friends. I never thought this would be such a sad party. It's almost like a memorial. That's all anyone can talk about - think about. Oh, I've been crying today as well."

"'I don't know why I came. I don't want to party. But I knew that her friends might be here. I wanted to share, I guess. I wanted to know if there's a way to make sense of this. I wanted… ' I couldn't find the words."

"Oh, my dear man. In the few minutes that Mary phoned me, I heard how close you were, and how you reconnected. I can imagine what's going through emotionally. Please, I'm sure this party is not going to last long, under the circumstances. I'd like to talk to you, in private, just the two of us. Can you stay? Have some appetizers. Let's not let the food go to waste. I'll bet you haven't eaten all day. I toned down the food - what I could - it was too late to cancel and besides, I'm sure her friends would want to commiserate together. They are all sad. May I introduce you, please?"

"I didn't really say yes, but Alice was such a kind sounding woman, who you knew cared, not just for Mary, for almost any artist."

"Everyone, please, may I have your attention? We are all so sad to hear about Mary. Mary was a gifted artist, a most endearing sole mate. I know you are as sad as I am. I want to introduce you to someone, Felix Peters. Felix was a very close friend of Mary's in California, and they just reconnected. Unfortunately, Felix arrived just a moment too late but saw the murder from a distance. Anyway, Felix is a special friend of Mary's, so now he's our friend, and I want you to welcome him as we all mourn our loss."

"With that, Alice walked me around the room and introduced me to everyone, one by one, giving a one-sentence description of each person. Everyone was nice but obviously, it was a bit awkward under the circumstances."

"They assassinated her, that's what they did," said a young artist in a nice jacket over a paint-spotted T-shirt and blue jeans. Others nodded in agreement. They were depressed about Mary but almost all were also angry. Angry with whom? They all knew of Mary's connections to the late President. They knew enough to suspect Charles for something. They just felt that the government was involved. Some thought that the government was incompetent. Others were more militant in their accusations."

*****

"Georgetown parties were quite fussy affairs. Lots of catered appetizers, lots of booze, of course at least a dressed waiter or two making sure drinks were filled and all were happy, and one person at the door, signifying that someone important was inside so that the door person could prevent unwanted intruders. Artist parties were different. At best, there'd be pizza and beer in some studio. 'Art' parties were not parties hosted by artists, but parties hosted by gallery and museum patrons, who wanted to mix with the artists, or in the case of Alice, who wanted to honor them and support them, so they were quite elaborate without going over the top.

Most hosts were moneyed, at least enough to have a maid helping to prepare the food before going home. In those days, no one had to be super rich to be an art patron; paintings which ten years later sold in the many thousands of dollars, at that time sold in galleries for a few hundred dollars. There were many who bought on an installment plan that the gallery would devise just to make a sale. Often collectors were junior lawyers who bought works on paper at first, but bought big original after they eventually worked their way up to become partners of a firm. The parties nurtured these early patrons and encouraged them to buy more."

"No one greeted guests until they had coats off and had managed to find the bar and pick up a glass with wine or hard liquor and something solid. Then it was just an insider's session, with some gossip about whoever was not within earshot. If the weather was warm, and if the host or hostess had a pool, under dim lighting a few might go in "a-natural." Of course, by that time, the joints were passed around and most of the partygoers had attained a new level of meditation."

"Alice's party would have been no different that night except that everyone was depressed upon the news of Mary's death, and then their depression turned to anger. The more they drank, the more they smoked, the more they discussed it and the angrier they became."

"Matt-what's-his-name, a painter struggling to get a bit more recognition even within the small D.C. community, who was also slightly high and slightly drunk, started to go at it with me about how Johnson didn't like the arts and didn't like Kennedy's people and used whatever tactics to clear the decks."

"That loud comment got the attention of Alice, who defended Johnson and said that while history showed Kennedy had renewed the flame to help the arts, it was now Johnson who was doing the dirty work of pushing programs through Congress. But then some poor soul mentioned Mary's name in the same sentence. It just came out - basically accused Johnson of having Mary killed. Alice became enraged by the implication that Johnson was the trigger, a President who Alice had just supported. That it was mentioned in the same sentence as Mary's death - even though most of the art community at the party had silently or maybe had whispered in agreement and had concluded that the murder had been a hit job by secretive government operatives, just like they might have gotten rid of a president and who knows who else- well, Alice couldn't stand that. And it was her party!"

"It was too late to try to separate the two opponents of the conversation, and perhaps with deep seeded doubts or anger, several now joined and did as much as accuse Johnson of directing both assassinations. That now implied that Alice, the hostess, by supporting Johnson in his public policies, was allowing murderers to go unpunished. A few guests rose to defend Alice, not about her support of Johnson but just her support of artists."

"The voices got louder, the emotions got stronger until there were fights, and throwing glasses and spilling whatever. By the time the party was over and the guests had left, the living room was in shambles. It will go down in local history as one of the most unsuccessful parties of all time."

"Alice was exhausted and I was in a state of mild shock. We looked around at the aftermath; Alice seemed calmer than I even though it was her house that had been wrecked. We each poured another glass of wine and sat down."

"You know, I never got a bite of the food. It's all on the floor now."

"'Let's go out for a bite,' I suggested."

"I'm hungry but not much is open at this hour."

"Chinatown is always open-- at least 'til 2 or 3."

"'Bravo Felix,' replied Alice. 'My house is a mess but I'm not going to deal with it until tomorrow. Can you drive?'"

"'Sure.' Alice found her purse in a drawer that had gotten pushed but not upturned and we walked out without even locking the door. 'Won't make any difference at this point,' she said almost with some humor."

"We drove across town in about ten minutes with an absence of traffic since it was almost midnight. We took P Street over to Massachusetts Avenue, one of the main arteries through the city. With lights running in our favor, the tunnels under the circles clear, we turned off at 7th Street and parked the car near a favorite haunt on H Street."

"'You can never go wrong at Tai Tung,' said Alice who had been to Chinatown scores of times after art openings. Chinese food was affordable for artists on a limited budget, and the restaurants were the few eateries open after ten or eleven o'clock."

"'It's a treat to have something other than Mexican. Can we order Chinese broccoli?' I asked. 'I need to have my dark greens.'"

"'What's that? Is it different than regular broccoli?' asked Alice."

"Different and better. Close to Italian rabe but better. The Chinese usually have it with oyster sauce, but I like it in their garlic sauce."

"I ordered the dishes without looking at the menu; I knew the dishes were not mentioned on the regular menu for tourists, and I couldn't read the menus written in Chinese. With Alice's approving nod, I added crabs in shell in oyster sauce, and a noodle dish."

"'We have enough food to feed a few more people,' said Alice who was surprised how much food filled the tabletop."

"We were both accomplished eaters using chop sticks the proper way, putting some food from one dish on top of the rice and holding the rice bowl closer to our mouths as we ate, then replenishing with a serving of a different dish on the rice.

By the end of the meal, the party disturbance seemed like a dream, although Alice knew she'd have to deal with the reality the next day."

"Can you believe being accused of wanting Kennedy assassinated just because I've agreed to support the White House with some new programs? After all, they will help the arts generally, which will also help these struggling artists."

"'They had too much to drink, or smoke, perhaps both,' I postured."

"No, there's some tension that has never gone away, ever since Kennedy's death. There's funny business going on with the government. We know that. I know that. Mary knew that, too. Even Kenneth O'Donnell mentioned that to me, at one of those Georgetown parties I attended last month. You know, Ken bridged the gap, was one of Kennedy's insiders and is now working for Johnson, as I am being supportive, too. But he seemed worried. We chatted about that at a Georgetown party. Mary was there. Elizabeth Taylor was being honored and Ken was worried how the Johnson team was distrustful of her. Seems like she was too close to Kennedy for them to feel she would be supportive of Johnson. Of course, she wanted to help as much as I wanted to help. But I only have some money and social ties. Taylor has international ties."

"Liz? Liz was there?"

"You sound like you know her!"

"I do. And it's funny how her name pops up."

"How well do you know her?"

"Very well. She and Richard have vacation homes in Puerto Vallarta."

"'I just realized the connection,' exclaimed Alice with a grin. 'That movie. I saw it. That iguana movie that John Huston made. It was filmed in Mexico. Where you live, right? I get it.'"

"Right in the same town where I live. They were filming for three months. *The Night of the Iguana*. I saw everyone everyday. And Maria and I got close to Liz and Richard. We helped them buy their properties."

"'Mary mentioned that you were in with the Hollywood crowd; I didn't know you were in that one,' quipped Alice."

"Well, I'm not sure I'd call it 'in,' but Liz and Richard do own two of my works."

"Then you are in alignment with the new crowd."

"Kennedy had many supporters. What difference does it make if Liz was so involved with Kennedy? Why does Johnson, or at least his people, seem so worried about her?"

"'Like at the party tonight,' answered Alice, 'there are those who are pointing fingers, accusing Johnson of being involved somehow with getting rid of Kennedy in the first place, or perhaps the cover-up, or what not.'"

"But they don't know, really, they're guessing."

"Someday, there'll figure it all out. It's hard to keep a secret forever. There must be a least a couple of people out there who know who did what; you know, whether Oswald was alone or had accomplices; if someone higher up was behind it all."

"'And do you think Mary's killing was connected to any of this?' I asked."

"I haven't had time to digest it. When I think about it, it makes no sense. But robbery makes less sense. There's no question Mary was inside this world, but she was just an outsider making some noise. I'm not sure how someone else might view it. Of course, there are government men out there who see conspiracy in almost anything and then want to remove it. Only they aren't very smart about how they go about removing unwanted elements. Very messy. What do they think? Killing a lovely woman and leaving her body on the C&O canal. Like no one will know that she smoked pot with the President? What did they think?"

"Alice finished her meal even sadder than when we left the party. It was all about Mary and her senseless death. Senseless and deliberate, what a combination we agreed. When we paid and walked out of the restaurant, it was well past 1 AM. The sidewalks were virtually deserted. I had a funny feeling and looked both ways before turning with Alice to walk just a short distance to the car."

"'Are we becoming too paranoid?' I asked rhetorically."

"I'm afraid not. You know, I was one of Mary's best friends. Sure, we had an age difference, but we were simpatico. I was her confidant. I kept warning her… to be quiet. You can't say what you feel, not in this town. You have to be careful. But Mary was too outspoken. She wanted progress too quickly. Charles has a more realistic gage on how the system works. Mary thought you could take short cuts. At times, I thought she was right. After all, she was close to Kennedy. That's something. But you know, it's not a Kennedy crowd anymore. She finally listened to me. I know. When she called me yesterday, she said she had good news and that she was going to change. She said all she wanted to do was work on new masterpieces and not worry about the world. I believed her. I saw how she was trying to set up a new approach to life. She told me how you appeared, suddenly. And it was clear that she was on the right track. She even told me she kissed you."

"She did?"

"Yes, but I hope you realize, it was only a test. She was testing herself. Her discipline. She wanted to know if she was still weak. She wasn't. She was just happy that she could connect with you and not feel like it would spin her off in a different direction. I know, you just happen to be there. It's not you. You just came - actually Felix - at a good time. A good time for her. She needed that confirmation. You gave it to her. And I did. But they didn't get the message in time."

"They?"

"They, our government, the ones we vote in and the ones who just get in. They. They got to her, just like they got to Kennedy."

"Do you believe that?"

"Unfortunately, there's no evidence to believe otherwise. I heard the radio reports. Tomorrow, I'll read the same spin in the newspapers. They did a cover-up on this. You know that too, but if you're smart, you'll never mention that to anyone. If the police come back to you, just say you were too far away."

"They already got my statements; I don't think I can say any more. They don't want more."

"What was her big news? Did she tell you?"

""It was personal in nature. I don't know if I should say it to anyone."

"Oh, I can guess. She told me that she and Charles were trying to conceive. I'll bet that was it. But don't tell me, Felix. I don't want to know. It'll just complicate my feelings. And I'll have to see Charles. If I know, then I'll feel obliged to tell him. I don't want to, so please don't tell me. Spare me that one aspect. Poor, poor Mary. They didn't know that they had already won. She had already decided to be a team player. There was no need to silence her, after all."

*****

"I stayed a few extra days, enough time to attend Mary's memorial service. It was held in the Unitarian Church on 16th Street. Mary was never religious, as far as I remembered, so I guess this was as open of a ceremony as they could arrange."

"About two hundred people came, a mixture of artists and governmental folks. Rarely does one see that combination. I was in the back, quiet, but afterwards, in the side hall, there was a receiving line. I went through and was instantly recognized by Mary's mother and father, and her younger sister and brother. They were from Omaha but had visited Mary a couple of times in San Diego."

"'Felix, why are you here, my gracious,' her mother exclaimed. 'It's been years. Oh, so sad.'"

"'Gretchen, I'm sorry, my condolences. I was here visiting my Dad. He was sick; okay now. I saw Mary, the day before, by accident, in the gallery.' Her father and siblings were overhearing me. Then Charles, standing a few feet away, broke ranks and came over."

"I'm Charles. Mary told me a lot about you."

"'Charles, I'm so sorry. I....' I couldn't really find anything else to say."

"'Thank you for coming,' Mary's father said when he noticed that I couldn't continue."

"'Felix was there. At the time,' Charles said to them, and then turning back to me, 'Can we talk, for a minute, in private?'"

Charles put his arm about my shoulder and we strolled down to a corner where no one was standing near.

"I read the reports. About you calling for help."

'I was too late. I bumped into Mary at her show. We chatted and agreed to meet. You were coming back that afternoon. She wanted me to meet you. At Alice's party - that night. But this happened."

"You were the last person she talked to. Did she…?"

"What?"

"I found out that she was pregnant. It was in the autopsy. What I want to know is, I mean, did Mary mention…"

"Mary told me that she was expecting. It was your baby. She just found out. She was so excited. She was going to tell you when you got back that afternoon and then announce it to her friends at the party. She wanted to change her name to yours and settle down, and just make art and be happy. I ….."

"If only I had known…."

"She wanted you and the baby to someday meet my wife and my daughters-- she was so positive about the future."

"The bastards. The dirty, god damn bastards. I'll get even someday, I swear."

"Do you know who did it? It wasn't a robbery. I saw it from afar but I could tell that. I told the police that it was not a robbery."

"I read the report. They caught some black fool a few blocks away. They are trying to pin it on him but they have no evidence."

"I was too far to see details, but it seemed like a white guy in a suit. Who else might have done this?"

"It's hard to tell for sure…but I'm making it my mission to find out."

"Charles, I was only here to see my Dad and ran into Mary. It was bad timing. What happened. But I'll tell you from our talk, she loved you. She wanted to be with you and raise a child."

"I guess I wanted to hear that. Thank you. Felix, it was good that you were here for her."

"'I don't see what Mary did to deserve this…it's not fair,' I lamented."

"Charles gave me a hug and returned to the receiving line. I later talked about the good times I had with her folks and sister and brother, but they were all in tears. It was too close to what had happened. People were going through the motions in public, but behind closed doors, no one had stopped crying. Nesta came up to me, too. She almost couldn't talk. Mary's work was still up in her gallery and would remain up for an extra month."

"I left Washington quietly. I tried to focus on the rest of my trip and getting back to Maria and my daughters, ever more grateful for what I had, but it was difficult. As I sat on the speeding train going to Penn Station, I had a few hours to gaze out of the train window and to think about my life. How distant it felt compared to what I had just experienced."

CHAPTER 8

"Anyway, most people know about the film. *The Night of the Iguana* was a great success when it came out in 1964. The filming was one of the easiest, according to Huston. He was proud of the work. Of course, I never really saw much of the film for quite a while. I did see some of the rough cuts, but the real editing was done back in L.A. When the film came out, there was no theater to play it in Puerto Vallarta. About a half-year later, when Huston came back for a visit, he arranged for a private showing and invited all the workers and their families to see the film. It was in English, so 98% of the audience had no idea what it was really about. They just recognized a few of the extras used, especially the young Mexicans who go chasing after the iguana. Maria and I saw it, leaving the girls at home with Mama; I had caught the film playing in a theater in Los Angeles on my way to Washington and knew that the movie was intended for an adult audience."

"The year the film came out, the Beatles had invaded the United States, Johnson had committed more troops to the Vietnam effort, and believe it or not, Liz and Richard actually got married. It was a quiet ceremony held in Montreal and a reception in Boston. Liz actually invited us, knowing that we couldn't go, but it was a nice gesture and Maria appreciated it. She felt that the two of them had bonded during all their shopping trips, and Liz had stressed that she hoped Maria would remain in touch, even if it were limited to a postcard or call once a month."

"That's what was happening in my world. As I said, I had returned from my Washington visit in a state of shock. Mary's murder was not fading from my mind."

"On the other hand, I was excited and I suppose re-energized after the recent exposure I had. I heard the new music and saw so much art during my trip. I had toured the new galleries in Washington and then, for my return, I had purposely booked a cheaper flight from New York, so I could go up a couple of days early and tour all the New York galleries. I was a fast and vigorous walker and I started on Madison around the high 70s, making sure Castelli was one of my first visits in order to see the Pop artists, and zigzagged down Madison hitting every gallery I could. Then over to 57th Street for the biggies- Emmerich, Marlborough, Pace, Jackson and many more. I would take a gallery break by going into the Guggenheim and then I'd end up in MOMA. I saw an entire world of art condensed into one day of walking into perhaps as many as fifty galleries and at least two museums. Most galleries I'd stay for a couple of minutes, but some would take me much longer to digest. I saw in person - for the first time - the stained canvases of Frankenthaler and Louis, work that had influenced Mary's work, and I saw the early work of some of the Pop artists that Castelli was showing and whose work seemed to be in a similar camp as mine. I paid special attention to some of the older artists like Gottlieb, Newman and Gorky who had pioneered new art. The exhibitions were dazzling; I began to wonder if I was making the correct choice to be so isolated from where the action was. I would have been showing with these guys on the same level, I thought, if I were living in New York. On the other hand, I was building up a body of new work, and I went back to Mexico determined to produce larger and in my mind, more important works. My goal wasn't about making art that a tourist could hang over the couch; I wanted to make art so wonderful that a collector would buy it for an entire wall and eventually donate it to a museum. I wanted to be in the league of some of the artists I really admired - Picasso,

Rivera, Kahlo, De Kooning, Kline, Goldberg, and others."

"At the same time, witnessing the murder of my friend Mary, caused me to not only wonder if the United States would survive such turmoil, a view that was voiced the loudest by John Huston, and perhaps also by Liz - in a sense - by the way she still grieved her loss of President Kennedy. I realized how dangerous life could be. I was willing to isolate myself in a way that I could deal with these emotions without exposing my family to them. And the fact that the police questioned me the way they did, also made me scared of the government forces. I had no idea why Mary was killed or by whom, but she told me enough to feel a connection to Kennedy's enemies, and they had to be very powerful people."

"Am I telling you too much about the history of the United States and not enough about how I fit in all this?"

"I've been very intrigued with your story so far. Do continue but I need to ask you, did you think you were on someone's hit list after you witnessed the killing?" asked Bart.

"I didn't know at first, although the thought did cross my mind. I don't feel I know much about that world, do you? I figured, these are very tough guys; if they wanted me dead, I'd be dead. I was alive so maybe they didn't know what I knew or had seen, and I wanted to leave it that way. You know, when something dramatic happens, eventually life's routine takes over and the event starts to drift into the background. That was happening for me. I got back to Puerto Vallarta, more excited about the art I saw and the ideas that I wanted to paint, and less scared about the tragic event I had witnessed. Minds can shape events to fit their conveniences, and I guess that's what I did as well."

"I poured my energy into some of the best paintings I had done in my life, and I pushed the rest away, except for my efforts to be a good husband and father. I wanted that positive reinforcement from my family, and they gave me encouragement. So I was very content for many months."

"At the same time, I didn't want to continue to have so much isolation. Liz was my key, more so than Richard who seemed to be observant when Liz was about, but Liz would write or call more often on her own. I told her what I was doing, and she didn't hesitate to make a couple of calls, which resulted in galleries having interest in my work. I soon got commitments for a couple of gallery showings for the following year, and that gave me enough reason to work extra hard and to have enough work for those upcoming exhibitions."

*****

"John Huston would call me from time to time when he was in town and I'd go over to his house. It was a bit of a jaunt -maybe an hour door to door - and I couldn't take Maria because of the girls, so I'd most often opt for an afternoon lunch with him. He wanted to talk art, and how his movies fused with my type of art. I think in one sense, he regretted not continuing as a painter. On the other hand, he recognized that his success would probably not have happened as a visual artist. Nevertheless, he truly believed that filmmaking was as much of an art form as painting or sculpture, even though it had such a commercial aspect to it. Distributors were always pushing for the happy endings to increase audience share, and not for what was right for the story. That was his main conflict -not the medium - only how the money folks seemed to get their hands on the artwork to manipulate it."

"I reminded him that museums and galleries did the same thing, or tried. The only saving grace was that artists for the most part worked alone, without a censor standing by, and the problems usually developed after the work was completed."

"I enjoyed those talks because it was what I sometimes missed in my isolation. I mentioned that to him and he seemed to feel that my life was not going to remain in Puerto Vallarta forever. 'You're too talented not to be mainstreamed soon,' he kept saying. 'Puerto Vallarta will always be with you, but you'll need more fertile ground at some point.'"

"We talked about politics. He had escaped the States once, to live in Ireland, when McCarthyism tried to take over the country by accusing everyone with ideas that they were Communists. And he thought that he'd need to flee once again. Kennedy had been eliminated and the bad guys are everywhere, he'd remind me. They'd infiltrate the arts, anything. He lectured me on the ways that the United States was spying and overthrowing governments around the world, but especially in South America and Asia, often by supporting the worst dictators ever. He was sympathetic to the causes of people who wanted their freedoms, and saw them as underdogs in their fight against the super powers. And the bombs, the ever larger bombs that we were developing and stockpiling. How long until one of them went off by accident?"

"Most often, we talked until dark, and then I had to get back home. 'Practicalities take precedence over saving the world,' I would apologize to him often when taking my leave."

"He acknowledged how we all had our realities. Anyway, it was a real contrast. Here was a guy who could be living in a glamorous Hollywood mansion with swimming pool and servants, where I'd be among the last to visit him, and instead, he was secluded in a remote hacienda on the Mexican coast, about an hour away from real civilization, and we were talking, as friends, together. That meant something to me."

*****

"Liz and Richard only came a few times a year, and usually for less than a week, but they squeezed in a lot of shopping and projects, while also, or so I suspect, they had some truly private time away from the limelight and press, at least compared to their lives in Los Angeles."

"When the movie came out and *The Night of the Iguana* was an overnight success, it was their affair that made more headlines than anything else. It put Puerto Vallarta on the map, and quickly enough I could hardly keep up with requests for tours, real estate and investment advice. When they were here, people would spot them."

"Locally, they were stars, at least Richard Burton was. Residents instantly recognized him from the movie posters that had been put up in almost all the retail tourist stores, and when they were together, especially after all the international headlines about their "affair in Puerto Vallarta," they could hardly walk the Malecon without tourists, now visiting more than ever, turning their heads and asking for autographs."

"'I'm sorry you don't get a break,' I said to them on one occasion."

"'You don't realize how it is in the States. This is a break,' laughed Richard."

"Liz and Richard were still my preferred clients, and when they came to town, I dropped almost everything. Liz ended up exploring north of the city and purchased a beachfront house in the small town of Bucerias. I tried to encourage her to look at Sayulita, telling her that someday in the future it would be discovered, and when the government finishes the new road, it will be only twenty minutes more past Bucerias. Since I had a boat, I offered her a boat ride so she could see the coastal development from Puerto Vallarta, around the point at Punta de Mita, and then up to Sayuillta. We could drive but Liz loved the idea of having the water experience."

"We decided to schedule a time when I could include them in one of Maria's folks' family Sunday dinners. Meanwhile, she kept purchasing craft items at almost give-away prices compared to dollar values, and ended up filling up the Bucerias house as well. In fact, that house became more of a warehouse than anything else, and I don't think she ever actually slept there."

"Several times Liz, or Liz with Richard, came over to my studio. They liked my paintings, leaning more for my newer ones. I had finally worked through non-objective art and was beginning to produce work that really had a look that was unique. I had also reversed myself; instead of mostly black and white with tiny highlights of color, I was using the brightest reds and oranges and yellows and blues, with accents of black and white. I never would have predicted that path a year earlier, but creativity flows in odd directions."

"'You have echoes of Diego Rivera,' Richard might have remarked, 'but now it's a Peters and no one else for sure.'"

"'Rivera died just when I was studying art in San Diego. He was one of my heroes,' I would say, as we got into conversations about scores of famous contemporary artists. Liz especially loved the paintings in which I had attached objects to the canvas. 'They come alive,' she used to say."

"They ended up buying quite a few small drawings from me, and two major paintings, one for their Puerto Vallarta house and one for Liz's L.A. house."

"'Just tell prospects that your paintings are prominently displayed in the collections of Elizabeth Taylor and Richard Burton. That'll help make more sales,' Liz would remark."

"She was right. A newspaper printed in English meant for the expats and tourists started and they did an article on Maria and me and when that came out and tourists found out that connection, they would knock on my studio door and want to take back a small painting, whatever they could fit in their suitcase. Very few wanted to deal with a wall-sized painting and few could be rolled up since I was attaching objects to the surfaces. It wasn't the type of sale I had in mind, but since I did so many small studies, I had hundreds to sell. The sales helped me maintain my studio and limit the number of hours I had to spend on my other work, except of course, when Liz and Richard were in town. Then I dropped my brushes to be at their disposal."

"So for the next Sunday on one of their infrequent visits, when they planned on staying a few days longer than usual, Liz proposed a boat trip with the kids to Sayulita. By this time, our daughters, Daniela at 5 and Silvia at 3 years old, were old hands on a boat. Liz and Richard were enamored with the girls, as were the girls with them, so they looked forward to spending the day with my family."

"'We've heard so much about this village of yours, it's about time that we had a visit,' said Liz."

"'Take a sweater; it's cooler on the water and we'll be coming back a bit late,' I advised. Even in March, the weather could be cool, especially when the wind picked up. Both had several layers, although leaving the dock in Puerto Vallarta, we were all in short sleeve shirts. Maria held the girls until Liz insisted on helping, and I dealt with the outboard and steered the boat. We had upgraded to a stronger Mercury motor, made in the U.S. and brought down by the film company and then 'sold' to me as part of my payment, so our boat speed was the envy of the locals."

"We ventured far out from shore and crossed the bay, heading to the very point called Punta de Mita, named because it's almost the middle of Mexico and the most western part except for the Baja peninsular. Rounding the point, we came near two small islands, called the Marietas Islands, and there we spotted several whales even though it was rather late in the season when they come down to the Bay for winter mating and birthing. Then up the coast on the other side, we could see the point that hid the Sayulita beach. However, just before the point, I landed the boat on a small beach."

"'There's no town here,' said Richard. 'Where Sayulita?'"

"'Just around the next point. Maria and I wanted to share something with you,' I said."

"We took off our shoes, rolled up our pants and disembarked onto the white sand."

"'It's beautiful,' said Liz."

"'See that building up there? That's where we are slowly building our house. This is our future home,' boasted Maria, after helping both girls off the boat."

"'Well, it's not much of a home now, but it's going to grow,' I added."

"'It's pretty impressive,' responded Richard."

"'Not ready to invite folks to yet,' I said."

"Felix is just starting. He wants to build a mansion."

"'Not a mansion,' I protested."

"Well, the size of a mansion. Room for his work and room for our family. We're doing it slowly, as we earn money."

"As the girls ran and played along the beach, Maria explained, 'my folks gave this to us as a present. Half of the beach. We can't live here now because of work, but we come on weekends or slow days or off-season. Someday, we'll spend most of our time here.'"

"'It's absolutely among the finest beaches I've ever seen,' said Richard. 'You must feel very lucky.'"

"'The beach in Sayulita is not bad, but it's not private like this,' I said."

"'Is the other half for sale?' Richard asked although Maria and I were not sure if he was serious or joking."

"'You want to buy up Mexico!' I joked in return."

"'No, I'm serious,' Richard said turning to Liz for agreement."

"Liz nodded, 'Absolutely'."

"'We won't ruin it for you,' said Richard. 'Maybe we'll want to retire here ourselves. You never know. I'll tell you what, if we buy it and we don't use it, we'll never sell it to anyone but you or your family. How's that?'"

"'You haven't even seen Sayulita. It's not much of a village to look at,' Maria said."

"'But it will change as Puerto Vallarta has changed in just a few years. I don't need to see it to know what's happening in this part of Mexico,' stated Liz. 'We just arrived on a direct flight from Los Angeles, and walked into the new international airport lobby. It's pretty obvious what's going on. Besides, one house way over there will be better than a hotel, which is what this beach will attract.'"

"'I'll inquire,' I said. 'I can't imagine it'll be much money in dollar terms. This land is not practical land for locals.'"

"'Ah, not yet but one day, they'll appreciate the meaning of a peaceful sandy beach, sunsets and privacy,' said Richard smiling and looking at Liz."

"After putting the kids in, we all pushed the boat off, Richard helping me the most, getting a bit more wet than he had bargained for - laughing nonetheless. It only took ten minutes to round the point and land at the south end of the Sayulita beach, where the fishing boats all congregated because the waves were smallest. As with the fishermen, I roared in a bit fast in order to get sufficiently up on the sand so the waves couldn't reach it enough to take it out. We once again disembarked."

"'Not much to look at, Felix' said Liz, 'but another beautiful beach. Such potential. It needs a nice big restaurant to attract tourists.'"

"'I don't know if tourists are ready for Sayulita,' I remarked, 'but Maria's Mama and Papa have probably cooked enough food to ruin your careers.'"

"'What's that guy doing over there?' asked Richard."

"'In the water? Surfing. A few hippies drift into the village with surfboards. I'm told the surf is perfect here,' I said."

"'If this is a surfing beach, then more will come. It's gotten quite a few fans in L.A. already,' said Liz."

"We walked about two blocks inland, past the main plaza and to the first hill facing the water. Up only a few feet, we entered a well-maintained whitewashed house, with a big terrace that faced the front."

"'They must be waiting on us,' said Maria as they all heard the talking and laughing."

"As soon as we entered, the entire family stood up to greet the famous visitors. 'Mama, Papa, I want you to meet Elizabeth and Richard. They are movie actors from the United States. They live some of the time in Puerto Vallarta and Felix and I have been helping them,' said Maria in Spanish but slowly enough so Liz and Richard could follow."

"'Call me Liz, por favor. Mucho gusto,' said Liz."

"'It's a very great pleasure to finally meet you,' said Richard shaking their hands. 'Liz and I have heard much about you, and Sayulita. And I might add, you have a very charming and intelligent daughter. Oh, not to mention a very enterprising and talented son-in-law.'"

"Mama and Papa just smiled, not knowing what was said until Maria translated in Spanish."

"'I could probably say it in Spanish, but the food will be cold by the time I get through. I'm not that fluent, yet,' said Richard grinning."

"Upon hearing the translation, both parents started saying how welcome the visitors were and how happy they were that Liz and Richard could join our Sunday family dinner. Maria quickly introduced our guests to her brothers, sisters, nieces and nephews. I was sure that they didn't quite absorb all the names and relationships, but the intentions were very obvious.

With a gesture or two, everyone sat down at the table, or actually three tables pushed close together, along the terrace. The kids ate at a separate table where they could also play. Parents were standing as much as sitting, attending to the kids and refreshing everyone's plates. The day was beautiful - blue cloudless sky and a bright sun warming the terrace, but not too much since the trellis gave us adequate shade. The table was set as if for a banquet. Everyone ate like it was a banquet. The sea was a hundred meters or more away, but the salt air felt like it was closer."

"'Huachinango fresco,' bragged Mama."

"'That's fresh red snapper,' translated Maria. 'It was probably swimming in the sea three hours ago. Snapper and Mahi-mahi are the two best local fish.'"

"After dinner, which was really a late lunch, we walked about the village while the girls napped and Maria's folks watched them."

"'This village is a few years behind the rest of the region,' I remarked. 'In addition to the surfers who wander in, there are a few Americans living here, but only a handful. They stay pretty low-key. The kinds of guys who want a very tranquil place away from everyone.'"

"'How can you expect that to last when the road will bring thousands here? Perhaps it's sad about the road, but not everyone can come by boat like we came,' said Richard."

"'There's talk about the government fixing things in town, too,' responded Maria. 'Then we might regret what comes. Many of us like it tranquil.'"

"'There'll be a stampede here if your folks ever open up a restaurant,' laughed Richard. 'Surfing, restaurants, don't you see? It will happen and it won't be that long.'"

"'If it changes the village, don't let anyone ever change that special beach of yours. We'll help protect it if you can see how to purchase the other half,' Liz repeated."

"Upon returning, Maria quickly told her parents how Liz and Richard wanted to buy the rest of the beach partly to protect it from development. She indicated we were in favor of it and wondered if that would be possible, might the current owners sell? Her father nodded, with a slight tilt of his head and crunching his lips together in a way that Maria thought was positive."

"'The girls are probably awake by now. Come. Let's get you back while the sun is still high and warm. Papa will inquire about the land,' I said."

"The boat ride back was uneventful but Liz insisted we drift a while in front of the beach. 'You've picked the best spot for a house, but the other end has room for a small house that would be private from each other. If we can buy the land, we'll build but only something that you are happy with. We want to be good neighbors. What's the name of this beach?'"

"There's an old Mexican name, 'Playa Carracitos,' but Maria and I call it 'Secret Beach.'"

"'How can anything stay secret if Elizabeth Taylor buys there?' quipped Richard."

CHAPTER 9

"You know how life just gets into a routine? We were doing fine. Working hard and finishing the final touches of our place so we could stay there when we visited Sayulita for an overnight, rather than rely on Maria's folks to cram us in, and then of course, everything revolved around the girls, their education, their play, giving them the experiences we wanted them to have - it was a busy life. Each night when we got the girls into bed, Maria would try to catch up with housework and I would try to add at least a full hour of studio work, but by the time I washed my brushes, we were exhausted. I was worried that we were trying to do too much. Maria noticed the same thing."

"'We must have more time for us!' she said one evening. Let's plan two evenings a week, no work. Just us. OK?'"

"I smiled. She knew how to keep a balance better than I."

"And you need more time for your work. You spend too much time making money for us, but what about your art? You are selling more and more. I can take over a lot of the tourist work and you can spend more time in the studio."

"'I'm doing okay,' I protested."

"You're an important artist. Liz and Richard can see that. They don't give you compliments just to be nice. They know good art and they say how good you are. Liz tells me that all the time. I want you to be famous. But you must work more. I know you want to. I don't want to see you sacrifice your career. But once in a while, a bit of time for us, too? Okay?"

*****

"You must be wondering how any of this relates? Let me tell you what I only heard, and of course, how I then got involved with intrigue."

"While I've enjoyed hearing about the celebrities, and your life, I was wondering how any of this translates into something dangerous," replied Bart. "Do tell me the rest."

"I'll jump ahead in my story, at least to the event that eventually pulled me into it. This is what happened sometime before I went to Washington. I realized later that the rumors about Liz in D.C. had to do with what I'm going to relate to you, although I was not a part of it. I was drawn in later - many years afterwards. Only when I discovered on my own what Liz never told me, did she tell me these details. But I sense your impatience, so I'll tell this to you now."

"What I'm about to divulge is what Liz told me happened. You know, Andy Warhol-- you must know the artist Andy Warhol? He's the artist who painted the Campbell soup can. He's one of the main artists in the Pop art movement, which I've described to you. Anyway, Warhol made portraits of rich patrons and famous celebrities, in his Pop art style. He loved that world. The more famous they were, the more he loved to paint them. He did portraits for anyone if they paid enough, but for the celebrities, he often made a deal. If he wanted to do someone, he could always find a newspaper photo that was already in the public domain, but he preferred his own custom photographs, often by using an inexpensive Polaroid. After all, the photos were going to be blown up into large silk-screens, so he didn't need to have fine detail, and he enjoyed seeing the results instantly so he could re-take shots until he was satisfied. Remember, digital cameras had not yet been invented."

"If the celebrity agreed, he'd create a series of paintings and the celebrity would get one of the paintings in exchange for posing. Of course, posing was simply going to his studio, which they called the Factory, and posing for some quick photographs. Later, Warhol would select the best photo and have it made into a large silk screen, then print the image over a painted canvas, and then sometimes he would take a brush and put loose brushstrokes on it. Sometimes he would do a second or third layer of silkscreen, for example, to make a shape around the lips a different color. The paintings were always colorful. He wasn't going for realism; the use of the photograph gave enough of an impression."

"Anyway, I'm not trying to give you a lesson on how an artist did his work, other than to say that he hooked up with Liz and Liz agreed to pose on one of her New York visits and Warhol, as it turned out, painted a number of Liz Taylor portraits. So they got to know each other that way."

"Liz was back in L.A. a few days after her portrait was done when the phone rang. Liz's housekeeper answered. Andy was on the phone pleading to talk to Liz immediately, it was life and death. Liz got on the phone."

"Liz, is that you? Is that really you? This is Andy. Andy."

"Hi Andy. I thought you had all the photos you needed for my portrait."

"Oh, Liz, I do, I do. Thank you," said Andy his soft, wispy voice. He never raised his voice and was easily diverted from saying why he had called. "The portraits are perfect, just perfect. After you get your painting, the rest will be bought up by the best collectors and they will all be in museums. Really! Leo says that! Leo knows how to sell for the best prices."

"That's good, Andy. Is that why you called?"

"No, Liz, I'm in trouble. I need your advice. You did tell me that I could call you if I ever needed anything?"

"'That was three days ago,' laughed Liz on the phone."

"Liz, I don't think this is funny. I'm in trouble."

"What's going on?"

"Do you think it's safe to talk on the telephone? Do you?"

"I'm sure no one cares about us. Tell me what's going on."

"Well, you know I've been doing the Kennedy assassination paintings? Do you?"

"Yes, you showed me, remember?"

"Yes, yes of course. Well, my manager purchased - and with real money Liz, I mean I paid a lot - he bought a roll of negatives taken at the time of the motorcade. One of the photographs was aimed at the book depository. It's such a great image, as good as the ones in the newspapers. I was going to, you know, use the newspaper ones, but you know, if I used them, I'll spend so much on lawyers fighting lawsuits. It's really a pain. Campbell soup, they were nice but some of those people who think they own commercial images, well, they send their lawyers after me."

"Yes, so?"

"Well, so I did it right, this time. I really did. I purchased some fellow's roll. No one wanted it. It was just like the published ones, just people in confusion, you know, the bystanders, and one of the shots showed the building. Oh, I could have gone there and photographed it afterwards, but it wouldn't be the same. The building is the same but I wanted the event. But we got this roll of negatives, and I now own it. So I blew two of the images up big, into one of my silk screens, and now I'm in trouble, Liz. I'm afraid."

"Of what, Andy, are you afraid of?"

"Well, you know how these people are rough. I mean, they killed our President, didn't they? They got to Oswald, too. So they can get to anyone. And Johnson, I don't like that man, he's not our kind of president, is he Liz? Anyway, Johnson doesn't want anyone to know the truth about the assassination. It was just Oswald, and no one else. Well, we know that's a fable, but who's going to argue, except for the nutcases? Anyway, my photo, the one of the building, Liz, it shows something. It's… it's not what the government is saying. "

"You see, Bart, Andy Warhol discovered something that he was afraid of revealing. He wanted publicity in one hand, but he was so afraid about his life and what would happen - he chose to clam up. I'll tell you in a bit what was revealed, but at that moment, he only confided with Liz about what he had. It was the last thing he thought he'd be mixed up with. All he was doing was making some art. Anyway, he realized what he had once he blew up the image."

"Felix, you must tell me. Please don't drag that out. I must know what he saw," pleaded Bart.

"Liz, I made six paintings," continued Andy, "or at least this image is screened on six of them. I painted on two of them and then I spotted the image. On the first painting. I did the rest but I covered up that window. It's only on one of the paintings."

"Andy, for God's sake, what is?"

"Liz, I spotted the second gunman! Not the window where Oswald was. On another floor, there's another shooter. It's clear. But if I reveal it, they'll come for me too. Liz, I know I'm not a brave man. I don't want this on me."

"Andy, if you're right, that changes what they are saying. It's important for the world to know the truth, isn't it?"

"No, Liz, not when the world doesn't want to know the truth. I know what the truth is, Liz. It's whatever someone says it is. They've already announced that, haven't they? And those men in politics, they only want their truth."

"Why don't you simply destroy the images, Andy? Then your hands are clean."

"Liz, I can't destroy my art. It'll be in museums. I want the world to know, but not when I'm around to be killed. I want to protect this, somehow."

"Andy, why can't you do that?"

"Too many people come through my factory. I can't hide it here. Can you hide it? Liz, can you hide it for me?"

"Hide all the paintings?"

"No, I painted out the second gunman in all but one. Just the one painting. That's the one that will become famous someday - but not now - not when Johnson is in power."

"I know the Johnson people. I can talk to them, if you want."

"No, no, no, please no. Not even you can control them. It's much too dangerous. No one will want to backtrack now that the official version is out. And from Warhol? They'll laugh and then they'll destroy the evidence, and probably me, too. You need to hide it for me."

"How can I hide it here any better than you?"

"Liz, you are smart - the cleverest woman I know. Surely you have an answer."

"Well, let me think. You want to let the world have your art, but just not now. You want it both ways! So we need to tuck it away somewhere, where it won't be seen. For a while, until you decide what to do. Is that correct?"

"Yes, yes, that's it. We'll figure it out, but not today. I need time."

"Okay, I know of a way. Listen carefully. I'll buy the painting. It'll look like a normal sale. No one will know the truth, but you must prepare it a special way."

"Anyway you say, Liz. You are my savior. I love you Liz, I love you."

Bart was listening intently. When Felix paused, as he liked to do just to let his mind catch up with his mouth, Bart blurted out, "Well, what was her plan?"

"I didn't know at the time. She never wanted me to know what happened to the painting with the image. She hatched a plan that she thought would do the trick."

"She eventually told you?" asked Bart.

"Not until I had discovered it by accident. Then I contacted her and she told me the details of what had happened. But I kept it a secret. I didn't want the world to know until the day of the exhibition. That's in two days."

"But when did you find out?"

"Not for quite some time," continued Felix. "In fact, I didn't know until several years later, about the painting, Liz's plan or the implications. The second gunman? I was never told until I finally figured it out. And then I never told anyone. Not yet. That's why I'm flying to New York. To open an exhibition that will reveal the truth. At the time, Andy and Liz considered it a dangerous secret. And poor Andy, we'll never know the truth why that girl shot him. He survived that, didn't he? But then we'll never know if his hospital death really was an accident."

"Elizabeth Taylor never got killed. We know that," said Bart "It was reported in the movie magazines that she was heavily into pain killers and had a chest full of medical ailments, so she wasn't killed. Are you sure your suspicions are really well founded?"

"They never really made the connection to Liz. All she did was buy a painting from Andy, and it wasn't anything different than the other four in the series that were sold to various collectors. She hung it for a year in her house until everyone knew the painting - knew it wasn't anything special except a nice Warhol, and then she quietly stored it away. She wanted it known that the painting was sold or given away and was out of the country and certainly out of Liz's house. That's where I come into the story again. I was still in Mexico, and she came down for one of her visits."

"You know," said Bart, "Kennedy's assassination was before my time. I only know the basics-- he got shot from a rifle by a guy named Lee Harvey Oswald while he was in a motorcade in Dallas. That's about it. Tell me what this means."

"After the assassination, out came more conspiracy theories than there are gas stations in America. Really! Who did it? Who planned it? Was Oswald alone?

Was he part of a Cuban plot? After all, Kennedy had tried to get Castro out. A Russian plot? After all, Oswald had gone to Russia and married a Russian woman. Was there a Mexican connection? After all, Oswald was in Mexico City shortly before the assassination. A Mafia connection? Well, we know of the money connections and Robert Kennedy's zeal going after the Mafia. Were there several gunmen? Or at least a second gunman?"

"The newly sworn-in president had to calm down the nation. Within two weeks, he formed the Warren Commission, with Earl Warren, then the Chief Justice of the Supreme Court, as the Chairman. They investigated the entire event, and months later, published their conclusions in an 886-page book and at least two-dozen volumes of supporting evidence. It seemed very impressive. The upshot of it all - Oswald acted alone. That was the best answer they had. Oh sure, they also implied that he might have been stimulated by Soviet philosophies, but no one else was involved. It was the cleanest conclusion."

In contrast to that theory, there have been more books and articles questioning the accuracy of just about everything. Many have hinted that the government is simply doing another cover-up, possibly to hide their own involvement. And for some, if they can name a group, nation, political party, race or religion that they don' t like, they are likely a co-murderer and conspired with Oswald.

"That's the background on the event. Now, why were there so many doubts? The most obvious reason was that as the shots were analyzed, there were experts who claimed that one man could not have fired three bullets when one bullet missed in the time period that was necessary, that one bullet that struck both victims couldn't have done all that damage, and if there were more bullets, like the four that are most often suggested, then one man could not have fired that many in such a short time, therefore he needed someone else to help shoot. It seemed very improbable that one "magic" bullet - that's what it's called - could have injured so many body parts in two men sitting on different seats and have penetrated at so many angles. There's one scenario that answers everyone's questions - If there had been a second gunman making additional shots, the bullet analysis would have made more sense. Many reporters and witnesses testified that they heard four shots. And the questions and doubts continue ad nausea."

"And why is that so important, you may wonder? Because more than one shooter means planning - deliberate and careful planning - and not the actions of a mad, insane person who decided to do this at the last minute. If that's the case, that there are others involved, then it opens up so many more possible evil partners, and at the same time, slams down completely the work of that entire committee with it's 886-page report and neat conclusion. And that, my friend, opens a firestorm, once again."

"I would think that gun experts could determine where the shots were fired from," suggested Bart.

"In a simple case perhaps. But the moving motorcade made things more difficult. There was a famous amateur film made, very grainy, that they used to see the body movements at each partial second. They also analyzed photographs of everything in the area to see if they could spot anyone suspicious. There was a famous theory that behind the grassy knoll, behind a fence, there might have been a second gunman. Most of those theories, while they never went away, didn't get more credible simply because no one could point to a second smoking gun. Therefore, the obvious conclusion was that Oswald was the only gunman, was highly skilled, got very lucky, and the magic bullet hit, bounced, ricocheted, twisted, or whatever and did all the damage that was known. He did it by himself, with no outside help. And that a bar owner named Jack Ruby was also a lone gunman who also got incredibly lucky to get inside the area where the police, under heavy guard, were moving Oswald and shot him dead before he could be interrogated. Now, incredible coincidences do happen all the time, even bad ones, just not in front of millions of people on live television involving the killing of a President of the United States."

"Felix, you sound like you don't believe that Oswald was the lone gun?"

"You know, I really did believe that. I was an average citizen who believed what those distinguished gentlemen had concluded. That is, until I understood the Warhol painting. That began later; my entire world turned upside down when Liz came back to Puerto Vallarta."

CHAPTER 10

"Liz knocked on my door, one morning. 'Hi Felix. Are you free for a moment?' she asked. 'Just got in yesterday from L.A.'"

"You didn't call to tell me. I would have picked you up."

"Got in late. Taxi was fine for me. Diego brought his truck. I had a lot of stuff. I didn't want to bother you with that."

"Is Richard here?"

"No. He might join me in a couple of days. Thinks I'm coming just to do more shopping. Anyway, he's busy enough rehearsing for a new film. But something is more important; I have something to talk to you about. May I come in?"

"I was slightly embarrassed that I had not invited her in right away. I guess I was a bit surprised and curious that she had come without requesting something in advance."

"Where's Maria? And the girls?"

"They're out on a school trip. Back late this afternoon, I suspect."

"I want to see them. But Felix, first I have to get your help on something."

"'Sure,' I said again."

"I have a painting. It's done by Andy Warhol. Do you know his art?"

"Of course. He's a genius. He'll be in the history books for sure."

"Well, after he did my self portrait, he did the Kennedy assassination paintings. You know how much I liked Kennedy. Anyway, I bought one and had it in my house. Now it's here. I managed to bring it down with me. It barely fitted in the plane, but it's here. I brought it with some furniture I wanted for the house. I want to give it to you to hold. Not here, but take it to your beach house in Sayulita. Just hang it on a wall so not many people will see it. Perhaps it'll be yours someday, but for now, just keep it for me, but tell no one that you have it or that it came from me. If anyone asks, just say you traded for it and you are not sure who the artist is."

"Is it stolen or something?"

"No, it's mine. I have all the papers. But if someone finds out about it, it could be dangerous. For you. And for me. Really. I shouldn't be asking you, but you are my friend and I know I can trust you. I don't want to make it dangerous for you, but I didn't know where else to turn. Can you, for me?"

"Sure," I said again. She knew I would say yes, and I didn't really mind. I was more curious than afraid of her words. How could one painting get someone in danger? I speculated. A stolen work was the only reason I could think of, but Liz said it wasn't. Since it was a Warhol, it was quite valuable. So why would she want it in a place like Sayulita? Kind of the last place to put valuable art, I would think, although I did hang a few of my paintings there; they were not valuable in that sense, but to me they were; I treasured my own work. "

"Can you pick up the painting and take it to Sayulita today?"

"I can. I have the afternoon free. Are you coming with me?"

"No, I don't want to be seen with it, even from a distance. I'll go with you to get it. It's in my house now, but I want to get it out right away."

"'Let's go get it, and I'll take it to the boat and get it to Sayulita. No one will see me unload it if I go by the beach. Give me a few minutes to gather up my stuff,' I said with a smile, as I was quickly putting together the stuff I needed."

"You are too good to me. Really!"

"We drove to her house in the van I used for business, even though it was only a few blocks away. I walked into her house and saw the painting in her foyer, wrapped in brown paper."

"Take this, too. It's a letter I wrote on the airplane stating that I've given you the painting as a surprise birthday gift. It'll mean that you had no knowledge about it. And no one can accuse you of stealing it."

"'Will I be allowed to see the painting?' I asked."

"Of course, but unwrap it when you get it to Sayulita. Hang it just like you might hang any of your paintings, if you want. That way, if someone sees it, they won't think it's anything special since artists have lots of paintings about. But a wrapped painting, that might look like something of value. Or just store it. I know you store your paintings there."

"And you won't tell me the secret behind it?"

"'Not now; maybe another day,' replied Liz firmly but with warmth. 'If you know, you'll put yourself in more danger. For now, it's best that you forget the intrigue. Just think of it as an innocent gift from me.'"

"Is this long-term?"

"Yes, but why?"

"If it's long-term and it's valuable, then I need to install an air-conditioner. Like I did in my studio here. The summer humidity is not good for long-term storage. My paintings are not as valuable, so I take a chance. But even so, it should be done right."

"I'll pay for that.

"That's not necessary. I was going to do it anyway, to help with my own paintings. The electricity is not so great in Sayulita. It goes off often, but I'll have Gris check it daily to make sure it's working."

"I'm grateful."

"But Liz, how do I accept this painting, even on a loan, if it's valuable?"

"I'll take the chance. Felix, it's valuable and it might get more valuable someday. If I'm not around, then it'll be yours to figure out what to do. I trust you. Sometimes, it's not the money that directs someone's actions, but to do the right thing."

"Do I need insurance on it?"

"We'll take a chance. It's best not to call attention to it."

"I don't really understand but I'll do it your way. I trust you."

"'I know you'll take care of it. Thank you, Felix. Thank you very much.' With that, she gave me a kiss on my cheek. 'I'm hoping I'm not getting you into trouble with this, but you were the only person I could turn to… whom I could trust.'"

*****

"I drove the painting to the dock and loaded it into the boat, covered it with a tarp so it wouldn't get splashed on in case I ran into some choppy water, even though it seemed well sealed in a plastic wrapping under the brown paper, and ran it over in less than an hour. I landed on the beach in front of the house. The house was just about completed and Maria and I and the kids had even slept there a few times. Not a soul saw me, and if someone had been on a boat nearby, no one would have thought anything was different this time than on any previous trip when I'd taken stuff to the house - especially my paintings - people were used to seeing me with canvases; I had taken several back and forth."

"I lifted it out of the boat and carried it right up the slope and into the house. During the boat ride, I kept trying to imagine what was Liz's reason for giving it to me for safekeeping. When I finally cut the string and unwrapped the brown paper wrapping, I stared at the painting. It was under clear plastic but clear enough to see it. It was of the Kennedy assassination series, the building where Oswald had taken his shot. I remembered hearing from Liz that Warhol had done a series of paintings using the assassination as the subject. What was so secretive about this painting, I wondered? It showed the Book Depository. I assumed that Andy had appropriated the photos being printed in the newspapers and magazines, and then brushed on some paint strokes to make it more artistic. I thought it strange that Liz didn't continue to hang it in one of her houses, either here or in L.A. It was a powerful painting and Warhol was now a status symbol for the well heeled. Why hide it? Nevertheless, it looked great among my paintings."

*****

"That painting became more and more valuable as the years and decades went by. Probably a million dollars if it ever went to auction today, but the paperwork from Andy to Liz to me would probably inflate the normal value. I was somewhat concerned however, about securing the papers to prove who was the rightful owner. A painting that valuable has to have proper documentation. Liz eventually gave me a more formal letter that had been notarized."

"When Liz passed away, it was forgotten about and no one from her estate even asked. If they had, I had both letters that she gave me, so I knew that no one else could claim ownership."

"For many years, it was safe in my house in Sayulita, away from all limelight. But in recent years, I didn't know what to do. I didn't want to transport it into the U.S. but I feared keeping it in Sayulita should I die. Also, for a few years, I wasn't in Sayulita as much as I used to be. I did build an air-conditioned storage room so the humidity would not do harm to the painting."

"Finally, I consulted an attorney who advised me on the best way to transport the painting through customs into the United States should I want to do that. I managed, however, in making my Sayulita house as secure as it needed to be. I have a good system in place; it's worked for half a century! I enjoy having the painting with my own art. When the painting is not hung up, it's wrapped and protected with a plywood crate, so nothing can accidentally puncture it."

"Why didn't you sell it? That money could support your old age," asked Bart.

"I couldn't bring myself to do that. There was more to the painting than its art value, and soon I'll tell you why."

"I don't understand - why didn't the artist put it on exhibition?"

"Andy was really afraid, and for good reason, as it turns out. Liz was friendly with the Johnson administration. She had transitioned from Kennedy to Johnson because she was passionate about Kennedy's goals and reasoned that she could keep that agenda alive through the Johnson folks. In many ways, she was right although she didn't know how much the war would get all efforts off track. But in any case, Andy just couldn't keep a secret. He was very child-like. He wanted attention, so he kept hinting. Liz made overtures to the White House about reopening the investigation. They didn't want to hear that kind of nonsense. And Andy, what could he do?"

"I'll pause my story and I'll tell you my Andy theories. Andy was a damn good artist. He was also a good promoter. Andy was also very selfish. He knew the historical value. I don't know how frightened he actually was, but he certainly used that as his excuse. If he had revealed what he had found in someone's photograph, he would have been just a small footnote as the one who first saw it. But later, once it came out via his art, his painting would be the most famous in the world. He knew how to get the most publicity for himself, and his hunch was to delay letting the world know about the discovery. He has his own "King Kong" story and he wanted the public to see it in his theater with the proper buildup and glamour, and that was not meant for an immediate showing."

"Less than four years later, when Andy was shot, I think his entire approach to the world changed. The painting and secret had gone underground, and for Warhol, after that attempt on his life, it could stay underground as far as he was concerned. He had other fish to fry."

"Anyway, once the painting was hidden, if Andy had never opened his mouth, nothing would have happened. But that wasn't his personality. All this is a way to say that word that Liz's Warhol painting might reveal something else, got to folks in the government. At some point, Liz got a visit and she freaked. She knew that even her ability to call the President directly might not stop actions from those in the CIA or who knows where. So she decided to take action and get that painting away and out of her house and life."

"Once it was safely in Mexico, at my house in Sayulita, out of Liz's house, out of Andy's factory, and out of any chance of publicity or premature discovery, things seem to settle down again. And I forgot about it, as well. Oh, I knew it was there, but it just wasn't something I thought about much. But you know, things such as this tend to resurface, as it did a few years later. But that was after my personal life changed in a very tragic way."

*****

"Keep in mind that this painting and its eventual arrival in Mexico, was just one thing and not necessarily the major event going on. I was busy with my life, as a painter and as a tourist guide or new resident guide or fixer of whatever someone needed in Puerto Vallarta, and especially, for about six years, my wife and I spent a good chunk of our time dealing with Liz and Richard's extensive holdings. They needed quality management and they got it. Along the way, we also became friends. We seemed to be their best link in finding that balance between helping them find privacy, which they wanted when they visited, and giving them some connection to the local residents and bay life. We would tell them about special gatherings and local festivals, and they enjoyed going to those."

"Maria and I worked hard as we raised a family. That's something that all families go through. And financially, since we often charged American rates, it was like getting several times the normal Mexican pay."

"We managed to purchase the beach land for Liz and Richard with funds that Liz had her accountant send me, along with additional money to keep her houses going, since they had no intention of coming during the off-season."

"Before the law changed, foreigners had a difficult time taking title to property near the coast. I had become a duel-citizen - that process was easy since my mother had been born in Mexico, which was more direct than being married to a Mexican, so I was entitled to citizenship. The land and houses that Liz and Richard purchased were put into my name and I served as their "presta nombre" which basically meant I was the legal owner of the land but for their benefit; we had Power of Attorney papers drawn up so all was up and up. They also made me the beneficiary of the beach land and executor of their other houses in Puerto Vallarta if anything should happen to them."

"Summers were never fun in Puerto Vallarta. Sayulita was a bit better situated to receive the breezes coming from the north, and at times on weekends we slept in our almost completed phase-one house at Secret Beach. For our house in Puerto Vallarta, we finally were able to purchase two air conditioners, brought down with stuff that Liz and Richard needed for their place, and finally, I could sleep at night without getting up to cool myself with a wet towel. Maria only wanted to use them on the hottest of nights; she thought that our ceiling fans were more than adequate. In a funny way, I didn't mind the heat either. Keep in mind, Washington D.C. during summer months was often like a steam bath, and so I had long before become acclimated to hot humid nights. Still, air conditioning was a luxury that one quickly got used to. On those breezeless, long hot nights, the girls piled in with us, until we installed the second unit in their room, at sacrifice to my studio needs. Of course, they had to put up with a lot of my drawings and canvases stored in their room; I didn't want the humidity ruining them and air-conditioned rooms were best."

"The future was looking bright; we were a congenial family, had lots of family support and we were doing great financially. Most important, Maria was happy with the entire package and I was producing paintings at an impressive clip. Production is not everything, but often when an artist is in a groove, masterpieces get made one after another. I was excited about my work and so each day became a variety of activities that culminated with at least three hours of concentrated studio work. I often spent the entire day, but never less than those three hours. You know, it's physical exercise - to paint. The concentration, the energy, the excitement, the physical work -- after three hours, I was usually ready for a break. Instead of resting, I simply switched to another activity, whether it was to deal with our business or to help the girls when they came home from school."

"Finally, I should mention that Liz's recommendations about my work, both in the area and to her friends in Los Angeles, started to bring results. I had a handful of shows lined up and, more importantly, several curators had contacted me about museum group shows. I would soon be considered as a serious and perhaps important new artist."

*****

"I don't know how to narrate the next chapter of my life other than to say it rather quickly."

"Each summer and fall, hundreds of people got dengue, a very hard consequence of being bitten by an infected mosquito. Usually it results in a nasty two-week flu-like episode, which is more dangerous to the old or people with other issues. Maria got it that summer, after having had it two summers previously. Some people insist it's even worse to have it a second time. Her condition got so bad we ended up going to the hospital at everyone's insistence. We got her to San Javier, the main private hospital in Puerto Vallarta. In hindsight, it was a mistake. Hospitals are dangerous places, and perhaps she picked up a fungal infection in her lung after staying there a couple of days. Five days later, she was dead."

"She was only 28 years old, leaving our 5 and 7-year old daughters to be raised by me. I was distraught beyond belief. She had been healthy and young. How could she die from something so easily? I couldn't get over it. Liz and Richard somehow heard about her death and expressed to me their sympathies by cablegram. I had to plead for Dad and Beatrice not to come. Maria's family was all over me, having taken the trouble to come in repeatedly to Puerto Vallarta. Her mother stayed with us, helping with the girls, while I just tried to get over my severe depression. I was at a lost. We had been a team, we had been in love and our passion and dreams were as alive as ever. None of it really worked without the other, and now I was alone. Not alone in that sense, for I had the girls and I had Maria's family, but it was all meant to be shared with Maria. It was all so sudden - I just couldn't get a grip on anything."

CHAPTER 11

"I'm very sorry for your loss," said Bart, sounding like it had recently happened.

"Oh, it was so many years ago. But, yes, my eyes get moist just thinking about it even now. I'll spare you the agony of describing the next several months; I'm sure you can imagine it. It's no different than the grief that any spouse would go through having lost someone so close and so young. My Dad kept in close touch with me. He had gone through a similar death with my mother, who at the time had been only a few years older than Maria. It's funny how our lives, which were on completely different tracks, still had that similarity. I remember how Dad got through it and so, I suppose, I had to as well."

"A year later, I had moved to L.A. Maria's parents seemed very understanding and I promised to visit with the girls, but I decided that with Maria gone, staying in Mexico to make my art wasn't worth it. Even though business was expanding, my passion wasn't in the business. I wanted to make important art, not just tourist art, and besides, I rationalized, schools weren't great in Puerto Vallarta and even worse in Sayulita, which was actually in Nayarit, a different state that had less money than Jalisco, the state in which Puerto Vallarta was located. I wanted my girls to have some American education standards, without denying their Mexican heritage. So I decided that a year, at the least, in the United States, with summers or vacations spent in Mexico, would allow them to get the best of both worlds or at least the best I could offer without their mother in the picture. My biggest worry was making a living in a much more expensive environment, and not having any family support as I had from Maria's family."

"I was not pulling up stakes completely. I had a couple of friends who had helped me a lot and they would take over my business and give me a percentage. One would also rent my house. The studio in Puerto Vallarta was to remain, serving as my storage for the time being, and the house in Sayulita, well, I hoped to use it as often as possible on visits. If the move was unsuccessful, I could ease back into the same lifestyle if need be. That was my conservative planning at work."

"Liz and Richard's relationship had its down spots and both of them were busy making films, but after five years, they were holding pretty strong I thought, and at times, with as much passion as I had with Maria. I could tell from those little things, like how Richard would give Liz a compliment about something very unimportant, perhaps the way she poured a drink or smiled, or the way that they held hands, in a loving way, like Maria and I used to hold hands. In a way, I almost felt jealous that I lost my love through no fault of our relationship, simply by some random chance - bad luck that turned tragic."

"Nevertheless, when considering all the obvious spots to go - back to San Diego where I had studied, or to New York City where the art action was really happening, or to Washington where my father was still living and there was a crumb of an art scene developing, Liz cast the deciding vote and insisted that L.A. would give me the best opportunity for my art and they offered me a year's use of a Venice apartment that a movie studio owned and which was available for their use. Venice was an up and coming beach area that was just beginning to get trendy among artists, writers and actors. It was much cheaper than elsewhere in L.A. while having a cultural feel to it. By car, it was only a half hour to Santa Monica and Hollywood. It was a gift that was hard to refuse, and closer by plane than any other option to Puerto Vallarta."

"So we packed up our van, putting on the roof as much studio equipment and paintings as could be bundled up, after going through countless hoops to get the immigration papers for the girls, and more work to get the proper insurance forms so the car would be allowed into the United States. A fellow from John's film crew helped me do since they had transferred all sorts of vehicles and equipment through customs in both directions. We drove to the border, crossed at Nogales, got up to Phoenix and then headed west to Los Angeles."

"The girls enjoyed the drive and even though they had to sit long hours on open stretches of desert, we stopped often enough to break up the trip. The roads were at times asphalted fine while other stretches were less than fine resulting in long periods bouncing on dirt roads. The van got filthy and a few times, I stopped just to let the engine cool in the shade somewhere; it actually held up fine but I feared breaking down with the girls out in the boondocks. I was only sorry that Maria was not alive to share our trip; we had planned a U.S. trip - even an extended stay so the girls could experience a year of American school, but we thought it would be best to wait until the girls were a bit older. I never thought Maria wouldn't be around to share that experience."

*****

"I suppose I'm rambling too long now. You see, it's been sixty plus years, and yet, when I talk about those days, I feel like it was yesterday. I can cry now like I cried then. There aren't many marriages where the love of a spouse remains so strong, after so many years. We were supposed to grow old together. Isn't that every couple's plan? The girls? They are grown, with children and grandchildren of their own. One stayed in the States and married a New Englander, and is as American as you might expect; the other eventually met a Mexican guy temporarily living in Los Angeles, originally from Guadalajara, and they split their time between Guadalajara and L.A. Her kids grew up in Guadalajara but ended up moving to the States. They are more Mexican than not. They all visit me on occasion and I used to make the rounds, as well."

Felix paused and Bart interjected, "Do you want to take a break? Why not have a drink. I'll buy you an alcoholic drink if you want."

"That's very kind of you, Bart. Yes, that might be a good idea, but not now. Before we land, I'd love something, maybe a glass of wine. Ah, here is the attendant."

Felix waved the flight attendant over. "I'll just take a diet coke for now. Thanks."

"We have more to talk about. Then a glass of wine before we land would sooth my nerves - if I make it to then, of course. If I'm still alive, I'm being picked up so it won't matter if I'm slightly relaxed. It's a rather long drive to my destination. But I want to continue with my story and not doze off, so a coke will do for now."

The attendant reached over Bart to hand Felix the drink. "Sir, would you like peanuts or a sandwich."

"Not now. I'm fine, thanks. Maybe a sandwich and a glass of red wine in an hour. We have a couple of hours to go, don't we?"

"Yes, sir, we aren't due to land until 5:50 local time, and it's not even 4 o'clock now. There's plenty of time."

Felix took a few sips of his coke and turned his attention back to Bart. "I suppose I should tell you a bit more about the early L.A. years. That was in the mid 60s."

"In Mexico, I was working like crazy, in my studio, helping with tourists and helping Liz and Richard. I was their main assistant in Puerto

Vallarta. They ran everything through me. But then there came a point when everything got built, they visited infrequently, and they needed me less. Then Maria died. So I was then in L.A. and busy being a single Dad to my kids and finding a permanent place to live and work. Liz contacted me a few times. Liz was worried that I wasn't working, but then she saw my studio that I had found in Venice about ten blocks from our apartment - a little concrete building in an alley where the front was a welding shop but the back was perfect for my work and I had it for a reasonable rental rate. While the girls were in school, I worked feverishly."

"'My, look how much work you have!' remarked Liz in one of her surprise afternoon visits after a couple of hours of shopping and in need of a diversion."

"Liz, I've been trying to produce my masterpieces since coming to Los Angeles. A lot of ideas going on. And the big ones; I'm closer to the galleries, so transporting them isn't the headache it was in Mexico. All this work is not done in five minutes. But my funds are running low and I need to sell or find some way to have an income. Maybe teaching but that's what every artist wants to so. There's a lot of competition for those jobs."

"You shouldn't get over-committed; that'll be bad for your art. You need studio time to keep this up."

"I'm pretty set for a show; I have a gallery or two nibbling in New York - one of the ones you called. And one show here - you know at the Atlas Gallery. But if I don't sell soon, I'll need to find more storage space for my paintings. Adding objects increases their depth and that makes them more difficult to store. Alas, artists rarely take the practical route."

"They need to be shown so you can sell them....to the right people. Felix, you were successful in Puerto Vallarta and you'll be successful in Los Angeles. Let me spread the word about your show. I'll get Richard to help - it'll be tough because they are shooting a film and are behind schedule - but our involvement will help you a lot. We owe that to you, for all you've done for us, although it's enough that we are friends and I admire your work and believe in you! And the girls - I trust I'll see them on my next visit. I haven't seen them for months. They must be thriving in school here, no?"

"You are very sweet to me, and of course, the girls miss you, too,' I said to Liz. 'They are growing up fast.'"

"I'm having a private party for a great artist - that is, in addition to you. I want you to come. You'll be exposed to a lot of people. Andy Warhol. Have you met him in person? You must. The Pasadena Museum is showing Andy's work. It's the first museum showing of his work on the West Coast. And I want you to meet Walter Hopps, the director of the museum. He's interested in avant-garde artists. You'll fit right in."

"I'd love to come."

"But Felix, please don't mention the painting. I don't want anyone to know it's in Mexico, or that you have anything to do with it. Andy knows of course, that you have it now, but no one else."

"It's safe. Of course I won't mention it."

"You know, Andy's fear was legitimate at the time. I tried to feel out the White House about reopening the Warren Commission. I might as well been yelling "fire" in a theater, the way they reacted. But all has been quiet for quite some time. I think the world has lost its concern for discovering the truth and has moved on. But if we should bring out these questions, I'm afraid Lyndon's aggression will start all over again."

*****

"The party was going strong when I arrived. Liz and Richard had quite a spread in Beverly Hills - high gate with security attendant checking the guest list, long driveway up to large parking area for guest vehicles and a granite walkway to a formal entry door with columns. I knew it would be somewhat dressy, so I opted for my dark blue velvet jacket over a dress shirt and dark blue jeans that almost passed for slacks. I greeted Liz and told her that I was lucky to find a babysitter. She instantly pulled me to the guest of honor."

"'Hello,' Andy Warhol said in almost a whisper elongating the one word."

"Liz was a great hostess. 'Andy, other than you, I'd like you to meet one of the greatest artists I know. He's terrific. He has lived in Mexico until recently, but the world will know about Felix Peters. Trust me. We have one of his earlier paintings in the dining room. You can't miss it. It's the one that covers the entire wall!' she lauded."

"I instantly put out my hand. He hesitated, then put his hand to mine, as limp as I've ever felt in a handshake. I was a bit embarrassed that I even offered my hand; it was apparent that Andy didn't shake hands except to be polite. Liz left us to greet other guests, so we small-talked. I dropped a few names so he knew why I was attending the party, and he was instantly impressed."

"Liz is so supportive of artists she likes. She must like you a lot."

"Well, I spent a lot of time with Liz and Richard, in Mexico. They came to my studio a lot and seemed to like my work. They bought. That's a good sign."

"'It is, it is. Liz came to my Factory for her portrait. Have you seen it? You'll enjoy seeing it,' Andy offered."

"'Believe it or not, I've seen it several times, and,' lowering my voice so only Andy could hear, 'I've seen the one she purchased from you. The assassination painting.'"

"By his expression, I then realized I shouldn't have mentioned that even though it wasn't a secret to Andy. Warhol froze. His party grin vanished. He glanced around the room, and saw that no one was listening. Almost in a whisper he said, 'Oh, you're that artist - the one in Mexico. That one. Be careful. Be very careful.'"

"About what? I'm just storing the painting for her."

"Oh, that one will make me famous all over again. But I won't show it. Not for many years. I open my mouth too much. I'm so sorry. Let's forget I said anything."

"The waiter came by with hors d'oeuvres, and Andy helped himself to one. 'Try one of these. Oh, they are so delicious. Really, Liz knows how to throw a party.'"

"Obviously, he was trying to change the subject."

*****

"A tall middle-aged man with dark hair, dark-rimmed glasses and a pitch-black suit over a white shirt with a narrow black tie walked up to us. A few feet away, I saw that Liz gestured to him to meet us. He looked like a bureaucrat, maybe more of a FBI agent from his demeanor, but his face didn't quite have that look. He had thick eyebrows that hovered above the rim of his glasses, which became animated as he was talking. Walter gave Andy a pat on his shoulder and immediately turned to me and held out his hand. 'I'm Walter Hopps. Liz told me that I had to meet the other artist invited to this party.'"

"'Walter, I'm pleased to meet you. Felix Peters,' I said."

"'Oh, Walter, he's a real artist and Liz loves his work,' Andy said in a soft squeal. 'Felix, Walter is a genius director. He was the first to show my work at the Ferus Gallery, way before anyone else. And he's the first museum in California to show me. He's my hero.'"

"Liz came over and joined us just while Andy was relating this. 'Ferus is where I first saw your work, remember Andy?'"

"'I do, Liz, I do,' smiled Andy."

"'What kind of work do you do?' Walter asked, not wasting time for small talk."

"'Abstract. Early on, maybe a Rivera-influence from my years in Mexico, but I've drifted to large format forms on bright backgrounds and I collage on things that I pick up at markets. Sorry, that doesn't tell you much. My studio is in Venice if you'd like to take a look,' I offered."

"Walter, there's an early Felix Peters in the dining room."

"'I saw it. That tells me a lot. Love to come. I'll come over soon. Actually, I've heard about you. Not just from Liz, from others. It's a small world - the art world - hard for a good artist not to be talked about - and I hear everything. I try, at least. Nice to meet you,' Walter Hopps said, before turning the subject back to the star of the evening whom he was showing at the museum. Andy was generous in allowing a few seconds of attention to be on someone other than himself, but it was obvious that he was happier when Walter started chatting about Andy's upcoming show."

"Andy's show looks great. L.A. will be surprised to see it. You know, not one of Andy's paintings have been publicly shown in California. Not one museum has a Warhol. That's shameful. I'm trying to get them to acknowledge the new art. I'm pushing the West Coast art, but how can they not acknowledge what has been happening in New York? Pop art is certainly here to change perceptions. And Andy's work, really, is the best of the best."

"Andy smiled in a dazed look. He really said very little but mumbled a few words just to show he was listening. Then he spotted another celebrity, and he pulled Liz and Walter away. I turned to get another drink. Walter, seeing the awkwardness of Andy's move, turned and deliberately said, 'Felix, it was a pleasure to finally meet you. I'll talk to you in a bit.'"

"I was feeling a bit shy without having a partner, especially at events such as Liz's fancy gathering. The girls had started teasing me about finding a date, but it had been less than a year and I was still in mourning. I did find a few folks from the crew and cast whom I met during the *Iguana* filming, and so I had something to talk about with them. Even John Huston was in attendance although he came in late and didn't stay very long, I gathered to make a quick appearance before going off to have a drink somewhere in private. But he was gracious upon seeing me and started telling me about his new expansion to his house near Mismaloya. I don't think he remembered about Maria's passing and I didn't bring it up, but when he asked why Maria was not with me, I finally had to tell him. He was absolutely aghast at having forgotten."

"'Old age will do that, I'm afraid,' he apologized. 'But I'm not that old. It must be too much drinking. I'm very, very sorry. Really I am.'"

"I changed the subject and we talked Mexico and haciendas and Margaritas."

"You know, I've been so busy and I know Liz and Richard have, we just don't seem to be in Puerto Vallarta at the same time. And now you are here. Why don't you come over to my hacienda here? Soon. Give me your number and I'll pick a time when Liz and Richard can come, too. We can have a small *Iguana* reunion. That'll be fun."

*****

"My studio was almost 1,800 square feet, about a 30 by 60 foot rectangular space, and in the back corner, a small bathroom and outside work sink. The floor was smooth but old concrete, with a wooden floor in the corner that had been a former office. I was most delighted with the ceiling height - a whopping sixteen feet at the peak and sloping down to a still respectable thirteen feet. This enabled me to make a painting as large as fifteen by fifty feet-- ample for my ambitions. The side of the one-story building faced a dead-end alley and had previously been used as some sort of mechanic's shop, I deduced as it had lots of oil stains on the floor. That wall had four good windows that gave me some natural light; the other main walls were dingy painted and marked up brick, which I painted pure white and then installed a plywood wall so I could easily put up and take down the canvases I was working on. Without neighbors abutting, I had privacy."

"Walter Hopps called and we set up a time for his visit the following week. Walter arrived by taxi and walked in with barely a knock, nodded his head, and just walked all around the studio, bending over at times to better view smaller works stacked against the wall, and moving one or two so he could step back and see the larger paintings."

"I was working on one of my biggest canvases to date, a billboard-sized painting smothered with yellow paint, with the words spelling out "Pacifico" buried in areas and jumping out in other areas, marching across the width of the canvas."

"'Strong work,' he said at last. 'Very strong work. Interesting,' he repeated after a few more stares. 'I see some Mexican influence but you've pushed it into an area that the new Pop artists are exploring-- very interesting'."

"'Thank you,' was all I offered in return."

"You seem to be Andy's California counterpart. This is pure L.A. Pop at its best. I want to show you. The museum is booked for a year, but I used to run Ferus Gallery. I can recommend you to them. They'll want to show you sooner. Let's go for a coffee. I want to know more about you."

"We headed about a block away, to a very non-descript diner that I frequented when I needed food and the girls were in school. Walter insisted on it. He liked simple places where artists ate. 'Artists seldom have money for better places, unless they're being treated out,' he said, although all he ordered was coffee. 'So tell me about your life. How the hell did you end up in Mexico? And then with Elizabeth Taylor?'"

"He liked gossip, especially how, in Los Angeles, Hollywood and money mixed in with the art scene. He revealed all kinds of insights about people. Andy was basically a shy and lonely person, so he kept himself busy surrounded by celebrities. Liz was considered sexy to artists, had that certain appeal and the art world appreciated her interest in their undiscovered creations, and Walter revealed that he liked people who liked artists who were not yet famous. His specialty was helping new collectors. 'If these guys buy the right works, then every one of those purchases will end up in museums some day. When I help a collector, I'm really helping a future curator. The curators who are in the museums today are behind the times. Art goes from the artist studio to the gallery to the collector and eventually to the museum. That's the system. I just help it along so the best ones get chosen. Someday, a curator will brag about a painting the museum has, but that curator will never realize that I was the one to first recognize the work when it was in the artist's studio and then helped to get it into a gallery, then hung correctly to sell it to a substantial collector to preserve that work until the museum is ready to accept the donation, which by that time is a no-brainer.'"

"Walter also liked the ones whom he thought had already made history, like Warhol was doing - like Clifford Still and Joseph Cornell - although both were still too minor of a name for his taste and deserved more prominence - like Marcel Duchamp and Man Ray, who were probably the superstars of all time in Walter's book. They were just names I'd read about - super heroes, to me - but Walter assured me that I'd be in the club one day, and I'd be meeting some of them soon enough."

"As famous as they were, they were prominent only in small circles; the outside world cared little for contemporary artists. Therefore, all of these artists were quite accessible to almost anyone who wanted to knock on their door. Walter knew the habits, the wishes, the frustrations of artists, as if he documented their hourly activities. He was concerned if one artist needed a lot of dental work because the pain was preventing the artist from working; he once helped an artist find the cash to get two new tires for a pickup truck, so the art could be hauled from a barn three hours away to the gallery in time for the opening - at which time he encouraged a newly successful assistant producer to go all out and purchase the biggest painting in the show. That was how Walter operated behind the scenes, but academically, he knew more about the history of art than anyone with whom I had ever talked with."

"My life now became his new interest. He was very intrigued how I managed to do so much painting while also trying to make a living and raising two daughters on my own. My fairly simple story about how I became an artist and got to where I was, took a good two hours and two more cups of coffee, by the time Walter stopped asking me detailed questions about my life. He apparently liked to connect the dots - my life to how my art was created. He saw influences I didn't even think about, and he articulated aspects of my work in ways that I could only visually sense but never explain."

"'Keep working, especially on those large ones. They will be the ones that will end up in the museums,' he finally concluded."

"If your girls are still in school, come with me; I'm supposed to meet a New York artist whom I'm sure you know, Barnett Newman."

"'Only from a few art magazines,' I said. 'He's doing very interesting work. Ahead of me.'"

"He's at least twenty-five years older than you. Don't be so impatient. Anyway, you've gone past that era. You're pioneering a new style."

"I tagged along. In fact, I drove Walter who didn't like to drive which made living in L.A. challenging enough, to a hotel in Santa Monica where Barnett Newman was staying. Newman was waiting for us in the lobby, overdressed with a tie, coat and monocle on. If he'd been an actor, he'd have been typed-cast to play an English butler in a mansion from the last century, yet he had pioneered radical art. Walter introduced me and then ushered us out. 'I'm hungry. I hope you are, too,' he said."

"The three of us went to yet another hotel cafeteria. 'I like hotel restaurants,' explained Walter. 'People are just in for a day or two, doing business. And they are open late. I often don't eat until close to midnight. Now how many places can you get a good meal at that hour?'"

"We chatted about art - New York versus L.A., who was creating what, and drank two bottles of house red wine. Barnet was in town for a small show of his work at the L.A. County Museum and Walter and he were going to meet the next day to see how it had been installed. Walter was doing this as a favor, because Barnet trusted Walter more than the curators at the museum. Barnet was chubby, wore an almost white wavy mustache, and was really the nicest artist, as a person, I've ever met. More than once, he asked me to visit him when I got to New York, and seemed interested in what I was creating in my studio. Of course, Walter sang the praises about my work."

"'When you are in New York, look me up,' he repeated. 'I'm in the phone book.'"

"I was amazed that such a famous artist was so casually inviting me to visit and didn't bother with an unlisted number. I managed to get home just when Angie, a young woman who picked up the girls and took them home for snack before I would get back from my studio, was ready to leave."

"'Girls are all set; their dinner is ready in the refrigerator. Yours too,' she said with a satisfied smile."

"'Muchas gracias,' I responded, although we tried to talk English in front of the girls."

CHAPTER 12

"I won't bore you with the next few decades. These connections helped me make more contacts, with an important gallery in New York, with a better gallery in L.A., and with a few museum curators and directors whom Walter pushed my way. My income grew some, as did my expenses, but I managed to maintain a decent life-style for my kids and kept expanding my studio work. I traveled to New York for a few shows, my girls grew, we visited Mexico often - how nice it was to get away when they had vacation especially in the winter months, and although I didn't love the summers, it was still nice enough to spend a month and allow the girls to really improve their Spanish and maintain their family connections. And my love life? Well, I had relationships, but nothing leading to marriage. I came close to one young woman; we even lived together for a year. Just didn't stick. After that, nothing for many years, at least not someone who I felt I needed to take to Mexico with me. I can't say I didn't date, only that I never met the one that could replace Maria. Or perhaps I didn't want to. I was busy being a father and an artist."

"My career did fine, although I supplemented my art sales with some teaching. Nothing that spectacular. I kept in touch, from time to time, with Elizabeth and Richard, even when they were apart. Liz, especially, followed the growth of the girls and my art exhibitions. Her presence always helped, how could it not?"

"Liz and Richard gradually pulled out of Puerto Vallarta; they couldn't get there enough, then they split up and that made it more awkward, and when they got together again, they were just too busy to get there. They eventually just handed me the rights to their half of the beach. So now I owned the entire beach cove. Every time we went, I took the girls there and we tried to spend time and plan additions to our vacation house the way that I use to plan it with their mother. I missed Maria and although her parents of course knew that I dated other women, for a long time, I hesitated bringing anyone down to Sayulita. I didn't want to offend Maria's family with someone else, although I think after several years, they would have welcomed whomever I might have brought-- after all, they were concerned about my happiness as well, and they knew the girls were missing a mother figure in their lives."

"I then did something that angered Liz and Richard. Well, not Richard, he didn't care. No, not angered, but I fear annoyed Liz quite a bit. Not that she said anything to me directly. And I think Richard knew that it was an innocent mistake, or not really a mistake but silly on Liz's part. Anyway, I befriended another actress, a Miss Lillian Lamour. Miss Lamour was an up and coming star, and I just had no idea that it would cause jealousy. After all, Liz was very established, very famous, but you know, we all have our insecurities. I heard Liz was the same way about Marilyn Monroe. And Liz was not the only one. Jackie, as in President Kennedy's wife, the first lady, had been jealous of Liz and feared her husband would have (or maybe already had) an affair with Liz-- which was complete nonsense but you can't be logical about these kinds of things. It was Liz who used to tell me how stupid Jackie had behaved and now she was doing the same thing. In Liz's case, I guess it was convenient that Miss Monroe died, and that conflict went away. But then it was replaced by Miss Lamour, or I don't know for sure, but perhaps others before. But it was Miss Lamour whom Liz saw me with, and she just didn't want to acknowledge my presence, not at the time, and not since. Richard just went along with whatever Liz wanted, so while I was not removed completely, I felt more distant. Is that a polite way of putting it? We did bump into each other a few times, but our friendship never was so intimate again."

"Am I rambling a bit? I'm sure you are now wondering when I might be coming to the point?"

"No, it is quite interesting, although I don't understand why you think I need to hear this with such urgency?" answered Bart.

"Let me jump ahead a few years and tell you what is really the reason that I'm in such a predicament."

"Just take note that the Kennedy presidency had been a game-changer. It brought in all sorts of new intellects as well as glamour folks. A realignment of the powers had quickly gone on-- and many folks don't like change, especially those who were the stewards of power before. That was before you were born, but I'm sure you heard a bit about the Kennedy era."

"Of course. I grew up during the Clinton and Bush eras, but we studied him in school," responded Bart.

"When Kennedy ran for office, he created quite a stir in the Hollywood community. And friends raised a whole bunch of money for the man. When he won, well, it was like the actors all won Emmys. One by one, they found a reason to be in Washington and their managers or agents would let the White House know, so they would receive those invitations for quiet dinners. Kennedy also hung out with the art crowd in Washington, which was not that large, but enough."

"Enter the assassination of Kennedy and then our increasing involvement in the Vietnam War. They seem such distant political acts but you know, even Presidents have strange bedfellows. By now, Johnson was out, and Nixon was in power."

"Why do I repeat about Kennedy even though we were now in the end of the decade, perhaps around 1968 or 1969? Because of what happened next."

"It was about that time that I ran into Andy at a New York function. I had a small work in a large group show of West Coast art at the Guggenheim, and I was negotiating about a show with my SoHo dealer. Andy remembered meeting me a few years earlier, and that I was a friend of Liz's although he didn't really know that I didn't see Liz or Richard anymore after I had accidentally insulted Liz with my acquaintance with Miss Lamour. Perhaps he remembered that Walter had been promoting my work. And he remembered I had something to do with his painting that Liz bought but he couldn't remember that I was the one storing it."

"But Andy tells me that he just started a magazine and that all sorts of reporters are doing interesting stories and one is about Kennedy and the arts, and he mentioned that somehow I knew Kennedy or someone and they were going to contact me."

"He had no real memory of Mary's killing nor that I knew her or witnessed it, but only remembered that somehow I was involved enough to be interviewed, after all, his magazine was called *Interview*, and I was a reputable artist and the magazine tried to include all the celebrities it could, and it would be good exposure for me, and besides, maybe Liz would agree to be interviewed as well, since she was close to Kennedy and that's when all sorts of neat stuff was going on for the arts - well, that's about how he presented it - completely mixed up. He only wanted some names that would look good in his magazine, but you know, once in print, it was not that different from any legit magazine. The fact that a story was produced on glossy paper and distributed nationally on the newsstands gave it credibility."

"I can't say I agreed to be interviewed. I probably just didn't refuse. But that's how the whole thing started. I wondered if he even knew that all this might stir things up again. After all, this was a year after that girl shot

Andy. She was a frustrated writer-actor of some sort. He survived, but I'm sure he didn't want to invite danger. Nevertheless, he was so excited about the magazine, I think he just went with stuff he was familiar with and didn't really think through the consequences. Was he also testing the waters to see if this was the time to reveal his secret?"

"So this very young reporter, a kid really, maybe just out of college, was told to write a story on the Kennedy connection to the arts and to talk to celebrities. Andy gave him all sorts of names, as did the magazine's editor - names to use, to namedrop if need be. Andy told him I was in town so why not interview me."

"The kid called me and I did agree to meet him. We met at a coffee shop in SoHo, down the street from my gallery dealer. We chatted. It was clear he had no idea the theme of the story and was just fishing around for an angle. We discussed how Kennedy had brought in all sorts of supporters from the Hollywood and arts community, how there was talk for the first time in getting the federal government to support artists and museums and cultural projects; how they were starting a new performance space in Washington, new museums there, and a new federal entity to give grants. Clearly, this was ancient history to this reporter, who had been a teenager when all this was going on. It was also pretty dry stuff, as far as he was concerned, for that magazine."

"He then surprised me and asked about Mary's death, and he asked about Warhol paintings and how they connected to the tragic death of the President. Andy must have clued him in on that."

"He asked me about specific folks, like Marilyn Monroe and her affair and death, and like Elizabeth Taylor who was supporting Kennedy and later working on some projects under Johnson - at least showing support. And did I hate Johnson as much as many artists did? And how did I react to the Nixon folks? He brought that up to contrast how Kennedy operated - that he heard that Nixon's staff was censoring all kinds of shows in the D.C.

museums. They even stopped the Corcoran from putting a large sculpture outside because it could be seen from the White House offices, and they didn't like abstract art."

"The more he asked, I could see how he was setting it up for a 'Kennedy was good and Johnson and now Nixon were evil' story."

"Anyway, he came around again to Mary's death, and asked if it wasn't a suspicious death since she was known to have been "intimate" - his word - with Kennedy, smoked pot with him, and was then "taken out" in the manner that she was, and that I was actually there at her killing - kind of like witnessing the Kennedy assassination, he thought. So that opened up all that again, kind of like pulling off a band-aid from a flesh wound that hasn't healed. It hurt."

"I ventured there very carefully but he had the tape cassette going and he kept asking questions. I didn't want to walk out but I couldn't really steer him differently. He wanted to hear more about the gossip. Not much different from any of the cheap dailies that printed crap gossip, except this would be in a four-color magazine and read by the sophisticated art crowd over coffee and bagels."

*****

"The magazine prepped two months ahead, but once this kid reporter had enough stuff to assure a future story, they were able to squeeze into the next issue that was being closed on Monday, a big promo-teaser about what was going to come out in the following issue. So that magazine with its promo - mentioning names - came out a few weeks later."

"Meanwhile, this reporter was figuring out a way to make it more and more interesting, and the more he got into it, the more it looked like the government was into it deeper than anyone had really previously connected them to it. He was new to the reporting game and the more calls he made, the more it got around that the magazine was investigating the relationship with Mary and Kennedy and that there was an artifact out there that would blow open the assassination case. I was aghast that he even mentioned that someone in the arts community was holding a secret that could unravel the Kennedy assassination case. That had to have come from Andy and I couldn't fathom why he wanted to make that known."

"Rather than keep all findings to himself, the reporter thought of me as a friend, and kept me apprised as to the article. Even though I was back in L.A., whenever he got more information that he wasn't sure how it was connected, he called me for either a reaction or for guidance. He managed to dig up all sorts of interesting gossip about Kennedy and artists and Mary's murder. The process he used for his article was like painting on a blank canvas where one stroke would lead to another, but in this case, one sentence led to another, one idea or fact led to five others, and before anyone knew it, he had filled 10 magazine pages with interesting names."

"He had purposely left out any connection to Liz because I'm sure that Andy didn't want that aspect to come back to slap him and so he had that deleted, but I'd imagine that his editor couldn't have helped but to include all the rest of the names. That would have sold copies. The article, full of arty aspects of openings and after-opening parties, did mention a bunch of influential politicians, collectors, museum board members as well as the usual group of well-known artists and Hollywood folks. Prior to publication, Andy called me personally and said it was a fun piece. He sort of said that it didn't really make the matter go away and instead just gave it new life, but heck, that's what his magazine was all about. He really congratulated me on my cooperation, when in fact I said that I was as discouraging to that reporter as I could be. He just laughed. He said that Walter was right about me, as was Liz. After I hung up, I realized that Walter must had been involved with Andy's including me to begin with."

"It was ten days after the teaser was seen in the issue that had just been distributed, as I was crossing Sunset Boulevard, when a dark sedan swerved and came right at me at a high rate of speed. I'd be dead except some pedestrian saw it before I did and pulled me back, behind a lamppost. The car sideswiped the lamppost, almost toppling it, but managed to speed off."

"'That nutcase tried to kill you!' shouted several people around me, and offering to get me off my back."

"I ducked into a store, pretending I was looking at an expensive jacket, to think hard about the implications. Clearly, I was in over my head. I wanted to call someone, Andy, Walter, even Liz. I hesitated. I knew they would not want to be dragged in. Maybe a car was already heading for them? I tried to assess who might be targets based on the story that was being written. Suddenly, I knew that writing words was much more treacherous than painting strokes.

I tried to laugh it off as crazy Hollywood, but you know, it was the first time that I felt that someone had attempted to kill me. My first thought was for my girls; who would take care of them? I started to walk back to my car to drive home and all I could do was to look over my shoulder. Even while driving, I was watching my rearview mirror as much as the road ahead. I think I was sweating a lot. I just didn't know what I had gotten myself into."

"I got back home without incident and luckily the girls were out for the afternoon at a school field hockey game that they were both in. As I walked through the door, I could tell that my place had been ransacked and all my papers had been carefully rifled apart. Nothing had been stolen that I could see."

"I packed a few bags as I waited for the girls. As soon as they appeared, we gathered their school papers and a few clothes and I took them in the car. We went out for dinner and then I checked into a hotel in Santa Monica, several miles from Venice. I was afraid to stay even in the neighborhood."

"The girls were happy watching television and going to bed, while

I analyzed the situation. I had to think quickly what to do. I'm pretty good at envisioning big projects, breaking them down into workable chores, and getting things done. And I'm pretty good about making large decisions quickly. Once I had decided the main question, it didn't take me long to think through the mechanics."

"I had a close friend, Pete, who sometimes assisted me with making stretchers, and with one phone call, I was able to outline my plan. I told him how to look after my place and rent it out, to save most of the money for me but to keep enough to keep him paid for his time. He was a struggling cabinetmaker and I knew he could use the cash and that he was trustworthy. I told him that I could only communicate in a funny way. I assumed that it would be too easy to trace me, so I told him to call his friend, Matt, whom I knew but was not close to, but to wait for 3 weeks. I figured in three weeks, I could send a letter to Matt's address and Pete could go over and pick it up. I also told Pete that I was heading east, near New York, where I had contacts. It was a lie, but I didn't want to take chances. The next morning, I dropped off the girls at school for a short day; I told the school that there had been a family emergency and that we were moving back East for the year, and they would finish the school year there. Meanwhile, I drove home, carefully looked around the block to make sure no one was hiding in wait for me, packed the van to the brink in about two hours, met Pete there to go over some details, picked up the girls at their lunch period, stopped at the bank for cash, and then drove away."

"In actuality, I headed to familiar turf. I drove south to Mexico and went over the border at Tijuana where it was so busy with tourists that not all passports were scrutinized. All that and I was across the border by the evening of the second day.

I kept driving until I got to Sayulita. Remember, in those days, there were no cell phones and cash was used to buy gas. Mail was the primary means of communicating, if one couldn't use a pay phone. If I needed to contact Pete or someone else, I figured I could post a letter by giving it to a tourist to mail once he or she returned to the U.S., and putting a New York address on the envelope. How I could receive a letter or call was more difficult; that would have to wait for a month or two, until I knew someone who might be coming to Mexico on holiday, and if I knew enough in advance, I could give that person's address to Pete by sending it to Matt. That would take a couple of weeks advance notice, but it was possible. All this was to buy us some time. I figured things would settle down after a few weeks, that although perhaps I was a target, I was probably not worth killing after a while. I hoped, at least. Meanwhile, I would be settled in Mexico and long gone from Los Angeles and not easily accessible when the full article would come out."

"Staying near Maria's family had advantages; the village was small enough so that every gringo or stranger coming in was easily spotted and word would get to them immediately if someone looked suspicious. No one knew the details of what had happened to me in the States, only that some bad guys were looking for me and I wanted to stay scarce. In Mexico, that's not so uncommon."

CHAPTER 13

"It was feeling a bit sticky, not yet summer but even in spring, one could sense the coming rains. The sky had enough clouds in the distance to suggest they could congregate into rain although I knew that we were still several weeks away from the first rainfall. The girls were in a private school that had recently opened just south of the airport, a mixture of kids of academically concerned local parents and Americans or Canadians, with just a sprinkling of kids from other countries whose parents had decided to stay in Puerto Vallarta for one reason or another. I was commuting back and forth since driving them to and from school from Sayulita still took almost an hour, although the road was being improved and once the construction concluded, it would cut the drive down to forty-five minutes. It was the one-lane delays that really caused the problems. At times, I took the dirt road the other way, which was about twice as long but at least I could keep moving. Either way, it took almost an hour. In any case, one early afternoon, two hours before I had to go fetch them, a tourist knocked on my door. I say tourist because he was a youngish man in his early 30s, dressed casually in shorts and a T-shirt that was wet in his chest area, holding a bottle of Pacifico in his hand, a Nikon camera around his neck and a brown daypack on his back."

"'Hi, are you Mister Peters?' he said. 'I heard that you used to give tours.'"

"'Why are you all the way out here? I don't give them anymore,' I replied."

"That's okay, because I really want to talk to you about something else."

"My guard went up and I quickly glanced to see if he was with anyone else, or if there was a car or some buddies waiting nearby."

"He sensed my concern. 'Please, don't be alarmed. I walked here by myself from town. I'm here by myself, and what I have to say to you might be of interest. Certainly, nothing to be afraid about,' he stated."

"'What about?' I asked."

"I know why you are here. I know about the men who went after you in L.A. I know about the government connection. But I can tell you that that is over with. No one cares anymore, except for a few folks who think there was an abuse of power. And that's not the way it should be done in America."

"'That's quite a mouthful,' I said, 'especially after coming all this way. If you say it's over with, why did you come to Mexico to find me?'"

"Because you are in interesting key in my story. I'm working for the New York Times and I must say, it wasn't easy to get them to pay for this trip. They thought I wanted a free vacation. But I think there's something you know that will give me what I want. And things in sunlight tend to be safer."

"You mean, advertise my involvement and you hope they won't come after me. Do you know how fast I had to leave?"

"I do. It was not easy to find you. But when one digs deep, one finds the past and your past led me directly here."

"I'm just hoping you don't have a gun in that bag of yours?"

"Go look yourself. I'm a reporter. Not a hit man. Certainly not a CIA guy. Here's my card. I'm Steven Green. A reporter. Here's the number for the Times. Call my office, they'll tell you."

"I eyed him up and down. I didn't invite him in. We just stood in the doorway. 'That's kind of impossible to do from here. Okay, I'll accept what you are. But why do you think that I'm involved in anything of interest? I'm really on the outside.'"

"Well, if I may jump to the point, I'd say the main reason is that you knew Mary Meyers. And you were the witness to her murder. But there's more about you. You knew the story in Washington D.C. You knew the artists who knew Mary. You knew Andy and agreed to be interviewed about this for his magazine. And you were a marked man who had at least one known attempt on your life."

"Andy was crazy asking me to be interviewed. It was because he thought Liz wanted me to have some attention. He didn't know what he was doing, quite frankly. That young reporter went way over the top with gossip. That's all it was. And the attempt, I don't know. I assumed it was an attempt. It could have been a drunk driver, too."

"And did that drunk driver ransack your house?"

"Alright. Someone wanted to get to me, or find my notes, or something. I panicked. Maybe I didn't need to, and maybe I wouldn't have except that I was worried about my girls."

"Indeed you had a right to be worried. What you don't know is that two other people were probably killed as well. And then there are the mysteries. The Marilyn Monroe death. That happened much earlier, but it might have been their early attempts to use undercover agents and to get rid of potential witnesses."

"They? The government?"

"She was connected to Kennedy and Johnson's people knew."

"So why would anyone from the Johnson administration care about that?"

"Because all roads lead back to Texas, I'm afraid."

"You know, Nixon is in there now. That's now ancient history."

"'Not if there's a smoking gun to this.' And he went on to give me lots of background on his research. 'What I want from you are some details--they might not mean much to you but they'll fill in some gaps I have.' I would like it to be on the record, but if not, I'll settle for what you can tell me off the record."

"I ended up talking to him on my terrace. I was careful about what I said. He promised to keep it off the record. At least whatever I added to the story; he wouldn't promise to keep my name out of the information he had prior to coming to Mexico. I wouldn't tell him about the painting. I couldn't. I trusted he enjoyed the extra two days he had to spend on the beach in Sayulita. At the same time, I knew that others would be following. If one reporter found me, others had to be close behind."

*****

"The elders, called Ejidoterianos or Ejidos, gathered in the small white one-story cement building just off the plaza at dusk. This was the equivalent of a town hall. The large room held a capacity of about thirty chairs. With the double doors wide open, wooden and woven straw chairs could be added into the small foyer area and even out onto the sidewalk if needed. The Ejidos annually elected a president, and it was more an honor than anything else. The background was that when land was nationalized and given back to the peasants in the early part of the century, there had been only eight families laying claim to the land, and they were called Ejidos. The village was tiny. Over the years, the families had multiplied, until there were about 200 family members. When the group sold land, the proceeds were divided up. When someone purchased or transferred land, they had to pay a fee-- whatever the Ejidos could reasonably demand - and this income was eventually distributed to the members, according to family rank."

"They'd meet twice a year about town matters; they were the closest thing to a local government although the regional government really had the legal control over the town. The Ejidos would also meet if there was an emergency or if a response was needed to a governmental action or if a member insisted on a meeting for some other reason. It was the result of an urgent calling by my father-in-law that the Ejidos gathered that evening."

"Papa had once been the president and spoke first. 'It is with a heavy heart that I must tell you that strangers might come to our village to injure my late daughter's husband and the father of two of our grandchildren. I want to tell you tonight the background and why we must protect him, and to protect our granddaughters. It is in our self-interest as well.'"

"According to Papa, for the next fifteen minutes, although most was already known to the members since it was a small village, Papa went over the history of 'Felix Peters,' how I fell in love and married their daughter, Maria, had two daughters, how Maria feel ill and died from dengue, how I moved back to the United States but kept visiting Sayulita, and how I was befriended by famous actors in Puerto Vallarta and then how some of my acquaintances were connected to both President Kennedy and then to President Johnson, but how the death of Kennedy and at least one and probably several connections to Kennedy had also met tragic deaths, and how I had sought safety again in Sayulita, but how one reporter tracked me down and that we were fearful of others coming to do harm."

"Several men asked why I could not simply go somewhere else for a while; that there were many places in Mexico where it would be difficult to find me."

"Because Felix knows the connections which have become very valuable, so they will find him again no matter where he goes. Is it not best for Felix and my granddaughters to be among family and friends, who can watch out for them and who can help protect them?"

"'Besides,' Papa continued, 'as you know, he is staying at his place that he built on his land at Playa Carracitos. He is as protected there as anyplace in Mexico.'"

"'And what is this secret that is so valuable?' asked the senior elder of the Ejidos."

"'Felix knows who killed President Kennedy. Not the shooter, but the men behind the shooter,' replied Papa solemnly."

*****

"Papa didn't quite understand how little I knew of anything that might be of importance, but he did understand that I had to take the girls and flee the States, and that one reporter had followed me here. Right after the meeting with the reporter, I knew I needed more distance - at least for a while. I talked to Papa, not Mama. Papa was more realistic about something like this. I told him I wouldn't tell him the specifics, but just generally, I'd be taking the girls away for a few days. My boat had been loaned to Maria's brothers, and I told them that I needed to have it back."

"Unbeknownst even to Papa and Mama, while Papa was preparing for the meeting, I had already prepared the night before for a morning departure. I stocked the panga that still had my Mercury outboard motor attached with oars, two extra metal containers of gasoline, life jackets and other provisions for my girls and me, including three containers of food, warm clothing, lighters, two tents, blankets and an assortment of fishing gear."

"Early that morning, just as the sun was rising, I got the girls ready, and set out on the boat, first going out with the other fisherman and then getting considerable distance before heading south. The waves were a bit rough to get out, but once beyond the breaker, the sea seemed quite calm. I motored around Punta de Mita so the fishermen would assume I was heading to Puerto Vallarta. As we rounded the point, I could see a huge chain link fence where the government was clearing out part of the town in order to sell the land to a big development corporation for a new resort, a sure sign that progress was heading to Sayulita as well. Across the bay, the land curved around like a horseshoe, forming the Bay of Banderas, where Puerto Vallarta anchored the midpoint. Instead of going near the city, I steered the boat dead across the bay and headed towards a small town called Yelapa. Although there was a road to Yelapa, it was so rough, the locals teased that only donkeys could make their way; instead, all building and daily supplies were delivered by boat from a dock south of Puerto Vallarta, near where my friends had made the movie a few years earlier. I got near the shore and then continued south, about another hour, past several long barren beaches where there was hardly a house or building in sight, then stayed away from the rocky shore where breakers exploded with white foam as they slammed into the protruding rocks, and then around yet another small point until I motored into a small inlet nestling a tiny white beach. There we landed on protected waters, to the side of a tiny hamlet that contained no more than a handful of small houses and shacks."

"We beached the boat in front of some vacant land, where I saw a flat space about twenty meters above the beach. Tying the boat to a palm tree in case waves came that far in, the girls and I dragged all the supplies to the flat area and quickly set up camp. To them, it was just a fun camping outing. As we were securing the second tent, four men came up and asked me what we were doing."

"Camping here for a few days. Is that all right?"

"Sure. Where'd you come from?"

"'North of Puerto Vallarta. Near Lo de Marcos,' I replied, being truthful but also avoiding pinning myself down as being from Sayulita, in case anyone came round asking. 'I heard that Tehuamixtle has good red snapper,' I continued, 'are they easy to catch near shore?'"

"'Sure,' repeated the men. 'Good fishing here. Welcome amigo,' they said."

"'Gracias,' I replied in perfect Spanish so they had little hint that I was actually an American. 'These are my daughters.'"

"They smiled and the girls waved in return. We stayed there for almost a week."

CHAPTER 14

"We can take a break here, if you want. Maybe you need to use the bathroom?" said Felix.

"I'll do that. I'll be right back." Bart headed to the front bathroom that was not used as much since almost all economy passengers used the rear ones. He was back in a few minutes, while Felix relaxed.

As he approached, Felix stood up. "Maybe I'll do the same. It's a good time."

Felix was much slower than Bart had been, of course, and elected not to use his cane but returned soon enough. Bart stood up to allow Felix easier access to his seat.

"Thank you. Do you want to rest now? I have more to tell you, but of course, I don't want to push too much on you."

"I'm fine and I'm fascinated with your story. It seems like there were folks who didn't want to hear the truth. Are you convinced that Oswald didn't kill Kennedy by himself?" asked Bart.

"Okay, here's the official answer. Yes, Oswald did it. Alone. He was capable and he had access. All those theories about another gunman and all that, well, that's all bullshit to sell books. That's the government's conclusion. Do you buy it?"

"Not according to your story."

"The actual? He was not alone. There was another gunman. Two. That makes it a conspiracy. That means that they were part of a plot, and part of a group. And that, my friend, opens up a can of worms."

"What type of worms?"

"What they haven't focused enough on, is that Oswald and his accomplice didn't do this in a vacuum. They were encouraged. Perhaps someone else worked it out or perhaps no one planned it except the two gunmen, but they were encouraged to go and find a way to fire those guns. Perhaps a group figured each gunman had a 5% chance. You know, sometimes you win on 5% chances. Either they won on Oswald or they won on the other gunman or they won on both - big time."

"Who are 'they?'"

"They? They are men who decided that Kennedy had to go; they decided that some inside people who were weak or were too talkative had to go."

"And Johnson? Was he involved?"

"This is just my opinion. Conspiracy theorists are looking too hard. No, Johnson would never do it. Would never allow it. Would never authorize it. But, and this is the big but, he wouldn't go out of his way to stop a movement if he only had a hint about it. Any solid evidence, yes, he'd have stopped it all right. But he didn't bother going after groups he didn't know in detail. He must have known that there were loyalists working on his behalf. Not the details, never to pin something on him, because loyal people around him just allowed what they thought needed to be done. And that was encouraging a few Oswalds to become gunmen. If not Dallas, then perhaps this might have happened during a visit to Atlanta, or Detroit, or Miami. And when they succeeded, they panicked, so they encouraged another guy to take out the captured shooter. But it was never one person who planned it; it was a group that simply encouraged it."

"And who was this group?"

"Well, what has not come to light is the Mexican connection."

"I thought there was a Cuban connection?"

"Yes, but from Cuba, men gathered in Mexico where it was easier to access their American contacts - the ones who had the cash. Cuba stimulated a lot, after all, they wanted revenge for Kennedy's attempted coup, but there were other interests who for their own reasons wanted Kennedy out of office. It doesn't take that many to make things happen. That's what most people don't understand. History changes with just a handful of people doing something. So why was Oswald in Mexico City shortly before the assassination?"

"He went there, to Mexico?"

"That's right. Mexico was the meeting ground. He went to the Russian consulate there. Others were there as well, from Cuba, from Columbia, you know, from several countries where folks were unhappy with American intervention. They don't just meet. They get inspired. They get riled up. They get energized. Nothing specific, mind you, but the hatred is stimulated."

"I think I've seen some recent articles in magazines about this. Why now?" wondered Bart.

"Documents are just now being released. They had been classified and buried and now they are being released. It's been decades, so few people care much about them, if the one-gunman conclusion holds up. They are being released based on that conclusion. Once they go over all those documents and then look at them under the new light of a second gunman, well, it might be old, but heads can roll again."

*****

"When I returned from hiding with the girls on my so-called camping trip, this story was told to me by a resident of Sayulita. I'm not sure he knew all the details, but here's what I surmised."

"The men rented a car in Puerto Vallarta, and with a map, found easily their way to Sayulita. But from the village, they then needed to go to one of the beaches; they were told Playa Escondida. Go from the cemetery, past Playa Los Muertos, and take the left onto the small jungle road; don't turn right to the coast because that will be a dead end. Bear right, and then bear right again to miss the point, and then once on the other side, bear right and then bear left. Follow the road down and then up and then down and then up and the second hill, turn right onto a smaller driveway, and that will eventually take you to Playa Escondida. Got that?"

"'Yes, of course. Not a problem,' they replied in unison. They headed out and immediately, they were lost, as the small dirt jungle road twisted around huge rocks and palm trees growing wherever, forcing the road to go around them rather than the rocks and palms yielding to the road. Each quarter kilometer, the path divided and they had to choose which path to take."

"They had no idea, asked the few folks walking the way, each pointing to a new direction. After a while, they thought they were close. They parked their car into the side, brushing the jungle growth against one side of the shiny car, and walked a well-worn path towards the sounds of the waves. After ten minutes of going under palms and on top of trampled growth, they could see the blue ocean squeaking between the trees. Heading down the path, they found a deserted beach, with no houses or people or signs of life, except the constant sound of the waves pounding the sand."

"'There's no one here,' one of the men said. 'We've been bamboozled.'"

"They managed to find their way back to Sayulita. And around the plaza, they spotted the original residents whom they had asked the way."

"No one was there."

"'You didn't ask to find anyone. You just asked to find the beach. We told you correctly,' was the confident reply."

"Yes, but you could have pointed out that Felix Peters would not be there."

"Felix? Why Felix hasn't been seen in - what - two, three months?"

"The men drove off, presumably heading back to the rental agency at the airport in Puerto Vallarta, while the advisor looked at his friends as they all laughed. They had fooled another investigation."

*****

"As they drove off, I appeared. 'Thanks for giving me the heads up.'"

"Why are you here, then? You should still be camping across the bay"

"I was. I came back two days ago. How long can I camp? I didn't know they'd be here today. It could have been next month. That's a long time to camp. Besides, sometimes it's safer to hide in plain sight. They were looking for an American in a remote beach, but not in town. Anyway, you sent them to the wrong beach. They'd have to hike a half-day to find me and by that time, I had come here. I could have kept that up indefinitely."

"Ha, and so you could have. What about the girls?"

"'They went from school to Mama's house. They blend in nicely in town as well. You know what those Gringos say? Mexicans look all alike!' I said with a laugh."

CHAPTER 15

"That was our year in Mexico, my girls and mine. It was actually good for the girls. They saw their grandparents regularly, went to an international school and reconnected with their heritage. I had actually worried that the L.A. scene was spoiling them. That year was a very productive year for me. Having the studio in the house made it easy to work while being there for the girls, who were more independent and helpful to me. I didn't need to spend time earning money by touring tourists. I had rental income both from the Puerto Vallarta houses and my Venice loft, and I had about a dozen major galleries handling my work. Each one made several substantial sales and even after deducting the fifty percent commission, I had a decent income. Remember, unlike most folks, I didn't have any mortgage to pay. But after a year, I knew the experience had run its course and it was time to return, to resume our lives in Los Angeles, and to have the girls finish their school years there so they'd be ready for any college."

"When we resumed our life in Los Angeles, we landed running in place; my kids were thriving in high school and my life was back into a productive groove.

In the latter part of the year my Dad died. I was sad that we didn't have a closer relationship only due to distance and his health. That last year, we spoke on the phone at least twice a week and I managed to get Beatrice and Dad to Los Angeles for a one-week visit early on, before his health problems prevented all traveling. He did the flight fine and we had a very easy schedule while he was there. I was so happy to see Dad reconnect with Daniela and Silvia, and I couldn't say more about how nice Beatrice was. They toured their school, went through our photo albums with them, which was filled with photos of Maria when the girls were toddlers, and I think, in their own way both of them, but Dad especially, came to respect my artwork. As a builder, he certainly was impressed with the production and the size of my large paintings; he appreciated the craft if he didn't understand the historical significance. And when we walked around Santa Monica and peeked into a gallery that had one of my paintings with a $10,000 price tag, that seemed to give my life extra validation - that I had made it."

"When he died, he left Beatrice and me a fair number of assets to divide, so that made being a single father much easier. I went back for the memorial service and Beatrice asked me to go through some family items that she thought were of more value to me than to her."

"You see, these dramatic times do pass. Months and then years roll by. I had almost forgotten about the dangers; the magazine article was a faded memory. I was settled. I think most was forgotten about by the time we got into the 1970s. There had not been a mention from anyone, either publicly or even in a party chitchat."

*****

"The following year, I received an invitation to be in a major show at the Corcoran Museum in Washington D.C. I was excited about showing at a prestigious museum in my old hometown. I was only sad that my Dad was not alive to see me there. I had quickly flown there for a small memorial service, keeping the girls at home. They had had a nice visit by him and I wanted them to remember that. Even after that visit, Dad always sent them letters and presents. I reminded them that Dad had stepped up to the plate as much as he could after their Mom died; he did as much as he could. When his health limited his traveling, I wanted the girls to have exposure to the East Coast for a visit, but then we ran out of time. So I went myself, and dealt with the family household items and tried to help Beatrice. There wasn't much I really could do. I also got together with Alice, and she had not changed; she was still the hostess of the art community, but she had run out of walls in her house to buy much more. Besides, she would remind me, as so many artists made bigger and bigger work, she'd have to buy a warehouse to live in. Her artist-friends thought that was actually a nice idea."

"Among the people I wanted to meet with was Walter Hopps. He had issued the invitation for a show. He had transferred to the East Coast, first by being invited as a fellow at the Institute for Policy Studies in Washington and then, just because he was a genius, soon knew the entire art scene, was asked to direct a fledging new museum of contemporary art, which then merged into the Corcoran Museum which then needed a new director - so was then asked to take that position. Inside of eighteen months, Walter was director of one of the best museums in the United States showing contemporary art in addition to its collection."

"I saw Walter in his office, at the rear of the hall of offices, which was almost a maze to find. The Corcoran, named after the founder and collector, is a distinguished Beaux-Arts building built at the turn of the century to show off the banker's collection. It faced the side of the Executive Office building and one park over, faced the back yard of the White House. To the fear of the Secret Service who observed all the questionable artists roaming about, the White House was within rifle shot of the Corcoran, which made it a building under constant surveillance. The Corcoran had one of the best collections of early American art in the country. Of more interest to me, the Corcoran was the main museum to collect contemporary art and to also show the best of the Washington artists. Gradually, traditional galleries had been repurposed for installing huge paintings and sculptures by contemporary artists, which caused the remaining small spaces to be turned into all sorts of tiny administration offices. To add to the demands for space, about a third of the building belonged to the Corcoran School of Art, which crammed its classes and its own administration into whatever was left in that wing of the museum. Despite this added strain, the school gave the museum a lot of energy with faculty and ambitious art students roaming about."

"Walter had teased me in L.A. that one day he'd curate a show called 'The Mexican Connection.' He was very aware, being from Los Angeles, how much influence resonated from just south of the border. He was interested in artists who were either born there, lived there, or somehow associated with Mexican art. In fact, Walter was as much of an archeologist as an art scholar; he was always classifying artists into various groups by everything other than style. My Mexican background, even though I grew up in Washington, absolutely made me a Mexican artist in his mind. I speculated that if I had never left D.C., he still might have grouped me that way. But the fact that I lived in Mexico, had married a Mexican woman - well, it all added to the allure of my art. Added to the recipe, I was of a specific generation - creating the new art - the next generation of contemporary art, he called it, like a version of the East Coast school - Warhol, Rauschenberg, Dine, Lichtenstein, Oldenberg, those guys. He saw the West Coast school beginning to make their mark. The older guys --Still, Diebenkorn, and guys my age like Kienholz, Ruscha, Irwin, Moses, Bengston, McCracken, Kauffman, Price. I was one of the L.A. Pop artists and he liked to think about the differences in the Pop of New York compared to Pop that was being made in Los Angeles."

"Bart, these are just unknown names to you, but I knew most of them. Artists tend to gather at openings and parties. It was a family of sorts, all doing different things but somehow related. You know, despite all the differences in style and medium, Walter was interested in how a group of us, working at the same time period, made a difference in one city. I was a West Coast artist, but I was also of a specific generation, and I had that Mexican connection."

"'I want six or so of the best artists whose work is linked to Mexico,' said Walter almost as soon as I greeted him. 'Only two will be American. You, and Luis Jimenez. He's like you, born in El Paso, so he's technically American, but he has that pedigree, and was influenced strongly by Diego Rivero and Mario Orozco. I might include Rivera, but his work is hard to get. Kahlo, too, but getting her work is almost impossible. I want to ground this historically, but we'll see. I'm still putting it together. It'll introduce a new name perhaps, the next generation now working in Mexico. What a nice mix that'll be - Rivera, Orozco, Peters, Jimenez, and two surprises. Two deceased and four much-alive artists!'"

"I could tell that Walter was constructing this as he talked. He had not really settled on a final list."

"He wouldn't tell me the others being considered, but he told me for sure that I was to be included. I was definitely in - and this was a big deal - a career changer. He was thinking of a big show at the museum, with only six artists. That would give each artist a lot of exposure and an opportunity to show some big things. I loved the idea. What artist wouldn't? "

"The exhibition was planned for the next year. Of course, in art, there are politics and money issues, no different than any profession. The beauty of this show was that it met Walter's high standards for art, and it had some interesting connections, to the Mexican embassy and to some companies that might be sponsors that dealt with Mexico a lot, and of course, the White House always was interested in putting its two cents in, not surprisingly, often in a subtle way, especially as it pertained to foreign relations, and this seemed to fit their aims to make better ties to Mexico to increase trade. Not to mention that, although I was only one-quarter Mexican in nationality, the fact that Hispanic artists would be included showed that the museum was reaching out to other minorities, as a grand gesture and not as a token afterthought. Grants were being offered to encourage these types of exhibitions. This was important to museums, not just for the money, but because for too long, most museums had been run by the white male Wasps who showed the European-influenced art made by white males. Hardly a female, or black or Hispanic or even an Asian were included in most shows. People had to fight for equal consideration. Walter was different. He liked those who he felt were overlooked. But they had to be good; he wouldn't tolerate showing anything not of museum quality, and Walter's standards were higher than most."

"All this was a win-win. Walter knew my work pretty well, having visited my studio at least a dozen times, and had already thought of a few works he had remembered. He had a photo memory for art, uncanny because at times he remembered a work of mine that I barely remembered myself until he showed me a slide of it. Anyway, he mentioned two paintings that were in my studio, and three that were in collections, and guess what else?"

"I'll want Pacifico. That's your masterpiece. That one will knock them dead. And the Beach Umbrellas; I want those colors here. "

"Which one? I did four big Umbrella paintings."

"Hmm. Not sure. I saw the one in your Santa Monica show. That one. Okay. Those two for sure. And Liz's painting. The one that fills her dining room. It's a bit earlier so it shows how you developed. She'll lend it for sure. Those are three definite ones. And your Boat painting. You know, the one where you attached the fishing boat on the right side. That's your biggest, isn't it? It'll cost more to get here due to the weight and size, but it'll be worth it. That's where - in Oakland isn't it? They'll lend it. That's four. We'll go through your slides and figure out the others. I'll pick some medium sized works to balance the show."

"That's how he worked; he did in two minutes what a young curator would take a month researching. I could see Walter's eyes mentally hanging the works on the museum walls as he was thinking about them. He was creating the list of works and curating the finished show within the same thought."

"His instincts were right on, both on the art and practical. For Liz's painting, I think he liked both the painting itself and the idea that the label would show that it was on loan from actress Elizabeth Taylor. Owners often liked to lend to museum shows; it gave their works prestige and often increased the values. The museum would arrange for the transportation and insurance during the three-month exhibition, and for any venues the show might travel to after its first date at the Corcoran."

"The show was planned to open the night of the Corcoran Ball. That was the biggest art fundraiser in the city, the 'social event of the season' as they say, so it would be a special opening, black tie with food and drinks to no end. Everybody who's somebody would be attending, even White House officials. Maybe the President would attend although he was not known to enjoy museum visits, but his press people forced a few to make him seem well-rounded. You need to understand that an incredible forty percent of Americans are active somehow in the arts - as amateurs - they paint, play in a band, sing in a choir, take photographs, write, act, and so forth. As it turns out, not everyone has a dim view of artists, much to the dismay of the right-wing politicians."

"Walter outlined all this to me as he got more and more excited about the project. He preferred to continue chatting in his office, and so sandwiches were ordered and delivered to us. I chose the tuna salad and he had the roast beef."

"It's really curious. I'm doing a Mexican theme and here you are, in my show, and a Washington native, no less. Strange if I think about it."

"Well, only as a kid. I grew up here. I came to the Corcoran a bit, but really, I was happier in the National Gallery. I could slide my shoes along that smooth marble and look at Rembrandts and Titians and I even got my first view of a Van Gogh."

"That was before sneakers became popular!"

"That's right; we all wore leather-soled shoes then - great for sliding.

When I came back to D.C. on a visit as an art student, the jewel, of course, was the Rothko room at the Phillips. That and then a real introduction to the Corcoran, which I never paid attention to in my youth."

"I wonder why you didn't go to art school here?"

"I simply wasn't ready. Or my Dad steered me a different way. Mom died when I was a teenager so I never had her guidance. I think she was more into the arts. I'm glad I changed. I didn't really get any encouragement to see or participate in new art. I think the schools here were a bit traditional, at least back then. When I was being introduced to abstract art on the West Coast, schools here were still teaching still life painting. Most likely I got better exposure being where I was."

"Washington has matured. It's a different town now."

"Indeed it is. You're a driving force here. Please let me know what you need from me for the show."

"'I will. By the way, whatever happened to your Warhol painting?' he suddenly remarked."

"The what?"

"The painting that Taylor gave to you?"

"You know about that?"

"Andy told me. I haven't said a word. But you know, someday, that painting in this museum would create a great show."

"But it's been seen, in her house. Why is it so important?"

"It's the history. Somehow, the history has to come out."

"Do you know that history? I mean, what did Andy tell you?"

190

"Too much, perhaps, for your comfort. Enough to make me interested. Oh, I don't know it all, so that makes me more curious. I know that there's a secret attached to it and all he kept saying was that I have to see it for myself and then I'd know. He almost couldn't contain himself he was so excited. Yet he just couldn't tell me what it was. It's my business to know about important art. Do you know more?"

"I really don't. I was asked to do a favor and I have it. That's about it. I know that there are connections. I once had to flee L.A. because of a reporter writing too much about it and putting my name down. They tried to kill me. Ransacked my house. I was fearful of my two daughters, so I scrambled out of there so fast it would have made your head spin. I stayed away for almost a year before I thought I'd be safe to return. Not sure why I thought the smoke had cleared…but it did. And the longer I was back home, the more I forgot about it. Just you mentioning it brings back disturbing feelings. Not just there, but here in D.C. I wonder how many others Andy has confided in? It's less of a secret now, isn't it?"

"That's hard to say. Most people don't really pay attention to Andy. He can barely articulate a paragraph in public. But I listen, carefully. I know how to connect the dots."

"I'm sure the government knows how to connect the dots as well."

"They might. This can be a rough town, I know."

"You know about Mary, too, I suspect?"

"Yes, I know all about her and what happened. I'm also a good friend with Alice. But I had heard about that connection while in L.A., just after I met you, when I wanted to know more about you. And now as director of the Corcoran, her work has come again to my attention. It deserves to be protected - to be shown? Don't you think?"

"More than most, I would want that. She didn't deserve to die. I'm angry with the government. I must confess I am of the opinion it was a hit job. It had to be."

"You've had your toes in some intrigue, haven't you?"

"Not of my asking, really."

"Well, it's the butterfly magic."

"What do you mean?"

"The butterfly. This guy Lorentz, he first theorized it. A butterfly flapping its wings in Brazil can cause a tornado in Texas. Well, the places have changed in each version, but that's the idea."

"So I might be that one butterfly that can cause a political tornado in D.C.?"

"I don't know. The trouble is, it's never possible to trace back the path - to find out where that first flapping occurred. But I wonder. It's sometimes possible to believe that the flapping can lead to something important."

"You know, in the middle of Mexico, there's a place that my late wife and I visited, about three hours past Guadalajara, near Morelia. It's a national park called El Rosario. You have to go to a tiny village called Angangueo to get there, then climb up a mountain. There, each winter, millions upon millions of Monarch butterflies migrate, to the same place, always to bask in the sun but not to get overheated. It's a delicate balance of environment that they demand. Cool at night but not too cold, and warm during the day but not too warm. They choose this one tiny area in all of Mexico. And not the same butterflies return. I mean, it takes four generations for the mariposas to make the journey, so they are fourth generation butterflies that resume their place in the same trees in the same patch of forest year after year. The other generations die during the long migration."

"How does that generation know where to return to each year?"

"That's the big question. Millions upon millions, traveling 3,000 miles from northern U.S. and Canada, and finding their way back to one small area. They bunch up on top of each other for warmth during the nights, and when the sun starts to come out, they flap all the time. They then fly about. When you peak at the sky between the tall pines, there are so many that they look like snow flakes drifting about. If each can cause a tornado, I wonder if they keep things in chaos in the world? That's your theory, at least."

"So what's the Mexican version?"

"The locals believe that the Mariposas contain the spirits of those departed. They're ghosts, so to speak, flapping about in the breeze. It's a wonderful part of the world, high up in altitude, away from the big cities. It's hard to walk up there - it's about 3,000 meters."

"You, my friend, are my Mariposa. I see Rivera's spirit in you. You are the generation who's doing the flapping now."

"And you, Walter, are the guy who loves to find that first flapping."

"Yes, that might be true. There are Mariposas all over. Only a few will cause something to happen, but they must be protected - all of them. After all, they are all very delicate."

"You mean Mariposas or artists?"

"Is there a difference? And you say that this is now a park. So the area is protected?"

"It is. You have you walk very carefully; you aren't even allowed to step on one of them."

"You see? This museum…it's my park. It's to preserve your work. It's to allow you to flap to your heart's content. I should call the show, 'El Rosario.'"

CHAPTER 16

"A year later, I took the girls and we flew straight to Washington. They were both old enough, 'young ladies' I referred to them as, and this was their first long gown event. They had been to many art openings but this was something different, like a Hollywood premiere. They looked so grown up. I was one of six stars in the show and one of three artists attending. I was as proud of them as they were of me."

"Imagine walking up the stairs to the main entrance of the museum. Limousines were parked outside, the lights of the building lit up the street, and everyone donning black ties or long gowns. The Ball committee had made no compromises on lobby and table decorations, for the food and drinks, for the service - they knew how to throw a party."

"Walter had only joked about the title. He stayed with "The Mexican Connection." The art was displayed prominently. Each artist had a photo and bio enlarged and mounted downstairs along with the director's statement and the acknowledgement of the sponsors. Then up the double marble stairs to the main galleries, Walter had given each artist one or two galleries, depending on the size of the work. My work was hung just to the left of the stairs, in one of the better galleries, I thought, with twenty-foot sky-lit ceilings, the original inlaid wood floor, and big beautiful white walls that made my paintings - all done in the past six years, with one earlier work and one very recent work - look like a million dollars. Three of my paintings were among my largest; one was ten feet by thirty feet wide and two were twelve by eighteen feet wide. I say paintings because they were hung up on the wall, but in fact, all but one had objects attached, that's often called a relief, so they stuck out about a yard or more. I had only seen these paintings on my studio wall where I could back up about twenty-five feet, and here they were in a major museum exquisitely displayed. They were impressive from the far side of the museum's atrium as well as close up. I had seen them during the day when the show was being installed, but the bright lights - with the skylights dark since it was evening and with all the people dressed up - gave everyone's work an extra glow. It was quite something, if I may say so myself."

"I couldn't help to think that if my reputation were ever in doubt, it would be getting a big boost from this show. The show was scheduled to travel to four other cities - Miami, Cleveland, Houston and San Francisco. That would be quite a lot of exposure over the next year and a half. And then Walter had arranged for a smaller version to go to secondary university museums in Milwaukee, Wilmington, Williamstown, Omaha and Phoenix during a two-year period."

"At the Corcoran Ball, there must have been over a thousand people attending. I was one of the stars of the evening - so many people were coming up to me to congratulate me on my work. Of course, not everyone knew who I was. The museum failed to give me a flower or nametag or somehow to let guests know that I was one of the artists. They finally made a brief presentation in the downstairs lobby, and I had a chance to stand up and be recognized."

"After the remarks, everyone wandered the museum galleries. Alice was a great help and escorted the girls around the exhibition and introduced them to a few friends who had patience to talk to teenagers, allowing me to be free to stray into other galleries and mingle. I learned to answer the most standard questions with sound bites - mostly, my stimulation came from the bright Mexican colors and items found in Puerto Vallarta, and yes, Elizabeth Taylor came often to my studio and purchased that painting herself, and it wasn't easy to attach the top portion of an actual Mexican panga boat to the painting, and yes, Mexico is actually safe and you don't have to get sick if you are careful about eating cooked food and bottled water or beer, and yes, Pacifico is actually a beer that's popular all over Mexico and in fact, more popular than Coke."

"That was the bulk of it, but it was nice that people were genuinely excited about my work. Some guests, of course, were highly sophisticated, and they were pleased that the Corcoran had ventured south of the border for such an exciting result."

"As I kept sipping white wine and nibbling on the tiny desserts being passed out, someone I almost didn't recognize came up to me. I automatically smiled as I had smiled at everyone that evening."

"'Felix, I want to congratulate you on your work?' With that, he held up his glass of wine and clinked on my glass."

"'Charles!' I said suddenly realizing who he was. 'I haven't seen you since the…. memorial. How have you been?'"

"As best as I could. I hear you went through the loss of your wife, too. I'm very sorry."

"Thank you. It was several years ago. Did they ever - I shouldn't ask - but did they ever find out?"

"No, not officially. They tried to pin it on some poor sap who was in the area, but the judge threw it out of court. I just want to tell you that I saw your name on a list. Be careful. Stick to your art, and you'll be okay."

"A list? Why me? I'm just an artist."

"That's all you might be, but you have friends. Taylor. And Warhol.

They drag your name in. And your connection to Mary."

"Why does the government care about artists?"

"If all you did was paint or perform, they wouldn't. But when you meddle in our field, the boys don't like that. Too out of control, you are. When you try to influence how government works, and when you do it by going to the top, well, there are those who can't stand by to watch that happen. I'm not saying it's right. It's just the way it is. Like Mary."

"I don't see what Mary did to deserve that."

"She didn't deserve it. I'm still so angry. She might have had her work on these walls."

"Walter Hopps mentioned that he wants to show her work. That's at least something that can be done."

"That's generous of him. I'll follow up on that. Thank you for your support….of Mary. That meant a lot to me. Listen, even here, they might be watching us. We've been talking long enough. Better you drift off and greet others."

"With that, he spotted someone else, and dashed off to make an obvious greeting. I turned my head to pretend I was going to talk to someone else but it was hard to stop thinking about Mary. Then two women came up to me. 'We heard you live in Mexico. Do you speak Mexican?'"

*****

"I loved the Corcoran and I loved how Walter put the exhibition together. But Walter's tenure barely survived my show. He was just too talented - probably too independent, in my view. That was the heyday of the museum. Being in Washington, there were all sorts of pressures on the board members. He was shortly afterwards forced to resign, but thankfully picked up by another museum. The Corcoran had many political scandals, and almost went down the tubes when a right-wing husband of a subsequent director conspired with a Senator to cancel a controversial photography show by a gay-black artist, whom the Republicans didn't think measured up to the sanitized standards of their party, and consequently they got negative press around the world, and once again, stirred up the art world to the degree that artists actually organized protests outside the museum. The museum continued to slide, until eventually it went bankrupt and was sold to the National Gallery of Art. So I was lucky, in a moment of time, to have a great museum doing great exhibitions under a great director-- those things do not often come together and when they do, they don't usually last."

"As we flew home to Los Angeles after the Corcoran opening and some after-reception parties, I couldn't help but think about Walter's inquiries about my Warhol painting. That gave birth to the idea of how to introduce it to the public - as part of an exhibition - but at the time, I didn't know how important showing the painting might become."

"Alas, if Walter were still at the Corcoran, or still alive and directing some museum, I'd be dealing with him instead of negotiating this show myself. But he passed away many years ago. So I had no choice. At my age, almost all my peers - artists or curators or patrons - are retired, senile or dead. Walter would have done all this for me, but instead, here I am, flying by myself to New York to get ready for a show that I had to arrange. Maybe I waited too long? Maybe I made things difficult for myself?"

As Felix paused, Bart asked, "that Charles - Mary's husband - I gather he really was CIA and all that?"

"That's what Mary implied. He never said. I don't know for sure."

"What ever happened to him?"

"The last time I talked to Charles directly was at that opening. He must have realized why Mary was killed. But the baby - his unborn baby - that would put anyone over the edge. I'm sure he was going to follow through and get even. Remember, those were the years when all sorts of unsavory stuff that the government was doing got exposed in the newspapers. Those investigative reporters had insiders giving them tips. Remember the Pentagon Papers? It wasn't many years later that Nixon fell because of Watergate. Do you suppose an angry inside informant would have been the catalyst for Nixon's downfall? I always wondered if Charles had a hand in those scandals."

"That's very possible, I suppose," said Bart. "Never underestimate someone who wants revenge, I always say."

"I did hear a few years later that Charles left the State Department, or the 'agency' depending on what you believe. Maybe he retired or maybe he was forced out. I lost track of him after that."

CHAPTER 17

"You know, Felix, about the Kennedy conspiracy theories, that's pretty much old stuff. It was in my high school history book. No one my age questions that anymore. The report seemed to have nailed that coffin shut."

"Perhaps. The government had their official investigation and tried to end the speculation, but there are still lots of questions. Maybe not from your generation, but from my generation - from the folks still alive. Do you really think there's only one conclusion?"

"The one gunman theory?"

"Yes. That Oswald acted alone, dreamed it up alone, and so forth? Yes, yes, perhaps he got stimulation from his ideology and such, but in the end, he was the gunman? That's the final answer. And all other theories then become wild speculation to sell books, to sell newspapers, to keep the dialogue going, and that those who question are kind of radical or oddball speculators compared to the sober, intelligent, diligent, solid investigation that the government officials carried out and that the administration gave credibility to?"

"So that's not the end then?" asked Bart.

"The problem is that life is rarely so simple. It just isn't. One party doesn't like another party, or wants something where other parties are becoming an obstacle. So this party suggests things to others that a certain party is impeding success, usually financial success, and that another party then takes the suggestion that someone has to be dealt with to another party, who then undertake an independent plan to perhaps do something a lot more drastic than the first imposed party had ever considered, but now it's late to reconsider because things are already in motion, so this new party then thinks, hey, we can't get into this dirty stuff ourselves, but we can certainly advocate certain ideas to some fall guy, someone stupid enough to do it just for the glory, or for some implied reward, most likely not monetary but in changing history, so by the time the methods are suggested, it's five, six, perhaps ten moves away from original parties, and so when this lone gunman went to work there really was no one you could point to who had the plan, initiated the action or knew what was going to happen. No, perhaps all the way down the line, it was as much of a surprise - let me correct that, a pleasant surprise - as it was a tragic surprise to the public. But if the government had been able to have enough time with Oswald, perhaps they could have learned of the most recent stimulation which then might have led them to the next in line, and so forth, but again, we would have had the same process all over again, investigating a second stunning success in taking out the gunman by still another radical, who probably doesn't even remember who or how the idea ever got suggested to him that he could become the judge and executioner for the greatest murderer in history and that the American public would call him a hero. No, just a couple of stupid men who were easily manipulated by a chain of parties who really had no plan when they started but probably hoped that if they suggested enough, something would eventually happen."

"But when does the money come in? None of that is free, you know," stated Bart.

"There are so many political action groups, at some point it goes down the line and someone feeds some money to keep the so-called "research" going. Only at one point, research morphs into gun purchases, airline tickets, hotels, and stuff - it's just part of the chain."

"So are they all guilty of murder? That is, if you found the members of the chain?"

"Yes, in my mind. Legally, that's a tough question because just by saying that someone is causing you a political or financial headache, and then four months later someone shoots that person dead, does that mean you are guilty of murder? No court would ever say so, so they are the smart ones. They must know that something not right will eventually happen."

"It sounds like we can't win, the good guys, that is?"

"I can tell you that once in a blue moon something goes wrong, something blows up in their faces, and then it's pretty obvious. But the public is slow at putting the pieces together to see how often it happens. Why just a few years later, it happened again but it blew up right near the middle of the process. You must remember the Watergate fiasco. That was the same process but the chain was much shorter and it pulled in White House folks. Even so, the President could have been saved but he was stupid enough to insert himself into the mess and you know how that ended. But you know, that process could have continued and ended up with a murder or two and by that time, no one would have connected the dots back to the White House. But they bungled a burglary and so history was altered. In Kennedy's case, he was dead and the chain had gotten too long to figure it all out, especially since they got rid of the main source. That's the real history. Not exciting stuff. No one saying, 'Go out and assassinate a President, and here's a half million dollars.' That's just fiction, for movies. That's not how it really happens."

"So it's a complicated process. No obvious bad guys?"

"Lots of bad guys, but so many that there are few ringleaders. At least the ringleaders end up being so far removed they are never caught."

"Never?"

"Hardly ever. Take the two Mexicans on this plane who want me dead."

"You really don't know that, Felix. Let's not hang them before we know."

"Not for sure, but let's pretend I'm correct....and they kill me. Then what? Let's pretend that they screw up and get caught. They'll claim what? That it was a robbery attempt? The murderers will say that I tried to kill them and they defended themselves."

"Against a ninety-four year old? That's a pretty lame defense, don't you think?"

"It doesn't matter really. Some lawyer will find some story, some technicality, and they'll never say who paid them to be on the plane to begin with. Maybe someone will put a knife into them while in prison and that will end that. How many links up the ladder could anyone possibly go to find someone who first had the idea that it might be better if I'm not around to announce to the world that there's proof that other people were involved in eliminating a President? It'll just never come out - unless, as I said, something blows up in someone's face prematurely. Then it's a newspaper's dream, like Watergate, but even that took time to come out."

"And you think that once a few names are questioned in this new investigation, that much more will come out?"

"The problem is, it happened more than half a century ago. Probably some names have long since been lost in the shuffle. Many suspects are dead. We might have suspicions but we will never be able to make the accusations to their faces. It's possible that a few of the main characters are still quite alive and active, perhaps in their eighties. Where are they now? What might they be thinking?"

Bart nodded in agreement with Felix's point. "It's not like a movie ending. The thing is, they never show the stars twenty years later. Maybe they are too old and feeble to care anymore? Maybe the public is too?"

"Someone cares," responded Felix. "If not the principals, then their children, or whoever took over the business. Someone will care."

*****

"So my story moves through the years - I showed regularly and once in a while I would hear from someone like Walter or Andy, not Liz but Alice, and someone brings up these events, and about these connections and perhaps something about my painting which I had hoped the world has forgotten that is stashed at my beach house. It's out there. Maybe a rumor gets heard by the government, and maybe by the other side. How could they not hear? If it's chatted about, rumors take off. Andy forgets to be careful and spills the beans to someone. Alice, still in the middle of society and art in D.C., does she ever forget what they did to her friend Mary? Charles, he wants revenge; do you think he ever stops looking for the killers? If he opens some doors, do any of his actions backfire and get traced back to me? He said I was on a list - how does my name get off that list? Liz, I doubt she said a word to anyone, but you never know, drinking, taking too many meds and talking about old times… and Walter, he still wanted to build a show around that painting. He knew enough and figured if he did a show, all of what he didn't know would be revealed. He was very curious. He had a good nose for a good show and good art and a historical spin. For my part, I kept worrying about the bad guys. They were out there. Someone or some group could ignite the fires all over again."

Felix took another pause and Bart decided to ask, "You think there are bad guys? You've been so involved with this for so many years, surely they'd appear by now if they existed, so maybe they don't exist. And where are these ringleaders, or whoever might be left? After all, if there is danger, then they must be around somewhere."

"Look, I think you consider this to be just the wild imagination of an old man, but I know how it works. My end can come anytime - at my home, as I walk the street, or even now, as I sit in this airplane. How is it planned? It can be a small group sitting in a modern office building, or in a government office, or it can be in someone's home. They could be meeting in hush tones or they can be playing cards and chatting as casually as you and I are talking. If you want to know how I think it's happening, I'll give you a reasonable scenario of how they might be operating, even after so many years. I think there's a Mexican group behind it and I think they are still around. You know, cartels and Mafia gangs and evil political groups are made of people who live daily lives, go home for dinner, go to bed each night and even tuck in their children. Here's my version."

*****

"Eight friends, including spouses, visit San Cristobal, Mexico. They had traveled there for a weeklong vacation, taking in the sights, shopping for amber jewelry and knitted clothing, enjoying beers and tacos and feeling the bright warm days and the cool nights, needing just the lightest of jackets or sweaters. At 2,000 meters high, San Cristobal is far away from the international tourist routes, located in south Mexico with the most convenient airport being almost two hours away at Tuxtla Guierra, but still popular with Mexican tourists who love the clean and charming city that was named one of Mexico's top authentic destinations.

"Although mostly retired and on vacation, the four men had much to talk about during a lunch in a restaurant, while their wives went out and surveyed all the stores, especially eyeing the best amber jewelry in the world at very affordable prices."

"'This new investigation thing, it's good to sell some newspapers, but not for us senior citizens. Now I hear someone is going to prove that we were involved,' said Mario, who clearly held the senior position both in age and influence."

"'That could bring back all sorts of new inquiries,' said Leon, a small person physically who used to control all the finances for the cartel's activities. 'I just don't want to go through that again. I don't want the attention and I don't want to work to keep some of the gang mum.'"

"'Besides,' added the third man, a big, rotund guy named Sam, 'we are really out of the action now.'"

"'Yeah. How we gonna find new talent? All our guys are dead by now,' agree Leon."

"He said it seriously, then thought about what he had said, and thought of a few names and then laughed out loud. 'Can you see the Stealer holding a gun now? He has the shakes! If he's still got his thing pumping. He might be dead as far as I know.'"

"The fourth was a quiet, serious man named Luis. Luis was the loner, and usually didn't like to travel with others, but was persuaded to come with the group. In some ways, because it was a new experience to be so social, he was enjoying himself, and enjoying the fact that his wife was enjoying the trip, but disturbed at the conversation. 'I don't think we have a choice,' he said with a grim look. 'If that evidence turns up, we won't stop an investigation. Those documents have done enough damage, but they don't point to us. But my man showed me a notice that we will be named - that we were involved. If that happens, then all those we haven't controlled or silenced will start to speak up. And new talent? I can find that. Don't worry about that.'"

"Say, whatever happened to that guy we couldn't find?"

"They were many. Which one?"

"Not so many people who are left."

"Oh, the one that fled to the coast. You know, the one that was close to that actress."

"Elizabeth Taylor? That one?"

"Yeah, that one. He's got some sort of evidence against us. You remember? Maybe he's goin' talk?"

"We gotta stop him. How we gonna find them anyway?"

"That notice says where he's going. I hear it's going to be a one-way ticket there."

'So if some of our guys are still kicking, we'd better do something? But how? We ain't been so active these days."

"We'll call in a specialist. We're too old."

"That guy who went to Puerto Vallarta area. He's close by, but we didn't find him then, how we gonna find him now?"

"All this time, we thought he's dead. He'd have to be our age at least. Maybe older. Maybe his ticker ain't working no more."

"Hey, someone that old. It can't be hard, can it?"

"Sam finally spoke. 'Look you guys. We're old. Why are we so worried? Won't matter what they find. We'll be dead soon enough.'"

"'Maybe you at your weight,' replied Leon who often teased Sam at weighing three hundred pounds, 'but not me, I hope. Hey, I'm turning 79 next week. I have a decade or more. That's a long time. I don't want to spend that time in prison. Or even in court. I don't even want to see a policeman show up at my door. Neither do you. I don't care after that. I don't care how my name is remembered. I just want to enjoy the warm weather and freedom. I'm not rich but I have enough to relax. I don't need a new commission smelling around old sealed boxes, if you get my drift. And the only thing that will get them excited is if they find a few of the survivors.'"

"'Yeah,' said Mario, 'only the ones that they can drag into the AG's office and in front of a grand jury. And as I think about who those names are, I can only come up with a handful.'"

"'Who? Who are they?' asked Sam."

"You know who they are. That guy we called the enforcer. He supplied the guns. That older guy who was the spokesman. He made sure it all went together. That guy who fled to Mexico; he knew the connections. Never found out how he got into that, but he knew the names. That back-up shooter. He also fled. The others, they're dead. Maybe one or two of these guys, too. I know the spokesman and the enforcer are alive. Not sure on the two who fled."

"That back-up shooter. He died. I'm sure."

"So that leaves three."

"The spokesman, he also moved to Mexico. I hear Acapulco."

"And since we are in Mexico, we'll go talk to him. I think he can be found."

"What about the other? Do you know where he is?"

"When we tried to get him, we were told Puerto Vallarta. Couldn't find him but we were told he went to one of the towns just north. It's been a long time, but you know, I'll bet his guard is down and I'll bet we can pick up his scent easy. Just because we lost the trail before, don't mean we won't find it now."

"We can find them. Then we hire some help, if you know what I mean. There's a lot of talent out there."

"Then we have a few days work to do. The wives can stay and shop. Just tell them we need to go on a three-day business trip."

"How about we go on a three-day fishing trip on the coast? They'll buy that."

"Give them a fistful of pesos and they won't ask nothing."

"So, you see Bart, they send their man to go looking for me. I'm the one that seemed to have escaped notice, the one that got away only because the need to eliminate me diminished before I was assassinated. My good luck. That's all. Others didn't have such good luck. But now everything is stirred up again. And I did the stirring - I'll have to admit that."

"But you are here, alive and well," said Bart.

"Yes, they probably found me but they are too old to do the job. So they must have hired someone, maybe to do it quietly. I don't know. Maybe those two sitting in economy class."

"Or maybe it's just your imagination, Felix. Really, you are in a safe airplane, you'll be landing at a secure airport with police all over, and then you say you'll be picked up and taken to where you are going. It's a slam-dunk. I wouldn't worry so much, if I were you."

"If something happens to me now, it's probably my own fault. I could have left the painting hidden. If I had died naturally, no one would have ever discovered the secret. I certainly could not have left the answer with one of my kids, or grandkids; I would never put them into danger. No, I had to do it while I still could do it."

"I saw the two men come aboard - the ones you eyed; they didn't look like killers to me."

"I got a good impression of those two men in the airport. I'm not being paranoid about that."

"Then why did they let you get on the plane rather than eliminate you at the airport or even before you left home? I'm not claiming to be an expert in assassination techniques, but it's more likely that those two men are not your killers."

"If they are not, someone else might be."

CHAPTER 18

"So let's assume you are correct and your life is in danger," said Bart, "you still haven't told me why someone would want to kill you. Where was that proof, that piece of evidence that you claim will bring out all the bad guys again? It has to be more than a painting and in any case, you say that painting disappeared."

"Ah, the big discovery? I'll tell you now. You'll finally know why I'm on this very airplane. Years later, I was back at the beach house. The girls were past college, married, with their own families by then. Since they were independent, I had a flexible schedule. I had my exhibitions, I had my studio work progressing but if I wanted to, I could work for a month, six months, even a year in Sayulita and mothball my L.A. studio."

"Even with the growth of Sayulita, my private beach was a good mile away from the hubbub, and few tourists bothered to walk the jungle roads to get there. The studio I constructed on the spot where Liz and Richard were going to build was a perfect and quiet studio retreat for me. That didn't mean that occasionally I wouldn't see a person or two strolling the beach, but more often than not, it'd still be deserted and all my own. Even if a few people did make it there, they would not climb up the steps to my house or studio, which had fences and gates and signs proclaiming it was 'off limits' and 'privado.'"

"There was nothing special about that day. I had worked in the studio and had a visitor who left shortly after lunch. Late in the afternoon, after I had wrapped up a couple of smaller drawings, I took my usual glass of wine and sat in my swing chair, trying to relax and enjoying that magnificent sea vista that was always awaiting me from my terrace. I happened to see a figure in the distance, and for some reason, that made me apprehensive about whether I'd see others strolling below on the sand and who they might be. It was just my imagination running wild, but I wondered about all the events, and in my mind, I had to go back many years, through many memories, to make sense of where I was. Why would the bad guys or the government guys or even some investigative guys want to find me, and perhaps to kill me? What made my life so special? And why come all the way to Mexico? What else was going on?"

"I recalled my life during the early 60s, about Maria and about my relationship with Liz and Richard, and then my L.A. days, and then my Washington D.C. connections, and to the obvious events from that period. I poured myself a second glass of red wine - Argentina Malbec most likely - and as I did so, I looked up and saw through the door opening into my office a slice of the large Warhol painting that had been hanging all these years. I recollected the circumstances of Liz giving me the painting and asking me to hide it here, and giving me the letter and then much later, giving me an typed legal document of ownership. The painting had not been touched in all these years except for the times when I moved it out from the storage room to display it, depending on whether I was in residence, and then back again. For some reason, and I don't know why, I put my glass down, walked into the room and pulled the painting off of the hanging hooks. I carefully stood it down against the doorframe so I could peek at both sides of the canvas. Especially, I was curious anew about the back. On the raw canvas were the usual signature and notes about the name and date and artist done in permanent ink marker - nothing unusual. The frame was a simple strip frame, popular at the time, with a dark walnut side and a painted gold-leaf on the very narrow front, nailed onto the edge of the canvas with a thinner black strip serving as a shadow spacer."

"I wanted to get it into a better light, so I moved the painting about two feet to my left. Funny, I had moved and hung this painting a few dozen times over the years. Why did I just now notice that it felt a bit heavy? Perhaps because I was older and not as strong, I wondered? At least it felt heavier than the stretcher and canvas should have been. Warhol didn't use very thick paint, so that would not have added to the weight. And the frame and shadow strip were standard moldings - flat and light weight. Why did it feel a bit off to me? I was used to lifting and handling canvases. I often used #10 cotton duck, which was unprimed canvas that I then primed with gesso and then painted on. #10 is pretty thick, probably as thick as anyone would use for a large canvas. This just felt heavier, which made no sense. I could see Warhol using a lighter weight canvas, but certainly nothing thicker and heavier. Why was this abnormally heavy?"

"As I picked up the painting by the side frame to reposition it for better light, the side strip frame pulled off a bit, enough to get a finger in. As I was about to push it back onto it's nails, I noticed a funny extra bump on the canvas material that was normally hidden by the frame."

"I might have just pushed the frame strip back in and be done with it. Instead, I gently pried the frame strip off that side of the painting, and then pulled off the thinner shadow strip of wood painted black on its edge. Once those two strips were removed, I saw that there was a vertical edge - a bump really - running down the entire side of the canvas. The wood stretcher should have been smooth. Something was under the canvas. I then found my hammer and a flathead screwdriver, and removed the frame strips from another other side. This odd edge seemed to run around the entire canvas. It was as if the canvas was stretched over something that didn't extrude farther than the middle of the side stretcher."

"This was a million dollar painting now that Warhol was dead and his reputation had soared into the stratosphere, so I wanted to be very careful before I pulled apart anything else. Yet how could I not investigate? This painting seemed to hold a clue.

You know, sometimes I do things in stupid ways. Although I often stretched and framed canvases in my studio, it's not really smart to deal with something of that value and size without proper preparation of space and help. Here's a valuable painting, and yet, without help or the proper conditions to undertake conservation work, I pried off the remaining pieces of the strip frame and shadow. In those days, most people used finishing nails rather than screws to put the flat stripping on. Nails made it easier to get off. Then I started to pull the staples off with nose pliers, one by one along two sides of a corner until the corner was loose enough to lift a few inches- being careful not to crease the canvas - and I peeked into the narrow space."

"I saw another layer! It seemed like it had been painted on. Was it just a support backing of some sort, since when I looked again at the back of the painting, the signature and gallery information was attached as if there was only one layer of canvas? This seemed like it had been painted on but it didn't make sense that Warhol would use another painting as a backing. I continued removing the staples until three sides were flapping in the breeze, as they say. I didn't remove the fourth side, because I didn't want to get the painting out of alignment. Then I lifted it up carefully, far enough to fully view the second layer, and do you know what I saw? It revealed a second painting underneath! Definitely a Warhol, almost the identical painting although I then noticed much different brush strokes on top of the photo image. Warhol would take brushes and paint loose strokes on top of some of the images. He might also silkscreen areas of the image in a different color. For example, in the portraits that he did of Liz and of Marilyn Monroe, he silkscreened the lips a bright red or a different color than the background or face color. What I was looking at was the same image of the Book Depositary building, but Andy had painted on top of it differently. It was simply a different painting from the same series. The brushwork had been done by hand and so each was different as a result of the brush process he used."

"Why did he stretch a similar painting on top of one another? The only logical reason might be that the painting below was a reject and the painting on top needed some extra support. Neither seemed to make sense to me. The painting below, as I stared at it, was a complete painting. I couldn't see any obvious flaws in it. The painting on top, the one I was used to viewing, its canvas seemed fine. Then I noticed that the painting on top had its own signature and label on it's back. This was a label I had never seen, since it was behind the first layer. The label I had seen for all those years really was intended for the hidden painting. Two paintings each had their own label; I was looking at the top canvas image but looking at the label for the hidden painting. As I looked at the top painting's back - which I had to stoop a bit to see - in addition to its label there was an additional paper, only it wasn't a label but a thin envelope. What did it contain? I carefully peeled it off and put it aside, as I wanted to continue to look at the hidden painting, the image that I was seeing for the first time."

"In the top painting, Andy had circled two windows with his brush. In the hidden painting, Andy had circled three windows with his red brush. It was supposed to feel artistic; in all candor, it simply pointed out what a viewer might have missed. In a fifth story window was a figure, caught in that instant by the photographer. When I compared both paintings, I saw that the fifth story window was covered over with paint in the top painting but left alone in the second."

"The window that everyone had looked at was where Oswald had stood and fired. It was on the 6th floor and Warhol had emphasized that with his brushwork. But the hidden painting had a window with a figure on a different floor. There was a stick shape with the figure. Could it be a gun? Was this image taken at the same time as the President was going by? I knew enough about the image that Andy had used that it was a photograph taken at the time of the assassination by one of the bystanders, and not a photo that was taken some time later. Including an authentic artifact from the historic moment in time was critical to Andy's work."

"I knew at that instant the reason for all the fuss about this painting. I realized why Liz had been both secretive and concerned that the painting should be quietly hidden. I realized why Warhol had been so timid and, in retrospect, afraid of mentioning the painting to me when I first met him. And I realized, based on the zilllions of studies, conspiracy theories, books, magazine articles, television documentaries and governmental reports, that I had evidence that something else was going on that day - that there was someone other than Oswald involved with the assassination of the President of the United States."

Bart stopped Felix. "You mean that all this time, you had the secret and it was in the painting? That there was a second gunman?"

"Yes, the secret was contained in the painting and in the envelope. I had to call Liz to confirm it all. A voice from the past, she said, but we had a good talk after all, and she told me all the details that she and Warhol had been hiding."

"And what was in the envelope? Please do tell!" urged Bart.

"Now we get to the real essence of my story. The envelope contained the roll of negatives that Andy had used to create the large silkscreen. His image, done in silkscreen, is a bit rough due to the process of making the screen and then applying the image onto the canvas. But the actual negative of the photograph, well, that has details like one couldn't believe."

"What did you do with the negative?"

"Patience my friend, because that will conclude my story. At the time, only Andy and Liz really knew. And Liz never saw the actual negative. Only Andy, working one night by himself to finish the paintings, knew the truth because he saw it, used it, then covered it up, and then was too frightened to reveal what he had found."

"All he had to do is call a reporter, or the FBI, or someone?"

"You're right, he should have. The world would have known when it should have known this. But he was scared. Not his thing. Imagine the reality. He was a big time artist but only in some very small circles. To the general public, he was a gay weirdo with funny hair dyed platinum blond who whispered funny sentences that the average person would not understand or have patience to interpret. If he had called the New York Times and told them what he had, they'd think he was just doing one of his performance acts. And the bad guys, they'd know the difference. They would know the truth. He'd be dead by the next day. That's what he believed and you know what, he was probably correct with his assessment."

"At the same time, he couldn't keep a secret. I mean, Andy keeping a secret so big is like asking a five-year old not to tell someone that there is a clown hiding in the closet. Do you see my point? How did someone else find out about it? We'll never know, but even at the party when I met him and he realized I had the painting, he started to blab. He wanted his name in the limelight, but he wanted to be safe. I'm sure he told friends. I'm sure he just couldn't keep something so big to himself. Even Walter hinted about it to me. And who knows - one person tells another. Once the secret is out to one additional person, you can almost bet that it'll get published one day."

"So only you know of this now?"

"Yes, only me - about the negatives. The painting, well, the director of the museum knows about that, but no one will pay attention to that without the negatives. Paintings aren't evidence. Negatives are. I'm the holder of the key. Liz is dead. Andy is dead. And I have the transparency. I guess I should have revealed it before now, but I promised Liz that I wouldn't until after she was gone. I'm not sure why she thought that she would predecease me. I was tempted to reveal it then."

"Why didn't you? Why didn't you do what you accuse Warhol of not doing?"

"For one simple reason, by that time, there were books on every conspiracy angle known to man. No one would pay hoot to me. I wouldn't be as crazy as how they'd take it if Andy had revealed it, but I'd be just another conspiracy nut looking for my 15 minutes of fame, no pun intended."

"Surely there'd be one newspaper interested?" questioned Bart.

"That's what I thought, too. I wondered which media outlets I could approach, but I didn't know anyone at the top. I thought about newspapers, television news, magazines, and later, online news organizations. None of them were approachable. The ones who did respond to some initial overtures, just wanted a quick story and headline. They weren't serious. Finally, I went back to what I know best- art museums. The blue chip museums come off more credible than any type of organization I could think of. So I took my time to arrange for an institution to stage an exhibition - a museum that would have academic credibility - one that the media would not suspect of doing it for attention. I had to rule out the Warhol Museum - too much self-interest there. I also stayed away from any that had recent shows that seemed like they were after sensationalism. I ruled out college museums; they wouldn't take the students seriously; well, perhaps Harvard, but I didn't think a university by itself was the best choice. Eventually, from talking to some art contacts, the Clark Art Institute surfaced. They are often partnered with Williams College, so I could get the academic side as a bonus. That was it. Once I felt confident about their sincere interest, I enticed them with the painting. Actually, I offered them two paintings to display. It all made sense because the Warhol work that I owned, and was willing to lend, was genuine. These particular paintings had never been publically displayed. And then there was the historical connection. I told them that they would be getting international attention. It was an attractive offer."

"Do they know all this? Did you reveal all of what you had? Of what you knew?"

"Only a hint that there would be an historical unveiling as a bonus to the show. That was enough for the time being. Not about the negatives. Not yet. I've planned this very carefully, but it will not be revealed until the exhibition opens. I concluded that a premature unveiling, even to the museum staff, would perhaps jeopardize my plan. When I arrive at the museum, I'll help them put the final and critical part together."

"Wow," exclaimed Bart. "That's something all right. So you are the main player?"

"For now, yes."

"Are you ready for your sandwich and glass of wine yet? I can ask the flight attendant, if you are."

"Sure. My story is nearing the end. I would like something to eat, thank you."

Bart pressed the button to call for the attendant. "How did you ever persuade a museum to do a show when they don't know the entire story?"

"They knew enough. They do know more is coming with me. But the process evolved rather quickly from the very beginning, although as you might expect, all shows have to be planned at least a year in advance."

"So all this happened a year ago?"

"More than a year. I first wrote and then called the director of the Clark Art Institute. I had met him briefly at an opening in Los Angeles. A nice guy. Sincere. You probably don't know about the Clark? It's a relatively small museum, located next to a prestigious liberal arts college in Williamstown, Massachusetts. That's about three hours north of New York and the same distance west of Boston - in the boon docks compared to having it in a large metropolitan area, but the Berkshires has several important museums and performance venues."

"Anyway, once I focused on that museum, since I had met him, it was pretty easy to contact him. Mentioning that I owned two important Warhol paintings that had come from Elizabeth Taylor did open some doors for me, I'll admit. One painting alone, without any of the historical connections, is enough to justify a nice exhibition. But I hinted to him that there were other things I could bring to the table, the all important second painting by Warhol - one that has never been seen in public, as well as some historical artifacts that would make headlines. Needless to say, David was intrigued. He wanted to see them in person. I offered to host him if he cared to come to Mexico. Well, suggesting that to someone in February is like asking an addict if he wants a fix. He couldn't wait to come."

"I'll bet. So the paintings are in Mexico?"

"Wait. There's more."

"Where is the painting? Where is the film negative that's so important in all this?"

"That's what is in my bag, that magic envelope containing a never-before-seen strip of negatives. The painting has been shipped; both of them but as one painting, as I had them. They don't know about the hidden painting yet. All this will come out when I arrive in Williamstown. They only know that one painting was shipped."

"I'm not sure I'm clear that the museum knows what's happening."

"I'll tell you the more recent events. How I arranged this show. Then you'll know where the artifacts are. But I might be skipping ahead again. Did I tell you my current situation?"

CHAPTER 19

"You asked why I'm not taking more precautions since I feel like my life could be in danger. I'll tell you why. Do you know what I fear even more than death? At my age, I fear losing my independence. I can't tell you how many of my friends suffered in their final years, with memory loss, with impaired vision, incontinence issues, even the ability to eat without someone spooning food into their mouths."

"I've been very fortunate, as to my physical health. I'd like to die with my boots on, so to speak. I don't want to suffer the indignity that I've seen others go through. So I don't have that much to fear, when I rationally stack my age against the odds. And my life has been more than satisfactory the past several years, at a time when I expected much less."

"You know, I last returned to my house in Sayulita more than a year ago, and I've not traveled since. I like it in Sayulita. I celebrated my 93rd and 94th birthdays there. My daughters called, and they urged me to come to celebrate with them but they have busy lives, and I wanted to be where I felt most at peace. The town residents, many of them know me; they even gave me a fiesta last month. I know it was Griselda or Dany who reminded them, but I was brought to the Casa de Cultura expecting just to check on a painting that they said needed attention, and about forty folks were there, about half Mexicans and the rest from the expat community. It was a nice surprise birthday party, and they knew me well because they served small Margaritas with the food. So I was pleased. As one gets older, it's nice for people to remember you on those special occasions. It also encourages me to stay in Sayulita. I really don't need to go back to Los Angeles anymore. My family knows that I have plenty of room at the beach house and they are welcome to visit. My studio space suits me there and there's no advantage anymore working elsewhere."

"Over the years, my dwelling had grown. After the girls were older, I was able to spend more time in Mexico. By then, I had all my gallery connections and I simply enjoyed being in warm weather, especially during the winter months. After my father died, I inherited some money, not a fortune since no one made that much money compared to current values, but a decent amount. I purchased the building that I was using in Venice and I took over the area formerly used by the welding shop and added living quarters. In Sayulita, I kept adding to the beach house and abandoned the Puerto Vallarta houses. With the roads well paved and tourists zooming in, my beach became my escape and sanctuary. It also kept my connection to Maria through her family, and I was a regular at her folks' house until they passed. I still give gifts to all of my nieces and nephews."

"I'll tell you, I have had other women in my life, after all, years roll by and one does have other relationships. Once the girls were off in college, I felt more open about dating. One woman, Jytte Thomsen, lived with me for almost ten years. She was Danish - slender and blond - and we traveled a lot to Europe. I had not seen that part of the world, and I must have visited every cathedral in Italy. Traveling there filled a gap in my studies, for I studied Western art but I never stepped foot in Italy, France or Spain to see the actual works in their natural habitats. That was something a longed to do. Jytte and I visited the major art museums to view the classics, and I saw what my European peers were doing. Well, that's a polite way of saying that I dragged her everywhere, but she was a willing companion. We spent summers in southern Spain, so at least my Spanish came in handy. That was in the late 1970s and 80s. We talked about marriage but it just didn't happen. I don't know why it evaporated. I'm not difficult but whoever loved me had to buy into my lifestyle. I needed Mexico and I needed L.A. and I worked very hard at my art. Being attached to an artist sounds glamorous but in reality, I'm working by myself for hours at a time - much more than a normal forty-hour week - not socializing, not happy much of the time - after all, making important art is a hard task. The fun moments - the openings and parties and celebrity sales - come very seldom if you stack them against all the hours involved in the studio, making the art."

"Loving someone at middle age is so much different than first love. Maria and I had been young and naïve and adventurous. The world awaited us. Early love has a passion and energy that only a young body can have. Love much later, is sincere and also has passion, but there's baggage now attached. Jytte had her family and I had mine. It's a merger of sorts, rather than developing something from nothing. I was settled in my work, with my Venice studio and with my Sayulita house. I couldn't abandon either. Jytte had her work, as a writer, and obligations and adult kids as well, which eventually meant both of us had grandchildren. So our playbook simply doubled in complexity although we tried to find new opportunities from all of it. Those were the unique moments, like our summers in Europe. For the rest of the time, we were set in our ways, and we each accommodated each other's needs. It was good but different, if you know what I mean."

"I can imagine. I, too, was married once. Not now. We had our plans. They didn't work out. I know meeting someone now is different," said Bart as if he was disturbed by this thought.

"Anyway, after Jytte and I separated, I expanded the house even more. Building with locals who Maria's family knew kept costs at a fraction compared to building in the States. I added a second floor with 3 bedrooms with a special master bedroom suite for myself. I can see the sun go down and the moon pass before my terrace windows without lifting my head out of the pillow. The downstairs bedrooms became den and studio, and I built a simple but large building where Liz and Richard had planned a house. That became my main studio for large work."

"It's a nice villa, actually. If I survive, you can come visit me. Really. You'll like it there."

"That's very kind of you. I'm sure I'll try to do that the next time I'm in Puerto Vallarta," responded Bart.

"The rough concrete walls are painted a sand color - just blending into the sandy beach a few meters at the front. I planted palms and plants that flower to extend the jungle feel into the interior spaces. Adding more plants was easy by placing large clay pots at strategic points."

"Then years later, I added something I thought I would never need-- a swimming pool, and I made it long enough so I could do laps. That was my way of compromising. My body became too weak to fight the ocean waves; on many days, the waves can be vigorous. Now I can still dip into the pool water and get my exercise, all the while gazing out onto the ocean horizon."

"Although my house is simply furnished by local crafts, my paintings fill up all the large walls, along with photos of my family and memories. Of course, in my office, that is always locked when I leave the house, I hung my most valuable paintings - Andy Warhol's JFK Assassination; on the opposite wall, I hung my own painting, one that I carefully selected and is one of my best from that period. It was the one that Maria commented on, and said that it would make me famous. She joked that I would forget her and fall for some art groupie after I became a household name. She was teasing me about that but she was sincere in appreciating the work. That painting is my connection to all those years with her."

"A Warhol and a Peters facing each other!" commented Bart. "Sounds like history to me, and I still know little about art. But you've gotten me so interested that I would like to see those paintings someday."

"You can, at least in two days - they are both in Williamstown as we speak. The director wanted my painting close by. I'm not famous like Andy, but my painting stands up to his. And I think my work took off after that painting. That's when I matured with a distinctive and innovative style."

"What else can I tell you about my paradise? My kitchen is open, but I have windows to control the breezes. My electricity has been in since I brought the Warhol painting over. I needed dependable air-conditioning; I had to make a few payments to various folks at the CFE - that's the Mexican electric company - so they'd run a line about a half-mile to my house, but they did. You know, one appreciates more the comforts of civilization when you don't have it. Electricity. That allowed me to enjoy all sorts of items of comfort. "

"It seems like a lot but all this was done, a tiny bit at a time over thirty or forty years. When you come and visit, you'll think it's quite a house."

"And of course, it's not in such a remote destination anymore. When I first arrived, there probably were half a dozen old trucks in Sayulita. Most could only make the road to Puerto Vallarta during the dry season. In the past few decades, Puerto Vallarta and then all the coastal towns have been discovered. Those who ventured first up the coast were the hippie surfers, then by some adventurous types, and later by anyone who wanted to build a house with ocean view in fun Mexican towns that were different than gated communities."

"To entice developers, the government renamed the coast Riviera Nayarit, which stimulated all kinds of upscale development. What was fertile jungle or pristine sand turned, almost overnight, into golf courses, condo-resorts, swimming pools, parking lots and guard gates protecting the visitors inside from any outside interference. Those folks are spending big bucks to be in the warmth of the beach."

"And guess what funky little village, located just a few minutes by taxi away, has blossomed in all this? You guess right-- little ol' Sayulita.

It's become one of the hot spots in all of Mexico-- that combination of beach and the right kind of surfing waves, a village that was saved from being bulldozed to make way for box condominiums, and a town that is small enough to give everyone, young and old, that fun experience. Of course, in the plaza, there are a few too many bars with loud music for my taste. My grandkids love the night scene, but I'm glad I'm far enough away to not hear anything but the waves, the frogs and the birds. The government was smart in preserving Sayulita. It made selling the nearby international-styled glamorous condos and resort rooms easier-- because the developers could advertise an "authentic" Mexican experience of Sayulita as part of the vacation package. With the growth came many benefits - more services, the Internet, more places to eat, more stores - it was a compressed version of a larger resort city. Some of my friends, the older folks, are not too happy with the changes. It's too busy, they say. But that's progress, and it happens around the world. I remember Liz and Richard telling me how quickly it could come; they sure were on the mark."

"My old Sayulita friends, who once had to struggle to make money but never had to struggle to provide food for their families because all they had to do was throw a net, drop a fishing line, or pull up a crop, soon had jobs- waiting on tables, cleaning hotel rooms, selling every sort of Mexican craft that all came via Guadalajara. By Mexican standards, they made pretty good money. But the downside was, they now needed more money to buy food that no longer was as cheap or as abundant except in the stores."

"For the most part, the younger generation cashed in on the new opportunities. The older generation did too, those who were smart. Some were fools who sold their land quickly, bought a new truck and five years later, were out of luck when the truck would start breaking down and they were left out on owning appreciating land. The smart ones opened up businesses and sold very little, if any, of their land. Or they sold their land a small piece at a time, over many years, at higher and higher prices. Gringos were snapping up lots all over and building half-million dollar houses with pools

- all on the steep hills surrounding the village, so they could get that ocean view. It was all about being close to the beach and having a view. Prices climbed astronomically."

"I suppose I found myself with a million-dollar house on a million-dollar beachfront estate-- but the thought of selling didn't cross my mind, not even for one second. Nowhere in the entire world, with ten million dollars in my pocket, would I find such a perfect place. So I came as often as I could and I was happy, for the most part, and at ease with the world. Perhaps at my age, I wasn't going to make any more marks - my energy level was no longer strong enough for that - but I was proud of my life, as I appraised it via quick memories, like looking through a photo album. I could think about the past and even with a limited future, I could plan projects."

"All in all, I'm happy with my life. I knew that a beast surprising me was something I had to be weary of - life can throw a curve at any time - but I think I got through the worst. Sitting in my house, with all that I need, sipping my Margarita which Dany purposely makes pretty weak because my daughters call him and nag him about my health but it still has enough punch for me, I can say, yes, life is peachy and I'm generally satisfied."

"I'm well cared for. Griselda and Dany come in every day to take care of the place. They come in late morning, careful not to disturb my early mornings and my late afternoons when the sun goes down and I want to be by myself. Unless I have guests; then they come more so I don't have any extra work."

"Ah, Griselda. She thinks she's my wife, to the dismay of her husband. She'd tuck me into bed at night, if I allowed her to. When I'm in residence, she keeps my refrigerator filled and offers me prepared meals. More than I can possibly eat. And she knows I really like going out. Of course, the extra food encourages me to invite friends from the village. I still have a quite a few, and of course, relatives from Maria's family; I seem to have guests almost every other day, some for lunch or drinks, others, like relatives, come for week-long visits."

"My generation has died out, the next generation is almost too old, and the younger generation has less interest in the 'old American.' That's what some of the local relatives have nicknamed me. I don't mind. Nevertheless, I try to be friendly and helpful and I quietly give some money now and then to those who need help to further their education and for those emergencies that all families seem to have at some point."

"It's not a bad life. Until the past few years, I was active in L.A., traveling somewhat; I traveled around Mexico, too, you know. I was honored with a show that the museum in Guadalajara organized. It traveled to Mexico City, Guanajuato, San Miguel and Veracruz. But that was years ago. Even the art scene in Puerto Vallarta grew, and one gallery insisted on giving me a show each season. That's now history; life slows down. But all in all, I'm settled being in Sayulita."

"Do you know that I still work? Artists really don't retire! I try to paint every day. How much longer can I do that? I hope until I don't wake up. The bigger question is - where do I want to be when I die? That's been decided. I'm happy where I am, even during summer. I have the ocean breezes and air-conditioning does the trick even on the hottest and most humid of days. I don't mind the summer rains; I've got plenty of work to do inside."

"For the most part, the rains mostly come in the late afternoon, the pre-rain show that I can see on the open sea is like watching a grand fireworks display in the far distance, and when the rain finally comes down with a vengeance, after an hour or two it's mostly gone and I can be outside on the patio again. Except for the times when the rain comes at me horizontally due to a strong wind, I can even be outside on the terrace without getting wet. When the wind blows too hard, I close the glass doors and watch the action from my tranquil interior. In this way, I feel as close to nature as I can, certainly for someone my age."

"I've condensed my actual studio space - not my storage but the area where I can actively paint and draw and make models. My physical capabilities are less than when I was younger, of course. A young woman named Carmelita comes in three mornings a week and preps my canvases for me. I don't have to do the physical work anymore. So I find the current arrangement very satisfying. I can walk into the side studio room, work on one of several projects going on at once - a couple of large canvases on special racks screwed to the wall and some paper works on my long drawing table. It's enough to do. Being adjacent to the rest of the house pays off because I find that my stamina lasts only an hour; then I can take a break, pace in a different space, nibble on whatever Griselda has left in the refrigerator for me, and go back to paint for a while more. Even walking to the other side of the beach to my main studio is not something I want to do everyday. I much prefer the smaller studio in my house that allows me better access to take naps and eat snacks. For many years, that quarter of mile to the studio gave me a nice walk and separation, but now, unless I'm really trying to tackle a large painting, which I don't do often, that studio is used more for storage or private showing and I work on smaller pieces in the house."

"I have my routine and I have enough guests and frequent invitations to vary my day. People in the arts who happen to be vacationing and hear that I live here do look me up. Ramos drives me when I want to go into Puerto Vallarta, but locally I don't need help. I can drive my golf cart into town and walk about the Centro."

"Did you know there's a small museum in town dedicated to me? It's tiny but has some of my work and space for other artists. I used to give talks there. In the beginning, I was invited by gatherings of winter residents who had houses in Sayulita, but eventually, they heard me often enough. But there are so many new visitors who come to Sayulita, some to vacation just at the beach but others come to participate in a yoga workshop or for a family or school reunion or they are part of some association. Then I'm often asked to give a talk in exchange for a donation to the museum. A little culture, maybe after a nice meal, gives their trip just that little added experience. Once in a while, I also allow for small groups to tour my house and studio. They think it's an extraordinary residence, although there are more elaborate houses that have since been built, but none are filled with so much art. For what once was a very modest, in fact a poor fishing village, I find it amazing how many million-dollar homes have been constructed over the years - many of them on challenging steep lots more suited for Billy goats - all to take advantage of the magical views."

"All in all, it's an interesting village that I can now enjoy. The local politics will always be what they are, as in any small town, but the town seems to have found its comfort level. Businesses are thriving, at least they make enough during the high season to carry them the rest of the year, and people work hard enough without getting too stressed. A balance, they say, is what makes life fun and long."

"I try to stay healthy and active. I can't tolerate people who constantly talk about their medical woes, or even to hear their miracle solutions when I know damn well that they have as many problems as anyone else, so I won't bother you with my occasional trips to the doctor. Needless to say, at 94 years old, I've had a few scares that fortunately turned out not life threatening. But it was a few years ago, maybe when I reached my ninth decade when I really started to panic about what would happen to all my stuff and to my secret should I not wake up one day. After all, I have friends in their early 90s but not so many who are in their late 90s. I can appreciate the realities. I felt I needed to come up with a plan and put something into motion."

"I did do some preliminary exploration of my resources, that is I looked at my bank account and I thought of my family and friends and contacts who might be able to deal with my affairs. For the Warhol mystery, I concluded I needed to do this on my own, without dragging in anyone. So once I formulated a plan, I started to make some calls and see what nibbles I might get. The museum in western Massachusetts took a bite on my hook. It's as simple as that. Once they got interested, it was easy to then plan out all the details and how the ending of my story would be executed. However, perhaps I had forgotten the danger element. After all, it's been many years and one tends to sanitize past horrible events. When I spotted those two fellows in the airport looking at me like they were, all of my worries came back to me. But I've always been a person who could bend with the conditions, and so I made a fast decision after sizing you up. I'm afraid, that's why you are involved. Or at least if you elect to help me - that is, if I need help - we'll see."

"Felix, I'm certain you will have a safe and successful trip and all this is an unnecessary precaution, but I'm happy to help you in whichever way I can. But I have to tell you. You think of bad guys like cops and robbers. I believe you see more than is there."

"But people get killed all the time."

"We're on an airplane. Before we boarded, we went through tight security," replied Bart. "I can assure you, no one has a gun on this plane and no one is going to shoot you. I can't tell you more but of that, I'm certain. I do some consulting in security matters for large organizations, and while I won't profess to be an expert on bad guys, I just don't think you should worry too much."

"That's very good of you. I'm sure you want to calm me down. And maybe you are right. I might be over-exaggerating the danger. On the other hand, I know what has happened in the past. Those were real events. Are all those folks dead by now and am I a forgotten footnote? I don't know, but my guard is up just in case. Anyway, a few more days and then it'll be all over. Now I must tell you how I planned my 'coming out,' shall we say, and tell you the last part of my story."

CHAPTER 20

"The director of the Clark Art Institute and I started to email each other. I had a notion of how an exhibition could be put together, and the director had a notion based on his museum's experiences. Together, we designed a pretty credible exhibition, but one that would take some expense and research time as well as they'd have to borrow additional works. That's a commitment that museums do not make lightly. Since the nucleus of the show was my Warhol paintings, the director really needed to be sure I had what I claimed. There was a limit to how much work he would have his curators do in preparation until there was a solid loan agreement in place for my Warhols. And for that, he needed to see them in person. So I sent out an invitation for him to come to Sayulita. About a year ago, he came."

"'I'm very grateful you sent the taxi for me,' said David Besland, the director of the Clark Art Institute. Besland was a good-looking chap with glasses that emit an academic professor look, someone pushing fifty. He was in a long sleeve, white and pink striped dress shirt, sleeves rolled up above light slacks. At least he had the sense to don grey sneakers. He didn't realize that most folks don't wear socks here, let alone long pants and long-sleeve shirts while the sun was out. Clearly in some degree of discomfort, he quipped, 'It's hotter here than I thought.'"

"Only standing in the sun. Come into the shade; it's actually quite delightful."

"David noticed first the absence of any street noise once the driver turned off the car and opened the rear door. David could sense an entire animal community hidden away in the dense jungle that they spent several minutes driving through. In the distance, various creatures were chirping or blipping or croaking away without rhythm, rising above the regular crash of ocean waves that he could hear just beyond the palms."

"Ramos fetched David's bag out of the rear of the SUV taxi, while David and I greeted one another. David noticed the tall palms through the openings into the house, just past an inviting and artistically crafted metal gate and carved wooden doorway. He stepped upon a concrete walkway infused with stone designs of various colors.

"'I'm more used to international travel destinations that ends up being taxied to a Hilton or Hyatt entrance, not a bucolic remote setting such as this,' he said with a smile."

"As he looked down, I pointed out some features. 'We try to incorporate stones and natural materials from the beach, and then incorporate local tile in colorful patterns. It's fun to mix and match. And there are practical reasons, in addition. These stones break up the surface and make it less slippery when it's wet. And the broken tile acts the same way - the extra grout makes it safer to walk on.'"

"Do you get a lot of rain?"

"Hardly a drop this time of year. But if you are here in the summer season, it hardly gets a chance to dry out. You came when the weather is perfect. No need for air-conditioning; it cools by evening. For Sayuilta, you are a bit overdressed for mid-day. Shorts and a T-shirt are more common. You did bring casual clothes?"

"Of course. And thanks again for the taxi service."

"Ramos does all my pickups. He's very reliable and he knows where to take my guests. Welcome to Villa de Playa Secreta."

"I don't know much Spanish; what does that mean?"

"Villa of Secret Beach. It was my late wife's nickname but Elizabeth Taylor made it official. Do you remember her?"

"Well, only as a movie legend. You knew her?"

"I think I can say we were close friends, when she was very young but still a famous actress. And that's why you are here! First, please, get settled and come by the pool terrace when you are ready. Did you bring your trunks? I'm sure you did. Have a swim later, or simply join me for an afternoon Margarita. But it's early yet. When you're ready, I'll give you a tour of the village. How does that sound?"

"Sounds great. You know, I've been to Mexico City once, for a museum conference, but never had time to really explore Mexico. I've been drawn by museum business to Europe and Asia, but not Mexico. And so close! Shame on me."

"As the crow flies from New York, we are not much farther than Phoenix. Closer than L.A. People just think of Mexico as a faraway land. It's not at all, except in culture, weather, food and drink!"

"In less than fifteen minutes, David had put his bag onto the shelf in the closet, inspected his bed (all to his delightful satisfaction) used the 'bano' ensuite, shaved, wondered about the open air shower but then felt how warm it was, saw the waves flicker and thunder beyond the palm trees not fifty paces from his bedroom balcony, and smiled to himself. He took off his travel clothes and put on a pair of khaki shorts and a flower patterned short sleeve short. He left the top button open, just because it was so warm. He discarded his travel sneakers in favor of open sandals. He thought not to wear a T-shirt until he knew what his host was planning although he did bring a couple arty T-shirts that the museum had designed for various past exhibits."

"Then he joined me by the pool. 'You have quite a spread here, I must say.'"

"'Advantages of coming before everyone else.' I was sitting in a Mexican-styled chair that could swing around from viewing the ocean to meeting David."

"And with beach front! This is a palace. You know, I narrowly escaped another half foot of snow in Williamstown. Just got out and to New York before it was too difficult to drive. Then non-stop to Puerto Vallarta- in what, about six hours?"

"Less. But traveling is always a nuisance what with security and all. Sit over here next to me so you can see the ocean. I assumed you wouldn't turn down a Margarita?"

"'Muchas gracias'" said David who obviously had refreshed his memory from a phase book on the plane. 'Not so bad. Really, I left this morning early and here I am - early afternoon in shorts! I'm afraid I'm a bit white.'"

"A few minutes of sun a day will take care of that, but be forewarned, not too much sun at once."

"It's so lovely here, with the beach and jungle. You must get inspired?"

"I'm not Monet. My work has different concepts at work. But yes, I must say that I've learned to be a connoisseur of color. It might be the Mexican sun, but colors just become so vibrant here. It's helped my paintings greatly. Look at that tree over there, with the palms behind, the plants in front and the bushes next to it. Within that single frame, there are infinite shades of green. I don't think there's more than a couple of leaves that share the same green - the textures, the angles to the light, the curves - all that variety even within one plant. I often think that I could spend a lifetime just investigating the color green."

"'And then you could spend equal time with the shades of blue on the water and sky. Just look at that view!' David said turning to face the ocean horizon."

"We drank our Margaritas and I let David acclimate to the terrace surroundings. When we were done, David followed me as I hobbled a bit with a cane but went fairly quickly. I got into a golf cart parked under a trellis by the side of the driveway. David got into the passenger's seat."

"Parking is a pain in Sayulita, so most homeowners use golf carts if they want to get into town. Tourists rent them. Much more fun and quiet. No pollution. Here we go."

"And with that, we zipped off, down my cobblestoned drive, onto a dirt road that meandered along the jungle. David had no idea if we were going deeper into the jungle or coming out. He couldn't hear any waves; in fact, it was peaceful within the tall jungle trees except for an occasional shriek of a bird or frog or some unidentified creature. But within ten minutes, he spotted houses up on the hills as we emerged next to a small beach."

"'Los Muertos Beach,' I told him. We drove through the town's cemetery, where most were buried above ground in tombs and family members had left plastic flowers wrapped in cellophane to honored deceased relatives."

"This is the main cemetery. When someone dies, most the town comes out to the burial. Remember, Sayulita has fewer than 3,000 Mexicans and most are related to one another in some way. It gets busy as hell because the population doubles with Gringos who winter here. Some stay most of the year, but the majority of them come for winter months. Then there are all the tourists; they come non-stop - most for a week. Sayulita has become a Mecca for the funky Mexican experience. The surf draws the young crowd and the shops draw the affluent older crowd. To accommodate all, there must be more than a hundred restaurants in this small village."

"'What a cute town,' exclaimed David. 'So lively. And no high-rises compared to the many I saw on the way from the airport.'"

"The government made Sayulita a 'Pueblo Mágico,' which means 'magic town.' There are about a hundred such designated towns in Mexico. We don't have the architectural interest, but we are a typical town that has preserved itself. That designation is a two-edge sword. It brings more tourists but it also preserves what we have. It's like being declared an historical landmark in the United States-- you can't destroy what's here. So we remain although we are bursting at the seams. Everyone wants to come but there's no more room to build. Unfortunately, folks keep raising prices - it's not the cheapest place to come to anymore. That's much tougher on the kids who want to camp and surf; only a few campgrounds remain."

"When did you come?"

"I came when there were just a few houses and buildings, when you couldn't get here easily by car from Puerto Vallarta - boat was the preferred method. When even Puerto Vallarta was a small fishing village. But you know, seventy years is a long time. Each year a bit more gets added and before you know it, you are in the middle of a Disneyworld."

"I think this feels a lot more authentic than Disney."

"To tourists, yes; to natives, maybe not. But you know, development means people come, and I get lots of fun visitors, like you. Now might you have come if I were in the middle of Iowa?"

"This was tempting. I had heard a lot about Sayulita. Truthfully, I might have come no matter where you were. Your offer was the real draw."

"We drove around the cobblestone roads. Tourists in beach clothes were wandering about, eating ice cream or popsicles, or dining on small tables set right at the edge of the road and on the crowded sidewalks. As we turned the corner, David exclaimed, 'Whoa, your name is on that building! What is it?'"

"It's a small museum of my work. The town honored me by turning their small cultural center into a museum. And there are two galleries of my work and two galleries showing the work of others, plus an activity room. But most people are here for the beach, not to see art. And funds are low for operating it properly. It works so far; they often do rotating exhibitions of local artists. It gives young people an inspiration. I give them a little support but I'm not going to live long enough."

"What will happen?"

"That's the problem I'm working on. I'm leaving enough for them to continue for a while, but it needs oversight. I trust it will work out."

"Can we have a look inside? I'd love to see more of your work in person."

"We parked in front, where it said no parking, and walked in. 'It's a small show but there are fifteen paintings and some drawings. That's about three from every decade. A mini-retrospective but for vacationers, a quick stop at best.'"

"I'm impressed. This could be in any city in the world. A museum gem indeed," commented David in a low voice because there were a group of six young people walking about, also viewing the works."

"While I stood in one corner, David walked about the two whitewashed galleries looking at each piece. Then I motioned to David and we went into another large gallery where there were works by other artists. 'I had something to do with this particular show. The art is by older artists who have worked in the region for many years but have not had proper gallery exposure. Of course, only old by most standards, not compared to my age!'"

"I sometimes give them some advice in how to curate shows. They are well intended but don't always have the museum experience. Even developing artists' work should be hung as if they were masterpieces. The next show is going to be ten artists under 25 years old. In the old days, one could never find young artists. Now, instead of fishing, many kids are interested in the arts- and a few into real art - not the tourist-stuff you find in the shops. I mean work that you will find serious."

"Did you teach here?"

"I gave workshops now and then, never for pay, just to get locals properly introduced. I also had interns helping me over the years. That's how some got hooked? They don't have an easy time making a living and doing art, but who ever did? The trouble is, too much regional art is geared for tourists. It's getting better; the gallery scene has improved, especially in Puerto Vallarta; there were enough half-million dollar condos and those buyers wanted something a bit more interesting than the folk art. That helped."

"'Well, as they say, beach towns are not where most go for culture. Not unless you are big like Miami or Los Angeles,' quipped David. 'Thank you for allowing me to view this. Just like anyone coming here, I never expected to see something so serious and well done, and you are right, we didn't spend that much time, but it did enrich my visit here. Do you know what was a first for me? It's the first time in my life that I toured an art museum in shorts!'"

"We have many visitors clad in bikinis!"

"How many people stop in?"

"Actually, visitation is quite impressive even though we are a beach town. The town gets over a million visitors annually. Since it's such a small town and we're only a block from the beach, almost every tourist walks by. When the building first was built by the Ejidos, being close to the beach wasn't any big deal. And since it's free, about one in ten walk in. It's only a 15-minute distraction, so we get over 100,000 visitors."

"A hundred thousand! Wow. Our museum does double that, but look how big we are and how much art we have. Maybe we should have a Clark Art branch here!"

"'Well, perhaps we can bring a young graduate to curate a show now and then, in between having surf lessons,' I seriously joked."

"We'll talk about that over drinks."

"Come see the town's main beach. We walked just a block down a pedestrian strip lined by palm trees and little boutiques, each façade painted a different color and all with zany logos and signs. We stood gazing at the Pacific Ocean. There were two dozen surfers on the right side waiting for their waves."

"The left side has smaller waves. Perfect for swimmers and those learning how to stand up on the boards. And that's where the fishermen still go out and come in with their boats."

"'Lots of people on the beach,' commented David."

"That's our main attraction. Everything else is just the icing on the cake."

"We headed back and this time went a few additional yards to the plaza. "It's not big but it's our main plaza. Everything happens here. This is the place to be seen and to see what's going on. It's busy almost non-stop."

"'It's almost wall-to-wall with restaurants,' said David."

"Swimming gets you hungry! Let's get back to the cart and I'll go back a different way. Anyway, that reminds me, I want some fish for Dany to grill for our dinner tonight."

"A few streets away, I pulled up in front of a fish market. The guys were loading up a truck with large fish onto large boxes of crushed ice. The owner came up to us and invited us to the back. There he pulled out a fresh mahi-mahi, about a meter long. I nodded approval and the man went about cutting off the head and tail, filleting it expertly and then slicing it into a dozen pieces."

"Muchas gracias," I said, as the man put the contents into a bag, twisted it carefully and then put it into yet another bag. Turning to David, I said, "this is the one aspect of Sayulita that hasn't changed. You can't go wrong. Don't worry, it's not all for tonight."

*****

"Back at the beach house, David finally couldn't wait any longer. 'So please let me look. It's very exciting, you know, to be offered to show two Warhols that have never been seen. Why us?'"

"Yes, why this museum, when you had so many other choices?" asked Bart.

"The Clark Art Institute is a most unusual, and highly regarded museum. It was started by Sterling and Francine Clark, he was heir to the Singer Sewing Machine fortune. He was an avid collector of art, often buying great numbers during his visits to Paris. Of course, on his frequent walks down Madison Avenue in New York, he was every gallery dealer's dream sale. When he bought, he paid generously, often overpaying it was thought. However, art prices climbed so steadily that it was only a few years later when his purchases seemed like bargains."

"The Clarks lived in New York and when World War II came, they feared that the city might get bombed, like London and other cities were being bombed, and so they sought a safe haven for their extensive art collection. Among the Clark's closest advisors were two professors from the art history department of Williams College in Williamstown, Massachusetts, and they suggested that the Clarks take a look at the Berkshires. They instantly fell in love with the idea of building a retreat there, but with the Clarks' ambition, it became much more than a safe storage facility - more of a Greek-revival temple that would serve as their country quarters and as a museum for their collection."

"Obviously, they left more money than most museums could only hope to be endowed with, and so the museum did fine. In the 1970s, they built a major expansion, since the purpose of the museum was not only to exhibit their art but to have a study program with a very extensive library free to art scholars around the world. They also partnered with an art conservation lab and with Williams College to offer a graduate level degree program. Using an internationally renowned architect, they expanded once again and fused the two previous styled buildings into a much larger complex. This gave the museum ample exhibition space to present temporary exhibitions of art that were outside the main collection. In fact, what was a modest but highly regarded museum became a national powerhouse, often compared to the Getty Museum in Los Angeles."

"I see," said Bart. "I never realized there were museums of that sort away from the big cities. Of course, I can't say that I've ever went to visit something like that. Please, continue."

"As I responded to David as to why his museum, I told him that I was leery of the big museums with Washington connections."

"This painting, David, rather the story behind the painting, will make national news for you. You will have to be prepared for that. Many years ago, when I visited Williams, I was impressed with your museum and studies program. And I was surprised; I thought your mission was limited to European art and early American art, but I saw your show of American Abstraction 1950 to 1975. It was very impressive."

"I remember; I was a new assistant curator and that show was the first one we did. The museum had just built an entire new wing and decided to push into modern art, at least the early foundation of modern art. We've now have had two decades of doing early modernist through the last century."

"'You've been very patient - have a look.' I took David into the office, the room where I hung the Warhol and one of my big paintings, along with a collection of smaller works on the two sidewalls. David carefully studied the Warhol without commenting."

"It is a beautiful painting. It will anchor the show perfectly. And the second Warhol painting? Where is it?"

"As I hinted to you, I can't show you here, but it will be in your museum prior to the exhibition. I also have documents that will bring all the art into historical perspective. As we've discussed by email, the only reason I'm being secretive is that I don't want to put anyone, including you or your staff, in danger. When all is revealed, there will be many people surprised, but perhaps a few will be upset that I've allowed all this into the light, so to speak."

"I'm trying to trust you, but I'd love to know all the details. Normally, I'd run the other way, but the fact that you have this one genuine Warhol, and with the papers from Warhol himself to Elizabeth Taylor to you, proves that you are the real McCoy. However, as the director, it's a bit awkward to tell my curators to do a show in which even I don't know all the artwork or artifacts that will be included."

"I know. I don't want to be difficult for a silly reason. I think I am doing the careful thing. The tie-in with Kennedy makes an important art exhibition and an important historical lesson."

"Well, Warhol is one of the great modern founders of Pop Art. It is the Kennedy association that grabbed the attention of the graduate program. Yes, that fits very well. But can you at least hint to me about the political dynamite that you propose to reveal?"

"I'm reluctant to at this point. It was a long time ago. Most of the people involved are dead, except families, mafias, and national interests have longer lives. I'm afraid that there could be remnants about. They attempted to kill me once, and that was before I even knew the secret. I've kept it a secret all these years and soon you'll be sharing it with the world."

"Dany came to the door and signaled that we should soon take our afternoon drinks on the terrace. 'We can go for a stroll on the beach first. I'm not the big walker I once was, but I still can stroll the length of my beach.'"

"The entire beach is yours?"

"Not the beach itself but the land, yes. Half of it was acquired by Elizabeth and Richard, but they split before building and eventually sold it to me at cost. That was our deal to begin with. It would cost millions today but in those days, it was not valuable land."

"How could it not be?"

"It's hard to imagine that Sayulita was a forgotten place. This land might as well have been a patch in the Sahara Desert."

"We took off our sandals at the walkway's edge as it terminated at the sand itself, and strolled northerly, about a quarter mile stretch. Huge rocks split up the plane as the waves pounded on them without rest."

"If I ever wanted to say something to someone, this is where we would discuss things. It's hard to use any sensitive listening device with the ocean thundering in the background. I gave David a bit more information about the meaning of the paintings, especially the second painting, but I didn't reveal to him about the second layer."

"'Why didn't you go public with this many years ago?' David asked me."

"At one time, I tried. But between the incompetence of the government, and the mess that a reporter caused, I gave up. And there were personal reasons of safety."

"For your own safety?"

"I suppose to protect my family, my kids. And to protect some others. Like Liz. Elizabeth Taylor. They might have killed her. But she's dead now, and I'm not long for this world."

"But you are very healthy indeed, from what I can see."

"Don't worry. I'm not dying today, or even this month, most likely. But I'm 94. I doubt I'll see 100. I'll be happy if I have a year or two more. Hey, maybe I'm being overly cautious, but you know, I've lived too long to be naïve about the evils in this world. At the same time, I'm a big believer in sunshine. The more the pubic knows, the harder it is to be corrupt or hide. I'd like to shed light on all this at the exhibition. I figured, once you saw the painting, you'll know I'm legit and that you have something valuable to show no matter what."

"My curatorial department reviewed your papers; there were no worries there."

"I knew your concerns. The paper was signed by Elizabeth Taylor herself, and she had it notarized. She wanted to be sure I had clear title to the painting, so no one could question it. The letter also described why and how Andy Warhol sold the painting to her, and I sent you his statement, also notarized."

"We have rarely seen this type of correspondence."

"Andy and Liz both knew the importance of this painting. They took no chances. They got it out of the United States and I hid it among my other art collection and my own work for these many years. I'm sure someone will come out of the gutter for this. For all these years I just thought to myself, let sleeping dogs lie. Maybe it's now just a bit of distant history, but I doubt it. And do you have no fear? You know, you can also be a target."

"I'm not afraid. I don't know who or what I'm supposed to fear, but as you requested, I've taken precautions. I, too, believe that once news gets out, it's too late. Too many are then involved. But now that I know the meaning, well, you are right; it will stir up some activity."

"For the second painting, I will give you instructions on space and frame needs. And I'm also going to have documentation ready for you in case anything should happen to me between now and the time of the exhibition."

"Now, now, don't worry about that of course…"

"I know the realities, David. Not only because of my age but because of the potential for someone to stop what I'm about to put into action. And I'm sorry to leave you in the dark about the second Warhol, but it's for your own good. You've seen this one so you know what I say is true. The only thing that I will hold for now is the second Warhol. But I won't disappoint you."

"I need to abide by your judgment. You've thought about this for a long time."

"For now, we'll just assume it's a normal show. We'll ship this painting very soon, so you'll have it under wraps at your museum, in safe storage; then you'll know that you have the basis for the show. I'll arrive two days ahead, you'll have the second work, and we'll make it all happen then. Is that agreeable?"

"Unusual, but agreeable. After your letter and our call, I did follow up with your suggestions and called some collectors. We already have enough art committed for a nice sizable show in our new space. It'll be for June, that's more than a year away. Are you okay with that time? We can have an opening around Memorial Day. That's when our main season begins and we'll have the most press."

"I can do that. We'll be in touch meanwhile. And the documents of which I spoke, will be at an attorney's office and they will be in constant communication with me; should I fail to get in touch for any reason, they'll have instructions to send to you the documents."

"'Felix, this is sounding more and more like cloaks and daggers,' said David with some added seriousness."

"This is a political statement, that's all. It'll affect history but only if you believe that one person can change the way the world acts."

"One person? Not an army?"

"Come, Dany's waving. Our Margaritas must be ready. We'll continue our discussion inside."

CHAPTER 21

"David and I sat for an early dinner, enjoying the fish that Dany had expertly grilled for us. We talked about the political implications of the show, and that was good since I was sure that a political debate would result, and David needed to be prepared for the many questions that would be asked of him."

"'There are political groups that believe in the actions of a few,' I remarked to David Bresland as we sat sipping our second glass of red wine, enjoying the lowering sun and the tide pulling the waves away from shore."

"How's so? That's one of my interests, you know."

"Well, a president or dictator or even a general can act in a way that will change history. But so can others. For example, in Concord, when the colonists and British were facing each other in a standoff, had not one person made that shot, perhaps the war would not have started and history might be different. We'll never know who made that shot, the one that historians call 'the shot that was heard around the world,' but we can surmise that it was just a farmer on one side, or a foot soldier on the other, just someone who perhaps panicked a bit prematurely."

"'Or it was inevitable,' countered David."

"Perhaps there are good guys who think they can make changes by trying to alter how one person, a person of influence, goes about leading. Imagine if you were the best friend of Bill Gates and you could have influenced how he invested all his money into worthy causes? But unfortunately, throughout history, there are those individuals who think they can alter fate and make political changes by just one person's actions. Those are the bad guys."

"What do you mean by bad guys?"

"The obvious ones - like assassins who eliminate leaders. They need not be of any position, other than the will to sacrifice themselves and most likely, to be able to pull a trigger to some degree of accuracy."

"My good man, I know your career has been in art, but I wonder how much you know about that side of life. I actually tripled majored in college, in history and political science. Art was my third interest, but ever since, I've tried to apply historical context to whatever art show I'm doing. So I'm very much into how politics and art have evolved side by side."

"You might have studied more, but I have age on my side; I've lived through more decades than you. I've been a witness, an observant, and a little bit of an activist."

"'Then I'll concede to you for the moment, while you tell me your theories,' said David."

"I think I know enough to draw conclusions, but these are shared by others. Much of this was originated by others. I am only a member in the belief society."

"'There are many political groups and voices,' David agreed."

"I think this is rather a large group of diverse individuals, from several walks of life, who have made this thesis their mantra. I must now bring up the historical connection of the Warhol painting and the mystery. It's a point of view that might not be shared by the majority of your audience, but when you see the evidence, you'll be a believer, as will they. It is a point of view that was first expressed to me passionately and I must say depressively so, by the famous movie director John Huston. Do you know that name?"

"Of course. One of the top ten directors in history, I'd estimate."

"He thought that the world was out of control when a few madmen could influence world events to the extent that they did. When I was introduced to that view, I began to study and think about it more carefully. Over the years, I have then updated his views by way of some more recent events, to prove the point."

"I grabbed a chip from the dish and offered them to David. He had poured another glass of wine, and so it was obvious that he was ready for a long discussion."

"It's my 'Lubricant Theory of World Politics,' a treatise on historical events you might say, and why the world is screwed up at times."

"Ha, ha. That's the most interesting title I've heard in that field. Do tell me, Felix," said David. "I want to hear your full theory on why the world is so screwed up, and how the bad guys fit into it all."

"Let's start with the artists of the world. There are talented but screwed up. Either they have a bad relationship with their mother or father, or they have a bad sex life. Either way, they are depressed. But if they are lucky, or smart, they take it out on their art and end up with something magical. Your curators will call it magical, but the initial motivation is usually a reaction to something bad. For example, I know an artist in Los Angeles, a top name now, who hasn't talked to his brother for forty years when I knew him. He got into art as an escape for the torment that his older brother gave him as he was growing up. Now if it weren't for that brother, he'd probably never have turned to art, nor been so motivated. I know others who have personal problems, many marriages or too much sex outside of whatever marriage they happen to be in. And they are a bit crazy. But they get away with it all as long as they produce credible art."

"Switch now to political leaders. They are messed up much the same, but they aren't allowed to behave stupidly. The public is watching. Instead of art, they put their drive into leadership - making things happen. But it gets down to what drives someone. Walter Hopps described it to me once as the butterfly effect. We were talking about how one person can sometimes alter history, but since, I've applied that to mean that one small personality defect, one small behavioral deviation, one small odd-ball element about someone's life and if that person happens to be in a position to affect history, either through creative means or through leadership means, that initial cause can have large consequences."

"'I've known my share of movers and shakers; they aren't all crazy,' said David."

"Of course not, but even the most normal of them have these small hidden skeletons. And it gets all blown up out of proportion by bad relationships or by bad sex."

"Sex, now that's something that's pretty much out there. It's in our world."

"It's in our world, but with the movers and shakers, it's their downfall."

"But your premise is that the world is screwed up. Some of us hold out a lot of hope for its future."

"There's always the upside and always the screwed upside, but for reasons that might surprise you. I'm old perhaps, but I've lived through a lot of history. I'm a keen observer. Macro views of world history are the norm, and certainly do best describe events like wars, revolutions, even the Arab Spring. Macro views will look at the length of suppressed societies, world trends such as social media that not only help elect someone like an Obama but fueled the Arab Spring as it got more and more traction, and might even try to take temperature readings of the population—its restlessness, anger, or economic hardship."

"'But for each large movement, there are individuals, and some are responsible for starting or stopping specific actions,' I added. 'When observed, in a most micro way and in this treatise, in a most personal way, biases as well as personality oddities can change the course of world history. There's a saying about how a butterfly's wings can produce a hurricane. Well, in Mexico, we have millions of Monarch butterflies, and it's clear to us how movements can begin. Mexico is full of energetic leaders.'"

"'But I know less about Mexico. Can you tell me how all this affects the United States?' asked David."

"Since for the past century or so, the United States has been the most influential player in world politics, although all this might be changing, it is easiest to take a look at a few blatant examples within our own royal court. In the early 1960s, a youngish man became president of the United States. Prior to then, we had Eisenhower, Truman, and Roosevelt. Well, two of the three were known to have had affairs, but only one while in office. John F. Kennedy was known as a ladies man, but there are scant concrete examples of venturing into other beds. There are more rumors and the main examples are vague liaisons with Marilyn Monroe, among a few celebrities. However, Jacqueline also gave birth while in the White House, and so during this period, there must have been some romance in the privacy of their bedroom. However, younger men in a time of dramatic experimentation, especially when money and access and power are part of the makeup, must have had temptations."

"In Washington DC, there was an art movement called the Washington Color School, which gained international recognition."

"I know it well; we did a show that included that group about five years ago."

"If you know the history of it, within the local artists, Morris Louis, fresh from a New York visit to the studio of Helen Frankenthaler, started to experiment with stained paint on unprimed canvas, where the emphasis was on how the color became part of the canvas, rather than sitting on top of the cotton duck for the purpose of illustration or illusion. As Morris' stained shapes became more and more limited and minimal, he never went so far as to use masking tape to define the shape. That was taken up by younger colleague Ken Noland, who started doing a few wide bands of color in circle motif, then used masking tape to make a few bands in a "chevron" or "V" shape, before continuing his career with horizontal strips and so forth. Others quickly joined the movement; Gene Davis spent decades doing vertical strips of thinner and thinner widths, Tom Downing got into colored large polka dots, and so forth. An early proponent of the color school was a woman by the name of Mary Meyers, who seized her own mark with colored pie chart shapes."

"Now you don't need to remember anything else about the Color School, but only about that artist Mary. There will never be any hard factual evidence, but it was well known within the artist community, which as in any city but especially Washington D.C. in the 60s was extremely small and close, that Kennedy liked to experiment with smoking marijuana with some artistic friends. I know it to be true from the direct source. Mary was one of his friends, and in fact, a very close friend of mine. Or had been, when we were in school. Now, even though Kennedy had already been assassinated, there was a messy trail. The rumor goes that either the CIA or the FBI didn't like messy trials and so one early morning, Mary was murdered along the C&O canal. Not only was this front-page news, but unbelievably, I was there. I saw it, too late to stop it. I was too far to see the face of the killer or the driver of the get-away car, but I saw the murder. But it was not a typical murder at all. It was a hit job. An assassination. No one has ever proved why she was killed or by whom. Of course, in usual cover-up fashion and despite my statements to the police, reports came out that this was just a robbery attempt, or a sexual rape attempt. If she was getting morning exercise, it is reasonable to assume that she wasn't carrying any money to speak. Besides, I saw what really happened. And maybe for witnessing that alone and not for the Warhol painting, my life was in jeopardy. I'll never find out."

"'I'm not aware of this,' said David."

"You must have studied this period; this was a time when folks within the government thought they could bend the rules to make national and international changes. They were wiretapping everyone from Martin Luther King to young, leftwing protestors."

"If this feeling was prevalent within the government, it must be assumed that it was prevalent outside of government as well, assuming that people are generally influenced by the times. And so, while there has never been any definitive conspiracy proof about the help that Oswald received, it seems pretty clear that there need not be a group planning of the exact assassination. It is sufficient to understand that Oswald was not acting alone that day, and was influenced by some prior encouragement, even unplanned but voiced goals, that to initiate changes in our government was within the bounds of a self-appointed group of individuals. What's good for the goose is good for the gander; if the government could eliminate what officials considered harmful influences to our president, they felt that they could also go to other countries and use similar methods to attempt regime change."

"Let's go down the line, and take a look at the presidents during the prime of my life.

Lyndon Johnson assumed the presidency upon Kennedy's death, and although he was also known as a womanizer, one shudders to think of the sprayed hair styled women who might be attractive to the ugly duckling, who happened to become the most important man in the world. Duties would seem to limit access to women and a more authoritative wife might also have a hand at that as well. Certainly, any womanizing would not capture the imagination of the American public as it had with the glamorous Kennedy clan."

"It is difficult to imagine much with Nixon. It was reported that he would sit with his wife Pat for meals without saying a word. It's hard to imagine much more in bed than a weekly attempt. Most likely, he might have jerked off in the privacy of a locked bathroom. But that too, would influence world events. A shy introvert, Nixon allowed his men to assume even more power, to both control national groups and of course, to go after protesters - even to expand greatly the efforts at regime change, especially in South America."

"Jimmy Carter, as the world knows, only lusted for sex, and the Baptist Sunday school teacher would never actually try it out outside the confines of his wife's bed.

Next came Ronald Reagan, who by virtue of the fact that he was involved with at least one other woman before he was fully divorced, made it pretty clear that the Hollywood rumors lived up to some of the hype. By the time he ascended to the White House, he was mature in age to have all that as past history."

"Then came Bill Clinton, the most infamous womanizer amongst the recent presidents. It got him into trouble during his governorship, during his campaign for president, and of course, during his presidency. So the question is, why? Why was he so reckless to allow himself to get into this position - pun intended. How was his relationship with Hillary?"

"Certainly they were an attractive couple, both physically and by the fact that both were well educated individuals rising rapidly in their world of Arkansas. It was one of those cases of, 'they had everything.' Yet for some reason, Bill couldn't get enough in his own bed."

"Obviously, when two people don't satisfy each other, there are many factors. Often money, or lack thereof, plays a role, but in their case, they were doing fine. Personality conflict is a major factor, but for most appearances, their marriage was solid enough to remain. Did Hillary really say to Bill something like, "Honey, I really don't want more sex, but it's alright with me if you go out and get it as long as I don't know about it and you are discreet about it?" Somehow, that's doubtful. Most wives wouldn't say that, and so while it can't be ruled out completely, what has become an accepted theory really doesn't seem logical when you say it 'out loud.'"

"Public life offers many opportunities, but it takes away many opportunities. What it takes away are those private moments with friends talking about inappropriate things. When people can't go to marriage councilors, they get advice from friends; people in high places don't get that type of intimate advice. If a president wants condoms, how does he go about getting them? Can he leave that personal choice up to a trusted aide? Women have the same issues. For example, one……"

"Wait a second, Felix. Are you saying that a president doesn't deal with the basics of sex very well?" asked Bart. "I mean, every kid knows that stuff."

"Not really. Let me back up for a moment and explain. Public school education is better today in teaching sex than during the 50s or 60s, a time period when Hillary and Bill were growing up. Almost everyone learned from fellow kids, and what they learned included some facts and mostly myths. Yes, a few parents 'talked' to their children, but in an atmosphere of puritan values, not a whole lot was ever passed down. Since that's the way it was, that was the way it continued. Most women were very ignorant about many aspects of sex and how their body changes with age."

"And so comes now the very heart of this treatise, using this one example to show the incredible consequences of personal failure. And in this case, not necessarily the failure of one person, but instead the failure of communication within a married couple."

"Let it be stated, with the belief that no scientific survey will come up with any accurate statistics, the following principle. The number of heterosexual women who want more sex than their partners is about the same as the number of men who are satisfied with a little sex. For instance, no more than 5% women desire sex on a daily basis and likewise only 5% of men are satisfied with much less than daily sex. Now the obvious exceptions are the newly dating, newly engaged or newly married who tend to engage in sexual relations more often than average. In the same way, specific strains of time pressure, whether from important work obligations or injury or celebratory family events or even travel, are events that interrupt the daily routine and deny couples the time necessary to enjoy sex. But generally speaking, married couples have sex one, two, three times per week on average, but not daily. And women are more okay with that amount than men. However, the testosterone levels of men push the majority - and here the percentage could be as high as 95% - to want sexual relief more often."

"While there are also physical factors which can contribute, for example, lessened hormone activity which occurs gradually in all females as they age, psychological bases might have a greater effect. After all, the ability to participate is simply one of pleasing her spouse. It is the same for the man to please his partner. And for equality sake, of course, how that is done should be determined by both parties. Moving beyond the political correctness of the discussion, the end result is that in most cases, the more a wife can satisfy her mate, the happier the marriage might be."

"Time restraints cause many obstacles - from work to children to economic pressures. At least there are accepted solutions for many of the physical causes. That's why Viagra is a billion dollar gross sales business. For women, as they mature, their ability to have spontaneous sex diminishes, and menopause can reduce it even more, making orgasm more difficult to achieve, and also causing vaginal dryness."

"There are a variety of products that come to the rescue. Many women take additional testosterone to help increase libido. And there are numerous products found in drug and chain stores to combat dryness. However, once again to put it into a micro-level, it's difficult to conceive how even close friends of Hillary might mention to the First Lady -when Bill was Governor and later, especially when he was President - something like, "Oh,

Hillary dear, you know, the next time you are in Walmart or CVS, pick up some "Astroglide," because it really makes the penis go in without the pain."

"As gross as you might find this statement in a political treatise, it is something so crazy as this that might have hurt their relationship. After all, I suspect that these products are not stocked in the medicine cabinets of the private bathrooms of the White House. Now, there has to be the willingness to use the products, and for that, a couple's counselor might have additional insight, but generally, even if two want to tangle, if one can't for physical reasons, that puts much more strain on the marriage."

"Couple all that history with ego boosting thoughts as a result of being the most powerful man in the world, and then add to the mix a 22-year old, plumpish but endowed and attractive young woman who admittedly went to Washington to try to give some powerful person a blow-job, and the rest is, as they say, history. But what really were the ramifications?"

"Let's give a brief outline in a few sentences. Clinton was willing but a girl urged it to happen, and it did, but isn't it funny how the dress was saved and all this got out? It didn't bring down his presidency, but it made him look so immoral, that Al Gore wanted distance from Clinton in his run against Bush. If it were not for this scandal, the Clintons would have been on the road much more for Gore, and that would have made the difference in the election."

"David finally interrupted my treatise. 'You concluding theme is that a single twenty-two year old girl, with nothing other than access, affected history for decades afterwards?'"

"That's it. There are other contingencies involved, of course. History has multiple layers. It can be argued that Bush didn't win legally, without funny games being done by Florida and then the Supreme Court, but aside from that, the election never would have been that close. So Bush wins, and a decade later, a million people are dead, we have invaded Iraq, we open up a hornet's nest of terrorists, and instead of a surplus, we are trillions of dollars in debt as we spend all our money on a useless war. When the economic meltdown happened, while that by itself was enough to allow Obama to win, it also wiped out the remaining hope that the United States would retain its position as the number one super power of the world."

"Would Al Gore have reacted with an invasion of Iraq? A reasonable conclusion says 'no.' Bush wanted - again on the micro-level - to out-do his Dad, who as president didn't go after Saddam, and that emotional feeling happened to fit Cheney's goals to transform the mid-east to a more oil/U.S. friendly state."

"In referencing the invasion, it's also important to show how weak leadership can indeed spark world changes. Do you remember that Peter Seller's movie, *The Mouse that Roared*? It was a farce; an antiquated ship filled with funny guys dressed in Victorian knight outfits, wage war upon the United States so that they could lose and their tiny kingdom would be given aid like all other countries who have lost to the U.S. Well, in the movie, they won because it was a national holiday, so they were able to land and somehow captured the biggest bomb in history and take it back to their country. The comedy dealt with their unexpected winning rather than losing the war."

"'How does the movie connect with anything?' asked David."

"In equal odds, nineteen men armed with razor blade knives captured four planes and two slammed into the World Trade buildings. 3,000 lives were lost and that was tragic. And tens of thousands more died as a result of the actions started by that event. That one event also steered history onto a new path."

"'I'd say in that case you have way underestimated,' injected David. 'Hundreds of thousands at least have died in that conflict. But is it not tragic that 50,000 Americans get killed in car accidents, or that same number from crime, or that 300,000 people die unnecessarily in hospitals, or that many from unnecessary prescriptions, and so forth?'"

"I think this is more tragic, David, because this was caused by deliberate actions. An intelligent president would have had the logical reaction of getting together with other countries to conduct what really should have amounted to an international police action - to go after the estimated 1,000 Al Qaeda potential terrorists. But in grand fashion, Bush went after Iraq while the U.S. was drowning in debt. The end result, losing more lives - the number of total dead from all sides, military and civilian, is estimated at one million human lives. The other result was that the U.S. served as their promotional tool - the terrorists multiplied in size with new recruits."

"Felix, history is full of overly aggressive leaders."

"For me, it starts with something more insignificant. If that 22-year old woman had not landed that intern job in the White House, the world would be different, and in most likelihood, better. If Hillary had known about lubricant, then the 22-year old sexual ambitions might not have been successful. Two tiny issues, one with a person, the other just perhaps not knowing about a simple item that most women use, that's what steered history."

"David got up and went to the side table for another wine bottle and filled both our glasses, before adding his comments. 'Often small things influence bigger movements. Felix, you are right that art is influenced by weird things, perhaps just a bad father-son experience as you suggested. But politics is different.'"

"That's true, as far as how the public views it. While most people do put domestic strains in the background of their lives, artists put them up front and center. Those emotional daily battles can become the inspiration for major and great works. So, true, leaders can fail to suppress domestic issues and they can influence their views of the world and eventually, influence their decisions. In recent history, the emotional view of 'out doing dad' seemed to have dominated the decision to instigate a full-fledged invasion of another country and to topple the regime of a dictator. The inability of a man to control his sexual fantasies, enhanced undoubtedly by the fact that he wasn't getting enough in bed with his spouse, encouraged the quick affair with one president, only for it to explode as a sex scandal of world proportions, allowing the election - or let's agree to the term 'near-election' - of Bush."

"Never will these suppositions be included in the history texts of the future, but they nonetheless remain forefront in the logical explanations as to why the world went the way it did. Tragically, in this case, rather than it inspiring something positive, a hundred or two hundred years from now, looking back, it could well be the critical bad decision - a major miscalculation that the United States took - which started it's decline as a world power. "

"'But that's not true either,' I continued. 'Every assassin thinks that his or her actions, just one bullet in one gun in one hand, can change history for the better. That anyone, just a lone gunman as they call them, can do as much to influence history as a massive movement involving millions of people. So whether it's done with criminal intent, or accidental intent, or just because a young girl wants the thrill of presidential sex, the result is the same. But it's not always so planned. An assassin knows what the result should be; the girl on the prowl most likely had no idea of the chain reaction that she was going to cause.'"

"'So,' concluded David, 'the chain reaction that we will cause, by exhibiting your paintings and exposing to the world the truth, that might be the butterfly that changes history?'"

*****

"That's enough about political theories," Felix said to Bart.

"I was following it. I've never thought about history like that, I'll admit. It makes one feel that perhaps an average 'Joe' can have some influence in world affairs after all. I need to sleep on that one," said Bart.

Bart wanted to see how high they were still flying but couldn't see much through the window that was past Felix's body except some clouds. He thought about what he wanted to say. "So from all this, it gets to the fact that you, as one person, are in procession of the one envelope containing a strip of negatives, that all these bad guys, as you call them, want from you."

"I guess that's right. Might I have said it like that, you would not have cared. If I succeed in presenting these negatives to the public, might I change history? Might subsequent investigations alter governmental agencies or perhaps affect mob or cartel operations? I don't know for sure, but they could. And I am only one person. I'm only a pawn in the game of politics."

"Oh, you are exactly correct; I think it could be a game changer. I'm very appreciative of your story, all the background and giving me the information that is pertinent to take on whatever you might ask of me and to make any action I take relevant to a successful outcome."

"You see, you do become vested once you know the background. I wasn't wasting my time. We need to let the bad guys know that they can't kill nice and sincere people and get away with changing the course of history. Can we?"

"So may I see this valuable strip of negatives?" Bart asked at last.

"Yes, of course. Let me take it out of the envelope so you can see the actual film. Here it is. Please be careful. And I ask you to take care of it, should anything happen to me before I board that car that has been sent to pick me up. The address of the intended receiver is clearly written both on the envelope and in a letter that is enclosed in the envelope. Why do I suspect something, you might still wonder? Well, those who have gotten killed before me, and the attempts on my life- all that happened. And now I have the real item, the proof that will bring trouble to them, and they will want this, that I'm sure."

"This flimsy piece of plastic? It's all about this?" asked Bart holding up the Mylar negatives for the first time but unable to make out the scenes.

"I've never seen an actual negative before. This technology was before my time."

"Yes, it's all about this. Hold it on the edge so you don't get fingerprints on the image part."

"'Like this?' asked Bart as he held up the strip to light to try to see the photos.

"There are six photos on that strip. The images are in reverse. The darks on the photo are light on the negative and the lights are the dark areas. With special light and chemicals, photos were printed this way in dark rooms."

"And what about the painting?"

"The painting won't matter if I'm gone and if this is gone. It's just a made up painting, created by a weirdo artist. But this gives it credibility along with my story. Do you believe what I told you?"

"You made it sound very plausible, I can't deny that. I'm just not sure you know the difference between the good guys and the bad guys."

"Oh, I can tell, when they come after me. When I see someone gun down my friend, or try to run me over by a car. Those are the bad guys. Do they have wives or children or say their prayers every night? I don't know the answer to that. But I know they are not about helping the world improve. They are working to preserve their own business interests."

"That sounds true," said Bart. "But any stranger may be a betrayer of your trust, or a savior. Jesus - I'm assuming you are not religious, but still - Jesus had his loyal followers but he was betrayed by one of his own. Do you see? One never knows."

"That's true but sometimes reaching out, good things will result. I have reached out to you."

"Why do you think these negatives are any different from those taken the next day? After all, it only shows a building."

"Warhol purchased the strip. I have not cut up the images into separate frames. At the time, he didn't know what image or images he wanted to use. So the others on the strip show the people just before and after the assassination. Now it did not show anything that the police were interested in, but it does show the time and date of the event, so that the photo of the book depository which is in the middle of the strip - the one with the images in the windows - can be proved easily to be at the exact time of Kennedy's assassination."

"Why didn't the police think it had something of value?"

"Well, the police, or I suspect the FBI, examined the film and didn't spot what Andy spotted once it was enlarged. They concluded that it had nothing of interest. There were the more valuable ones, showing the actual motorcade. Lots of people took photos after all the screaming started. So once they released the film back to the photographer - an amateur bystander who happened to be standing at the right place, or the wrong place at the right time, the owner decided to make some fast money. Andy 's guy looked at a proof sheet, saw a bunch of crowd photos and this one of the depository and told Andy. As an artist, he knew he could make it work. The significance was that the roll was taken at that moment- there was a connection to the event that no subsequent photo would have had. And I must say, I suspect initially he was more interested in the crowd images. But he had the images and decided to work with all that he had."

"I see the building; it's the third photo."

"How does it feel to be holding history?"

"After your story, I'd say a bit scary. Here, you shouldn't even trust me, I don't think."

Bart handed the envelop back to Felix.

"Felix, if I understand the essence of your thesis, it's that at times in history, even a pawn, a common man, such as you or me, can affect history."

"That's it exactly. From a series of accidents, I'm in possession of a secret that will be headline news. And should anything happen to me, I'm asking you to carry the torch. You are just someone randomly here, sitting next to me, but willing to listen to my story."

"And might all this really affect history?"

"Not in the same way that Oswald and his accomplice did, and not in the way that a 22-year old girl did when she tangled with Clinton, but who knows? There is a presidential election coming up. Perhaps the candidates will be asked about the government's role in these types of things, and perhaps one of them will put a foot in his or her mouth. Then someone will look back and say, if this secret had never been revealed, then 'so and so' would never have made such a stupid remark that lost a tiny percentage of votes to change the results of the election."

"Or nothing at all will happen," said Bart.

"That's also correct. However, I tend to believe that while butterflies might not create a hurricane with the flapping of their wings, some actions do have a better chance of causing a domino effect."

"So I'm going to be part of history. That is, if the negatives get into my hands and if I'm then able to carry out the mission. That's kind of exciting, in some ways. It's not often that an ordinary citizen gets that chance. Kind of like taking the bullet for someone, isn't it? Like for a president or someone?"

"It could be so, Bart. It could be so. The fact that you might be involved is really no different than the reason I'm involved. The reason Liz was drawn in, that was just by chance. Even Andy - Andy who discovered it - only got those negatives by chance. And so history goes, a lot of chance and some actions by individual players. That's what we are, just individual players."

"I don't know, Felix, sometimes I think we have just formed a team."

"That's a good feeling - to know there's support. Thank you."

Just then the attendant came with the food that Felix had requested. "Here comes your wine and sandwich. You need to get your tray down," reminded Bart. "Here, I'll hold your wine until you get it down."

Felix slid the envelop into his bag which was beside him on the floor. He put down the tray and took the sandwich that the attendant offered him. Bart held his drink and napkin. "Here's your drink. Bon appétit."

Felix set it down and adjusted his napkin to cover his lap. "Do you want something, too? Look, the attendant can bring you something too."

Bart turned his head to see the attendant's cart go past. "I don't eat much when I fly. Weak stomach or something. Thank you."

Felix took a bite of the sandwich. Then he picked up the wine and sipped. "See, over there, the attendants are already collecting trash. I'd better eat fast."

"No, there's plenty of time. They will be coming around again, not to worry," said Bart glancing at the steward going down the aisle again with a trash bag.

"Not the greatest wine, but what can one expect on the plane," said Felix. "Oh, it's not so cloudy now," he said turning his head to look out the window. He ate another bite, and turned his head again to look out the window. "Looks like we are a bit lower. Maybe we are getting close to New York," he said while drinking.

Bart noticed that Felix has drunk quite a bit already; the wine was half gone.

CHAPTER 22

The old gentleman, seated in 3A by the window, coughed and gagged and then let out a few spasms. With a little bit of saliva coming out of his mouth, he barely could get out a few soft moans. Quickly his head went down towards the window. He spilled the small portion of wine still left in his glass. He was out.

The static P.A. announcement was barely audible above the groan of the plane's engines, first in Spanish and then in English. "The pilot has reported that we are within 70 miles of JFK and should be on the ground in less than twenty minutes. Please put your seats and trays in their upright position, and make sure your seat belt is fully fastened. We will be making a final round to collect any trash that you might have. It has been a pleasure having you aboard our flight from Puerto Vallarta."

Bart Singleton, seated comfortably in his first class seat, observed that the old gentleman in the seat next to him had fallen asleep. Bart thought that he had heard a lifetime of stories during this flight. Bart picked up the gentleman's glass, plate and napkin and gave it to the attendant when she came up the aisle. "Sound asleep it seems," he said in a low voice to the attendant while handing her the trash. "He sure talked a lot."

The attendant smiled with sympathy. "Sorry if he was a bother.

Looks like he needs some rest. We'll wake him soon enough when we deplane."

"Oh, he was entertaining enough." Bart smiled and turned away to also get the old man's tray table into its locked position. He heard the metallic knock of the wheels going down from the plane and as he looked over the old man to see out of the window, he could make out buildings from the New York area. The sun was just beginning to set, causing a glow from the reflected sides of glass office buildings.

The plane landed with a whip-bump but soon enough was gliding on wheels and using air brakes. It took several more minutes before the second announcement came on, welcoming everyone to New York, with time and temperature, information about immigration, customs, connections and baggage, plus asking everyone not to get out of their seats until the plane had pulled up fully to the gate and the pilot had signaled that it was time to then unbuckle, opening the storage above carefully since items might have moved about, and that passengers were now free to use their cell phones. As the plane was slowing, Bart reached down to Felix's bag and pulled out the envelope containing the strip of negatives, and held it in his lap.

He then pulled out his cell phone and waited the minute or two for it to power up. He pressed his numbers, and said that he had just landed and all is well. There was no conversation beyond that.

Being towards the front, passenger Bart Singleton was able to get up and out early in the line, and he grabbed his bag from above before leaving. As he stood in the aisle waiting for the door to open to allow passengers to exit, Bart slipped the envelope into his bag and zipped it tight. The sleeping old man didn't move. Bart spotted the same attendant standing at the plane's exit and said, "I guess you'll have to wake him."

"He must need a wheelchair. We'll help him as soon as all the passengers have cleared. Have a great afternoon!"

Bart smiled and left with the rest of the passengers. Soon he would be among the first to go through immigration and customs, which as an American citizen would be no problem. His passport was genuine although for someone else, and he had others if the need arose in the future. He would then collect his suitcase in the baggage claim area, take out a sports jacket from the bag - which had a few other clothes in it to make it seem real in case he was inspected. Before forty-five minutes had passed, he was outside the terminal, in a taxi and heading for the city. He would eventually take three taxis so that no one could follow his route, crush and then ditch his disposal prepaid cell phone, rip his checked bag and remaining clothes into pieces and scatter the pieces into no fewer than six public trash containers, and disappear forever from anyone who might want to talk to the passenger sitting next the old man - just in case anyone suspected foul play; he was hoping that they wouldn't since it would be quite natural for a 94-year old man to die on a flight; if they did find out, they'd be looking for that passenger, and they'd never find him. Later, he'd change his hair back to its natural grey, in a shorter style. He'd do it on the train to Baltimore where his car was waiting for him. He had plans to drive back to San Francisco. He had work waiting for him there but he wasn't needed until a week from now. Meanwhile, he was going to have a pleasant drive across the country. He always wanted to see the Grand Canyon - just never had the chance. The strip of negatives? They were already en route, mailed to a Dallas post office address he had been given; sent normal mail, dropped in a city mailbox, the negative in an ordinary white envelope with a regular stamp; not even with a tracking number. He was told not to - everyone trusted the United States Post Office.

*****

As the flight attendants had waited patiently for all the passengers to exit the plane, and then had waited for the wheelchair assistants to line up just outside the entranceway to receive those needing a ride, the attendant assigned to the first-class section went to wake up the old gentleman.

"Sir, we've arrived in New York. It's time to wake up."

There was no answer. As she was gently shaking him, one of his arms went limp.

"Sherrie, come quick. I think he's ill."

As the second attendant rushed over, she whispered, "Is he dead?"

"Poor old man, " said the first attendant. "Maybe his time was up."

"He must be dead. He's not moving!"

The first attendant shrugged. She couldn't tell. "Oh my God, he's all wet. Call an ambulance. Just in case."

The second attendant hopped to the phone a few feet away and made the urgent call.

"Sir, are you alright? Are you alright?" repeated the attendant.

Finally she heard a slight moan. One eye opened halfway. In a low and raspy voice, the old gentleman barely was able to mumble, "I've been poisoned. Call a doctor. Call the police."

The attendant thought at first that he meant that he had some sort of food poisoning. She tried to remember what the gentleman had ordered, and if he had eaten it. As she was thinking this, the old man repeated his alarm in the same, barely audible voice. "That man poisoned me. He robbed me. Help me." He then fell out of consciousness.

"Sherrie, is the ambulance coming? "

"Yes, I've called."

"Call the authorities too. There might be a bigger problem here."

The first responders came within minutes, and with a minimum of commotion, they had the old gentleman out of his seatbelt and onto the stretcher. As they were carrying him out of the plane, the lead responder said to the attendants, "Find his carry-on and take it to baggage claim and tell them we have a passenger going straight to the hospital. They'll hold his belongings and notify immigration about the situation. There was no further explanation as the responders had enough to do to get the patient to the ambulance and get the basic vitals and perhaps some sort of treatment started. After the walkway, they used a different exit to get to the ambulance waiting nearby, without going where all the passengers had to go. The main responder didn't know if the old man was going to make it.

CHAPTER 23

Exactly two days later, David Bresland squeezed through the crowd and down the side aisle of the auditorium to the stage stairs. The hall was filled to capacity with interested art patrons and reporters from news organizations from around the world, almost all who were based in New York City, a reasonable drive from the museum. These reporters, some with their support crews of camera and audio technicians, had received the Clark's press release a week earlier. Embedded with the museum's art story was a real, hard news story-- an answer to the Kennedy assassination. This was not a statement that usually came from an art institute's exhibition press release. Few editors wanted to miss this opportunity and they had no reason to think the museum was bluffing.

David walked up the five steps to the podium, set off to the left side of the stage so the large projection screen would be in full view of the audience. For the start of the presentation, the museum's name and the title of the exhibition were projected onto the large screen. The audience quieted almost instantly.

"Ladies and Gentlemen, welcome to the Clark Art Institute. You are in for a treat tonight and to be part of an historic event. In addition to our supportive members and distinguished guests being present, there are press reporters here in anticipation. I don't think we will disappoint any of you."

"We are here to inaugurate our special exhibition titled, 'Warhol's Art and the Kennedy Assassination.' And in doing so, we think we can solve, or at least prove, one aspect of the mystery surrounding the circumstances of his death."

There was a loud whisper that could be heard throughout the gallery.

"That's correct. Tonight, in this museum and because of this very exhibition, we will bring a new focus to what happened on that day, November 23, 1963." David pressed the remote so the first image, that of the Kennedy motorcade, was shown. "Perhaps a few of you were alive and remember that date very well. All of you know its historical significance. It is one of the few dates in history that people will not forget."

"As you know, there have been hundreds, if not thousands of theories put forth over the past several decades. Today, I think we can put some of these theories to rest as well as to give new insight as to the particulars of that fateful day. Today we will stimulate a new investigation."

"We had invited the exhibition's guiding inspiration here tonight, the lender of these two never-before-shown Warhol paintings, Felix Peters, a well-known artist in his own right. I'm sad to report to you that I was informed two days ago that Felix died on a flight from Puerto Vallarta, Mexico to New York City; he was on his way to Williamstown to host this very event and to explain the implications of this show, and of his major contribution to the exhibition, the loan of two magnificent Andy Warhol paintings. These paintings, ladies and gentlemen, have never, in their entire existence, been shown to the public."

David projected a studio photograph of Felix working in front of his paintings and then projected the two paintings. "In the projection, you see the two Warhol paintings which are on display upstairs and which will be open for viewing after this presentation. The painting on the left was purchased by the actress Elizabeth Taylor directly from the artist; it was hung in her private home for a while and then stored. The painting on the right has never been seen by anyone other than the artist, Andy Warhol."

"The fact that the painting on the right has never been seen and the circumstances surrounding this fact will do nothing less than astonish you."

"Felix Peters was 94 years old. On my visit to his house and studio in Mexico, he seemed full of vigor and energy. He was a gracious host and I liked him a lot. We do not have confirmation on the cause of his death, but Mr. Peters was concerned that his life might be at risk in presenting this exhibition. He felt that there were those who might want to have him silenced. Nevertheless, he felt that history needed to be corrected. It is possible that Mr. Peters was murdered on his way to Williamstown."

This time, the chatter was much louder. The press snapped photos of the director and some of the audience as they reacted. Anyone would have known that this was headline material, no matter what was said after this. Murder was not a word that was often, and probably never, uttered at the Clark Art Institute.

"Because of the suspected circumstances of Mr. Peter's death, it is appropriate that we have hung in our main foyer an example of his work. That painting was hanging in Sayulita opposite to the left Warhol painting for many years, and the artist generously loaned it to us for this exhibition."

"Mr. Peters was a very intelligent and thoughtful person, both in his art and his life. He carefully preserved and maintained these paintings for more than 60 years, and he carefully planned how he wanted to finally show the paintings to the public. As insurance, he sent to me specific instructions and I feel confident, tonight, in telling you the secret that Felix Peters shared with no one for all those years."

"Ladies and gentlemen, the painting, at least the one on the left, arrived at our museum more than six months ago. We built this show around it. As you know, Andy Warhol, like much of the art and performance community, was drawn to the late John F. Kennedy. The President's assassination was a giant blow to the emotions of these artists, and many artists tried to grapple with its implications. Warhol did a series of paintings revolving around the Kennedy presidency. The most famous were his multiple portraits of the First Lady, Jackie Onassis. But he also used photographs taken in Dallas at the time of the motorcade for a series around the assassination."

"Much of Warhol's work used recognizable images such as Coca-Cola and Campbell Soup. Public photographs that he found printed in newspapers or advertisements also served as sources for the images in his work. However, due to the value of the assassination photos, some owned and copyrighted by smaller organizations or private people who happened to be standing there and taking amateur shots at the precise moment, Warhol assumed that he would be sued for years if he used them. So with a fairly ample budget - as you know, his reputation was solid by then and he was selling very well - he had one of his factory managers purchase a roll of film images that were taken by a spectator and offered for sale. This purchase was made several months after the assassination. This roll was not considered historically or criminally of importance, at the time. Remember, many people at the scene took photographs. Only a few captured what the government needed to analyze the event. Warhol only wanted to use images that were taken at the time of the historic tragedy. Because of the images on the roll and the reactions of the crowd to the assassination, he was sure - and we are also certain - that the photos he purchased were actually taken at the time the shots were fired at the motorcade."

"Now, there were six images in this one strip of negatives that Warhol purchased. Warhol used a couple of the crowd scenes for one series of paintings, but for this series, he settled upon using the image of the building where Oswald shot the President. This image seemed very similar to all the others of the Book Depository building and Andy didn't think much of it. He blew up the image to create the silkscreen that he needed.

He then silkscreened the image with black ink on a total of six canvases, each painted previously with a different background color. For his first painting, he painted the backdrop a very light and bright gold yellow, really gold with yellow, white and a speck of silver mixed in. This brought out the details of the photo to a greater extent, especially with the image now very large, filling a four by six foot canvas. As the artist was brushing on his loose brushstrokes, he backed away to see the result of his first painting in the series of six. At that historic moment, for the first time, Andy Warhol saw a detail in the photograph that no one else had seen. It turned out not to be in the photographs of the same building taken about the same time by other photographers. Now I say 'about,' because a fraction of a second can make all the difference."

"I will tell you in a moment what that discovery was. Please bear with me as I continue. Andy studied all the images carefully, and then studied the strip of negatives with a magnifying glass, and he confirmed his discovery. Andy didn't know what to do. He panicked because he knew that he had something very special, but perhaps very dangerous. Keep in mind, Oswald had killed the President, Ruby had killed Oswald, and there were other threats being made as well."

"Andy didn't have the notion of just calling the FBI, or calling the New York Times and just telling the world what he had. He was very paranoid and chose to just discuss it carefully with a close advisor."

"Now who would Andy call?" David waited to allow people to think about this before continuing. He wanted to pace out his remarks. "You or I would call a lawyer, a law enforcement person, or even tell a reporter. Not Andy. He called someone who happened to be a friend, and who had just chatted with Andy the evening before because he had just completed her portrait series. And in Andy's world, it was always a group of celebrities around him. Andy called his friend, actress Elizabeth Taylor."

"Elizabeth Taylor was so famous, she too had had nutcases after her and threats on her life. She warned Andy to be careful with the painting and the image. This made Andy even more scared, and so they formed a plan. Really, Ms. Taylor came up with the plan and together they executed it."

"Andy finished the last five canvases, and painted them in a similar way, but with one main difference. Can you see the difference in these two paintings?"

"Andy used paint to enhance elements of the photographs in most of his paintings. Look carefully at these two paintings, hung side by side. In the painting on the left, noticed that the artist didn't touch these windows, the ones on the second and fifth levels and the sixth level. He only painted around the image. He made a second painting also of a similar background color, printed out the image, and then wiped out the element in the photograph that was so potentially controversial. And he did the same with the remaining four canvases. His normal work method was to include brush variations over the same image. These four in the series were later sold by Andy's gallery dealer, Leo Castelli, and since have been shown at various museums. But the very first one, the one that was not wiped out, was the painting that showed what none of the other paintings revealed. But once Andy realized that, he wanted to hide it. He was afraid to let anyone see it, yet as an artist, he couldn't bring himself to destroy or even alter the painting. He knew it was dangerous but he also knew that it was gold. What was he to do?"

"Now this is the part that not even Felix Peters knew about for many years, which is why this got buried. Following Elizabeth Taylor's instructions, Andy attached the negatives from the roll of film, the only transparency that contained the fine details of the photographs, to the back of the second painting. He then stretched that canvas on top of the very first painting, and put a strip frame around it. No one, even viewing the back, would ever know that there were two layers of primed canvas. The plastic strip of negatives was so thin, and he used just a little tape, that it would never telegraph through to the surface of the canvas. This painting, which was one of only five known paintings in the series, at least the world assumed it was only one painting, was then purchased by Elizabeth Taylor and shipped off to her house in Los Angeles."

David took another break. He was grateful that they had enough seats for the museum's members; most were older. He didn't worry about the reporters; they were on duty anyway, whether comfortable or not. He never could have taken so much time to get into all the details for a standing audience. He could tell that they were interested in the story and were not yet fidgeting in their chairs.

A woman raised her hand in the back. "I'm sorry but I do have a question, David." The woman was Helen Gold, a wealthy Williamstown resident, and one who gave a substantial donation each year to the museum.

"Yes, Mrs. Gold, but please remember, I have a ways to go in my story."

"I'm sorry, yes, but I do have a question. Didn't Andy Warhol have assistants who saw this?"

"Yes, he did work with assistants. But they didn't spot the detail and when Andy spotted it, he sent them out of the factory - remember, Warhol's studio building was always referred to as The Factory. It was late afternoon and he told them to come back the next morning. Andy often worked by himself in the evening when he did the custom brushwork. But let me continue and you'll see how we get back to this. And in the end, if you have any questions, I'll be glad to answer them."

"So the painting got to Los Angeles, and into the hands of Elizabeth Taylor. Ms. Taylor knew of the double painting but you know, she had a busy life too. Remember, too, that there were national changes going on. Much of the American public, including all of Ms. Taylor's friends, were depressed, perhaps clinically depressed over the death of their hero, their savior, their only hope for a better future in the political world. And they were very distrustful of Johnson, and his people who quickly seized all control. While all were distrustful, the art and Hollywood community were divided as to what to do. Half of the liberals wanted to help Johnson. To the country, Johnson was carrying out Kennedy's goals, and perhaps better able to reach those goals than he would have been had the President lived. But behind closed doors, it was a vastly different world. Johnson wanted the support of the arts community and made overtures but he didn't understand that world; he had no rapport with them. In the contemporary art world, Johnson preferred his Remington sculptures and western paintings, not Warhol or anything like Pop art. He pulled some people in with the argument that he wanted to carry out the Kennedy goals, but there were those who thought his fingers had been dirtied. After all, the assassination had been carried out in Johnson's own home turf. So the other half just didn't trust Johnson; some even thought he might have had something to do with Kennedy's assassination and so wiped their hands of the White House and started to look for alternative candidates. That would take years.

In any case, Ms. Taylor was torn between whether to give President Johnson support or not. This came to mean something because a year later, there would be an election and we all know what elections are about- money. Hollywood had contributed a lot to help Kennedy, and Johnson wanted that same vein of gold."

"As you know, Johnson won handsomely against a weak Goldwater campaign, and life went on. Then, too, problems were increasing, in Vietnam especially. And soon thereafter, there were other assassinations, most notably Martin Luther King followed by Robert F. Kennedy. That decade had more than its share of political violence, as highlighted by Kent State and the Chicago Convention. Now if you are amazed that we are here at the Clark, revisiting those political issues, I will remind you that all of it goes back to this painting."

"In Elizabeth Taylor's mind, the world was getting dangerous. Someone had threaten her and broken into her yard, and in Washington D.C, one of artists who Ms. Taylor had met, and whom Felix Peters also knew, and an artist who was close to President Kennedy, had been killed on the C&O canal in Georgetown under suspicious circumstances. Well, let me be blunt. Many in the art world were convinced that the Johnson administration had ordered her killed."

"This may sound shocking today, but during those times, lots of stuff happened without proper explanation, in this country and as you all know, all around the globe where the U.S. government tried to influence and in some cases, steer which government or dictator would be in power. Later, this became the culture of the Watergate burglary, Irangate, and other Washington scandals."

"A few years later, inadvertently through Andy Warhol's publication, some of this started to get publicized. When someone got to Ms. Taylor, perhaps from the Johnson administration, Ms. Taylor panicked as well. She called her friend, an artist whom she knew very, very well who lived most of the time in Mexico. Ms. Taylor owned property in Mexico and she thought it safer to get the painting out of the United States. She arranged to transport it there, hidden along with other home furnishings. Once there, she wanted it out of her house, so she loaned but really gave the painting to artist and friend Felix Peters, with the promise that no one would see it during her lifetime and that he should keep it in his home there, a town twenty-two miles north of Puerto Vallarta. She thought she was continuing her promise to Warhol while distancing both of them from the painting."

"Now Felix didn't know the connection or what was under the painting. He knew that it was one of Warhol's first assassination paintings, and that Ms. Taylor had said there was an element of danger in owning it, and that was about all. He also realized, as Warhol's art grew in reputation, that it was very valuable."

"The years rolled by, and Felix Peters established his own reputation. After the death of Mr. Peter's wife who died quite young, he moved his two daughters to Los Angeles for their education, but he returned often to his home in Puerto Vallarta and to his bigger residence that he built in a town about an hour away, called Sayulita. It was there, in his Sayulita house, that Mr. Peters kept the painting, in a secure and climate controlled room."

"The town of Sayulita. Remember that name. Perhaps you know the town? It has since become a much traveled vacation destination. But it also is the home of Felix Peters and the home for 60 years of this Andy Warhol painting. I visited Mr. Peters and I saw the painting there, and the circumstances of its adopted home. But what I saw was only the painting and the image on the left, ladies and gentlemen. Felix told me of the second painting but was afraid to show it to me until right before the exhibition, for security purposes."

With that statement, people lifted their heads ever so slightly. They had been listening fine, but this was a revelation that made them want to view the image once again. Mrs. Gold started to raise her hand, but David waved her off.

"Wait with questions because I'm now getting to the juicy part."

"Upon word of Mr. Peter's death, I was able to open a package that had accompanied the painting. In it were instructions should Mr. Peters be unable to attend for any reason. The instructions told us what to do and how."

"We assembled our top conservators and with increased security to minimize risk of revealing prematurely what we were doing, our curators carried out his instructions and essentially discovered the secret in the same way that Mr. Peters had discovered several decades ago. The museum's Mr. Wickstrom videotaped the entire process so it would be well documented for this exhibition."

"What was so special about this painting? I'm going to tell you something that only two people knew for many years, until Felix Peters, in possession of the actual painting, discovered on his own. The reason that no one ever saw the first painting until tonight is that Andy Warhol, taking Elizabeth Taylor's advice, covered it over with the second painting in the series. So while it looked like one canvas, no one knew that it actually was two paintings on one stretcher with one frame around them."

"We carefully removed the double layer frame around the painting, and then we carefully removed the staples from the canvas. Just as Mr. Peters had advised us, indeed under the painting was a second layer, a second Warhol painting of the same subject. We left that painting on the stretcher and put in fresh staples. We had already prepared a stretcher of the same dimensions as Mr. Peters instructed, and we stapled the top painting to that new stretcher. Behind each painting are the original labels and signatures by the artist."

"Now the negatives which Mr. Peters first saw, had actually been removed and stored separately by him. In fact, his death possibly was due to the fact that the murderer assumed he was carrying the roll of negatives to this exhibition. And he was correct. The murderer is now in possession of the roll. It is most likely gone forever."

The audience again chatters. David raises his voice to get their attention. "But, ladies and gentlemen, Felix Peters was a very smart man. In the decades since the film had been taken, digital imaging has taken over. As an artist, and like any good artist, digitizing images of one's work is standard procedure. There's hardly an artist today, anywhere on the globe, who is not an expert at the best methods of getting digital images."

"We have that roll, reproduced and enlarged, in the gallery so you can see how the artist Andy Warhol, used the images and then, when they were blown up, spotted the astonishing discovery."

David signaled for the next projection, filling the screen with the image of the strip of negatives.

"And what is that discovery that was hidden in the second painting? Ah, now we come to the very climax of my remarks, and one that will put an additional interest for this exhibition, which is interesting just because of the art, but now is of historical importance. Andy Warhol, in his studio, discovered this fact. While everyone was looking at the sixth floor window, the specific floor and window where the assassin Oswald stood and fired those fatal shots, and who, by thousands of pages in the Warren Report was finally declared the sole assassin, artist Andy Warhol, using what he thought was interesting and timely but unimportant photographs, spotted a window on the fifth floor, and in that window, clearly stood a figure - with a gun!"

"Yes, ladies and gentlemen, there can be no doubt that the government report is clearly wrong. There was a second gunman. To what extent, we do not know, but we do know that there was some sort of conspiracy in the assassination of John Fitzgerald Kennedy, the 35th President of the United States."

David stood still. He knew everyone needed a minute to absorb what he had just stated.

"Look at the painting on the left. There is no figure because with his brushstrokes, Warhol painted over that window, at least with enough paint to make it unclear what was underneath. He did the same on the four additional paintings in that series. In the painting on the right, his first in the series, he left that area alone, and indeed, then saw that the image was in the window. I will tell you that the four additional paintings in this series and the one that Elizabeth Taylor received and hung and then stored, Andy made sure that he painted out that particular window. He wanted no one to know. He was tempted, according to what Mr. Peters told me who heard it from Ms. Taylor, to paint it over and be done with it, but he couldn't. It would be like breaking a Faberge Egg, or vandalizing the Mona Lisa. He could no more alter a finished painting that he had done than you or I could paint a black mark over one of our treasured Monet or Renoir paintings. The famous artist Andy Warhol, alone in his studio with his six paintings on the floor before him, decided to leave this first painting alone and let it be the only painting that would show the world the truth. But not then, not when he thought he might get killed in doing so. Giving the world this information was of less importance to him than his own life. So he panicked and called Elizabeth Taylor for advice and they hatched their plan."

"Now as the months and then years went by, Warhol had a hard time keeping this secret. It was too sweet not to share it with someone, but he never was direct; he just hinted. Ms. Taylor got some suspicious calls and some months later, decided it was safer - for her - to get the painting out of her house and out of the country, without destroying it. In fact, she wanted it known that it was no longer in her collection."

"Then a few years later, another episode happened. You might be aware that Andy was into all kinds of media projects. He took photographs, he made films, he did installations, and several years later, he started a magazine called *Interview*. It went on to attract a very sizable circulation. This magazine was a fun pet project of his. At one time, the editor came up with an idea for a story with the Mary Meyers killing and Kennedy association to the arts as its subject, and happened to chat with Warhol to get some ideas. Warhol got all excited but not enough to reveal what he knew, but enough to say something like, 'Oh, Elizabeth Taylor was a close friend with Kennedy and also knew the artist, and she knows a lot and she's a big celebrity, so interview her.' Or he'd say, 'that half-Mexican artist Felix Peters, knew something about that, so you can ask him. He was a witness, wasn't he?'"

"Did he also mention that he had a painting that would prove to the world that Kennedy was not killed by a single assassin? Was he unconsciously trying to get the secret out? Did he want Ms. Taylor to reveal in an interview that she held, or knew where it was stored, a painting that would change everyone's conclusion about the Kennedy presidency and the Kennedy assassination? Our guess, and that of Mr. Peter's, is that Andy just wanted to stir things up without going that far - just a taste of something without having to commit. But along the way, he also proved to be a valuable source to the reporter. After all, these were not seasoned newspaper reporters, but young kids, fresh out of school, with an art leaning, trying to write celebrity stories more than hard news. So just giving some names and access to a young reporter, meant he was way ahead of what the New York Times might have gotten in such a short time - no offense to the Times reporters who are here today."

"That kind of thing seemed innocent enough to Warhol, just enough gossip to make the magazine story of interest, but you know, when reporters asked questions, they brought things into the open which stirred up all kinds of rumors which got heard by all sorts of folks and before long, Mr. Peters almost gets run down by a car while his house is broken into, and the question is, how do you prove it had any connection to this painting and to this secret? It's impossible, but just as Ms. Taylor panicked a few years earlier, Mr. Peters had to flee with his children back to Mexico until things blew over--- it was hard to prove but he certainly felt the danger."

"And Andy, reckless with his gossip was even more paranoid about the dangers that would come his way if his secret got fully out. Remember, it was only a year before that Warhol was, himself, shot in his studio by a frustrated feminist writer. You, too, would be paranoid after that. Can you imagine wondering when someone might attempt to shoot you next? "

"And so was Elizabeth Taylor. She never had an assassination attempt, but there were plenty of shady figures around her. This was the decade when the word 'paparazzi' became so well known. By that time, Robert F. Kennedy and Martin Luther King had been assassinated. Violence in the United States was increasing, at least, that's how it felt to the individuals who held this secret. Mr. Peters wondered why this painting brought out these kinds of folks. He wondered and then, almost by accident, discovered the secret."

"Mr. Peters had the painting and eventually, getting a clue from just lifting the painting and realizing that it was a bit heavy, figured out the secret - the secret that I just revealed to you tonight. He had promised that he would never show the painting while Ms. Taylor was alive. Fast forward many years, and both Warhol and Taylor are no longer alive and Felix has to figure out how to make this secret public, but in a way that the entire truth would come out. He didn't want this to look like a publicity stunt to stir up yet another conspiracy theory."

"We are here to open this exhibition, although it was carefully planned many years earlier. I would like to also thank my curatorial and museum staff, and especially the William College graduate students who helped with the research, all done carefully under our Chief Curator, Ms. Caroline Vine. I would like to thank our videographer, Mr. James Wickstrom, who painstakingly documented our process of separating and uncovering the second painting so there can be no doubt as to how the second painting appeared."

"This is a concluding chapter in the painting's history, but a beginning chapter for what it reveals. But regrettably, the harm that Mr. Peters feared might befall him seems to have occurred and as a result, he is not with us sharing this moment. That fact alone gives even more credence to the facts that I've just related to you tonight."

"Ladies and gentlemen, thank you for your time and for coming out for the Clark's special summer exhibition. I welcome you to view the paintings in this exhibition, because all of them have art significance. But these two Warhol works, together with the prints that are blown up showing each negative on the film roll, and the extra large one showing the window and the second gunman, has a historic significance that I'm sure you can now appreciate. We are grateful to Felix Peters, for all that he has done, and I'm sure that his dedication will be richly received. I will take questions."

Hands flew up all over the room.

CHAPTER 24

Felix Peters lay in the hospital bed, looking up at the suspended ceiling with an array of emergency alarms attached. He didn't have the strength to even turn his head much to view the rest of the room. All he could do was think, about the events and about his life.

"I might die today," he thought to himself. "If not today, it'll be tomorrow. OK, there's a chance I'll drag it out. I suspected it was poison. Why did I put some to my lips? I couldn't let him know. Just a little. I turned my head and let most pour down my side. I was wet but he didn't see. The noise of the plane. The attendant walking the aisle caught his attention just for the second. It was enough, I think. I tried. They all think that old folks are senile. We get away with stuff. And most of us are a lot more aware of what's going on than people think. That guy thought I was out of it. He was wrong. But I had to let him believe I was a goner. Did I succeed? Ha. I'm here, aren't I? The doctors said a drop or two more and I wouldn't be here. They found the cyanide in the wine that drenched my clothes. They knew I wasn't crazy. Except that I didn't escape it all. That little bit got onto my lips and into my mouth and down my throat."

"Luckily, it was a tiny amount. Not enough, as it turned out. I'm still alive. The way the doctors have pinned my hopes, I might just make it now. What difference would it make anyway? My stomach is on fire, they've loaded me with painkillers, I can't move out of bed, they are feeding me some liquid stuff, and trying to make sure I'm somewhat comfortable."

"I should just sleep. I can't. My mind wanders. The problem is that I still have my wits about me. And I want to say a few last words if that's what I have. But my throat is sore. I can barely talk. I think I don't need to for a while. I did my preparations and David had my notes and gave his talk. I wonder how it went. He should be coming. My daughters, too. At least Silvia will come. She has always been the one to worry more about me. Daniela is retired and too involved with her grandchildren; she'll call me once Silvia makes her report. But a nurse told me something about Silvia - what was it? Silvia sent a message that she was on the red-eye and will be here later this morning. I think that was it. That's soon if I have my days right. I'm a bit mixed up. When did I come here? There's no newspaper here to even tell me what day it is now. Imagine, she dropped everything to come from Los Angeles. I'm not sure where I am; some hospital in the New York area, but I'm sure they took me to the closest one to the airport. Surely Silvia asked when they called her."

"I wonder if my obit went out, or if my death will get reported. David probably announced my death to the world. I know I'm not really dead. But that was our deal. The police cooperated. I remember something about that. Maybe they will now presume I am. At my age, it's something that I think about quite a lot. Will anyone really care? In Sayulita, they'll care. A few curators are left who might know my name. But the world keeps going and at my age, they probably think I've been dead."

"I hope the opening went well. I'm sure David did a fine job. He's smart. And the media. I wonder what they reported. Technology isn't perfect. He knows the story, even if I'm not around to tell it. I told it once. To that Bart. But that was a ruse. Some of it. He turned out to be my killer. How ironic. The painkillers are making my mouth dry, and I slur a bit. If I try to speak, I sound hoarse. My voice was never clear anyway and at my old age, it's worse; I can't sit up. They've given me this baby bottle with a straw, so I'm constantly sipping water to loosen up my tongue. It doesn't matter. I'm hooked up to an IV. I'm getting fluids whether I want them or not. They come in every hour but I've told them I want privacy. I want to think without interruption. I can see them peeking thru the door. They've left it open a few inches, just to see if I'm still kicking. Maybe they think my body will just give in any hour now. I asked for a recorder. I wanted to tell things to my girls, to my executors. I have new ideas. They brought me one but I don't know how to use it. I need help. New technology is difficult for me. I'll wait. They'll come soon. I've got more energy than they think. No miracles mind you, but maybe I'll be able to dictate into that recorder everything I've wanted to say. Who was it? Mark Twain or someone wrote an autobiography and instructed that it not be published for 100 years, which by that time, no one will care what he said about people—they'd all be dead too. Well, first, I'm not famous enough for people to line up to buy my words 100 years from now and second, I'll be dead very soon, so I don't think it will matter, and frankly, I'm pretty old—94 if you believe it, so I doubt there's many of my contemporaries around to give a hoot, and if there are, they are most likely too senile to care anyway."

"Ah, I just saw a face peek through that door crack. She saw me talking to myself. It's pretty obvious that I haven't expired yet. Am I scared? I'm sure she's wondering how I can be so calm. After all, there was an attempted murder. When you are 94 you tend to less frightened about the end. Maybe because old people just get tired and we don't mind an upcoming rest. Who else knows as much about dying? It used to be only a few unfortunates, like prisoners who were executed. Of course, perhaps they are delusional enough to think they will get a last minute repeal. Then there are thousands of terminally ill people. Some of them know when death is getting close. Of the millions of deaths, some were given death sentences by a doctor. They must know, perhaps in a month or two or perhaps within days. How do they face the eventual? Many of them are young. Surely they feel cheated out of life. Who else? Those who are intent upon suicide. They can know their death within seconds of the actual event, at least if they are successful. And though it doesn't happen much in this country as it does elsewhere, euthanasia determines the exact time of someone's death. I've seen the videos; those folks are very much aware of what's happening; they just have determined that they are in too much pain with no chance of relief, and they are at peace with the idea of ending it all."

"I can't think of many others who are in my position. Perhaps some accident victims who get an unbearable chance to know that whatever has happened will be fatal to them, like a skydiver whose chute fails to open. But I suspect that in such situations, there's a lot of panic going on, and perhaps a struggle to find a solution, rather than the tranquil opportunity to review one's life, to make arrangements about after-death affairs and to do what I want to do- to put down some final thoughts."

"I don't wish a young person to go through what I'm now going through. At least, I've lived a full life. I have decades of memories, not like a young person who knows he or she will soon die. I've had time to prepare."

"Now it should be apparent that perhaps I have an intended audience. One would think it would be family. My first wife died many years ago, our two daughters are grown, with small families of grown kids themselves, and although Silvia is coming later today, I really don't have any better words than I had for all those years of raising them and then helping them for the next dozen or two dozen years, as they went from one crisis to another. And for my grandkids, they really don't care much about an old guy like me, and their kids - yes, I have a few great grandkids - are too young to care. And as I said, I really don't have any contemporaries around whom I know or who are in condition to care about me. When my obit notice shows up somehow (these things get emailed around more than anything else), they'll just say something like, "Oh, I thought he had already died a few years back." I don't blame them. It's really hard to keep track of who's dead and who's alive. I was active with people twenty years in both directions of my age. Of course all those ten or twenty years older have all died, but of those who were younger, many are still around, but the distance has grown as I've been less and less active and I guess more withdrawn. It's just a natural decline in what a person is capable of doing. What do they say about generals - they just fade from sight, don't they?"

"Even before this recent attempt on my life, I had prepared for death. Most people do. I made a will and in my case, I spent too many hours with my attorney friend, before he passed away, setting up the trust, setting up the mechanisms so my ideas would continue to have some influence in this world. Notice that I said world, and not community, nor country even. This is not intended for a specific cause in the traditional way of thinking, not for a school or medical foundation, or for anything that one might normally think about. When you turn 80 or so, you have a rational mind to know that you might not made it another decade, and certainly not two. You also know that your ability to do new work will decline some and that after I die, people will have to deal with all that I've left. So I started to spend a lot of time thinking of a better solution to my life's work. I don't want my art to end up in a basement or attic. A lot of art just gets disposed of. I want it saved. But maybe no one cares enough. So what about me? Why should the world care that another old man passes away? In realty, no one of significance will care, save for one very small, but critical fact-- that I held a secret that will shatter people's imaginations!"

"Now at first glance, if I had something that important, it would have leaked out, or I would have sold it for millions, or someone would have wanted to steal it from me. How could I have anything of importance and not have revealed it up to now? Certainly, at my age, nothing that important could have come into my hands recently. So people will think, I'm 94, perhaps I learned something as a young man, so with easy math, perhaps 60 to 70 years ago. What might have happened that long ago, that a young man discovered an important secret and kept it almost to his grave? It must have been about someone famous, because he's not famous. Perhaps some dirty gossip for historians to care about? No, nothing like that. I assure you.

But you are getting warmer. We could play 20 questions. I used to like that game when I was young. Almost any secret in the world could be discovered within 20 questions, with just yes or no answers. How very simple to find out almost anything. But of course, the game depends on honest answers."

"Ah, I see the nurse, her name is Elena. 'Hello, Elena, please come here. I need to talk to you'."

"Mr. Peters, you seem perky today. You've been talking to yourself."

"Have I? I must be still out of it."

"You're a lot better than when they brought you in two days ago."

"My voice is weak."

"Weak? You are lucky, Mr. Peters. It'll get better. Give it a few days."

Just then, a woman in her mid sixties walked in, sandy blonde colored hair, a dark pants suit and wheeling a large carry-on bag with a nametag still tied to the strap.

"Dad, how did you get poisoned?" asked Felix's daughter, Silvia, walking to the bed and looking at the monitor instead of greeting her father.

"'Hola, Dad' might be more appropriate." Felix said in a barely audible voice.

"He had a close call," explained the nurse. "They didn't believe an older gentleman coming from an airline flight would have been poisoned. That's what you told them, remember Mr. Peters? But a doctor spotted that wet stain on your shirt and then smelled almond and suspected cyanide. He was lucky the emergency room doctor was so observant."

"Cyanide! Honestly, Dad. " She went over and kissed and then hugged Felix. Then she started to cry. "They said it was close. Why on earth would someone have you poisoned? Is that why there are two policemen outside in the hall waiting to talk to you? What do they need to talk about? Do you know who did this?"

"¡Calmete! ¡Calmete!"

"¡Ay, Caramba, Papa! ¡Mi Dios!"

"My darling, calm down," said Felix in a paced whisper. "I can't talk over your crying."

"I'm surprised I have any tears left. I've been crying ever since the hospital called me. Thank goodness I insisted you put my number in your wallet. And I've been crying half the night. It's hard enough to sleep on the plane, but then to think what you've gone through, and for what? You must know what's going on…"

At that point, Silvia noticed David walking into the room, who obviously was not part of the hospital's medical team.

"Felix. Oh, I'm so happy to see you, alive!"

"Are you a detective?"

"That's a first. No, I'm the director of the Clark Art Institute."

"So you are the one to put Dad up to this!"

"Well, I wouldn't put it that way."

"Silvia," said Felix trying hard to be heard. "I called David, not the other way around. David, this is my daughter, Silvia."

"Will one of you explain to me what's going on?"

David was the first to talk. "I'll let Felix tell you the story if he's up to it. I've just come down from Williamstown, Massachusetts. It's about a four-hour drive, due north of here. I didn't tell my staff where I was going or why. No one knows that I'm here in a New York hospital. Two days ago, we had an opening, where your Dad's Warhol painting was on exhibition. You must know the painting?"

"Of course. I grew up with that painting around. But what does that have to do with my Dad being poisoned?"

David looked at Felix who smiled. "Darling daughter, the world thinks I'm dead. Let's leave it that way for now."

"Why, Dad, why?"

"It's a long story. Set me up so I can have more pillows on my back, and I'll tell you. You might as well let in the policemen. If I have to tell the story, I'll only tell it once. Not even David knows the entire history."

Silvia went out and talked to the policemen and the three reentered the room.

"Mr. Peters, I am Detective Evans and this is Detective O'Reilly. Detective O'Reilly is from the NYPD and I am an investigator for the FAA. We are here because the hospital told us that your admission was caused by poison and it was not an accidental incident. They found traces of cyanide on your clothing. You were half conscious when they brought you but they said that you mentioned off and on in your daze that you were purposefully poisoned on the Aeromexico flight 397 from Puerto Vallarta to JFK. That puts the matter into my hands since it was an incident that occurred while you were airborne, and Detective O'Reilly is here since the alleged perpetrator presumably escaped in New York. Are you up to giving us specifics?"

"Or I can ask you some questions," suggest Detective O'Reilly. "We can wait if necessary but the sooner we have some information, the sooner we can start the investigation."

"In order to understand the motive, it's a long story if you care to hear it."

"Yes, we would like to hear your version. May we record it? But first, I need to understand who is in this room, other than your daughter who introduced herself to us out in the hall."

The nurse came in and did some readings and checked Felix's fluid bag and said she'd return with the doctor on duty. David introduced himself and asked if they wanted him to leave.

"That's up to Mr. Peters," replied Evans.

"David can stay, of course. David knows a lot if not all of what I have to say. So that's why there's a recorder in my room. I thought it was to allow me to say my final goodbye."

"We're sorry you thought that," said Detective Evans. 'You were not awake when we first came."

As the men turned to David, he formally introduced himself. "Officers, my name is David Bresland. I am the director of the Clark Art Institute, a museum up in Williamstown, Massachusetts. I am here because two important paintings owned by Mr. Peters are on loan to us for an exhibition. Apparently, it is the reason why one or more persons tried to kill Mr. Peters."

"Why would anyone want to kill Dad? Dad is an artist. Why was he a target? Dad, tell me!"

Just then, the doctor walked in. "Mr. Peters needs to rest a bit. Can you come back in the morning and I'm sure he'll have the energy to speak with you?

"Gentlemen, I can give you the background and then you can question Felix tomorrow, " suggested David.

After consultation with the medical desk, they agreed to convene back in Felix's room at 10 AM. That would give the doctors time to do their morning rounds and examine Felix. "Besides," declared the doctor on duty, "he's old and needs more rest. His body has been through a rough time. By tomorrow he'll be much improved."

David and Silvia and the detectives went to a private conference room used by the doctors and sat down. There, David explained everything that he knew, including the reason behind David reporting that Felix had died.

"If Mr. Peters is wary about the government controlling the press, perhaps he should appreciate the fact that we sometimes can help in that way," said Detective Evans after listening to David's story. "We'll confirm the report that the victim died, in a way that we can later say it was just a hospital clerical error, and the patient didn't die. That'll give us a few days to flush out whomever we can."

CHAPTER 25

Felix stared up at the ceiling. He heard the footsteps and knew the visitor without even looking to his side.

"Hi my dear," he said.

"Hello Dad. I see you are a bit more chipper this morning."

"I feel much better. And why are you dressed so elegantly today? Going to have lunch with one of your friends?"

"Why? I'm just visiting you. You aren't used to seeing people in city clothes. Too much time in Sayulita."

"They are refusing to let me go. They are keeping me here like a prisoner. I might be old but I'm not crazy, I'm not dying, at least not today, and I want out of here. What can you do? You used to be assertive in these kinds of things-- what can you do for your Dad now?"

Dad, yesterday you could barely talk. The day before, you were barely alive. Rest a day. I'll talk to them, but I'm sure they want to keep you here at least a day longer."

"Get them to release me. I'm fine. Really. Do something. You know the system."

*****

They all assembled in Felix's hospital room, pulling two additional chairs from an office across the hall, and the detectives leaned on the wide windowsill.

"David, what happened at the Clark? You haven't finished telling me," asked Felix.

David stood up and was eager to continue. "I told the background to the detectives in the hall lobby, yesterday while you were resting."

"But Dad didn't hear about the reception," said Silvia.

"Our auditorium was packed. I gave the background. The whole story was condensed and I told it. After the presentation, everyone assembled in the main gallery where I pulled the cord so the drape could drop and reveal both Warhol paintings at the same time. They saw it projected on the screen, but there it was for the world to see in person. It was pretty dramatic, if I may say so."

Felix interjected. "I told David in my email exactly what to do. You see, for all these years, the painting that you and Daniela and others knew and saw and assumed I was holding, was a genuine Warhol painting, but it was stretched by Andy himself on top of the second painting, the one that had the image of the second shooter preserved."

"David said it covered a second painting, and one that showed a second gunman at the Kennedy assassination?" inquired Silvia to see if all that was true.

"Yes, the original blowup of the negatives showed the second gunman in the adjacent window of the Book Depository. You see, the existence of the second gunman now brings down all the official reports of Kennedy's assassination. They will have to start from the beginning."

"And between the two paintings Andy taped the original negatives" said David. "It was so thin, no one could tell from the front of the back.

"But you said that the passenger sitting next to you took the transparency," objected Silvia. "Why did you let him?"

"My dear, do you think all old people are also fools? I discovered the negatives quite a few years ago. I knew the value of it. I wasn't about to put it back in the stretcher and leave it to chance that it would survive. I had it digitally scanned several times, for the best quality. I was only bringing the original transparency to the opening just for "show and tell." It was something to hold up to the media and audience, that's all. By now, that image has been emailed to every newspaper and conspiracy investigator in the world. That man stole a meaningless icon. A souvenir, that's all. I wonder who he gave it to and what that person will think once he sees the image in tomorrow's papers."

"Correction. You've lost your sense of time. The papers have already come out. I picked up a couple of them on the way here," said David. "And it's gone viral on the Internet."

"I must have been sleeping quite a bit here."

The doctor wanted you to rest. He kept us from asking you much until now," injected Detective O'Reilly.

"You see, I wanted the Clark to host this show in order for this image to be taken seriously. The Clark gives the Warhol paintings absolute authenticity. If I had just invited in a reporter or two, the story would have been buried in the back pages as just another crack theory. But not with the Clark Art Institute behind it; they are not the type to make up stories to get more publicity."

"You reported that you told that man that the museum didn't know about the second painting," said Detective Evans.

"So I lied; so what? I had to drag out my story. Bart had to realize that I had something valuable. I wanted to wait until we got close to landing. I knew I needed to get him off the plane and then to get help. Once I returned to my seat from using the bathroom, that's when I finally saw the light - or at least my suspicion. But sitting next to him, I didn't know how to call for help without alarming him."

"If you had told him it was too late, that the museum had it all, might he have changed his plans?" inquired Detective O'Reilly.

"He was a hired gun, so to speak. He was not hired to think. If he knew that, I feared he would have attempted to kill me sooner. Of course David knew. I told him the entire story when he visited me in Sayulita. We decided to ship the painting as it was - or I should say as 'they' were - one on top of the other. Our plan was for the Clark to document the removal of the top painting to reveal the second one. But Bart didn't need to know all that, did he? I must say, it wasn't easy making my story longer. I mean, I know I like to talk but still, this was four hours non-stop - and I don't mean the flight. I made up stuff to entertain him."

"Like what stuff?" asked David.

Looking at David, "I told him about your 'Lubricant Theory of World Politics.'"

"You didn't? Felix! Tell me you didn't!"

"I certainly did. It was very entertaining!"

"I had had two Margaritas and we were on our second bottle of wine when I mentioned that to you. I was drunk!"

"It kept his interest, for sure. Anyway, I'm sure most of it is applicable, no?"

"What is that 'Lubricant Theory?'" asked Silvia.

"Never mind. It's not something for public consumption," said David quickly.

Felix laughed while David looked a bit embarrassed. "But David, I did you a favor; I didn't say it came from you. I told Bart that it was my theory."

"That's better then. So what happened next? Why did you finally suspect him?" asked David.

"He was a nice man. I have to say that. But you know, I talked for so long, he was almost too nice. I mean, people get edgy, but not Bart."

"You suspected the Mexican men that boarded, didn't you?" asked David.

"Yes, at first. I was wrong. Only about who it was - not about the fact that someone wanted to stop me. So I suppose my guard was going up about Bart the longer I got into my story. The mistake people make is that they think old people are also not observant. He seemed a bit too anxious for me to drink a glass of wine."

"How did you avoid taking more poison? Or a better question - why did you take any of it if you thought he was poisoning you?" asked David but the others were about to ask the same thing."

"I had some doubts. Perhaps I was wrong, I thought, but then I spotted him fingering something into my glass. That was proof. I had to think quickly. I had to drink some - I had to show him I was taking my glass up to my lips. But then I got him to look away - at the attendant -just long enough."

"But you could have refused!" fretted Silvia.

He had big strong hands. I'm sure he could have put his hand on my neck and done me in just as quickly. I'm sure that was Plan B - not the preferred method because that might have been noticed. His Plan A - I should say their plan, I'm sure he was just carrying out orders - which was to have me die and hope that it would look like an old man died naturally. After all, I suppose it happens all the time. No, I had to have some of the poison; he had to see a reaction. I took a chance, I realize. I had no idea if even a little sip would kill me.

"So you sipped some wine and then what?" asked Detective O'Reilly.

"When he turned his head, just for a second, instead of swallowing, I let the rest run past the side of my face. It ran down my shoulder, got my shirt all wet and my seat. But it was the side away from him. I didn't think he'd see it. You know, old guys can be cagey too."

"The doctor said that you took almost enough to kill you. You were not in the best shape when they brought you in. You were lucky, Felix," said the detective.

"Yes, lucky. I had to wait. He had to think I was dead, or at least dying. I had to wait until I was sure he had left the plane. Then I was barely able to talk. I guess I managed to tell the attendant enough. I mentioned poison, didn't I?"

"You did," confirmed Detective Evans. "The ambulance came and as soon as they got you here, they looked for poison. You did the right thing, I guess. But I'm not sure I would have even taken a drop of that wine. You were brave, as well."

"Dad, brave? No, stupid, stupid. You almost died."

"My darling daughter, I'm going to be around a while longer, so don't fret."

"So Dad, are you out of danger now? After all, it's all out. Right? Detectives, do you think they'll leave Dad alone?"

"Probably so, but let's give it some time," answered Detective Evans. "Can you stay somewhere else?"

"You can stay with me in Los Angeles."

"Gracias mi querida. I'm sure they don't know much about where my kids are. I'll return to Sayulita in a few weeks. By that time, it'll be old news, the image will be all over the world, new investigations will keep those guys busy enough."

"I doubt they'll waste time just on revenge," said Detective Evans. "They were dangerous only because they wanted to stop something from happening. Their hired gun had one duty. That's over. They failed. Like a Watergate, this one blew up in their faces."

Detective Evans added, "They'll realize that it's useless to spend energy that way. Now they'll spend energy in trying to suppress parts of the investigation. They'll be busy trying to hide some of the surviving participants. And you know what, they'll succeed partially. There aren't so many players left."

"Most likely this won't change much," said Felix, "but if it changes just a little, then it's important. History has played out. Kennedy was assassinated. Mary was murdered as well. Perhaps others were killed in the name of keeping the conspiracy a secret. Gradually, the public will know most of the truth, but never will they know all."

"But it's a new public. Not the public who cried when the news of the gun firing first was broadcast. It's the second and third generation. If the attendance yesterday is any indication, they still care," said David.

"At least they now know there were guns - not a single gun - but at least two guns pointed at the motorcade. That's a beginning."

David interjected, "Felix, let's follow up this exhibition with another, next summer, of your work. We have shown Tamayo and Rivera already;

your painting outside the show has generated a lot of compliments. A Peters exhibition would be a welcome addition. After all this, there'll be an extra interest in seeing your work."

"Dad, if you have that show, will you still want to play dead?"

"Maybe not, but by then I'll be 95. A year at my age is like a decade to someone of your age."

"I'm confident you'll be around," said David. "But in any case, we'll work out the logistics and which works are available next month. Just in case you meet any more killers on airplanes."

"I'm proud of you, Dad, do you know that? Let's get you home."

THE END